For an instant
went out of fo

Sunita could almost see a line being drawn in the sands of time—this was the moment that separated before and after. She nearly took the coward's route, and wondered if Frederick would swallow the lie that Amil was Sam's. Then she realised she could not—would not—do that.

'Yes. He is yours. Amil is your son.'

Now she understood the meaning of a deafening silence. This one rolled through the room, echoed in her ears until she wanted to shout. Instead she waited, saw his body freeze, saw the whole gamut of emotion cross his face, and watched as his expression settled into an anger so ice-cold a shiver rippled over her skin.

Panic twisted her insides. The die had been cast and she knew now that, whatever happened, life would never be the same.

CLAIMING HIS SECRET ROYAL HEIR

BY
NINA MILNE

HarperCollins
PUBLISHERS
Since 1817

First Published in Great Britain 2017
By Mills & Boon, an imprint of HarperCollins*Publishers*
1 London Bridge Street, London, SE1 9GF

© 2017 Nina Milne

ISBN: 978-0-2 92338-4

23-1017

Our policy is to use papers that are natural, renewable and recyclable products and made from wood grown in sustainable forests. The logging and manufacturing processes conform to the legal environmental regulations of the country of origin.

Printed and bound in Spain
by CPI, Barcelona

Nina Milne has always dreamed of writing for Mills & Boon Romance—ever since she played libraries with her mother's stacks of Mills & Boon romances as a child. On her way to this dream Nina acquired an English degree, a hero of her own, three gorgeous children and—somehow!—an accountancy qualification. She lives in Brighton and has filled her house with stacks of books—her very own *real* library.

To the memory of my very lovely 'Nanni'—
I still miss you.

CHAPTER ONE

August 15th—Online Celebrity News with April Fotherington

Who will be the new Lycander Princess?

All bets are off!

It's official! Lady Kaitlin Derwent is no longer a contender for the position of Lycander Bride—the people's favourite aristo announced that her new squeeze for the foreseeable future is Daniel Harrington, CEO of Harrington's Legal Services.

Who'd have thought it?

Exit Lady Kaitlin!

So Prince Frederick, ruler of Lycander, is on the lookout for a new bride.

Who will it be?

Will it be the type of woman who graced his arm and his bed back in his playboy days, before the tragic death of his older brother and the scandalous death of Prince Alphonse, his flamboyant father, in a house of ill repute propelled him to the throne?

FREDERICK II OF the House of Petrelli, Prince and Ruler of Lycander, stopped reading and pushed his screen across the ornate carved desk, resplendent with gilt—a royal gift from an English monarch of yore.

The phrase pounded his brain—*tragic death of his older brother*—but he forced his features to remain calm, and made himself focus on the man standing in front of him: Marcus Alrikson, his chief advisor. After all, he needed all the advice he could get.

'I don't understand what the problem is—this article is nothing more than a gossip fest. And it's old news.'

Marcus shook his head. '*That* is the problem. The article serves to remind the people of your past.'

'Don't you mean my sordid, scandalous and immoral past?' Might as well tell it like it is, he thought.

'If you like,' Marcus returned evenly. 'The bigger problem is that we both know you are holding on to the crown by your fingertips. The people did not want you on the throne because of your past—so any reminder causes damage.'

'I understand that.'

The all too familiar guilt twisted his insides—the people had wanted his brother on the throne. Axel had been born to this. He would have been the ideal ruler to bring prosperity and calm to the land after their father's turbulent rule.

But Axel was dead and buried—victim of a car crash that should have been Frederick's destiny. Frederick should have been in that car on his way to a State dinner; instead he'd asked Axel to step in and take his place and his big brother had—no questions asked. So Frederick had attended a party on board a glitzy yacht to celebrate a business deal…and Axel had died.

The dark secret tarnished Frederick's soul, weighted his conscience.

And now Lycander was stuck with the black sheep of the royal line and the people were threatening to revolt. Bleak determination hardened inside him. He would keep the crown safe, whatever the cost—he owed that at least to Axel's memory.

'So what do you suggest?'

'I suggest you find a new bride—someone like Lady Kaitlin. Your proposed alliance with Kaitlin was a popular one. It showed the people that you had decided to settle down with a suitable bride, that you'd changed—proof there would be no repeat of your father's disastrous marriages.'

'I *have* decided to settle down.' To bind himself to a lifestyle he'd once sworn to avoid and the formulation of a cold-blooded alliance undertaken for the sake of the throne. 'But Kaitlin is no longer an option—she has fallen in love with another man.'

Irritation sparked inside him. He wished Kaitlin well, but it was hard to believe that the cool, poised Lady Kaitlin had succumbed to so foolish an emotion.

'Which is not good news for Lycander.'

Marcus resumed pacing, each stride swallowing up a metre of the marble floor, taking him past yet another portrait of one of Frederick's ancestors.

'Kaitlin was the perfect bride—her background is impeccable and she reminded the people of Lycander brides of the past.'

Unlike the succession of actresses, models and gold diggers Frederick's father had married.

'The people loved her.'

Unlike you.

The unspoken words hovered in the air between them.

'I understand all this. But Kaitlin is history.'

'Yes. And right now the press is *focused* on your history. That article zones in on your former flames—the actresses, the socialites, the models. Giselle, Mariana, Sunita… Hell, this reporter, April, even tried to track them down.'

Frederick froze.

Sunita.

Images flashed across his mind; memory reached across the chasm of tragedy.

Sunita.

Shared laughter, sheer beauty, almond-shaped eyes of a brown that veered from tawny to light, dependent on her mood. The raven sheen of her silken hair, the glow of her skin, the lissom length of her legs.

Sunita.

The woman who had left him—the woman he'd allowed to go...

Without preamble, he pulled his netbook back towards him, eyes scanning the article.

But where is Sunita now?

This is where it becomes a little mysterious.

Mere weeks after the end of her relationship with the Prince of Lycander—which, according to several sources, she ended abruptly—Sunita decided to 'take a break' from her highly lucrative modelling career to 'rediscover her roots'.

This involved a move to Mumbai, where her mother reportedly hailed from. But the trail ends there, and to all intents and purposes Sunita seems to have vanished.

'Frederick?' Marcus's voice pulled him from the article and he looked up to see his chief advisor's forehead crease into a frown. 'What is it?'

'Nothing.' Under the sceptical gaze Frederick shrugged. 'It just sounds unlike Sunita to give up her career.'

Sunita had been one of the most ambitious people he knew—had been defined by that ambition, had had her career aspirations and goals mapped out with well-lit beacons. The idea of her jacking it all in seemed far-fetched at best.

Marcus drummed his fingers on his thigh. 'Could her disappearance have anything to do with you?'

'No.'

'What happened?'

'We spent a few weeks together—she moved on.'

'*She* moved on?'

Damn. 'We moved on.'

'Why?'

Keep it together. This is history. 'She decided to call it a day as she'd garnered sufficient publicity from our connection.'

Marcus raised his eyebrows. 'So she used you for publicity?'

'Yes. To be fair, she was upfront about that from the start.'

More fool him for thinking she'd changed her mind as time had gone on. He'd believed their time together, the long conversations, the laughter, had meant something. Well, he'd been wrong. Sunita had been after publicity and then she'd cut and run. Yet there had been something in her expression that morning…a transitory shadow in her tawny eyes, an errant twist of her hands that had belied the glib words dropping from her lips. But he hadn't called her on it.

Enough! The past was over and did not bear dwelling on because—as he knew with soul-wrenching certainty—it could not be changed.

Marcus's dark blue eyes met his as he resumed pacing. 'So weeks after this publicity stunt she disappeared off the modelling scene? That doesn't make sense.'

It didn't. But it had nothing to do with him. Two years

ago Sunita had affected him in ways he didn't want to remember. He'd missed her once she'd gone—an unheard-of weakness he'd knocked on the head and buried. Easy come, easy go. That was the Playboy Prince's motto. Sunita had gone—he'd accepted it. And then, mere months after her departure, Axel had died and his life had changed for ever.

'I'll look into it,' Marcus said. 'But right now you need to focus on this list. Potential brides. A princess, a lady and a *marquesa*. Take your pick.'

Frederick accepted the piece of paper but didn't so much as glance down. 'What do you mean, "look into it"?'

'If there is any chance of potential scandal we need to shut it down now. So I plan to find Sunita before April Fotherington or any other reporter does.'

'Then what?'

'Then I'll send someone to talk to her. Or go myself.'

'No!' The refusal came with a vehemence that surprised him. However it had ended, his time with Sunita had marked something—his last moments of joy before catastrophe occurred, perhaps. He didn't want her life tainted…didn't want Marcus or his minions to find her if she didn't want to be found.

'It needs to be done.' Marcus leant forward, his hands on the edge of the desk. 'I understand you don't like it, but you can't take even the smallest risk that there is a scandal floating around out there. The crown is at stake. The throne is rocking, Frederick, and if it topples it will be a Humpty Dumpty scenario.'

Great! A Humpty Dumpty scenario—exactly what he needed. Of course he could choose to ignore the warning, but that would be foolish. Marcus knew his stuff. The sensible option would be to allow Marcus to go ahead, investigate and deal with any problem. But for some reason every fibre of his being cavilled—dammit, stupid though it sounded, it wasn't the *honourable* thing to do.

A small mocking smile tilted his lips as he faced his chief advisor. Frederick of Lycander—man of honour. Axel would be proud of him. 'Fine. *I'll* check out Sunita.'

Marcus's blue eyes narrowed. 'With all due respect, that's nuts and you know it. The press will jump on it.'

'Then let them jump. I'm the boss and this is what's going to happen.'

'Why?'

'Because it's the right thing to do.' And for once he'd like to stand on a tiny wedge of the moral high ground. 'What would Axel have done? Sent you in to spy on a woman he'd dated?'

'Axel would never have got himself into a position where it was necessary.'

'Touché. But I have and I will deal with it.' His brain whirred as he thought it through. 'I can schedule a trip to Mumbai—I'd like to follow up on how the Schools for All project is rolling out anyway.'

It was a project set up by Axel, but Frederick had taken it over and had every intention of making it into a success.

'I'll locate Sunita, confirm there is no scandal, and then I'll come back and find a wife from your shortlist. No argument.' A mirthless smile touched his lips. 'Don't worry. I'll be discreet.'

August 17th, Mumbai

Sunita stared down at the screen and reread the article for approximately the millionth time in three days as a mini-tornado of panic whirled and soared around her tummy.

She told herself that she was climbing the heights of irrationality. April Fotherington *hadn't* found her—she was safe here in this spacious, anonymous Mumbai apartment, surrounded by cool white walls and the hustle and bustle of a city she'd come to love. Soon enough the flicker of interest the article might ignite would die out. No one had discovered her secret thus far—there was no reason to believe they would now. She was safe. *They* were safe.

But she couldn't help the sudden lurch of fear as she gazed round the living room and the evidence of the life she'd created. Signs of her baby son were everywhere— a wooden toy box in the corner, the cheerful play mat by the sofa, board books, beakers... She knew all too well how quickly life could change, be upended and destroyed.

Stop. No one would take Amil away. Alphonse of Lycander was dead, and he had been the greatest threat—a man who had fought virulent custody battles for four of his children and used his position and wealth to win them all. She had no doubt he would have done the same for his grandchild—would have used the might and power of his sovereignty to win Amil.

Just as Frederick still might.

The peal of the doorbell jolted her from her thoughts and a scud of panic skittered through her. It couldn't be her grandmother and Amil—they had only left a little while before. *Chill.* They could have forgotten something, it could be a neighbour, or a delivery or—

Only one way to find out.

Holding her breath, she peered through the peephole.

Shock dizzied her—she blinked and prayed the man at her door was a figment of her overheated imagination, brought on by reading the article so many times. The alternative was too ghastly to contemplate. But, however many times she blinked, Prince Frederick of Lycander was still right there.

What to do? What to do? Ignore him?

But what if he waited outside? What if he was still there when Amil came back? Or what if he went away and returned when Amil was here? What if he was here to take Amil?

Enough. She had not got this far to give up now. She was no longer that ten-year-old girl, reeling from her mother's death, powerless to stop the father she had never known from taking her. No longer that eleven, twelve, thirteen-year-old girl at the mercy of her stepmother and sisters who had graduated with honours from *Cinderella* school.

She'd escaped them without the help of a handsome prince and left that feeling of powerlessness far behind. No way was she going back there—especially now, when her son was at stake.

Adrenalin surged through her body as she did what life had taught her—moved forward to face up to whatever was about to be thrown at her. She might dodge it, catch it, or punch it, but she would confront it on her own terms.

True to her motto, she pulled the door open and raised her eyebrows in aloof surprise. 'Your Highness,' she said. 'What are you doing here?'

Stepping out into the communal hall, she closed the door behind her, searching his gaze for a sign that he knew about Amil.

'I came to see *you*. April Fotherington wrote an article saying you'd vanished.'

Sunita forced herself not to lean back against the wall in relief. Instead, she maintained her façade of reserve as they stood and studied each other. Against her will, her stomach nosedived and her hormones cartwheeled. Memories of the totally wrong sort streamed through her mind and fizzed through her veins as she drank him in. The same corn-blond hair, the same hazel eyes…

No, not the same. His eyes were now haunted by shadows and his lips no longer turned upward in insouciance. Prince Frederick looked like a man who hadn't smiled in a while. Little wonder after the loss of his brother and his father, followed by a troubled ascent to the throne.

Instinctively she stepped closer, wanting to offer comfort. 'I saw the article. But before we discuss that, I'm sorry for your losses. I wanted to send condolences but...'

It had been too risky, and it had seemed wrong somehow—to send condolences whilst pregnant with his baby, whom she intended to keep secret from him.

'Why didn't you?'

The seemingly casual question held an edge and she tensed.

'If all your girlfriends had done that you'd still be reading them now. I didn't feel our brief relationship gave me the right.'

Disingenuous, but there was some truth there. For a second she could almost taste the bitter disappointment with herself for succumbing to the Playboy Prince's charms and falling into bed with him. Hell—she might as well have carved the notch on his four-poster bed herself.

She'd woken the morning after and known what she had to do—the only way forward to salvage some pride and dignity. End it on *her* terms, before he did. It had been the only option, but even as she had done it there had been a tiny part of her that had hoped he'd stop her, ask her to stay. But of course he hadn't. The Playboy Prince wouldn't change. People didn't change—Sunita knew that.

Anyway this was history. *Over and done with.*

'I am offering condolences now.'

'Thank you. But, as I said, that's not why I am here.'

'The article?'

'Yes. I'd like to talk—perhaps we could go inside.'

'No!' *Tone it down, Sunita.* 'This is my home, Frederick, my private sanctuary. I want to keep it that way.'

He eyed her for a moment and she forced herself to hold his gaze.

'Then where would you suggest? Preferably somewhere discreet.'

'In case the press spot us and tips me as the next candidate for Lycander Bride?'

The words were out before she could stop them; obscure hurt touched her with the knowledge he didn't want to be seen with her.

'Something like that. You're my unofficial business.'

For a moment there was a hint of the Frederick she'd known in the warmth of his voice, and more memories threatened to surface. Of warmth and laughter, touch and taste.

'My official reason for this trip is charity business— I'm patron of an educational charity that is rolling out some new schools.'

The tang of warmth had disappeared; instead impatience vibrated from him as he shifted from foot to foot.

'Are you sure we can't talk inside? It shouldn't take long. All I want is the solution to April's mystery.'

Sunita checked the hollow laughter before it could fall from her lips. Was that *all* he wanted? Easy-peasy, lemon-squeezy.

'I'm sure we can't talk here.'

Think. But coherent thought was nigh on impossible. Raw panic combined with her body's reaction to his proximity had unsettled her, sheer awareness wrong-footed her. *Think.* Yet her mind drew a blank as to any possible location, any café where she and Amil weren't regulars.

Fear displaced all other emotion—Frederick must not find out about Amil. Not now, not like this. One day, yes, but at a time of her choice—when it was right and safe for Amil.

'I'll just grab a coat and we can go.'

'A coat?'

'It's monsoon season.'

Sunita turned, opened the door, and slipped inside, her mind racing to formulate a plan. She'd always been able to think on her feet, after all. If Frederick wanted a solution to the mystery of her disappearance from the modelling scene, then that was what she would provide.

Grabbing her phone, she pressed speed dial and waited.

'Sunita?'

'Hey, Sam. I need a favour. A *big* favour.'

CHAPTER TWO

FREDERICK WATCHED AS she opened the door and sidled out. Coatless, he couldn't help but notice. What was going on? Anyone would think she had the Lycander Crown Jewels tucked away in there. Hell, maybe she did. Or maybe something was wrong.

Disquiet flickered and he closed it down. He'd vowed emotion would not come into play here. He and Sunita were history—the sole reason for his presence was to ensure no scandal would touch Lycander and topple him, Humpty Dumpty-style.

They exited the building and emerged onto the heat-soaked pavement, thronged with an almost impossible mass of people, alive with the shouts of the hawkers who peddled their wares and the thrum of the seemingly endless cars that streamed along the road. Horns blared, and the smell of cumin, coriander and myriad spices mingled with the delicate scents of the garlands of flowers on offer and the harsher fumes of pollution.

Sunita walked slightly ahead, and he took the opportunity to study her. The past two years had done nothing to detract from her beauty—her hair shone with a lustre that should have the manufacturer of whatever brand of shampoo she used banging at her door, and her impossibly long legs and slender waist were unchanged.

Yet there was a difference. The Sunita he'd known had dressed to be noticed, but today her outfit was simple and anonymous—cut-off jeans, a loose dark blue T-shirt and blue sandals. It was an ensemble that made her blend in with the crowd. Even the way she walked seemed altered—somehow different from the way she had once sashayed down the catwalk.

Once.

And therein lay the crux of the matter. The more he thought about it, the more he recalled the vibrant, publicity-loving, career-orientated Sunita he'd known, the less possible it seemed that she had traded the life path she'd planned for an anonymous existence. His research of the past two days had confirmed that mere weeks after Sunita had ended their association she'd thrown it all away and melted into obscurity.

'How did you find me?'

'It wasn't easy.'

Or so Marcus had informed him. Sunita's agent had refused point-blank to respond to his discreet enquiries, but Marcus had ways and means, and had eventually procured the address through 'contacts'—whatever that meant.

'Was it my agent? Was it Harvey?'

'No. But whoever it was I promise you they did you a favour.'

'Some favour.'

'You mean you aren't happy to see me?' he deadpanned.

A shadow of a smile threatened to touch her lips and he fought the urge to focus on those lips in more detail.

'Pass.'

Raising an arm, she hailed a taxi and they waited until the yellow and black vehicle had screeched through the traffic to stop by the kerb.

Once inside she leant forward to speak to the driver.

'Sunshine Café, please,' she said, and then sat back. 'I'm taking you to meet the solution to your mystery. The reason I stayed in India.'

Her eyes slid away from him for a fraction of a second and then back again as she inhaled an audible breath.

'His name is Sam Matthews. He used to be a photographer, but he's moved here and set up a beach café.'

'A boyfriend?'

Such a simple answer—Sunita had given it all up for love. A small stab of jealousy pierced his ribcage, caught him unawares. *Get real, Frederick.* So what if she walked straight into someone else's arms, into the real thing? That had never been his destiny. *Know your limitations. Easy come, easy go.* Two stellar life mottos.

'Yes.'

'Must be some boyfriend to have persuaded you to throw away your career. You told me once that nothing was more important to you than success.'

'I meant it at the time.'

'So you gave up stardom and lucre for love.'

A small smile touched her lips. 'Yes, I did.'

'And you're happy? Sam makes you happy?'

Her hands twisted on her lap in a small convulsive movement. She looked down as if in surprise, then back up as she nodded. 'Yes.'

A spectrum of emotion showed in her brown eyes—regret, guilt, defiance,—he couldn't settle on what it was, and then it was gone.

'I'm happy.'

Job done. Sunita had a boyfriend and she'd moved on with her life. There was no dangerous scandal to uncover. A simple case of over-vigilance from his chief advisor. He could stop the taxi now and return to his hotel.

Yet…something felt off. He could swear Sunita was

watching him, assessing his reactions. Just like two years ago when she'd called it a day. Or maybe it was his own ego seeing spectres—perhaps he didn't *want* to believe another woman had ricocheted from him to perfect love. Sunita to Sam, Kaitlin to Daniel—there was a definite pattern emerging.

He glanced out of the window at the busy beach, scattered with parasols and bodies, as the taxi slowed to a halt.

'We're here,' she announced.

What the hell? He might as well meet this paragon who had upended Sunita's plans, her career, her life, in a way he had not.

Damn it. There was that hint of chagrin again. Not classy, Frederick. Not royal behaviour.

Minutes later they approached a glass-fronted restaurant nestled at the corner of a less populated section of sand, under the shade of two fronded palms. Once inside, Frederick absorbed the warm yet uncluttered feel achieved by the wooden floor, high exposed beam ceiling and polished wooden tables and slatted chairs. A long sweeping bar added to the ambience, as did the hum of conversation.

Sunita moved forward. 'Hey, Sam.'

Frederick studied the man who stood before them. There was more than a hint of wariness in his eyes and stance. Chestnut wavy hair, average height, average build, light brown eyes that returned his gaze with an answering assessment.

Sunita completed the introduction. 'Sam, Frederick— Frederick, Sam. Right, now that's done…'

'Perhaps you and I could have a drink and a catch-up? For old times' sake.'

The suggestion brought on by an instinctive unease, augmented by the look of reluctance on her face. Something wasn't right. She hadn't wanted him to so much as peek into her apartment, and she could have simply *told* him about Sam. Instead she'd brought him here to see him, as if to provide tangible proof of his existence.

'Sure.' Sunita glanced at her watch. 'But I can't be too long.'

Sam indicated a staircase. 'There's a private room you can use upstairs, if you want to chat without attracting attention.'

'Great. Thank you,' Frederick said, and stepped back to allow the couple to walk together.

Their body language indicated that they were...*comfortable* with each other. They walked side by side, but there was no accidental brush of a hand, no quick glance of appreciation or anticipation, no chemistry or any sign of the awareness that had shimmered in the air since he himself had set eyes on Sunita.

They entered a small room with a wooden table and chairs by a large glass window that overlooked the beach. Sam moved over to the window, closed the shutters and turned to face them. 'If you tell me what you'd like to drink, I'll have it sent up.'

'You're welcome to join us,' Frederick said smoothly, and saw the look of caution in Sam's brown eyes intensify as he shook his head.

'I'd love to, but we're extremely busy and one of my staff members didn't turn up today, so I'm afraid I can't.'

'That's fine, Sam. Don't worry,' Sunita interpolated— and surely the words had tumbled out just a little too fast. Like they did when she was nervous. 'Could I have a guava and pineapple juice, please?'

'Sounds good—I'll have the same.'

'No problem.'

With that, Sam left the room.

'He clearly doesn't see me as a threat,' Frederick observed.

'There is no reason why he should.'

For an instant he allowed his gaze to linger on her lips and he saw heat touch her cheekbones. 'Of course not,' he agreed smoothly.

Her eyes narrowed, and one sandaled foot tapped the floor with an impatience he remembered all too well. 'Anyway, you came here to solve the mystery. Mystery solved. So your "unofficial" business is over.'

Were her words almost too airy or had he caught a case of severe paranoia from Marcus? 'It would appear so.' He watched her from beneath lowered lids.

'So, tell me more about your official business—the schools project.'

'My brother set up the charity—he believed every child deserves access to an education, however basic.'

It had been a philanthropic side Frederick hadn't even known Axel had had—one his brother had kept private. Because he had been a good man...a good man who had died—

Grief and guilt thrust forward but he pushed them back. The only reparation he could make was to continue Axel's work.

'So, I'm funding and working with a committee to set up schools here. Tomorrow I'm going to visit one of the new ones and meet the children.'

'That sounds incredible—there's so much poverty here, and yet also such a vibrant sense of happiness as well.'

'Why don't you get involved? That would be great publicity for the organisation—I could put you in touch.'

For a second her face lit up, and then she shook her head. 'No. I'm not modelling at the moment and...'

'I'm not suggesting you model. I'm suggesting you get involved with some charity work.'

'I… I don't want any publicity at the moment—'

'Why not?'

'I… Sam and I prefer our life to be out of the spotlight.'

This still didn't make sense. Sunita had thrived in the spotlight, been pulled to it like a moth to a flame. But before he could point that out, the door opened and a waitress appeared with a tray.

'Thank you.' Sunita smiled as the girl placed the drinks on the table, alongside a plate of snacks that looked to range from across the globe. Tiny pizzas topped with morsels of smoked salmon nestled next to crisp, succulent *pakora*, which sat alongside miniature burgers in minuscule buns. 'These look delicious.'

Once the waitress had exited, Frederick sampled a *pakora*, savoured the bite of the spice and the crunch of the batter around the soft potato underneath. 'These are delicious! Sam runs an excellent kitchen.'

'Yes—he and…he has made a real success of this place.'

'You must be proud of him.'

'Yes. Of course.'

'Are you involved with the restaurant?'

'No.'

He sipped his drink, with its refreshing contrast of sharp and sweet. 'So what do you do now? Do you have a job?'

'I…'

Fluster showed in the heat that crept along her cheekbones, the abrupt swirling of her drink, the over-careful selection of a snack.

'I'm a lady of leisure.' Her eyes dared him to challenge her, but he couldn't help it—a snort of disbelief emerged. Sunita had been a human dynamo, always on the go, abuzz with energy, ideas and vibrancy.

'For real?'

'Yes.' Now her fingers tapped on the table in irritation. 'Why not? I'm lucky enough that I can afford not to work—I pay my own way.'

An undercurrent of steel lined her words—one he remembered all too well. 'Just like you did two years ago.'

It had become a standing joke—she'd refused point-blank to let him pay for anything, had insisted they split every bill down the middle. The one time he'd been foolish enough to buy her a gift, she'd handed it back.

I don't like to feel beholden. It's my issue, not yours. Keep it for your next woman. I pay my own way.'

Apparently she still did.

He raised his hands in a gesture of peace. 'Where you get your money from is none of my business. I just can't imagine you doing nothing all day.'

'That's not how it is. I have a very fulfilling life.'

'Doing what?'

'None of your business. You came here to find out why I disappeared. I've told you—I fell in love, I've settled down, and I want to live my life quietly.'

Instinct told him there was something askew with the portrait she painted. Tension showed in the tautness of her body; but perhaps that tension had nothing to do with him.

'My chief advisor will be relieved—he is worried there is some mystery around your disappearance that could damage me.'

For a fraction of a second her knuckles whitened around her glass and then her eyebrows rose in a quizzical curve. 'Isn't that a tad far-fetched? To say nothing of egotistically paranoid?'

'Possibly,' he agreed, matching her eyebrow for eyebrow. 'But it also seems extremely far-fetched to me that you walked away from your career.'

'Well, I did.'

Frederick waited, but it appeared Sunita felt that sufficed.

'So you confirm that your retreat and subsequent dramatic change of lifestyle have nothing to do with me?'

Her glance flickered away and then she laughed. 'We spent one night together two years ago. Do you *really* think that your charms, manifest though they were, were sufficient to make me change my life?'

Put like that, he had to admit it sounded arrogantly self-involved. And yet... 'We spent more than one night together, Sunita.'

A wave of her hand dismissed his comment. 'A publicity stunt—nothing more.'

'OK. Let's play it your way. I can just about buy it that those weeks were all about publicity for you, but what about that night? Was *that* all for publicity?'

These were the questions he should have asked two years ago.

Her gaze swept away from him. 'No. It wasn't. I didn't intend that night to happen.'

'Is that why you left?'

It was as though the years had rolled back—he could almost imagine that they were in that five-star hotel in Paris, where they'd played truant from the glitzy party they'd been supposed to be at. Attraction had finally taken over and—

Whoa! Reel it in, Frederick!

'Yes, that's why I left. I broke my own rules. By sleeping with you I became just another notch on your bedpost—another woman on the Playboy Prince's conveyor belt. That was never meant to happen.'

'That's not how it was.'

'That's *exactly* how it was.' Tawny eyes challenged him.

'And if I'd asked you to stay?'

'You didn't.'

Her voice was flat and who could blame her? The point was that he hadn't. Because it had been easier to believe that she'd never cared, to stick by his *easy come, easy go* motto.

'But this is all beside the point—there was never a future for us. People don't change.' Her voice held utter conviction. 'You were The Playboy Prince...'

'And *you* were very clear that you had no desire for a relationship because you wanted to focus on your career. Then, just weeks later, you met Sam and realised he was the one and your career was no longer important?' It was impossible for Frederick to keep the scepticism out of his voice.

'Yes, I did.'

'So you changed.'

'Love changes everything.'

Damn it—he'd stake his fortune on the sincerity in her voice, and there was that irrational nip of jealousy again.

'So, yes,' she continued, 'I met Sam and I decided to take a break, and the break has extended to a couple of years. Simple. No mystery. That's what you came here to discover.'

Now her tone had lost the fervour of truth—he was nearly sure of it.

'You promise?' The words were foolish, but he couldn't hold them back.

She nodded. 'I promise...'

He studied her expression, saw the hint of trouble in her eyes and in the twist of her fingers under the table.

'No scandal will break over Lycander.'

'Then my work here is done.'

Yet an odd reluctance pulled at him as he rose from the

chair and looked down at her, sure now that there was *more* than a hint of trouble in her eyes. *Not his business.* She'd made a promise and he believed her. He had a country to run, a destiny to fulfil...

'I wish you well, Sunita. I'm glad you've found happiness.'

'I wish you well too.'

In one lithe movement she stood and stretched out a hand, caught his sleeve, stood on tiptoe and brushed his cheek with her lips. Memory slammed into him—her scent, the silken touch of her hair against his skin—and it took all his powers of self-control not to tug her into his arms. Instead, he forced his body to remain still, to accept the kiss in the spirit it was being given—whatever that might be—though he was pretty damn sure from the heat that touched her cheeks that she wasn't sure either.

'I...goodbye.' Once again her hands twisted together as she watched him.

'Goodbye, Sunita.'

He headed for the door, stopped at her audible intake of breath, half turned as she said his name.

'Yes?'

'It...it doesn't matter. It was good to see you again.'

That only confirmed that she had intended to say something else, but before he could respond Sam entered and glanced at them both. 'All OK?'

'Everything is fine.' Sunita's voice was over-bright now. 'Frederick is just leaving.'

Minutes later he was in a taxi, headed back to the hotel. But as the journey progressed doubts hustled and bustled and crowded his brain. Something was wrong. He had no idea what, and it most likely had nothing to do with him. Quite possibly he had the wrong end of the stick. Undoubtedly wisdom dictated that he should not get involved. Sunita was more than capable of looking out for herself, and she had Sam to turn to. But what if Sam was the problem?

Hell.

Leaning forward, he gave the driver Sunita's address.

Damn it all to hell and back! Sunita strode the length of her lounge and resisted the urge to kick a bright red bean bag across the room. Venting wouldn't stem the onrush, the sheer *onslaught* of guilt, the veritable tsunami of distaste with herself.

Why, why, *why* had he turned up? Not telling Frederick for two years had been hard enough—lying directly to Frederick's face was another ballgame altogether. Especially as it was a face that mirrored Amil's—the angle of his cheekbone, the colour of his eyes, the subtle nuances that couldn't be ignored.

The guilt kept rolling on in and her stride increased. *Focus.* Concentrate on all the sensible, logical justifications for her actions.

The decision to keep Amil a secret had been one of the toughest she had ever faced, but it was a decision she still believed to be right. She'd done her research: the Lycanders had a track record of winning custody of their children and hanging the mothers out to dry.

Frederick's father, Prince Alphonse, had fathered five children by four wives; his first wife had died, but he'd fought and won vicious custody battles against all the other three.

Ah, pointed out her conscience, *but Alphonse is dead, and in any case Frederick is Amil's father.*

But Frederick was also his father's son, and who knew what he might do? The scandal of an illegitimate baby was the last thing Lycander's Prince needed at this juncture, and she had no idea how he would react.

She didn't like any of the possible scenarios—from a custody battle to show his people that he looked after his own, to an outright and public rejection of Amil. Well, damn it, the first would happen over her dead body and the second made her shudder—because she knew exactly how awful that rejection felt and she wouldn't put Amil through it.

But the Frederick she'd seen today—would he be so callous?

She didn't know. Her thoughts were muddled by the vortex of emotion his arrival had evoked. Because something had warmed inside her, triggering a whole rush of feelings. Memories had swooped and soared, smothering her skin in desire. Flashes of his touch, of their shared joy and passion…all of that had upended any hope of rational thought or perspective. Just like two years before.

When she'd first met Frederick she'd expected to thoroughly dislike him; his reputation as a cutthroat businessman-cum-playboy had seen to that. But when he'd asked her to dinner she'd agreed to it for the publicity. And at that dinner he'd surprised her. At the next he'd surprised her even more, and somehow, as time had gone on, they had forged a connection—one she had tried oh, so hard to tell herself was nothing more than temporary friendship.

Hah!

And then there had been that *stupid* tug of attraction, which had eventually prevailed and overridden every rule she'd set herself.

Well, not this time.

To her relief the doorbell rang. Amil's arrival would put an end to all this.

She dashed to the door and pulled it open, a smile of

welcome on her face. A smile that froze into a rictus of shock.

'Frederick?'

She didn't know why she'd posed it as a question, since it clearly *was* Frederick. Her brain scrambled for purchase and eventually found it as she moved to swing the door shut, to hustle him out.

Too late.

He stepped forward, glanced around the room, and she could almost see the penny begin to drop—slowly at first, as cursory curiosity morphed into deeper question.

'You have a baby?'

His hazel eyes widened in puzzlement, and a small frown creased his brow as he took another step into her sanctum. His gaze rested on each and every item of Amil's.

'Yes.' The word was a whisper—all she could manage as her tummy hollowed and she grasped the doorjamb with lifeless fingers.

'How old?'

Each syllable was ice-cold, edged with glass, and she nearly flinched. No, she would not be intimidated. Not here. Not now. What was done was done, and—rightly or wrongly—she knew that even if she could turn back time she would make the same decision.

'Fourteen months.'

'Girl or boy?'

'Boy.'

Each question, each answer, brought them closer and closer to the inevitable and her brain wouldn't function. Instead, all she could focus on was his face, on the dawn of emotion—wonder, anger, fear and surely hope too?

That last was so unexpected that it jolted her into further words. 'His name is Amil.'

'Amil,' he repeated.

He took another step forward and instinctively she moved as well, as if to protect the life she had built, putting herself between him and her home.

'Is he mine?'

For an instant it was if the world went out of focus. She could almost see a line being drawn in the sands of time—this was the instant that separated 'before' and 'after'. For one brief instant she nearly took the coward's route, wondered if he would swallow the lie that Amil was Sam's. Then she realised she could not, *would* not do that.

'Yes. He is yours. Amil is your son.'

Now she understood the origins of a deafening silence. This one rolled across the room, echoed in her ears until she wanted to shout. Instead she waited, saw his body freeze, saw the gamut of emotion cross his face, watched as it settled into an expression of anger so ice-cold a shiver rippled her skin.

Panic twisted her insides—the die had been cast and she knew that now, whatever happened, life would never be the same.

CHAPTER THREE

STAY STILL. FOCUS ON remaining still.

The room seemed to spin around him, the white walls a rotating blur, the floor tilting under his feet. Good thing he didn't suffer from seasickness. Emotions crashed into him, rebounded off the walls of his brain and the sides of his guts. His heart thudded his ribcage at the speed of insanity.

A child. A son. *His* child. *His* son.

Fourteen months old.

Fourteen months during which his son had had no father. Anger and pain twisted together. Frederick knew exactly what it was like to have no parent—his mother had abandoned him without compunction in return for a lump sum, a mansion and a yearly stipend that allowed her a life of luxury.

Easy come, easy go.

Yes, Frederick knew what it was like to know a parent was not there for him. The anger unfurled in him and solidified.

'My son,' he said slowly, and he couldn't keep the taut rage from his voice.

He saw Sunita's awareness of it, but she stepped forward right into the force field of his anger, tawny eyes fierce and fearless.

'*My* son,' she said.

Stop.

However angry he was, however furious he was, he had to think about the baby. About Amil. Memories of the horrendous custody battles his father had instigated crowded his mind—Stefan, Emerson, Barrett—his father had treated all his sons as possessions.

'*Our* son,' he said.

The knowledge was surreal, almost impossible to comprehend. But it was imperative that he kept in control—there was too much at stake here to let emotion override him. Time to shut emotion down, just as he had for two long years. Move it aside and deal with what had to be done.

'We need to talk.'

She hesitated and then nodded, moving forward to close the front door. She watched him warily, her hands twisted together, her tawny eyes wide.

'How do you know he's mine and not Sam's?'

The look she gave him was intended to wither. 'I'm not an idiot.'

'That is a questionable statement. But what you *have* shown yourself to be is a liar. So you can hardly blame me for the question, or for wanting a better answer than that. How do you know?'

Her eyes narrowed in anger as she caught her lower lip in her teeth and then released it alongside a sigh. 'Sam isn't my boyfriend. He has a perfectly lovely girlfriend called Miranda and they live together. I asked him to fake it to try and explain to you why I left the modelling world.'

'Is there a boyfriend at all?'

She shook her head. 'No.'

So there had been no one since him. The thought provoked a caveman sort of satisfaction that had no place in this discussion. Sunita had deceived him to his face in order to hide his son from him—now was not the moment to give a damn about her relationship status. Apart from the fact that it meant Amil was his.

Hold it together, Frederick. Shelve the emotion...deal with the situation at hand.

'Why didn't you tell me?'

Sunita started to pace. Her stride reminded him of a caged animal.

'Because I was scared.'

Halting in front of him, she looked so beautiful it momentarily pierced his anger.

'I know how hard this must be for you, but please try to understand I was terrified.'

For an instant he believed her, but then he recalled her profession, her ability to play to the camera, and he swatted down the foolish fledgling impulse to show sympathy and emitted a snort of disbelief.

'Terrified of what? What did I ever do to make you fear me?'

The idea was abhorrent—he'd witnessed his father in action, his delight in the exertion of power, and he'd vowed never to engage in a similar manner. Thus he'd embarked on a life of pleasure instead.

'It wasn't that straightforward. When we split obviously I had no idea I was pregnant. I found out a few weeks later and I was in shock. I did intend to tell you, but I decided to wait until I got to twelve weeks. And then your brother died. I *couldn't* tell you then, so I decided to wait some more.'

Now her expression held no apology, and her eyes met his full-on.

'And?'

'And obviously there was a lot of press at the time about Lycander. I did some research, and it's all there—your father fought custody battles over every one of his children except Axel, and that was only because Axel's mother died before he could do so. Your mother never saw you again, his third wife fought for years before she won the right even to *see* her son, and wife number four lost her case because he managed to make out she was unfit and she had to publicly humiliate herself in order to be granted minimal visiting rights.'

'That was my father—not me.'

'Yes, but *you* had become the Lycander heir. Are you saying your father wouldn't have fought for custody of his grandson? Even if you'd wanted to, how could you have stopped him? More to the point, would you have cared enough to try?'

The words hit him like bullets. She hadn't believed he would fight for the well-being of their child. She'd thought he would stand back and watch Alphonse wrest his son away.

He shook his head. *Do you blame her?* asked a small voice. He'd been the Playboy Prince—he'd worked hard, played harder, and made it clear he had no wish for any emotional responsibilities.

'I would *never* have let my father take our child from you.' He knew first-hand what it felt like to grow up without a mother. All the Lycander children did.

'I couldn't take that risk. Plus, you didn't want to be a father—you'd made it more than clear that you had no wish for a relationship or a child.'

'Neither did you.'

His voice was even, non-accusatory, but she bristled anyway, tawny eyes flashing lasers.

'I changed.'

'But you didn't give me the chance to. Not at any point in the past two years. Even if you could justify your deceit to yourself when my father was alive, you could have told me after his death.'

His father's death had unleashed a fresh tumult of emotion to close down. He'd had to accept that he would now never forge a relationship with the man who had constantly put him down—the man who had never forgiven him for his mother's actions. And on a practical level it had pitchforked him into the nightmare scenario of ascension to the throne.

But none of that explained her continued deceit.

'I read the papers, Frederick. You have had enough to contend with in the past year to keep your throne—the revelation of a love-child with me would have finished you off. You were practically engaged to Lady Kaitlin.'

'So you want my *gratitude* for keeping my child a secret? You've persuaded yourself that you did it for me? Is that how you sleep at night?'

'I sleep fine at night. I did what I thought was right. I didn't want Amil to grow up knowing that he had been the reason his father lost his throne, or lost the woman he loved. That is too big a burden for any child.'

The words were rounded with utter certainty.

'That was not your decision to make. At any point. Regardless of the circumstances, you should have come to me as soon as you knew you were pregnant. Nothing should have stopped you. Not Axel, not my father, not Kaitlin—*nothing*. You have deprived him of his father.'

'I chose depriving him of his father over depriving him of his mother.' Her arms dropped to her sides and a sudden weariness slumped her shoulders. 'We can argue about this for ever—I did what I thought was best. For Amil.'

'*And* you.'

'If you like. But in this case the two were synonymous. He needs me.'

'I get that.'

He'd have settled for any mother—had lived in hope that one of the series of stepmothers would give a damn. Until he'd worked out there was little point getting attached, as his father quite simply got rid of each and every one.

'But Amil also needs his father. That would be me.'

'I accept that you are his father.'

Although she didn't look happy about it, her eyes were full of wariness.

'But whether he needs you or not depends on what you are offering him. If that isn't good for him then he doesn't need you. It makes no odds whether you are his father or not. The whole "blood is thicker than water" idea sucks.'

No argument there. 'I *will* be part of Amil's life.'

'It's not that easy.'

'It doesn't matter if it's easy.'

'Those are words. Words are meaningless. Exactly *how* would it work? You'll disguise yourself every so often and sneak over here to see him on "unofficial business" masked by your charity work? Or will you announce to your people that you have a love-child?'

Before he could answer there was a knock at the door and they both stilled.

'It's my grandmother…with Amil.' Panic touched her expression and she closed her eyes and inhaled deeply. 'I don't want my grandmother to know until we've worked out what to do.'

Frederick searched for words, tried to think, but the enormity of the moment had eclipsed his ability to rationalise. Instead fear came to the podium—he had a child, a son, and he was about to meet him.

What would he feel when he saw Amil?

The fear tasted ashen—what if he felt nothing?

What if he was like his mother and there was no instinctive love, merely an indifference that bordered on dislike? Or like his father, who had treated his sons as possessions, chess pieces in his petty power games?

If so, then he'd fake it—no matter what he did or didn't feel, he'd fake love until it became real.

He hauled in a deep breath and focused on Sunita's face. 'I'll leave as soon as you let them in. Ask your grandmother to look after Amil tonight. Then I'll come back and we can finish this discussion.'

Sunita nodded agreement and stepped forward.

His heart threatened to leave his ribcage and moisture sheened his neck as she pulled the door open.

A fleeting impression registered, of a tall, slender woman with silver hair pulled back in a bun, clad in a shimmering green and red sari, and then his gaze snagged on the little boy in her arms. Raven curls, chubby legs, a goofy smile for his mother.

Mine. My son.

Emotion slammed into him—so hard he almost recoiled and had to concentrate to stay steady. Fight or flight kicked in—half of him wanted to turn and run in sheer terror, the other half wanted to step forward and take his son, shield him from all and any harm.

'Nanni, this is an old friend of mine who's dropped in.'

'Good to meet you.' Somehow Frederick kept his voice even, forced himself to meet the older woman's alert gaze. He saw the small frown start to form on her brow and turned back to Sunita. 'It was great to see you again, Sunita. 'Til later.'

A last glance at his son—*his son*—and he walked away.

Sunita scooped Amil up and buried herself in his warmth and his scent. She held him so close that he wriggled in protest, so she lowered him to the ground and he crawled towards his play mat.

'Thank you for looking after him.'

'I enjoyed it immensely. And thank *you*, Sunita, for allowing me to be part of Amil's life. And yours.'

'Stop! I have told you—you don't need to thank me.'

Yet every time she did.

'Yes, I do. I was neither a good mother nor a good grandmother. You have given me a chance of redemption, and I appreciate that with all my heart.'

'We've been through this, Nanni; the past is the past and we're only looking forward.'

Her grandmother's marriage had been deeply unhappy—her husband had been an autocrat who had controlled every aspect of his family's life with an iron hand. When Sunita's mother had fallen pregnant by a British man who'd had no intent of standing by her, her father had insisted she be disowned.

Sunita could almost hear her mother's voice now: *'Suni, sweetheart, never, ever marry a man who can control you.'*

It was advice Sunita intended to take one step further— she had no plans to marry anyone, *ever*. Her father's marriage had been a misery of incompatibility, bitterness and blame—an imbroglio she'd been pitchforked into to live a Cinderella-like existence full of thoughtless, uncaring relations.

'Please, Nanni. You are a wonderful grandmother and great-grandmother and Amil adores you. Now, I have a favour to ask. Would you mind looking after Amil for the rest of the evening?'

'So you can see your friend again?'

'Yes.'

'The friend you didn't introduce?'

Sunita opened her mouth and closed it again.

Her grandmother shook her head. 'You don't have to tell me.'

'I *will* tell you, Nanni—but after dinner, if that's OK.'

'You will tell me whenever you are ready. Whatever it is, this time I will be there for you.'

An hour later, with Amil fed and his bag packed, Sunita gave her grandmother a hug. She watched as the driver she'd insisted on providing manoeuvred the car into the stream of traffic, waved, and then made her way back upstairs... To find the now familiar breadth of Frederick on the doorstep, a jacket hooked over his shoulder.

'Come in. Let's talk.'

He followed her inside and closed the door, draping his dark grey jacket over the back of a chair. 'Actually, I thought we could talk somewhere else. I've booked a table at Zeus.'

Located in one of Mumbai's most luxurious hotels, Zeus was the city's hottest restaurant, graced by celebrities and anyone who wanted to see and be seen.

Foreboding crept along her skin, every instinct on full alert. 'Why on earth would you do that?'

'Because I am taking the mother of my child out for dinner so we can discuss the future.'

Sunita stared at him as the surreal situation deepened into impossibility. 'If you and I go out for dinner it will galvanise a whole load of press interest.'

'That is the point. We are going public. I will not keep Amil a secret, or make him unofficial business.'

She blinked as her brain crashed and tried to change gear. 'But we haven't discussed this at all.'

This was going way too fast, and events were threatening to spiral out of control. *Her* control.

'I don't think we should go public until we've worked out the practical implications—until we have a plan.'

'Not possible. People are already wondering where I am. Especially my chief advisor. People may have spotted us at the café, and April Fotherington will be wondering if my presence in Mumbai is connected to you. I want the truth to come out on *my* terms, not hers, or those of whichever reporter makes it their business to "expose" the story. I want this to break in a positive way.'

Sunita eyed him, part of her impressed by the sheer strength and absolute assurance he projected, another part wary of the fact he seemed to have taken control of the situation without so much as a by-your-leave.

'I'm not sure that's possible. Think about the scandal—your people won't like this.' And they wouldn't like *her*, a supermodel with a dubious past. 'Are you sure this is the best way to introduce Amil's existence to your people?'

'I don't know. But I believe it's the right way to show my people that this is *good* news, that Amil is not a secret. That I am being honest.'

An unpleasant twinge of guilt pinched her nerves—*she* had kept Amil secret, *she* had been dishonest. She had made a decision that no longer felt anywhere near as right as it had this morning.

'So what do you say?' he asked. 'Will you have dinner with me?'

The idea gave her a sudden little thrill, brought back a sea of memories of the dinners they had shared two years before—dinners when banter and serious talk had flown back and forth, when each word, each gesture, had been a movement in the ancient dance of courtship. A courtship she had never meant to consummate…

But this meal would be on a whole new level and courtship would not be on the table. Wherever they held this discussion tonight, the only topic of conversation would be Amil and the future.

And if Frederick believed this strategy was the best way forward then she owed him her co-operation.

'Let's get this show on the road.' An unexpected fizz of excitement buzzed through her. She could *do* this; she'd always relished a fight and once upon a time she'd revelled in a show. 'But I need to change.'

'You look fine to me.'

His voice was deep and molten, and just like that the atmosphere changed. Awareness hummed and vibrated, shimmering around them, and she had to force herself to remain still, to keep her feet rooted to the cool tiles of the floor. The hazel of his eyes had darkened in a way she remembered all too well, and now it was exhilaration of a different sort that heated her veins.

Stop.

All that mattered here was Amil and his future. Two years ago she had tried and failed to resist the magnetic pull that Frederick exerted on her—a pull she had distrusted, and this time would not permit. Whatever her treacherous hormones seemed to think.

Perhaps he realised the same, because he stepped backwards and nodded. 'But I appreciate you want to change.'

'I do. You need a show, and a show is exactly what I can provide. Luckily I kept some of the clothes from my modelling days.'

Even if she'd never once worn them, she loved them still. Silk, chiffon and lace, denim and velvet, long skirts and short, flared and skinny—she had enjoyed showcasing each and every outfit. Had refused to wear any item that didn't make her soul sing. And now there was no denying the buzz. This was what she had once lived for and craved. Publicity, notice, fame—all things she could spin and control.

Almost against her will, her mind fizzed with possibility. Amil was no longer a secret, no longer in danger—they could live their lives as they wished. She could resume her career, be Sunita again, walk the catwalks and revel in fashion and all its glorious aspects. Amil would, of course, come with her—just as she had accompanied her mother to fashion shoots—and Nanni could come too.

Life would take on a new hue without the terrible burden of discovery clouding every horizon. Though of course Frederick would be part of that life, if only a minor part. His real life lay in Lycander, and she assumed he would want only a few visits a year perhaps.

Whoa! Slow right down, Suni!

She had no idea what Frederick's plans were, and she'd do well to remember that before she waltzed off into la-la land. She didn't know this man—this Frederick.

Her gaze rested on him, absorbed the breadth of his body, his masculine presence, the determined angle of his stubbled jaw, the shadowed eyes crinkled now in a network of lines she thought probably hadn't come from laughter. Her breath caught on a sudden wave of desire. Not only physical desire, but a stupid yearning to walk over and smooth the shadows away.

A yearning she filed away under both dangerous and delusional as she turned and left the room.

CHAPTER FOUR

FREDERICK CHANGED INTO the suit he'd had delivered to him whilst he was waiting and prowled the flat on the lookout for evidence of Amil's life.

Amil. The syllables were still so unfamiliar—his only knowledge of his son that brief glimpse a few hours earlier. But there would be time—plenty of time—to catch up on the past fourteen months. Provided Sunita agreed to his proposition—and she *would* agree.

Whatever it took, he would make her see his option was the only way forward.

He paused in front of a framed photograph of Sunita and a newborn Amil. He looked at the tiny baby, with his downy dark hair, the impossible perfection of his minuscule fingernails, and the utter vulnerability of him twisted Frederick's gut.

Shifting his gaze to Sunita, he saw the love in her brown eyes clear in every nuance, every part of her body. Her beauty was unquestionable, but this was a beauty that had nothing to do with physical features and everything to do with love.

Perhaps he should feel anger that he had missed out on that moment, but his overwhelming emotion was relief—gratitude, even—that his son had been given something so vital. Something he himself had never received. *His* mother had handed him straight over to a nanny and a few scant years later had disappeared from his life.

For a long moment Frederick gazed at the photo, trying to figure out what he should feel, what he *would* feel when he finally met Amil properly, held him... Panic hammered his chest and he stepped backwards. What if he was like his mother—what if he quite simply lacked the parenting gene?

The click of heels against marble snapped him to attention and he stepped back from the photo, turning to see Sunita advance into the room. For a moment his lungs truly ceased to work as his pulse ratcheted up a notch or three.

Sunita looked... It was impossible to describe her without recourse to a thesaurus. *This* was the woman he remembered—the one who dressed to catch the eye. But it wasn't only the dress with its bright red bodice and gently plumed skirt that showcased her trademark legs. The bright colour was toned down by contrasting black satin panels and silver stiletto heels. It was the way she wore it—she seemed to bring the dress alive. And vice versa. A buzz vibrated from her—an energy and sparkle that epitomised Sunita.

'Wow!' was the best he could do as he fought down visceral desire and the need to tug her into his arms and rekindle the spark that he knew with gut-wrenching certainty would burst into flame. To kiss her senseless...

What the hell was he thinking? More to the point, what part of himself was he thinking *with*?

Maybe he was more like his father than he knew. Alphonse had always put physical desire above all else. If he'd been attracted to a woman he'd acted on that attraction, regardless of marriage vows, fidelity or the tenets of plain, common decency. The last ruler of Lycander had believed that *his* desires were paramount, and it didn't matter who got hurt in the process.

Frederick wouldn't walk that road. He never had—that, at least, was one immoral path he'd avoided.

His business with Sunita was exactly that—*business*. He had an idea to propound, an idea he would not mix with the physical.

'You look fantastic.'

'Thank you. I know it sounds shallow, but it is awesome to dress up again.'

She smoothed her hand down the skirt and her smile caught at his chest.

'You look pretty good yourself. Where did the suit come from?'

'I had it delivered whilst I was waiting.'

'Good thinking, Batman.'

Her voice was a little breathless, and he knew that she was as affected as he was by their proximity. Her scent teased him, her eyes met his, and what he saw in their deep brown depths made him almost groan aloud.

Enough.

Right now he had to focus on the most important factor, and that was Amil. Irritation scoured him that he could be letting physical attraction come into play.

He nodded to the door. 'We'd better go.'

Sunita wanted, *needed* this journey to come to an end. Despite the spacious interior of the limo, Frederick was too…*close*.

Memories lingered in the air, and her body was on high alert, tuned in to his every move, and she loathed her own weakness as much now as she had two years before. She needed to distract herself, to focus on what was important—and that was Amil.

The day's events had moved at warp speed and she was desperately trying to keep up. The truth was out, and it was imperative she kept control of a future that she could no longer reliably predict.

Frederick wanted to be a real part of Amil's life—he had made that more than clear. But at this point she had no idea what that meant, and she knew she had to tread carefully.

The limo slowed down and she took a deep breath as it glided to a stop.

'Ready?' he asked.

'Ready.'

With any luck she wouldn't have lost her touch with the press. In truth, she'd always liked the paparazzi. Her mother had always told her that publicity was a means to measure success, part of the climb to fame and fortune and independence.

They stepped out into a crowd of reporters, the click of cameras and a fire of questions.

'Are you back together?'

'Friends or lovers?'

'Does Kaitlin know?'

'Where have you been, Sunita?'

Frederick showed no sign of tension. His posture and smile were relaxed, his whole attitude laid back.

'At present we have no comment. But if you hold on I promise we will have an announcement to make after dinner.'

Next to him, Sunita smiled the smile that had shot her to catwalk fame. She directed a small finger-wave at a reporter who'd always given her positive press, a smile at a woman she'd always enjoyed a good relationship with, and a wink at a photographer renowned for his audacity.

Then they left the reporters behind and entered the restaurant, and despite the knowledge of how important the forthcoming conversation was a part of Sunita revelled in the attention she was gathering. The simple ability to walk with her own natural grace, to know it was OK to be recognised, her appreciation of the dress and the inner confidence it gave her—all of it was such a contrast to the past two years, during which she had lived in constant denial of her own identity, burdened by the fear of discovery.

The manager beamed at them as he led them past the busy tables, where patrons looked up from their food and a buzz immediately spread. Sunita kept her eyes ahead, noting the dark-stained English Oak screens and latticing that graced the room, the hustle and bustle from the open-plan kitchen where chefs raced round, the waiters weaving in and out, and the tantalising smells that drifted into the eating area.

'As requested, we've seated you in a private dining area where you will be undisturbed. My head chef has arranged a buffet for you there, with samples of all our signature dishes, and there is, of course, champagne on ice—we are very happy to welcome you both here.'

He turned to Sunita.

'I do not expect you to remember me, but when you were a child your mother brought you many, many times to the restaurant I worked in then. Your mother was a lovely lady.'

Memory tugged as she studied the manager's face. 'I *do* remember you. You're Nikhil! You used to give me extra sweets and fortune cookies, and you would help me read the fortunes.'

His smile broadened. 'That is correct—I am very happy to see you here, and I am very sorry about your mother. She was a good woman.'

'Thank you. That means a lot to me. And it would have to her as well.'

It really would. So many people had looked down on

Leela Baswani because she had been a single, unmarried mother, and a model and actress to boot. But her mother had refused to cower before them; she had lived her life and she'd loved every minute of it—even those terrible last few months. Months she didn't want to remember, of watching her mother decline, knowing that soon she would be left alone in the world.

But those were not the memories Leela would have wanted her daughter to carry forth into life. Instead she would remember her as Nikhil did—as a good, brave, vibrant woman.

Nikhil showed them into the private dining room, where a beautifully decorated table laid with snowy white linen held fluted glassware, gleaming cutlery and a simple table decoration composed of an arrangement of glorious white roses.

Sunita looked at them, and then at Nikhil, and a lump formed in her throat. White roses had been her mother's favourite flower—her trademark accessory—and as the scent reached her nostrils she closed her eyes for a second. 'Thank you, Nikhil.'

The manager gave a small bow. 'You are very welcome. Now, both of you enjoy the food. I believe our chef has excelled himself. And I guarantee you complete privacy.'

With one more beaming smile, he left, closing the door behind him.

'I'm sorry about your mother,' Frederick said.

'Thank you.'

'She isn't mentioned in any articles about you except April's most recent one. None of your family is.'

'No. They aren't.'

And that was the way it would stay—she would love to remember her mother more publicly, but to do that would risk questions about her father, and she'd severed her ties with him years before—the man who'd abandoned her before birth and then reappeared in her life only to make it thoroughly miserable.

'Anyway, we aren't here to speak of my family.' He raised an eyebrow and she bit her lip. 'I mean, we are here to discuss Amil's future.'

'We are. But first shall we help ourselves to food?'

She nodded. No way could she hurt Nikhil's feelings, but she sensed there was more to Frederick's suggestion than that. It was almost as if he were stalling, giving himself time to prepare, and a sense of foreboding prickled her skin—one she did her best to shake off as she made a selection from the incredible dishes displayed on the table.

There was a tantalising array of dumplings with descriptions written in beautiful calligraphy next to each platter— prawn and chive, shanghai chicken, *pak choi*… Next to them lay main courses that made her mouth water—Szechuan clay pot chicken, salmon in Assam sauce, ginger fried rice…

The smell itself was enough to allay her fears, and she reminded herself that Frederick had a country to run— other fish to fry, so to speak. Surely the most he would want would be to contribute to Amil's upkeep and see him a few times a year. That would work—that would be more than enough.

Once they were seated, she took a deep breath. 'Before we start this discussion you need to know that I will not agree to anything that feels wrong for Amil. He is my priority here and if you try to take him away from me I will fight you with my last dying breath. I just want that out there.'

There was something almost speculative in his gaze, alongside a steely determination that matched her own. 'Amil is my priority too—and that means I *will* be a real part of his life. That is non-negotiable. *I* just want *that* out there.'

'Fine. But what does that mean?'

'I'm glad you asked that, because I've given this some thought and I know what I believe is best for Amil's future.'

The smoothness of his voice alerted Sunita's anxiety. The presentiment of doom returned and this time her very bones knew it was justified. Spearing a dumpling with an effort at nonchalance, she waved her fork in the air.

'Why don't you tell me what you have in mind?'

His hazel eyes met hers, his face neutral. 'I want you to marry me.'

CHAPTER FIVE

'MARRY YOU?' SUITA STARED at him, flabberghasted. 'That's a joke, right?'

It must be his opening bid in negotiations designed to throw her into a state of incoherence. If so, he'd slammed the nail on the head.

'No joke. Trust me, marriage isn't a topic I'd kid about. It's a genuine proposal—I've thought it through.'

'When? In the past few hours? Are you certifiably *nuts*?'

'This makes sense.'

'How? There is no universe where this makes even a particle of a molecule of sense.'

'This is what is best for Amil—best for our son.'

'No, it isn't. Not in this day and age. You *cannot* play the let's-get-together-for-our-child's-sake card.'

That was the stuff of fairy tales, and she was damned sure that her mother had been right about those being a crock of manure.

'Yes, I can. In the circumstances.'

'What circumstances?' Her fogged brain attempted to illuminate a pathway to understanding and failed.

'If you marry me Amil will become Crown Prince of Lycander after me. If you don't, he won't.'

The words took the wind out of the sails of incredulity. Of *course*. *Duh!* But the idea that Frederick would marry her to legitimise Amil hadn't even tiptoed across her mind. The whole concept of her baby one day ruling a principality seemed surreal, and right now she needed to cling onto reality.

'We can't get married to give Amil a crown.'

'But we can get married so that we don't deprive him of one.'

'Semantics.' *Think.* 'He won't feel deprived of something he never expected to have.' *Would he?* 'Amil will grow up knowing...'

Her voice trailed off. Knowing what? That if his mother had agreed to marry his father he would have been a prince, a ruler, rather than a prince's illegitimate love-child.

'Knowing that he can be whatever he wants to be,' she concluded.

'As long as what he wants to be isn't Ruler of Lycander.'

Panic stole over her, wrapped her in tentacles of anxiety. 'You are putting me in an impossible position. You are asking me to decide Amil's entire future. To make decisions on his behalf.'

'No. I am suggesting *we* make this decision together. I believe this is the best course of action for Amil. If you think otherwise then convince me.'

'He may not want to be pushed into a pre-ordained future—may not want to be a ruler. Why would we burden him with the weight of duty, with all the rules and obligations that come with it?'

'Because it is his *right* to rule. Just as it was my brother's.'

His voice was even, but she saw the shadows chase across his eyes, sensed the pain the words brought.

'Axel wanted to rule—he believed in his destiny.'

'So you believe this is Amil's destiny?' Sunita shook her

head. 'It's too abstract. We make our own destiny and Amil will make his, whatever we decide to do. I want to make the decision that is best for his wellbeing and happiness—you don't need a crown for either.'

'This isn't about need—this is about his birthright. As my first born son he has the right to inherit the Lycander crown.'

'Even though he was born out of wedlock?'

It was the phrase her grandmother had used to describe Sunita's birth, to try and explain why her husband had thrown their pregnant daughter out.

I know it is hard to understand in this day and age, Sunita, but in our family a mixed race child, born out of wedlock, was a stigma. It wasn't right, but it was how my husband felt.'

A feeling shared by others. Sunita could still feel the sting of the taunts her half-siblings had flung at her— nasty, insidious words that had clawed at her self-esteem.

Focus. Frederick watched her, his hazel eyes neutral and cool; he was in control and she quite clearly wasn't. Her thoughts raced round a playground of panic, visited the seesaw, spent time on the slide. Being born out of wedlock would have no impact on Amil's life; it was not a reason to get married.

She forced herself to concentrate on Frederick's answer to her question.

'It makes no odds as long as we legitimise him through marriage,' he said. 'Lycander's rules are complex, but clear on that front.'

Oh, Lord. What was she supposed to do? How could she make a decision like this without the use of a crystal ball? Her mother had believed the right course of action had been to hand Sunita over to her father.

'People can change, Suni,' her mother had said. She'd

stroked Sunita's hair with a hand that had looked almost translucent, the effort of even that movement an evident strain. *'I have to believe that.'*

Sunita understood the uncharacteristic thread of sentimentality in her mother over those final weeks. Leela Baswani had wanted to die believing her daughter would be safe and happy, and so she had allowed herself to be conned again by the man who had already broken her heart. She'd allowed herself to believe that people could change.

Well, she'd been wrong. And so was this.

'This is impossible, Frederick. We can't spend the rest of our lives together.'

The very idea of spending a *week* with anyone made her skin prickle in affront—she could almost feel the manacles closing round her wrists. 'Maybe we should get married, legitimise Amil, and then get a divorce.'

Even as the words left her lips she knew how stupid they were.

'No. I want to give Amil a life with both his parents, and most importantly, if he is to rule Lycander, he needs to live in the palace, be brought up to understand his inheritance. And I need a wife—a true consort.'

This was becoming laughable. 'Really, I am *not* wife material—trust me on this.'

His broad shoulders lifted. 'But you *are* the mother of my child.'

Fabulous. 'So you'll make do with me because I come with a ready-made heir? And this whole marriage idea is because we are convenient?' The idea caused welcome anger—an emotion she could manage way better than panic.

'You don't care about Amil as a person—you only care about him as a commodity.'

'No!' Her words had clearly touched a nerve. 'I care about Amil because he is my son and I believe this is his right. I want him to grow up with two parents. And, believe me, this is hardly *convenient*. I intended to present my people with a wife and heir in a more conventional way.'

'Well, gee, thank you. That makes us feel *really* special.'

But she was the woman who had omitted to mention his son's existence—making her feel special would hardly be anywhere on his agenda.

His raised eyebrows indicated complete accord with her unspoken thought. 'There's no point in hypocrisy. If you expect me to go down on one knee, think again.'

'I don't expect anything—especially not a proposal. I don't want to marry you; I don't want to marry anyone.'

'I appreciate that. Until recently marriage has never exactly been high on my to-do list either. Back in the day I had a business to run and a party lifestyle to maintain. But circumstances have changed. For us both. *We* have Amil. *I* now have a country to run. I need a wife and I need an heir…to show the people of Lycander that I have changed. That I am responsible, that I offer stability, that I can put the principality's needs above my own.'

Sunita tried to equate this Frederick with the man she had known. '*Have* you changed?'

'Yes.' The syllable was bleak in its certainty, but despite its brevity it conveyed absolute conviction. 'You can choose to believe that or not, as you wish. But believe this: I need to get married.'

'Well, I don't. I prefer to be on my own.' She didn't want to be tied to anyone—she wanted to be independent and free to make decisions for herself and for Amil. 'Free.' *In control.*

'I understand that.' His jaw set in a hard line. 'But marriage is the only way to secure Amil his birthright and give him two parents one hundred per cent of the time.'

There was a strange undercurrent to his voice, and she realised just how important this must be to him. According to her research, his parents had split when he was three and his father had won sole custody. After that he'd had a series of stepmothers, none of whom had lasted more than a few years. So perhaps it was little wonder he wanted to give his son the kind of stable family he'd never had. For a moment, compassion for the little boy he had once been touched her and she forced herself to concentrate on the present.

'But it wouldn't be good for Amil to grow up and see his parents in an unhappy marriage.'

'Why assume it will be unhappy?'

'Because…' To her own annoyance, not a single reason sprang to mind that didn't sound stupid. Eventually she said, 'You can't expect me to sign up to a life sentence with a man I don't even know.'

'Fair enough. Then let's rectify that.'

He smiled—a smile of the toe-curling variety, like sunshine breaking through a grey cloudbank. And she couldn't help smiling back. But then the moment was gone and the stormy skies reappeared.

'Rectify it how?'

'Let's get to know each other. Bring Amil to Lycander and—'

'No! Once we are in Lycander I have no idea if we will be subject to Lycander law. Which, as far as I can gather, is *you*.'

The smile was a distant memory now, his face set in granite. 'You don't trust me?'

'I don't trust anyone.' After all, if you couldn't trust your own father, who *could* you trust? His promise to her mother that he would look after Sunita, care for her as only a parent could, had turned out to be a bunch of empty, meaningless syllables.

'So we stay here.'

He raised his hands. 'Fair enough. But I can't be away for too long. I can stay in Mumbai for a few days or... Wait, I have a better idea.' The smile made a return. 'How about we go away for a few days? You and me. Away from the press and the politics and the spotlight.'

'You and me?' Panic and horror cartwheeled in her stomach.

'Yes. You and me. I'll put my money where my mouth is—you said you couldn't marry someone you didn't know, so here's the opportunity to spend time with me. Twenty-four-seven, with no distractions.'

'Be still my beating heart.'

Now his smile broadened and this time she was sure her hair curled.

'I *knew* you'd like the idea. Would your grandmother be happy to look after Amil?'

'If I agree to this, Amil comes with us.' A frown touched her brow and her eyes narrowed in suspicion. 'Surely you want to get to know your son?'

'Of course I do. But before we spend time together as a family, we need to know where we stand. I know he is only a baby, but I want him to have certainty and stability.'

The kind of certainty she guessed he'd never known. Again for an instant she wanted to reach out and offer comfort. *What to do? What to do?* In truth she didn't know. She should close this down now—but was that the right thing for Amil?

Frederick wanted to be a real part of his life, wanted to make him his heir. She couldn't in all conscience dismiss it out of hand. More than that, insane though it might be, there was a tiny part of her that didn't want to. That same tiny part that two years ago had wanted Frederick to ask her to stay, to sweep her into his arms and—

Cue mental eye-roll and a reality check. Fairy tales didn't exist. This was for Amil's sake.

'OK. Two days. I won't leave Amil longer than that.'

'Deal. Where do you want to go?'

Sunita thought for a moment. 'Goa.' That would keep it all in perspective—her parents had spent some time in Goa; they'd been happy there, but that hadn't led to a happily-ever-after in any sense.

'OK. Here's how it'll work. I'll have my people pick up Amil and your grandmother now, and bring them to the hotel. Once we make the announcement about Amil the press will converge. I want my son safe here, under royal security protection.'

She could feel the colour leech from her skin and saw that he had noticed it.

'I don't believe he is danger, but his position has changed. No matter what we decide, there will be more interest in him and his life from now on.'

She inhaled an audible breath. 'You're right. I'll call my grandmother and prepare her.'

Pulling her phone out of her bag, she rose and walked to the opposite end of the room.

Frederick watched as Sunita paced the width of the room as she talked, her voice low but animated, one hand gesturing as the conversation progressed.

It was impossible not to admire her fluidity of movement, her vibrancy. At least she hadn't blown the marriage idea out of the water. But he'd known she wouldn't do that—for Amil she had to consider it. What woman would deprive her son of a crown? Yet unease still tingled in his veins. Sunita might well be the one woman who would do exactly that.

Ironic, really—his chief advisor had a list of women who wanted to marry him, and he'd proposed to the one woman who didn't even want to audition for the part of bride.

No matter—he would convince her that this was the way forward. Whatever it took.

His conscience jabbed him. Really? *Whatever* it took? Maybe that was how his father had justified the custody battles.

Abruptly he turned away and, pulling his own phone out, set to work making arrangements.

He dropped his phone back in his pocket as she returned to the table. 'How did your grandmother take it?'

'With her trademark unflappable serenity. I think she suspected—she may even have recognised you earlier and put two and two together. She'll have Amil ready.' Her chin jutted out at a defiant angle. 'I've asked Sam and Miranda as well.'

She really didn't trust him. 'Do you really think I will take Amil from you by force?'

Silence greeted this and he exhaled heavily.

'If you can't trust my morality then at least trust my intelligence. I want you to marry me—kidnapping Amil would hardly help my cause. Or garner me positive publicity in Lycander. You hid Amil from me for two years. I have more reason to distrust *you* than vice versa.'

'Maybe it's best if neither of us trusts each other.'

She had a point.

'Works for me. Whilst we are away Amil will be in your grandmother's charge, with Sam and Miranda as your back-up. But they remain based in the hotel, and if they go anywhere one of my staff goes with them. Does that work for you?'

'Yes.'

'Good. Once they are safely here I'll announce it to the press. We'll leave for Goa tomorrow, after my visit to the school.'

'Whoa! Hold on.' One elegant hand rose in the air to stop him. 'This is a *joint* operation. So, first off, *I* want to make the announcement. And we are *not* mentioning marriage.'

She drummed her fingers on the table and he could see her mind whir. This had always been her forte—she'd used to play the press like a finely tuned instrument, and had always orchestrated publicity for maximum impact with impeccable timing.

'Prince Frederick and I are delighted to announce that fourteen months ago our son Amil was born. Obviously we have a great deal to discuss about the future, which we will be doing over the next few days. My press office will be in touch with details of a photo opportunity with the three of us tomorrow.'

'Photo opportunity?' Three of us…? The words filled him with equal parts terror and anticipation.

'Yes. Better to arrange it than have them stalk us to try and get one. And I assume you want to spend time with Amil before we go?' She clocked his hesitation before he could mask it. 'Is there a problem?'

'No.' *Liar.*

Her eyes filled with doubt. He racked his brain and realised that in this case only the truth would suffice.

'I don't want to upset Amil or confuse him just before you leave him.'

He didn't want his son to believe on any level that it

was his father's fault that he was losing his mother. Even for a few days.

For the first time since his proposal she smiled—a real, genuine smile—and he blinked at the warmth it conveyed. If he were fanciful, he'd swear it had heated his skin and his soul.

'You won't upset him. Truly. How about we take him to the Hanging Gardens? He loves it there—the press can take their photos and then we can take him for a walk.'

'Sounds great.'

But the warmth dissipated and left a cold sheen of panic in its wake. What if the meeting didn't go well? What if they couldn't connect?

Then he'd fake it. If he could close his emotions down— and he was a past master in the art—then surely the reverse would be true too. 'My school visit is planned for seven a.m., so if we schedule the press for midday that should work.'

'I'd like to come with you to the school. It's a cause I'd love to be involved in, and now…now I can.'

Her smile broadened and it occurred to him that, whilst he couldn't condone what she had done, hiding Amil had impacted on Sunita's life heavily. She'd lost her career, had to subdue her identity and become anonymous.

Sheesh. Get a grip. Any minute now he'd start to feel sorry for her.

The point now was that Sunita would be an asset to the charity.

His phone beeped and he read the message.

'Amil and your grandmother are in the hotel. So are Sam and Miranda. So let's go and face the press.'

And then he'd face the music. He had no doubt his chief advisor had set up a veritable orchestra.

CHAPTER SIX

'YOU'VE DONE *WHAT*?' Marcus Alrikson, hot off a private jet, scooted across the floor of the hotel suite. 'The whole existence of a secret baby is bad enough—but now you're telling me you have proposed marriage!' Marcus paused, pinched the bridge of his nose and inhaled deeply. 'Why?'

Frederick surveyed him from the depths of the leather sofa. 'Because I have a son, and I want my son to live with me *and* his mother. I realise that flies in the face of Lycander tradition, but there you have it. I want Amil to inherit his birthright. The only way to achieve both those goals is marriage.'

'If this marriage loses you the crown he won't have a birthright to inherit.'

'It won't.' Frederick imbued his voice with a certainty he was far from feeling—but he was damned if he would admit that to Marcus. 'This is the right thing to do and the people of Lycander will see that.'

'Perhaps...but that doesn't mean they will accept Sunita or Amil.'

'They will have no reason not to. Sunita has proved herself to be an exemplary mother. And she will be an exemplary princess.'

Marcus shook his head. 'She is a supermodel with a reputation as a party girl. You have no idea what she may or may not do—she would never have made my list in a million years. She is as far from Kaitlin Derwent as the moon is from Jupiter.'

'And look what happened with Lady Kaitlin. Plus, don't you think you're being a little hypocritical? What about *my* reputation?'

'You have spent two years showing that you have changed. The reforms you are undertaking for Lycander are what the people want. You may have been a playboy with a party lifestyle, but you also founded a global business—Freddy Petrelli's Olive Oil is on supermarket shelves worldwide. At least you partied on your own dime.'

'So did Sunita. And her party days were over by the time we met.'

'Sunita has spent two years hiding your son from you,' Marcus retorted. 'There is nothing to suggest she will be good for Lycander and plenty to suggest she will plunge the monarchy straight back into scandal. She could run off with Amil, file for divorce before the honeymoon is over...'

'She won't.'

He couldn't know that, though—not really. He'd known Sunita for a couple of weeks two years ago. Doubt stepped in but he kicked it out even as he acknowledged the sceptical rise of his chief advisor's eyebrow. 'Or at least it's a risk I am willing to take.'

'It is too big a risk. The women on my list are open to the idea of an arranged marriage—they have been brought up to understand the rules. Dammit, Frederick, we *had* this discussion. We agreed that it was important for the Lycander bride to be totally unlike your father's later choices and more in line with his first wife.'

Axel's mother, Princess Michaela, a princess in her own right, had been a good woman.

'We did. But circumstances have changed.'

'Doesn't matter. You plan to present your people with a bride who may well cause a scandal broth of divorce and custody battles.'

'I have no choice—none of this is Amil's fault.'

'I am not suggesting you turn your back on Amil. Provide for him. See him regularly. But do not marry his mother.'

'No.' It was as simple as that. 'I will be a real father to Amil and this is the way forward. I'm doing this, Marcus— with or without your help.'

Silence reigned and then Marcus exhaled a long sigh and sank into the seat opposite. 'As you wish.'

Sunita surveyed her reflection in the mirror, relieved that there was no evidence of the tumult that raged in her brain. Frederick…discovery… Amil… Crown Prince… marriage… Goa….disaster.

There was potential disaster on all fronts—the thought of marriage was surreal, the enormity of the decision she needed to make made her head whirl and the idea of two days in Goa with Frederick made her tummy loop the loop.

A tentative knock on the door heralded the arrival of Eric, the Lycander staff member who had been dispatched to her apartment the previous night.

'Good morning, Eric, and thank you again for getting my things. I really appreciate it.'

'You're very welcome, ma'am. The Prince is ready.'

She followed Eric through the opulence of the hotel, with its gold and white theme, along plush carpet and past gilded walls, through the marble lobby, past luscious plants and spectacular flower arrangements and outside to the limo. There Frederick awaited her, leant against the hood of the car, dressed casually in jeans and a T-shirt, his blond hair still a touch spiked with damp, as if he'd grabbed a shower on the run.

'A limo? Isn't that a touch ostentatious?'

The flippant comment made to mask her catch of breath, the thump of her heart. 'I promised the children a limo after my last visit—they were most disappointed when I turned up in a taxi.'

He held the door for her and she slid inside, the air-conditioned interior a welcome relief against the humidity, with its suggestion of imminent monsoon rain.

'They are amazing kids—they make you feel…humble.'

Sunita nodded. 'I read up on the charity last night. The whole set-up sounds awesome and its achievements are phenomenal. I love the simplicity of the idea—using open spaces as classrooms—and I admire the dedication of the volunteers. I'll do all I can to raise the profile and raise funds. Today and in the future.'

'Thank you. Axel helped set up the charity and donated huge sums after someone wrote to him with the idea and it caught his imagination. I wish…'

'You wish what?' The wistfulness in his voice touched her.

'I wish he'd told me about it.'

'People don't always like to talk about their charitable activity.' She frowned. 'But in this case surely he must have been pretty public about it, because his profile would have raised awareness.'

'It didn't work like that. My father was unpredictable about certain issues—he may not have approved of Axel's involvement. So Axel kept it low-key. Anonymous, in fact. I only found out after his death because someone from the charity wrote with their condolences and their thanks for all he had done. I decided to take over and make it a more high-profile role.'

'Didn't your father mind?'

Frederick shrugged. 'I don't know. He and I weren't close.' His tone forbade further questions. 'Anyway, in the past two years the number of schools has increased three-fold and I've hired an excellent administrator—she isn't a volunteer, because she can't afford to be, but she is worth every penny. The schools are makeshift, but that has saved money and I think it makes them more accessible.'

His face was lit with enthusiasm and there was no doubting his sincerity. Any reservations she'd harboured that this was simply a publicity stunt designed to show that Frederick had a charitable side began to fall away.

This continued when they arrived at the school and a veritable flock of children hurtled towards the car.

He exhibited patience, good humour and common sense; he allowed them to feel and touch the car, and then promised they could examine the interior after their lessons—as long as their teacher agreed.

A smiling woman dressed in a forest-green and blue *salwar kameez* came forward and within minutes children of differing ages and sizes were seated in the pavilion area and the lesson commenced.

Sunita marvelled at the children's concentration and the delight they exuded—despite the open-air arena, and all the distractions on offer, they were absorbed in their tasks, clearly revelling in the opportunity to learn.

'Would you like to go and look at their work?' the teacher offered, and soon Sunita was seated next to a group of chattering children, all of whom thrust their notebooks towards her, emanating so much pride in their achievements that flipped her heart.

She glanced at Frederick and her heart did another turn. Standing against a backdrop of palm trees and lush monsoon greenery, he was performing a series of magic tricks that held the children spellbound. He produced coins from ears and cards from thin air, bringing gasps of wonder and giggles of joy.

Finally, after the promised exploration of the limo, the children dispersed—many of them off to work—and after a long conversation with the teacher Frederick and Sunita returned to the car for their journey back to the hotel.

'Next time I'll take Amil,' Sunita said. 'I want him to meet those kids, to grow up with an understanding of the real world.'

'Agreed.'

The word reminded Sunita that from now on Frederick would have a say in her parenting decisions, but right now that didn't seem to matter. This was a topic they agreed on.

'There's such a lesson to be learnt there—those children want to learn, and it doesn't matter to them if they have computers or science labs or technology. They find joy in learning, and that's awesome as well as humbling.'

'*All* of this is humbling.'

He turned to look out of the window, gesturing to the crowded Mumbai streets, and Sunita understood what that movement of his hand had encompassed—the poverty that was rife, embodied by the beggars who surged to the limo windows whenever the car slowed, hands outstretched, entreaty on their faces. But it was more than that – you could see the spectrum of humanity, so many individuals each and every one with their own dreams and worries.

'You really care. This isn't all a publicity stunt...part of your new image.'

'This is about a continuation of Axel's work—no more, no less. Don't paint me as a good person, Sunita. If it weren't for Axel I would never have given this so much as a thought.'

The harshness of his voice shocked her, jolted her backwards on the seat with its intensity. 'Perhaps, but you were hardly duty-bound to take over—or to come out here and interact with those children like that.' She couldn't help it. 'Axel didn't do that, did he?'

'Axel *couldn't* do that—he needed to be the heir my father wanted him to be.'

With that he pulled his phone out of his pocket in a clear indication that the subject was well and truly closed.

Sunita frowned, fighting the urge to remove the phone from his grasp and resume their conversation, to make him see that he was wrong—in this instance he *was* a good person.

Back off, Sunita.

Right now she needed to remain focused on whether or not she wanted to marry this man—and what the consequences of her decision would be for Amil. And in that vein she needed to look ahead to the photo call, which meant an assessment of the recent press coverage. So she pulled her own phone out of her pocket.

A few minutes later he returned the mobile to his pocket.

'OK. We'll fly to Goa late afternoon, after the photo call and the trip to Hanging Gardens. As you requested I've sorted out a room near your suite for Sam and Miranda.'

'Thank you. I appreciate that.'

Goa! Sudden panic streamed through her and she pushed it down. She was contemplating *marriage* to Frederick, for goodness' sake—so panic over a mere two days was foolish, to say the least. She needed to focus on Amil.

She glanced across at Frederick, wondering how he must feel about taking Amil out. Perhaps she should ask, but the question would simply serve as a reminder of the fact that he had missed out on the first fourteen months of his son's life.

So instead she faced forward and maintained silence until the limo pulled up outside the hotel.

Frederick stood outside the hotel bedroom door. His heart pounded in his chest with a potent mix of emotions—nervousness, anticipation and an odd sense of rightness. In two minutes he would meet Amil. Properly. Terror added itself to the mix, and before he could turn tail and flee he raised his hand and knocked.

Sunita opened the door, Amil in her arms, and he froze. He didn't care that he was standing in the corridor in full sight of any curious passers-by. All he could do was gaze at his son. *His son.*

Wonder entered his soul as his eyes roved over his features and awe filled him. *His son.* The words overwhelmed and terrified him in equal measure, causing a strange inability to reach out and hold the little boy. His emotions paralysed him, iced his limbs into immobility, stopped his brain, brought the world into slow motion.

Determination that he would not let Amil down fought with the bone-deep knowledge that of course he would. He wasn't equipped for this—didn't have the foundations to know how to be a parent, how not to disappoint.

But he would do all he could. He could give this boy his name, his principality, and perhaps over time he would work out how to show his love.

Amil gazed back at him with solemn hazel eyes and again panic threatened—enough that he wrenched his gaze away.

'You OK?' Sunita's soft voice pulled him into focus and he saw understanding in her eyes, and perhaps even the hint of a tear at the edge of her impossibly long eyelashes.

'I'm fine.'

Get a grip.

He had no wish to feature as an object of compassion. So he kept his gaze on Sunita, absorbed her vibrant beauty, observed her change of outfit from casual jeans and T-shirt to a leaf-print black and white dress cinched at the waist with a wide red belt. Strappy sandals completed the ensemble.

'Babababababa!' Amil vouchsafed, and a well of emotion surged anew.

'Do you want to hold him?'

'No!' *Think*. 'I don't want to spook him—especially just before the photo call.'

It wasn't a bad cover-up, but possibly not good enough to allay the doubts that dawned in her eyes.

'You won't. He's fairly sociable. Though obviously he doesn't really meet that many strange me—' She broke off. 'I'm sorry. Of all the stupid things to say that took the cake, the biscuit and the whole damn patisserie.'

'It's OK. I am a stranger to Amil—that's why I don't want to spook him.'

His gaze returned to the baby, who was watching him, his eyes wide open, one chubby hand clutching a tendril of Sunita's hair.

'We need to go.'

'I know. But first I have a couple of questions about the press conference and the Kaitlin question.'

Frederick frowned. 'What question would that be?'

'A couple of reporters said, and I quote, that you are "broken-hearted" and that perhaps I can mend the chasm. Others have suggested you would welcome a dalliance with an old flame as a gesture, to show Lady Kaitlin you are over her.'

'I still don't understand what your question is.'

'Two questions. *Are* you heartbroken? *Are* you over her?'

'No and yes. I need to get married for Lycander. My

heart is not involved. Kaitlin understood that—our relationship was an alliance. When that alliance became impossible we ended our relationship. Since then she has met someone else and I wish her well.'

Sunita's expression held a kind of shocked curiosity. 'That's *it*? You were with her for *months*. You must have felt *something* for her.'

Momentary doubt touched him and then he shrugged. 'Of course I did. I thought that she would be an excellent asset to Lycander.'

Kaitlin's diplomatic connections had been exemplary, as had her aristocratic background. She'd had a complete understanding of the role of consort and had been as uninterested in love as he was.

'I was disappointed when it didn't work out.'

'Yes. I see that it must have been tough for you to have the deal break down.' Sarcasm rang out from the spurious sympathy.

'It was—but only because it had an adverse impact on my position as ruler.'

And that was all that mattered. His goal was to rule Lycander as his brother would have wished, to achieve what Axel would have achieved. Whatever it took.

'So all you need to know about Kaitlin is that she is in the past. My heart is intact.' He glanced at his watch. 'And now we really need to go.'

A pause and then she nodded. 'OK. This is our chance to change the mixed reaction into a positive one. An opportunity to turn the tide in our favour.'

'You sound confident that you can do that.'

'Yup. I'm not a fan of bad publicity. Watch and learn.'

One photo call later and Frederick was looking at Sunita in reluctant admiration. He had to hand it to her. By the end of the hour she had had even the most hostile reporter

eating out of her hand. Somehow she had mixed a suggestion of regret over her actions with the implicit belief that
it had been the only option at the time. In addition, she had
managed to make it clear that whilst two years ago Frederick had been a shallow party prince, now he had morphed
into a different and better man, a worthy ruler of Lycander.

No doubt Marcus had been applauding as he watched.

Hell, even *he* had almost believed it. *Almost.*

'You did a great job. And I appreciate that you included
me in your spin.'

'It wasn't spin. Everything I said about you was true—
you *have* worked incredibly hard these past two years, you
have instigated all the changes I outlined, and you *do* have
Lycander's future at heart.'

The words washed over him like cold, dirty water—if
the people of Lycander knew where the blame for Axel's
death lay they would repudiate him without compunction,
and they would be right to do so. But he didn't want these
thoughts today—not on his first outing with Amil.

He glanced down at Amil, secure now in his buggy,
dressed in a jaunty striped top and dungarees, a sun hat
perched on his head, a toy cat clasped firmly in one hand.

'Amamamamam…ma.' Chubby legs kicked and he
wriggled in a clear instruction for them to move on.

Sunita smiled down at her son. 'I think he wants to get
going—he wants to see all the animal hedges. They seem
to utterly fascinate him.'

As they wandered through the lush gardens that
abounded with shades of green tranquillity seemed to be
carried on the breeze that came from the Arabian Sea, and
for a moment it was almost possible to pretend they were
an ordinary family out for the day.

Sunita came to a halt near a topiary hedge, one of many

clipped into the shape of animals. 'For some reason this is his favourite—I can't work out why.'

Frederick studied it. 'I'm not sure I can even work out what it is. I spotted the giraffe and the elephant and the ox-drawn cart, but this one flummoxes me.'

Sunita gave a sudden gurgle of laughter. 'I know what Amil thinks it is. Amil, sweetheart, tell Mu— Tell us what the animal does.'

The little boy beamed and made a *'raaaah'* noise.

Frederick felt his heart turn over in his chest. Without thought he hunkered down next to Amil and clapped. 'Clever boy. The tiger goes *"rah"*.'

'Raaah!' Amil agreed.

And here it came again—the paralysis, the fear that he would mess this up. He'd never managed any other relationship with even a sliver of success. Why would this be different?

Rising to his feet, he gestured around the garden. 'This is a beautiful place.'

'I used to come here as a child,' Sunita said. 'It's one of my earliest memories. I loved the flower clock.'

She pressed her lips together, as if she regretted the words, and Frederick frowned. Her publicity blurb skated over her childhood, chose to focus instead on her life after she'd embarked on her career. Almost as if she had written her early years out of her life history…

'Come on,' she said hurriedly. 'This morning isn't about my childhood. It's about Amil's—let's go to the Old Woman's Shoe.'

Five minutes later Frederick stared at the shoe—actually an enormous replica of a boot. As landmarks went, it seemed somewhat bizarre—especially when the words of the nursery rhyme filtered back to him.

There was an old woman who lived in a shoe.
She had so many children she didn't know what to do.
She gave them broth without any bread,
Then whipped them all soundly and sent them to bed.

'Isn't this a slightly odd thing to put in a children's playground?'

'Yes. But I loved it—I used to climb it and it made me feel lucky. It was a way to count my blessings. At least I didn't live with a horrible old woman who starved me and beat me!'

At least. There had been a wealth of memory in those syllables, and for a daft moment he had the urge to put his arm around her and pull her into the comfort of a hug.

As if realising she had given away more than she had wanted, she hastened on. 'Anyway, I looked up the rhyme recently and it turns out it probably has political rather than literal connotations. But enough talk. This is about you and Amil. Do you want to take Amil into the shoe? I'll wait here with the buggy.'

The suggestion came out of nowhere, ambushed him, and once again his body froze into immobility even as his brain turned him into a gibbering wreck.

'I think that may be a little bit much for him. He barely knows me.' *Think.* 'We haven't even explained to him who I am.'

The accusation in his own voice surprised him—and he knew it masked a hurt he didn't want her to see. Because it exposed a weakness he didn't want her to know. *'Never show weakness, my son.'* The one piece of paternal advice he agreed with. *'Show weakness and you lose.'* Just as all his stepmothers had lost. Their weakness had been their love for their children—a weakness Alphonse had exploited.

Heat touched the angle of her cheekbones as she acknowledged the truth of his words. 'I know. I'm not sure what you want to do. I don't know what you want him to call you. Dad? Daddy? Papa?'

In truth he didn't know either, and that increased his panic. Sunita stepped towards him, and the compassion in her eyes added fuel to the panic-induced anger.

'But remember, he is only fourteen months old—I don't think he understands the concept of having a dad.'

The words were a stark reminder of her deception.

'Amil doesn't understand or *you* don't?'

The harshness of his voice propelled her backwards, and he was glad of it when he saw the compassion vanish from her expression.

'Both of us. Give me a break, Frederick. Until yesterday it was just Amil and me. Now here you are, and you want to marry me and make Amil the Crown Prince. It's a lot to take in.'

For an instant he empathised, heard the catch in her voice under the anger. But this was no time for empathy or sympathy. Now all that mattered was the knowledge of what was at stake.

'Then take it in fast, Sunita. You chose to hide Amil from me and now you need to deal with the consequences of that decision. Most people wouldn't think they were so bad. *I* am the one who has missed out on the first fourteen months of my son's life. *My son.* I am Amil's father and *you* need to deal with it.'

There was silence, broken only by the sound of Amil grizzling, his eyes wide and anxious as he looked up at Sunita.

Oh, hell. Guilt twisted his chest. What was *wrong* with him? This was his first outing with Amil and he'd allowed it to come to this. Shades of his own father, indeed.

He squatted down beside the baby. 'I'm sorry, Amil. Daddy's sorry.' Standing up, he gestured to the Old Woman's Shoe. 'You take him up. I'll wait here with the buggy. I've upset him enough—I don't want to compound my error.'

Sunita hesitated, but then Amil's grizzling turned to tears and she nodded assent.

'OK.' Leaning down, she unbuckled Amil and took him out. 'Come on, sweetheart. Let's try some walking.'

Frederick watched their progress and determination solidified inside him. He might be messing this up big-time, but he would not concede defeat. At the very least he would give his son the chance to be a prince. Their outing to the Hanging Gardens might be a disaster, but going to Goa wouldn't be.

By the end of their time there Sunita would agree to marry him.

CHAPTER SEVEN

SUNITA LOOKED ACROSS the expanse of the royal jet to where Frederick sat. There was no trace of the man she'd glimpsed mere hours ago in the Hanging Gardens—a man who had exhibited a depth of pain and frustration that had made her think long and hard.

Another glance—he still looked cool, regal and remote, and she couldn't read any emotion or discern what thoughts might be in his mind. Which would make what she had to say all the more difficult.

For a moment she nearly turned craven. *No*. This was the right thing to do and she would do it.

'Frederick?'

'Sunita.'

'Can we talk?'

'Of course.' He pushed his netbook across the table, rose and crossed to sit in the luxurious leather seat next to hers. 'Shoot.'

'I've thought about what you said earlier. About me having to accept that you are Amil's father.'

He raised a hand. 'It doesn't matter. I shouldn't have said what I did.'

'It *does* matter. I don't see how we can even consider a future together until we resolve our past. So I want to say I'm sorry.'

She twisted her hands together on her lap, recalling Frederick's expression when he'd looked at Amil as if his son was the most precious being in the universe.

'I'm sorry you missed out on Amil's first months.'

However justified her decision, Frederick could never have that time back—would never be able to hold his new-born son in his arms, see his first smile, run his finger over his gum to reveal that first tooth.

'I'm sorry.'

'OK.'

'But it's *not* OK, is it?'

'No.' He closed his eyes, then reopened them. 'No. It isn't OK that you hid my son's existence from me.'

'I couldn't take the risk.'

'Yes. You could have. You *chose* not to.'

Rationalisations lined up in her vocal cords but she uttered none of them. Bottom line—he was right. Her choice had meant Frederick had missed out on something infinitely precious.

'Yes, I did. And all the reasons I gave you earlier were true. But it's more than that.'

She inhaled deeply. She had no wish to confide this to him—she wasn't even sure she wanted to acknowledge it herself. But there it was again—the memory of the way Frederick had looked at Amil, the fact that he wanted to be part of his son's life and wanted to create a stable family unit. He deserved a true explanation.

'I thought history was repeating itself. I thought you would be like…' Her voice trailed off, her brain wishing it could reverse track and pull the words back.

'Like who?'

The gentleness of his voice surprised her—gave her the momentum to carry on.

'Like my father. He was a Londoner, on holiday in India

with a group of friends when he met my mother. They fell in love—or so she believed. She fell pregnant and she *did* choose to tell him, and all she could see was a tornado of dust as he disappeared. Straight back, road-runner-style, to his fiancée in London.'

Even now the enormity of her father's selfishness had the power to stun her—he *must* have understood the repercussions. They would have been complex enough in any culture, but in India there had been added layers of complication that transcended even betrayal and heartbreak.

Understanding showed in the expression on Frederick's face. 'That must have been tough for your mother.'

'Yes. It was. It changed the entire trajectory of her life. Her family was horrified and threw her out—she was only nineteen, and she had to fend for herself in a society which by and large had condemned her. And a lot of that is down to my father and his rejection of her—and me. I know we were in different circumstances—you didn't lie to me—but I knew you didn't want children. I didn't want to hear you say the same words my own father had—I didn't want Amil to feel the sense of rejection I did.'

Sunita forced herself to hold his gaze, to keep her tone level. This verged on the excruciating—touchy-feely confidences were not her bag at all.

'It seemed better, easier, less painful, to bring Amil up on my own. I figured what *he* didn't know and *you* didn't know wouldn't hurt anyone.'

There was a silence, and then he reached out, touching her forearm lightly. 'I'm sorry for what happened to your mother and to you. I promise you—I will never reject Amil.'

There could be no doubt as to the sincerity in his voice, and in the here and now she believed he meant every word. But she knew that good intentions did not always turn into actions. Her father must have once believed the empty promises he'd made to make up for his past, to be a good parent.

'It will not happen,' he repeated, as if he sensed her doubts. 'And now let's put the past behind us. I wish you had told me about Amil earlier, but I do understand why you made the choices you did. I believe now that we need to move forward, put the past behind us and focus on our present and our future. Deal?'

He held out his hand and Sunita looked down at it. So perfect—strong, masculine, capable… Capable of the gentlest of caresses, capable of…

Close it down, Sunita.

Too late—images scrambled her mind and for a moment she was unable to help herself. She closed her eyes, let the sensation dance over her skin. But it was more than desire—she knew that this deal signified understanding and forgiveness, and that made her head whirl as well.

Then she opened her eyes and reached out, clasped his hand and worked to still the beat of her heart. 'Deal,' she said. The syllable emerged with way too much violence, and she dropped his hand as if it were burning her. Which in a sense it was.

She looked down, then sneaked a look up at him—had he seen her reaction? Of course he had. It didn't take a forensic degree to know that. Embarrassment flushed her skin even as she couldn't help but wonder if this stupid physical reaction was a mutual one.

Her gaze met his and against all odds her pulse quickened further. His hazel eyes had darkened, the heat in them so intense her skin sizzled as her hormones cartwheeled.

Nothing else mattered except this.

Her lips parted as he rose, and his eyes never once left hers as he held out a hand. Without thought she put her hand in his, and he tugged her up so they stood mere cen-timetres apart.

Oh, so gently, but with a firmness that neither expected nor brooked denial, his hands encircled her waist and pulled her body flush against his. The feel of him, of the hard, muscular wall of his chest, made her gasp, and she looped her arms round his neck, accidentally brushing the soft skin on his nape.

An oath dropped from his lips and then those self-same lips touched hers and she was lost.

The kiss oh-so-familiar and yet so much more than be-fore; the tang of coffee and the hint of strawberry jam, the sheer rollick of sensation that coursed her blood, made her feel alive and made her want more. He deepened the kiss and she pressed against him, caught in this moment that felt so damn right.

Stop. What the hell was she doing?

She wrenched out of his arms so hard she nearly tum-bled over, putting a hand out to steady herself against the back of the chair.

For a moment silence reigned, broken only by the sound of their jagged breathing. Sunita tried to force herself to think through the fog of desire that refused to disperse. She couldn't let herself succumb to him again—she *couldn't.* Two years ago she'd lost her self-respect—now she could lose even more than that. Her attraction was a weakness he could play on—something that might cloud her judge-ment when she needed it most.

'I'm sorry. That was stupid.'

He ran a hand down his face, almost as if to wipe away all emotion, all desire, and when he met her gaze his ex-pression was neutralised. 'No need to be sorry. That was a *good* thing.'

'How do you figure that out?'

'Because it proves we have physical compatibility. That's important in a marriage.'

His words acted like the equivalent of a bucket of ice-cold water and she slammed her hands on her hips. 'So that kiss was a deliberate ploy? A way to make the marriage more acceptable to me?'

'It wasn't a deliberate ploy, but it wasn't a mistake either. Mutual attraction is a benefit in a marriage. A bonus to our alliance.'

A benefit. A bonus. Any minute now he'd tell her there was some tax advantage to it too.

Sheer outrage threatened at his use of their attraction as a calculated move to persuade her. More fool her for believing he had been as caught up and carried away as she had. This *was* the Playboy Prince, after all.

'Well, I'll bear that in mind, but given that you have found "physical compatibility" with hundreds of women, I'm not sure it counts for much. Now, if you'll excuse me, I'll just go and freshen up.'

Frederick resisted the urge to put his head in his hands and groan. Then he considered the alternative option of kicking himself around the private jet.

Kissing Sunita had not been on the agenda—but somehow her beauty, her vulnerability, her honesty had overwhelmed him, and what he had meant to offer as comfort had turned into the type of kiss that still seared his memory, still had his body in thrall.

Dammit. He would *not* let physical attraction control him as it had his father—that way led to stupid decisions, poor judgement calls and people getting hurt. Yet during that kiss his judgement could have parachuted off the plane and he wouldn't have given a damn.

Then, to compound his original stupidity, he had

morphed into a pompous ass. Words had flowed from his tongue as he'd fought the urge to pull her straight back into his arms and resume proceedings. What an idiot. And then there had been her reference to his past. The truth was, even back then Sunita had been different from his so-called 'hundreds of women'.

He looked up as she returned to the room, her brown eyes cold, her expression implacable as she headed back to her chair and reached down into her bag for a book.

Hell. Now what? This was not going to plan and he didn't know how to retrieve it. Did not have a clue. He was so far out of his comfort zone he'd need a satnav and a compass to find his way back.

'Sunita?'

'Yes.'

'That kiss…'

'I think we've said all that needs to be said about it. As far as I am concerned, I plan to erase it from my memory banks.'

'Fine. But before you do that I want to clarify something. You mentioned my "hundreds of women"—for starters, that is an exaggeration. Yes, I partied hard and, yes, there were women, but not as many as the press made out. But, any which-way, those days are over and they have been for a long time. I was never unfaithful to any woman and I plan on a monogamous marriage.'

Clearly his default setting today was 'pompous ass', so he might as well run with it.

'So you'd be faithful for the duration. For decades, if necessary?'

The scepticism in her tone rankled.

'I am always faithful.'

'But your relationships have only lasted a few weeks

at a time—that's hardly much of a test. Variety was the spice of your life.'

'Very poetic. Let's take it further, then—I believe it's possible to have variety *and* plenty of spice with one woman.'

'Then why didn't you ever try it before?'

Damn. Poetic *and* sharp.

'Because short-term suited me—I didn't want physical attraction to develop into any expectations of marriage or love. I never offered more than I could give and the same goes now. I can offer marriage and fidelity, but not love.'

'I still don't buy it. Most people are faithful *because* of love—if you don't believe in love what would motivate you to be faithful?'

'I will not repeat my father's mistakes. He went through women like a man with a cold does tissues. Any beautiful woman—he thought it was his right to have her, whether he was already in a relationship or not, and it led to a whole lot of strife and angst. So I will not plunge Lycander into scandal and I will not hurt my children or humiliate my wife. That is nothing to do with love—it is to do with respect for my country and my family.'

'OK.'

Sympathy warmed her eyes and the moment suddenly felt too weighted, too heavy, and he cleared his throat. 'I thought you might want to know more about Lycander—after all, it will be your new home and your country.'

'I'd like that. I do remember some of what you told me two years ago. Rolling countryside, where you can walk and smell the scents of honeysuckle and almost taste the olives that you grow. You made the olive groves come to life.' She hesitated, and then asked, 'What happened to your business deal? The one you hoped would go through two years ago?'

Her words caused him to pause. Sunita had been one of the very few people he'd spoken to about his dreams. Ever since he was young he'd been focused on breaking free of his father's money—sick and tired of the constant reminders that he relied on his father's coffers for his food, his clothes, the roof over his head.

Then, at twenty-one, he'd come into the inheritance of a run-down, abandoned olive grove. And as he'd walked around it had been as if the soil itself had imparted something to him, as if the very air was laden with memories of past glories, of trees laden with plump lush olives, the sound and whir of a ghostly olive press.

That was where it had all started, and over the years he'd built an immensely profitable business. Two years before he'd been in the midst of a buy-out—he'd succeeded, and taken his company to the next echelon. That had been the deal he'd been celebrating—the reason he'd handed over the state function to Axel, the reason Axel had died.

Guilt and grief prodded him and he saw Sunita frown. *Focus.* 'The deal went through.'

'So who runs your business now?'

'A board of directors and my second-in-command—I have very little to do with it any more.'

'That must be hard.'

'That's how it is. Lycander needs my attention, and its people need to see that they come first. The principality isn't huge, but we have beaches, we have vineyards, we have olive groves. I know I'm biased, but our olives are the best in the world—they have bite…their taste lingers on your tongue—and the olive oil we produce is in a class of its own. As for our grapes—I believe the wine we produce rivals that of France and Spain. Lycander has the potential to be a prosperous land, but right now it is a vessel of past glories. My father increased taxes, lowered the minimum wage—did all he could to increase the money in the royal coffers without a care for the effect.'

'But couldn't anyone stop him?'

'No. In Lycander, the ruler's word is law—he has the final say on the governing of the land. Of course there are elected advisors, but they have no legislative power and the monarch can disregard their advice. So effectively everything hinges on having a ruler who genuinely cares about Lycander and its people.'

'That sounds like a whole heap of responsibility. For you. *And* to wish upon Amil.'

'It is, but I think it needs to be seen in context. In the past, when everything worked, it was easier—right now it is harder. But I will make sure I set things to rights. I know what needs to be done. I will make the laws fair, I will reduce taxation rates and I'll stop tax evasion. I want the divide between the wealthy and the poor to be bridged. I—'

He broke off at her expression.

'You can pick your jaw up from the ground.'

She raised her hand in admission. 'OK. Busted. I *am* surprised. Two years ago you were passionate about your business, but you didn't mention politics or social beliefs. Now your enthusiasm, your beliefs, are palpable.'

The all too familiar push and pull of guilt tugged within him.

'This isn't about my enthusiasm or my beliefs. It is about Axel—it's about fulfilling a promise. The people and the country suffered under my father's rule. The real reason there was no rebellion was that they knew one day Axel would succeed him, and that kept the unrest at bay. Axel had a vision—one that I *will* make happen.'

That had been the promise he'd made in his very first speech and he would fulfil it.

'What about *your* vison? The way you speak of Lycander—I can hear your pride in it.'

'I never had a vision for Lycander. I had a work hard, play hard lifestyle.'

'But you've changed?'

'Yes, I have.'

But the cost of that had been his brother's life.

Her frown deepened. She leant forward and he could smell her exotic scent with its overtone of papaya, could see the tiny birthmark on the angle of her cheekbone.

'I know you will be a good ruler. Whether you rule because it is your duty or because your heart is in it.'

There was silence. She was close. Way too close. And he had had a sudden desire to tell her the truth about his ascent to the throne—a desire mixed with the longing to tug her back into his arms and damn common sense and practicality.

Neither could happen, so he rose to his feet and looked down at her.

'Thank you. But the point I was trying to make is that I will ensure the principality Amil inherits will be a *good* place, with a strong economic foundation. Of course he will still have much responsibility, but I hope it will not be a burden.'

'What if he doesn't want the job? What if he has other ambitions, other aspirations?'

'I would never force him to take the crown. He could abdicate.' He met her gaze. 'Provided we have more children.'

'More children?' she echoed.

'Yes. I would like more children in order to secure the succession.' After all, there was no hope of his brothers ever having anything to do with Lycander. 'To take the pressure off Amil.'

'Is that the only reason?'

'For now. I haven't really got my head around having Amil yet.'

Right now he was terrified about his ability to parent *one* child—it wasn't the moment for a rose-tinted image of a functional, happy group of siblings.

'Do *you* want more kids?'

Sunita hesitated. 'I don't know...' A small smile tugged her lips upwards. 'I haven't really got *my* head around it all yet either. Until yesterday it was just me and Amil. My happiest memories are of my mother and me—just us. After—'

She broke off, looked away and then back at him, and he wondered what she had been about to say.

'Anyway,' she resumed, 'I'm not sure that the whole "happy family" scenario always works. Are you close to your other brothers?'

'No.'

His half-siblings... Stefan, who loathed all things Lycander, had left the principality as soon as he'd reached eighteen and hadn't returned. The twins, Emerson and Barrett, still only twenty, had left Lycander only days after their father's death and hadn't returned.

There was a definite pattern there, and it wasn't woven with closeness. The way they had grown up had made that an impossibility—their father had revelled in pitting brother against brother in a constant circus of competition and rivalry, and in the end Frederick had retired from the field, isolated himself and concentrated on his own life.

'But that was down to our upbringing. I hope that our children would do better.'

Perhaps it was a fruitless hope—there was every chance he would prove to be as useless a parent as his own parents had been, in which case perhaps a large family was a foolish idea.

But now wasn't the moment to dwell on it.

Relief touched him as the pilot announced their descent to Goa before Sunita could pursue the conversation further.

CHAPTER EIGHT

SUNITA'S EYES STRETCHED so wide she wondered if her eyeballs would actually pop out of her head.

'This is incredible.'

In truth it was beyond incredible—and she hadn't even seen the inside of the villa yet.

The drive itself had been unexpected—their chauffeur-driven car had traversed remarkably peaceful roads until they'd reached an idyllic village seemingly untouched by tourism. Winding lanes had displayed a number of villas draped with greenery, and now they had arrived at Sangwan Villa.

The Portuguese-built, newly renovated building was nestled amidst verdant grounds where teak and jackfruit trees thrived, giving the air an evocative smell of leather with a hint of pineapple.

Her gaze rested on the structure itself. With its pillared verandas and high roof it looked like a vision out of a fairy tale.

The thought jolted her. She needed to remember that fairy tales were exactly that—tales, fiction. And most fairy tales had a dark side, a grim under-story, and the myths they were built on didn't have any happily-ever-afters.

'How on earth did you get it at such short notice?'

'It was closed for maintenance—I made it worth the owners' while to postpone the work.'

A woman walked towards them, a smile on her face, her white and green sari very much in keeping with the verdant backdrop.

'Your Highness. Welcome. I am Deepali and I will be looking after you during your stay. Your staff have been settled in and your suites are ready, if you will follow me. I will show you your rooms and then I thought you may wish to have an evening drink by the pool before dinner. There are menus in your rooms—just call through when you are ready.'

'That sounds wonderful,' Sunita said. 'And thank you so much for making this available at such short notice.'

Minutes later she was looking around a sumptuous suite. 'It's beautiful...'

But it was more than that—it was quirky and cosy, with its warm aura countered by the cool of the tiled floor. The sitting area boasted comfy overstuffed armchairs, where she could imagine curling up with a book and a cup of coffee, or simply gazing at the courtyard outside, resplendent with shrubbery. Two steps led down to the bedroom, where a luxurious wooden bed sprawled against decadent red walls.

Her suitcases had been deposited by a large lacquered wardrobe and she opened one, needing the confidence fresh clothes would give her. A floaty dress with a vivid bird print gave her instant cheer, and as she made her way out to the courtyard she allowed herself to revel in the sound of kingfishers and the sight and scent of the opulent lilies in the ornate pond.

Frederick sat on a recliner chair, a frosted beer bottle on the small table behind him and his blond head slightly tipped back to absorb the rays of the evening sun. Her breath caught as her gaze snagged on the strong line of his throat, the strength of his jaw—Adonis could eat his heart out.

But enough voyeurism…

He turned as she approached and smiled, and for a moment the clock turned back, transported her to two years before, when that smile had quite literally bewitched her, causing her to forget common sense and every promise she'd made herself.

Not this time. This time she had her sensible head on.

So she forced her toes to uncurl and sat down next to him, stretched her legs out and exhaled. 'This is a fabulous place.' She swiped a sideways glance at him. 'And you've surprised me.' *Again.*

'Why?'

'It's not what I expected.'

'What *did* you expect?'

'Something busier—a five-star hotel on the beach, with a nightclub.'

'Is that what you wanted?'

'No.'

'I told you, Sunita, I've changed. Plus, this time needs to be for you and me. No distractions. You wanted to get to know me better. Here I am.'

So he was—and the thought had her reaching for the lime drink she'd ordered.

She needed to focus on the practical—on need-to-know, real-life information.

'I need to know what our marriage would mean on a day-to-day level for Amil. What it will be like for him to grow up in a palace, as a Lycander prince. Right now it feels surreal.'

'The state apartments are a bit more opulent than your

average home, I suppose, but otherwise his childhood will
be what we make it.'

'Will he go to a nursery?'

'I don't see why not—there will be a certain level of security arrangements, but I can't see a problem with that.'

'And he'll have friends round to play?'

How she'd craved friendship as a child—but there had
been no one. Her mixed race heritage, the fact that she was
illegitimate, the fact that her mother was a model, had all
combined to make school a miserable place of isolation
for her. She knew exactly what a solitary childhood could
be like, and she didn't want that for her son.

'Yup. Again, subject to security vetting.'

'Is that how it worked for you?'

She sensed the tension in his body.

'It isn't relevant how it was for me,' he said.

He had to be kidding. 'Of course it is. You are a prince
who grew up in a palace. You want Amil to do the same.
So, did you make friends, have kids round to play? Were
you treated differently?'

Discomfort showed as he shifted on his seat, picked
his beer up and put it down again without even taking
a sip. 'My life…my younger brothers' lives…weren't as
straightforward as I hope Amil's will be. There weren't
that many opportunities for us to make normal friends. It
was better for Axel, because my father sent him to boarding school, and—'

Whoa! 'That is *not* happening to Amil. I will not send
him away.'

'I won't rule that out.'

'Yes, you will. I don't care if every Crown Prince since
the Conquest was sent to boarding school. Amil isn't
going.'

'That is not why I would do it.' Frustration seeped into

his tone. 'In fact, I didn't say I *would* do it. It is simply a possibility I will consider in the future.'

'No.'

His voice tightened. 'Different children thrive in different conditions. Axel was educated at boarding school and it didn't do him any harm. I spent a term there and I loved it.'

'In which case, why did you leave?'

'Because my father changed his mind.'

'He must have had a reason.'

'I'm sure he did.'

Despite the even tone of his voice she could sense evasion.

'Do you know what it was?'

'My father's attitude to my education was a little hit and miss. Axel went to boarding school, but the rest of us... We had tutors some of the time, attended a term of local school here and there, or we ran wild. For my father, education wasn't a priority—in the palace or in the principality as a whole. I will change that, but it will take time—that's why I won't rule out boarding school if it is right for Amil.'

'That is *my* decision.'

'Amil is *our* son. *We* will make decisions about his future. Not you or me. Us—together.'

'And what happens if we don't agree?'

'Then we find a compromise.'

'There is no compromise between boarding school and not boarding school. It's black or white. What happens then?'

'I don't know. But we'll work it out.'

'Those are just words. Neither of us has any idea of how to work things out.'

Which was exactly why this was a terrible idea. Co-parenting sucked.

'Fine. Then let's work it out now,' he said.

'How?'

'You tell me exactly why you are so adamant that boarding school is not an option. The truth. My brother loved his boarding school, and the few months I spent there were some of the happiest times of my life. I will not rule it out without reason.'

'I…' Explanations sucked as well, but she could see that she didn't sound rational. 'I'm scared for him. School was an unmitigated disaster for me—because I didn't fit from day one. I was the only mixed race child in my school, and my mother's status didn't help. Plus, quite often she would pull me out of school to go on shoots with her—she had no one to leave me with, you see. I guess I was an obvious target.'

'Were you bullied?'

Although his voice was gentle she could hear an underlying anger, saw the clench of his jaw.

'No. It was much worse. I was ignored. Some girl decided that the best way to treat someone as low down the pecking order as me would be to pretend I was invisible.'

She could still hear it now. The high-pitched voice, so stuck-up and snobbish, the other girls gathering round to listen. 'It is demeaning to even *acknowledge* a dirty girl like her. So we will ignore her. Are we all agreed?'

'My whole experience of school was miserable. The only saving grace was the fact that it wasn't boarding school—that I could go home to my mother. Amil will be different too. He will be royalty—there will be people who are envious of him. I don't want him to be far away and miserable.'

Though in truth there was even more to it than that. There was her bone-deep knowledge that time was infinitely precious—she had had so few years with her mother, but at least they had had the maximum possible time to-gether.

'I don't want him to be far away. Full stop. He is *my* child—I want to see him grow, and I want to be there for him.'

Frederick's hazel eyes studied her expression with an intensity that made her feel he could read her soul.

Then he nodded. 'OK. You get the casting vote on the boarding school question.'

'Why?' Wariness narrowed her eyes at his capitulation. 'Does it matter?'

'Yes. I need to know that you mean it. That these aren't just words to sweeten the marriage offer.'

'Because you still don't trust me?'

She wanted to—she really did—but how could she when there was so much at stake?

'Let's say it would help if I knew what had changed your mind.'

'You've made me realise why I enjoyed boarding school so much. Why Axel thrived there. It was the opposite to your situation. For us it was an escape from our home life—boarding school was a haven of certainty after the chaos of life at the palace. Somewhere I knew what was what, where I had an opportunity to actually get an education. Our home life was erratic, at best. It won't be like that for Amil.'

Sunita's heart ached at the thought of all those young princes, buffeted by the fallout from their father's chaotic lifestyle. 'No, it won't.'

'And by the time he goes to school I *will* have turned education around in Lycander. Teachers will be better paid, the curriculum will be overhauled in a good way, and there will be more money injected into schools everywhere.'

As if embarrassed by his own enthusiasm, he leant back

with a rueful smile that flipped her heart again. A sure case of topsy-turvy heart syndrome. And it was messing with her head, making the idea of marriage more palatable. *Ridiculous.* Marriage equalled tying herself down, committing herself to a shared life, to a fairy tale ending. The idea hurt her teeth, sent her whole being into revolt.

Only that wasn't true, was it? Horror surfaced at the identification of a tiny glimmer of sparkle inside her that desperately *wanted* a fairy tale ending... Frederick, Sunita and Amil, living happily ever after in a palace. Princess Sunita.

'Penny for your thoughts?' His voice interrupted her reverie.

'They aren't worth it.'

They weren't worth even a fraction of a penny—she had lost the plot and it was time to get it back. This marriage deal wasn't off the table, but there wouldn't be any glimmer of fairy sparkle sprinkled on it.

She looked up as Deepali approached from across the courtyard. 'Your meal is ready. The chef has prepared a selection of traditional Goan food—I trust you will enjoy it.'

Sunita managed a smile even as her brain scrambled around in panic, chasing down that stupid, sparkly bit of her that advocated the ringing out of wedding bells. How had this happened? In a little over twenty-four hours he had somehow persuaded her that marriage was not only a possibility but a sparkly one.

Enough. She had to halt this before this fairy tale place wove some sort of magic spell around her—before that stupid sparkly bit inside her grew.

Frederick studied Sunita's expression as she looked round the dining room. Her eyes skittered over the colourful prints on the white walls, along the simple wooden table, and he could almost hear her brain whirring.

Deepali entered and put their plates in front of them. 'Prawn rissoles,' she said, and Sunita inhaled appreciatively.

'They smell marvellous—and I'm sure they'll taste just as good.'

The middle-aged woman smiled. 'I'll pass on your kind comments to the chef.'

Once she'd gone, Frederick watched as Sunita studied the rissole with more attention than any food warranted, however appetising.

'This looks great.' She popped a forkful into her mouth and closed her eyes. 'Fabulous! The reason why melt-in-the-mouth is a cliché. Cumin, with perhaps a hint of coriander, and...'

But even as she spoke he knew that her thoughts were elsewhere. There was an almost manic quality to her culinary listing, and he interrupted without compunction.

'So,' he said, 'you avoided my earlier question about what you were thinking.'

Her brown eyes watched him with almost a hint of defiance. 'I was thinking how surreal this situation is—the idea that two people who don't know each other at all could contemplate marriage. It's...mad.'

'That's why we're here—to get to know each other.'

'We can't pack that into two days—most people take years.'

'And there is still a fifty per cent divorce rate.'

'In which case we are *definitely* doomed.'

'Not at all. All those people who take years...they try to fall in love, decide they've fallen in love, expect love to last. Every action is dictated by love. They heap pressure on the whole institution of marriage *and* on themselves. Our approach is based on common sense and on us both getting a deal we think is fair. Two days is more than enough time.'

He leant over and poured wine into her glass.

'In days gone by it would have been the norm. Throughout Lycander history, rulers made *alliances*—not love matches.'

'Does posterity say whether they worked?'

'Some were more successful than others, but every marriage lasted.'

Until Alphonse had arrived and turned statistics and traditions on their heads.

'For better or worse?' Sunita sounded sceptical.

'I see no reason why we couldn't be one of the better ones—we'd go in without any ridiculous, unrealistic expectations, with an understanding of what each other is looking for.'

'I don't even know what your favourite colour is.'

'Does it matter?'

'I feel it's the sort of thing one should know before they marry someone.'

'OK. Blue.' He raised his eyebrows. '*Now* will you marry me?'

This pulled a reluctant smile from her, but it came with an attendant shake of her head. 'What sort of blue? Royal blue, because it's on the Lycander flag?'

'Nope. Aquamarine blue.'

'Because…?'

'Does there have to be a reason?'

Sunita tipped her head to one side. 'There usually is.'

'So what's *your* favourite colour?'

'Red.'

'Because…?'

'Because it was my mother's favourite colour—I like to

think it was her way of sticking two fingers up at the world that had branded her a scarlet woman. She always wore something red—her sari would maybe have a red weave, or she'd wear a red flower, or paint her toenails red. And as for her lipstick collection...'

'You must miss her.'

'I do. A lot.' She looked down at her plate and scooped up the last of her rissole. 'Anyway, why aquamarine blue?'

Reluctance laced his vocal cords—along with a sense of injustice that a question that had seemed so simple on the surface had suddenly become more complex. *Get a grip.* If this was a hoop Sunita had constructed as a prelude to marriage then he'd jump through it—he'd do the damn hula if necessary.

'It's the colour of the Lycander Sea. When life in the palace became too much I'd escape to the beach, watch the sea. It put things into perspective. Sometimes it was so still, so calm, so serene it gave me peace. Occasionally it would be turbulent, and then I guess I'd identify with it. As a child I was pretty sure Neptune lived off the coast of Lycander...'

OK, Frederick, that's enough. More than he'd intended in fact. But there was something about the way Sunita listened—*really* listened—that seemed to have affected him.

She watched him now, lips slightly parted, tawny eyes serious, but as if sensing his discomfort she leant back before she spoke.

'OK, next question. Star sign?'

'Leo.'

'Me too.'

'Is that good or bad?'

'I really don't know. We'd need to ask Nanni—she is an avid believer in horoscopes. Though I'm not sure why. I think her parents had her and my grandfather's horoscopes read to see if they'd be a good match, and the astrologer was confident they were compatible.'

'Were they?'

'I don't think they can have been. From what my mother told me my grandfather was a tyrant and a control freak, whereas Nanni is a kind, gentle woman. But Nanni herself never speaks of her marriage—and never criticises my grandfather. And she still believes in horoscopes.'

'What about you? Do *you* believe in horoscopes?'

'I think there may be something in it, but not enough that you can base your life decisions on them—that's the easy way out, isn't it? You can just shrug your shoulders and blame fate if it all goes wrong. It doesn't work like that—life is about choice.'

'Yes…' Bleakness settled on him—his choices had cost Axel his life. 'But life is also about the consequences of those choices. Consequences you have to live with.'

'Yes, you do. But in this case Amil's future is in *our* hands—he will have to live with the destiny *we* choose for him. And that is hard. But it's not only about Amil. It's about us as well. You and me. That's why this marriage can't work.'

Her chin jutted out at an angle of determination.

Frederick frowned—but before he could respond the door opened and Deepali re-entered the room, followed by a young man pushing a trolley.

'Fish *recheado*,' the young man announced. 'Made with pomfret.'

Deepali's face shone with pride. 'This is my son, Ashok—he is the chef here,' she explained.

'I thought you might want to know about the dish,' Ashok said.

'I'd love to.'

Sunita smiled her trademark smile and Frederick saw Ashok's appreciation.

'The pomfret is stuffed with a special paste. I used chillies, cloves, cumin and lemon. It is a Goan dish, but *recheado* means stuffed in Portuguese.' Ashok smiled. 'And there is also Goan bread, freshly baked. Enjoy.'

Frederick waited until the mother and son had left the room and then he looked at Sunita.

'Why not?' he repeated.

CHAPTER NINE

'WHY WON'T THIS marriage work?'

Frederick's voice was even, his question posed as if the topic under discussion was as simple as a grocery list rather than the rest of their lives.

Sunita took a deep breath and marshalled the thoughts she'd herded into a cogent argument throughout the starter. 'Would you have even considered marriage to me if it wasn't for Amil?'

There was no hesitation as he tipped his hand in the air, palm up. 'No.'

To her surprise, irrational hurt touched her that he didn't have to give it even a second's thought. 'Exactly.'

'But you *can't* take Amil out of the equation. If it weren't for Amil you wouldn't consider marriage to me either.'

'I get that. But it's different for you. I don't *need* to marry anyone. You do, and you need it to be the right person—for Lycander's sake. A woman like Lady Kaitlin Derwent. I am the *antithesis* of Kaitlin.'

For an insane moment the knowledge hurt. But she was no longer a child, desperately trying to measure up to her half-sisters and always failing. High academic grades, musical ability, natural intelligence… You name it, Sunita lacked it. But in this case she needed to emphasise her failings with pride.

'I haven't got an aristocratic bone in my body, and I don't have the *gravitas* that you need to offer the Lycander people.'

'You are the mother of my son.'

'Your *illegitimate* son. Plus, I was a model. Your father married or was associated with a succession of models, actresses and showbiz people, and all his relationships ended in scandal. Your people will tar me with the same brush.'

'Then so be it. I agree that you do not have the background I was looking for in my bride, but I believe you will win the people over. In time.'

'I don't think I will.' She inhaled deeply. 'For a start, I want to resume my modelling career—and I can't see that going down a storm with the people.'

Or with him. He masked his reaction, but not fast enough—he hadn't taken that into the equation.

'You don't like the idea either?'

'I neither like nor dislike it. I agree it might be problematic for the people to accept, but it's a problem we can work around.'

'But it doesn't *have* to be a problem. Don't marry me— marry someone like Kaitlin…someone with the qualities to be a true consort.'

Even as she said the words a strange pang of what she reluctantly identified as jealousy shot through her veins. *Jealousy? Really?* She didn't even know who she was jealous of. It meant nothing to her if Frederick married someone else. *Nothing.* As for being jealous of Kaitlin—that was absurd.

Sunita forged on. 'You know I'm right. Tell me about your agreement with Kaitlin. What else did she bring to the table apart from her background?'

'This is not a constructive conversation.'

'I disagree. This isn't only about Amil. This is about us as well. Your life and mine. You want to make me a princess—I deserve to know what that entails, what your expectations are. You said it yourself.'

'What I expected from Kaitlin and what I would expect from you are different.'

Ouch. 'In what way?' Ice dripped from her tone as she forked up a piece of succulent fish with unnecessary violence.

'You are two different individuals—of course I would have different expectations.' Frustration tinged his voice, along with what looked like a growing knowledge that he'd entered stormy waters and was in imminent danger of capsizing.

'Well, I'd like to know what you expected from Kaitlin.' *From your ideal candidate*, her treacherous heart cried out.

'Fine. Kaitlin was brought up for this role—she has dozens of connections, she speaks four European languages, she has diplomacy down pat. I planned to use her as a royal ambassador—she would have played a very public role. I also hoped she would be influential behind the scenes—play a part in turning Lycander round, in shaping policy.'

For Pete's sake! Sunita didn't think she could bear to hear any more. Lady Kaitlin had obviously been on a fast track to royal sainthood, and the role of Lycander princess would have fitted her like a silken glove. Whereas Sunita was more fitted for the lost sock that languished behind the radiator.

The realisation hollowed her tummy and she shook her head in repudiation. 'There you have it. I think you owe it to Lycander to marry someone else.'

Surely she'd made her case? She understood that Frederick wanted to be part of Amil's life, but he *had* to see that Sunita was quite simply not princess material.

'No.' His voice was flat. 'I have already considered everything you've said. And, incidentally, you and my chief advisor are in complete agreement. But you are Amil's mother, and that trumps all other considerations. He is my son. I want him to live with me—I want him to be Lycander's Crown Prince after me. I also want him to live with his mother. So marriage is the only option.'

'No, it isn't. What if I decide not to marry you?' He couldn't actually *force* her to the altar. 'You would still be an important part of Amil's life.'

'Stop!'

'What?' Her stomach plummeted as she saw the expression on his face—weariness, distaste, sadness.

'Don't do this.'

'Why not?'

'Because if you don't marry me I will fight for joint custody.'

Joint custody. The words sucker-punched her. 'You promised that you wouldn't take him from me. You said he needs me.'

'I also told you I will be a real part of his life. What would you suggest? A weekend here and there? He is my son as well.'

'Yes. But you'll marry someone else—have another family.'

'And you think that should make me want Amil less— is that the message you want to give our son?'

'No!'

Damn it—she couldn't think. Panic had her in its grip, squeezing out any coherent thought. All she could think of now was losing Amil for half of his childhood. Of Amil in Lycander with a stepmother—whichever new multilingual paragon of virtue Frederick eventually married—and half-siblings.

History on repeat with a vengeance.

Memories of her own humiliations, inflicted by the

hands of her stepmother and her half-sisters—the put-downs, the differentiation, the horror—were chiselled on her very soul. No way would she risk that for Amil.

'I won't agree to joint custody. I *can't.*'

But she could see his point. She had already deprived him of fourteen months of Amil's life—how could she expect him to settle for the occasional week? Regular phone calls and Skype? Would *she* settle for that? Never in a million years.

She inclined her head. 'All right. You win. I'll marry you.'

It looked as if Princess Sunita was about to enter the land of fairy tales. It was a good thing she knew that happy-ever-afters didn't exist in real life.

CHAPTER TEN

'ALL RIGHT. YOU WIN. I'll marry you.'

The words seemed to haunt his dreams, and by the time the distinctive fluting whistle of a golden oriole penetrated his uneasy repose it was a relief to wake up, hop out of the slatted wooden bed and head for the shower. He could only hope the stream of water would wake him up to common sense.

He had won, and there was nothing wrong with winning—it meant he would have a life with his son, would be able to give Amil his principality. That was *good* news, right?

The problem was Sunita's words had not been the only ones to permeate his sleeping mind. His father's voice had also made a showing.

'Every woman has a price. Find her weakness, exploit it and then you win, Freddy, m'boy.'

He switched off the shower in a savage movement. Time to man up. Yes, he'd won—and that was OK. It was a cause to celebrate—*not* the equivalent of what his father had done. *He* was striving to keep Amil with Sunita full-time. He hadn't destroyed a family—he'd created one. Ergo, he was not his father. It wasn't as if he had *threatened* her with joint custody. It had been the only other option—an option he'd known she would knock back.

Rationally, the facts were undeniable. Sometimes in life you had to choose between the rock and the hard place, and he'd done his best to make the rock a comfortable choice for her. He'd offered her the chance to be a princess—most women would have grabbed the baton and run with it.

End of.

Now it was time to figure out the next step.

He pulled on chinos and a navy T-shirt and headed into the courtyard and the early-morning sunshine.

'Over here.'

He heard Sunita's voice and spotted her sitting under the shade of a tree, simply dressed in a rainbow-striped sundress, sunglasses perched atop her raven hair. Sunlight filtered through the green leaves of the banyan tree, dappling her arms and the wood of the table, lighting up the tentative smile she offered as he approached.

It was a smile that seemed to bathe his skin in the warmth of relief, pushing away any lingering doubts about his actions.

'Hey.'

'Hey…' He sat down opposite and surveyed the array of fruit. 'Wow.'

'I know, right? It's hard to know where to begin!'

'I'm not even sure I can name them all.'

'*Chiku*, papaya, guava, pineapple, *rambutan*. They all taste different and they are all delicious.'

He reached for a *chiku*—a fruit he'd never heard of. 'It looks like a potato.'

'Wait until you taste it.'

He halved the fruit to reveal pinkish flesh seeded with a mere three black seeds. He scooped out a spoonful and blinked at the intense sweetness.

'Better than cotton candy.'

She smiled, and once again relief touched him.

'About last night…' he said. 'I know marriage isn't your ideal option, but I am very glad you said yes.'

'It isn't, but it *is* the best option on the table and I've decided to make the best of it. Perhaps if I'd been more upfront two years ago we wouldn't be in this mess. But we are, and I'll do my best to be positive about the marriage idea.'

'Our marriage doesn't have to be a mess. I think we can make this work. For Amil *and* for us.'

A pause, and then she nodded. 'I'll try. So, what's the next step in Project Marriage?'

There was no room for further doubts or any more discussion with his conscience. Project Marriage was what he wanted and what he believed to be right for them all. Yet for some reason he felt restless, as if the beauty of the surroundings was somehow tainted. This was the sort of place where *real* couples should sit and plan their future—couples foolish enough to believe in the concept of love.

'We need a plan, but I suggest we move this discussion to somewhere else. Is there anything you want to see in Goa? We could hit the beach…visit the old quarter…'

In truth he didn't care—he needed to move, to get on with the business of the day away from this tranquil fairy tale setting that seemed to accuse him of having behaved like his father, however much logic told him he hadn't.

Sunita thought for a moment, her tawny eyes dreamy, as if the question needed deeper consideration than it appeared to warrant.

'I'd like to go to the Dudhsagar Falls.'

There was a nuance in her voice he couldn't identify. 'Any reason?'

For a second she hesitated, then she shrugged. 'My parents came to Goa together and they visited the falls. It's one of the few memories my mother ever shared about them both—she said it was important sometimes to remember the happy memories or they would all crumble to dust.'

She picked up a *rambutan*, rolled the lychee-like fruit almost like a dice.

'I'm not entirely sure what she meant, but I'd like to go somewhere she was happy. Even if that happiness was no more than a mirage.'

He had the feeling that right now Sunita missed her mother—and who could blame her? She was about to step into a whole new world that she didn't want to enter.

'I'm sorry you lost her, Sunita.'

'Me too. But I do feel lucky I had her for the time I did.' She hesitated. 'I don't know the details, but I'm guessing you didn't have much time with *your* mum.'

'No.'

Even before the divorce his mother had spent minimal time with him—at least until the divorce proceedings were underway. Then it had all changed, and even now he could remember the glorious happiness his three-year-old self had felt—not the detail, but the joy that finally his mother wanted his company, would hug him, take him out… And then abruptly it had all ceased. She'd gone before the ink had even dried on the papers. The whole 'loving mother' act had been exactly that—an act undertaken to up her settlement.

'I'm sorry.'

'No need. You can't miss what you've never had.'

The words came out rougher than he'd intended, but he didn't want her compassion. He'd got over his mother's abandonment long ago, buried those emotions along with the rest.

Pulling out his phone, he did a check on the falls, scanned the information. 'The falls it is—I'll speak to Security, see how close they can get us. Looks like the official road is closed off because of monsoon season, but I'm sure we can get something sorted.'

'Actually, I wondered if we could do what my parents did and walk along the railway track to get there. Just us— no security. I know they're discreet, but today I'd like to be just Frederick and Sunita—before we get caught up in the reality of being a royal couple.'

The wistfulness in her voice decided him—alongside the fact that, however much he trusted his staff, it made sense to thrash out the details of this marriage in private. Plus if he was being honest with himself, he too wanted to be 'just Frederick and Sunita' for one day. To put aside the burden of ruling and his complex need for this marriage for one day.

'Sounds like a plan.'

Surprise etched her face. 'You're sure?'

'I'm sure. Tell me the route they took and I'll figure it out.'

She grinned. 'I think they came back on a goods train.'

'We can manage that.'

'The Prince and his future consort hopping on a goods train? I like it.'

Her smile broadened and it caught at his heart, causing a sudden unfamiliar tug of hope that perhaps this might all work out.

Sunita glanced up at the sky, and for the first time in the past forty-eight hours her thoughts slowed down as she absorbed the grandeur of the bright grey monsoon clouds.

Most tourists flocked to India in the summer months, but she loved monsoon—always had, even as a child. Loved the drum of the rain, which brought the country much needed water and succour from heat, and lavished verdant green to the trees and fields.

'It doesn't seem possible that there can be so many different shades of green—it makes me wish I could paint, somehow capture all this.' Her outswept arm encapsulated the winding track, the surrounding green and the skies above. 'Photos never seem to catch the reality of it—they look fake, somehow.'

'Then commit it to memory,' Frederick said, putting out a hand to steady her as she stumbled slightly over an awkward rock.

The touch of his hand against hers almost made her gasp out loud, adding an extra level to her already over-crowded senses. In an almost involuntary movement she clasped her fingers around his.

'Like my mother did. She described this walk to me so many times it almost felt like a story.'

Perhaps a real-life fairy tale, in which a moment of happiness had *not* led to a lifetime of happily-ever-after.

'It's odd to think that they walked here once…maybe took the exact same steps we're taking now.' She turned to him. 'You must feel that a lot as a ruler—the idea of history being always around you. Your ancestors' spirits looking over your shoulders.'

For an instant she'd swear a small shiver shot through him, and understanding smote her. Perhaps for him it was the spirit of his older brother that haunted his every move and decision.

Yet his voice was light as he answered, 'I am more worried about current judgement and the opinion of posterity than the line of my progenitors.'

He slowed as they approached a tunnel, half turning for evidence of any oncoming train.

They stepped inside the dark and now it was her turn to shiver at the dank confines. Water trickled down the damp mossy walls and he tightened his grip on her hand. Without thought she moved closer to the strength of his body.

'It's safe. Even if a train does come through there is ample space as long as we keep to the side.'

Yet suddenly it didn't *feel* safe—though it was no longer the train she was worried about. Frederick was too close, and that proximity was playing havoc with her body.

Did it matter any more? They were to be married—their physical attraction could now be acknowledged. The idea jolted a funny little thrill through her—one she short-circuited instantly. Two years ago physical attraction had lambasted her self-control and her pride. No way would she enter *that* thrall again.

As they emerged into sunlight she dropped his hand, under the pretext of tugging her hair into a ponytail, and then turned to him.

'I think we were talking about current judgement and public opinion—and on that topic we need to decide how to announce our engagement.'

For an instant his gaze locked on her hand and then he nodded. 'I think we keep it low-key. I don't want to announce this as a romantic fairy tale—that would be disingenuous, and way too reminiscent of my father's marriages. Every engagement, every wedding was an extravaganza, with proclamations of eternal love.'

'Did he love *any* of them?'

'According to his own criteria he did—but in reality I believe it was little more than lust and an ability to kid himself.'

'Perhaps he did it for children?'

'My father never did anything unless it was for himself.' His tone was factual, rather than bitter. 'But that isn't the point. I don't want to lie and present our marriage as some sort of perfect love story. I'd rather be honest.'

Sunita stared at him. 'That is hardly the most gripping headline—*Prince Proposes to Legitimise Heir.*' Irrational hurt threatened at his reminder that this was the only reason for their union. Well, so be it. 'I don't believe in fairy tales, but I *do* believe in good publicity.'

'So what would *you* suggest?'

An old flame is rekindled. Prince Frederick of Lycander and Sunita decide to wed! Both the Prince and his bride profess delight at the prospect of being a real family.' Her pace increased slightly. 'I mean, that is just off the top of my head—I'm sure your spin people can work on it. We don't have to profess undying love, but anything is better than indifference.'

Admiration glinted in his eyes and warmed her.

'I'd forgotten what a natural you are with publicity. You've definitely not lost your touch.'

'Thank you kindly, good sir. Publicity is an incredibly powerful tool. I agree that we shouldn't lie to your people, but what you are doing is a good, principled action for your son—the people should know that. Of course they'll be interested in a bit of fun and glitz and a celebration too.' She glanced sideways at him. 'Fun is important—for all of us. I want Amil's childhood to be full of fun and joy—I want him to have a happy path through life.'

'So do I.'

'Good. Then let's show your people that. Let's make sure the engagement announcement is honest, but happy. We've decided to do this, so we need to make the best of it.'

With impeccable dramatic timing the skies chose that moment to open up, and before Sunita could do more than let out a warning cry the rain sheeted down in a torrential downpour.

Sunita tipped her face up and let it gush over her, revelling in the sheer force of Nature as it provided one of life's essentials.

Mere moments later the rain ceased. Blue skies replaced the grey, and sudden shafts of bright golden sunshine shot down, illuminating the droplets of water that hung everywhere. The smell of wet earth permeated the air and it seemed impossible not to smile.

'It's as if someone switched the tap off and the lights on,' Frederick said, a note of wonder in his voice as he looked round.

'That would be Varuna, the god of water. Nanni says that he listens to what the frogs say, and when they croak enough he gives us rain.'

'I think I'm going to like Nanni.'

'Of course you are.'

'So I take it your mother's family eventually relented and took her and you back in?'

'No…' Sunita sighed, feeling the familiar ache of regret and sadness. 'I wish that was how it had played out, but it didn't. They didn't relent.'

Even when they knew her mother was dying.

Anger was suddenly added to the mix. Her grandfather hadn't even told Nanni that their daughter was ill—hadn't given her the chance to say goodbye.

'I met Nanni for the first time when I was pregnant with Amil.' She glanced across at him. 'I don't expect your sympathy, but when I found I was pregnant I felt very alone.'

His expression hardened slightly, but to her surprise she could see an element of frustrated sympathy in his creased brow. 'So you decided to find your mother's relatives?'

'Yes. My mother had left enough information that it wasn't too hard. It turned out my grandfather had died two years before, and Nanni agreed to see me.'

That first meeting was one she would never forget—her

grandmother had simply stared at her, tears seeping from her brown eyes, her hands clasped as if in prayer. And then she had stepped forward and hugged Sunita, before standing back and touching her face as if in wonder, no doubt seeing not just her granddaughter but her daughter as well.

'She was overjoyed and so was I. She has never forgiven herself for not standing up to my grandfather, for letting my mother go, and I think she sees me and Amil as her second chance.'

'It isn't always easy to stand up to a partner if he or she has all the power. Your Nanni shouldn't be too hard on herself.'

'I've told her that. My mother didn't blame her either. Nanni was totally dependent on her husband—money, clothes, food, everything—and he made sure she knew it. If she had left with my mother he would have cut her off from the rest of her family, her children…everyone.' She paused and then turned to him, willing him to understand. 'I won't *ever* let myself get into that position.'

'You won't. Our marriage will be nothing like that.'

'I understand that, but I did mean what I said yesterday— I intend to resume my career. You saw what happened to your mother, your stepmothers. I've seen what happened to Nanni—I will *not* be dependent on you.'

'You won't be. We can set up a pre-nup.'

'In a principality where your word is law? Any pre-nup I sign wouldn't be worth the paper it was written on.'

'OK. You will be paid a salary that goes directly into your personal account—you can move that into another account anywhere in the world.'

'A salary essentially paid by *you*—one you could stop at any moment?'

His lips thinned. 'You really do not trust me at all, do you?'

There was a hint of hurt in his voice, but it was something she could not afford to listen to.

'I can't trust anyone. Think about it, Frederick. What if I decided to take Amil and leave? Would you still pay my salary? What if you turn out to be like your father? What if you fall in love with another woman?' Life had taught her there could never be too many 'what ifs' in the mix. 'Then I'll need money of my own.'

The easy warmth in his hazel eyes vanished, and now his brow was as clouded as a monsoon sky. 'None of those things will happen.'

'That's what you say *now*, but times change—we both know that.'

A shadow flickered across his face and she knew her point had gone home.

'So I must make sure myself that I have enough money in the bank for whatever life throws at me.'

To ensure there was always an escape route—that she would never be trapped like her grandmother had been, as *she* had been as a child.

'That is non-negotiable.'

'Understood.'

'Also, I want to leave Amil with my grandmother when we go back to Lycander.'

'Why?' The syllable was taut. 'Because you think I will snatch him the minute we land on Lycander soil?'

'No. But I won't risk taking him there until we have worked out how our marriage will be received. Also, I can get things ready for him; it will be a big change for him and I'd like to make his transition as easy as possible.'

The idea of not having Amil with her hurt, but she could not—*would* not—risk taking him to Lycander until she was sure of his reception there.

'I'll come back to Lycander with you, and *then* I'll get Amil.'

'OK. But *we* will get Amil.'

She nodded and then there was a silence, broken by a roar in the not so far distance.

'Dhudsagar Falls,' Sunita said. 'We're close.'

By tacit consent they quickened their pace.

CHAPTER ELEVEN

THE SOUND OF the monsoon-inflated waterfalls pounded his eardrums, but even as Frederick anticipated the sight his brain couldn't banish Sunita's expression, the realisation that she still didn't trust him.

Not that he blamed her—after all, his father had used his wealth and power to grind his wives to dust in the courts. All except his mother, who had played Alphonse at his own game and duped him—an act his father had never forgiven her for. Never forgiven Frederick for, come to that. But he wished that Sunita did not think so badly of him. *Enough.* Her opinion shouldn't matter, and in truth she couldn't judge him more harshly than he deserved. But…

His train of thought was broken by her gasp from next to him. 'Any minute now,' she whispered, as they emerged through a tunnel and onto a railway bridge already populated by a few other visitors.

But they had no interest in Sunita and Frederick—because it was impossible to focus on anything other than the waterfalls, both mighty and terrible. No image could do them justice as the four tiers cascaded and roared in torrents of milky-white water, leaping from the edge of towering cliffs and gusting and gushing down the slippery rock slopes.

The spray drenched him but he didn't move, utterly

mesmerised by the power and glory of Nature's creation, cloaked in a rising mist that mixed with the shafts of sunlight to create a rainbow of light.

'It's beyond description.'

Frederick nodded and moved by awe, on instinct, he reached out and took her hand in his. He wasn't sure how long they stood there, but it was long enough that the other tourists dispersed, long enough that another group came and went.

And then Sunita shook her head, as if coming out of a trance. 'We'd better go.'

He wondered what she'd been thinking all that time—perhaps she'd imagined her parents standing in the same spot, their thoughts and emotions, their hopes and dreams as they'd gazed at the might of the waterfalls.

They continued their trek along the railway tracks in a silence that he instinctively respected until he motioned to the adjacent forest. 'Shall we explore in there—it looks peaceful?'

'Good idea.' She glanced up at him. 'Sorry I've been lost in thought—it was just such an awe-inspiring sight.'

'It was.' He reached into his backpack. 'Time for food—or is that too prosaic?'

'Nope. I'm starving. And this looks idyllic—if a little damp.'

'I've brought a blanket, and if we spread it here, over this branch, we can perch on it.'

'Perfect.'

She accepted the wrapped sandwiches.

'Goan green chutney,' Frederick informed her. 'I promised Ashok to tell you the exact ingredients. Coriander leaves, coconut, chili and a little sugar and salt.'

Sunita took a bite. 'Glorious. That boy is talented.' She

surveyed him. 'So you went to the kitchen yourself? I'm surprised that was allowed.'

'Meaning?'

'Meaning your staff seem to think you shouldn't lift a finger for yourself.'

'I've noticed. I *am* trying to re-educate them—in fact I've given them all the day off today. The problem is my father expected to be waited on hand and foot, and that is what all Lycander staff seem conditioned to do. I even have someone who chooses all my clothes.' He grinned. 'Though, to be fair, Kirsten does a better job of it than I could.'

'Well, for the record, no one is choosing *my* clothes for me. That would drive me nuts. I need to fit my clothes to my mood.'

They ate in companionable silence and then Frederick leant forward, unsure why he felt the need to say his next words, but knowing he had to take heed of the urge to show her that their hopes and dreams didn't have to be built on an altar of falsehood and misunderstanding.

'Sunita?'

'Yes.'

She turned her head and his heart did a funny little jump. Dressed in simple khaki trousers and a red T-shirt, with her hair pulled back in a high ponytail, her features make-up free, she looked absurdly young and touchingly vulnerable.

'I understand why you want to go back to your career, and I understand your need for independence, but let's not go into this marriage expecting the worst. We'll be OK,' he said, even as he realised the ridiculous inadequacy of the words.

'You can't know that.' She lifted her shoulders in a shrug. 'But I appreciate the sentiment.'

'There are some things I *do* know, though. I won't turn into my father.' *Please God!* 'I won't fall in love with someone else and take Amil away from you.'

'You can't know that either.'

'I don't do falling in love, and that will not change. As for Amil, I will not take him from you. You have my word.'

'Words are meaningless.'

Her fierce certainty told him that someone had lied to her with devastating consequence, and increased his need to show her that he would not do the same.

'Sunita, I couldn't do it.' The words rasped from his throat. 'I would have done anything to have a mother. I witnessed first-hand what my father did to his wives, how it affected my brothers. I could not, I *will* not let history repeat itself.'

Her whole body stilled, and then she rose and moved towards him, sat right next to him, so close a tendril of her hair tickled his cheek.

'I'm sorry—I know what it's like to lose a mother through death, but for you it must have been pain of a different type…to know she was out there. And your poor mother… to have lost you like that—I can't imagine how it must have felt. Not just your mother but Stefan's and the twins'.'

For a moment the temptation to let her believe the fiction touched him. To let her believe the false assumption that his mother had been wronged, had spent years in grief and lamenting, that his mother had loved him. After all, he had no wish to be an object of pity or allow the ugly visage of self-pity to show its face.

But as he saw the sympathy, the empathy on her face, he realised he couldn't let her waste that compassion. 'My mother didn't suffer, Sunita.'

'I don't understand.'

'My mother sold me out for generous alimony and a

mansion in Beverly Hills. She played my father like a fine fiddle—conned him into believing she would do anything to keep custody of me, would be devastated to lose me. At the time he was still worrying about his popularity— many people hadn't got over the way he'd married my mother mere weeks after his first wife's death. He wanted to hurt her by taking me away—however, he didn't want to come across as the totally cruel husband again, so he offered her a generous settlement and she skipped all the way to the bank.'

'But…' Disbelief lined her face, along with a dark frown. 'How *could* she?'

'With great ease, apparently. Hey, it's OK. I came to terms with it long ago. I didn't tell you because I want to discuss it, or because I want sympathy. I told you because I want you to know that I could never take Amil from you. I know first-hand that a child needs his mother. From my own experience *and* my siblings'. Stefan, Barrett, Emerson—they have all been devastated by the custody battles and having their mothers torn from them. I would not put you or Amil through it. You have my word, and that word is not meaningless.'

'Thank you.' Shifting on the branch so that she faced him, she cupped his face in her hands, her fingers warm against his cheeks. 'Truly. Thank you for sharing that— you didn't have to. And I do believe that right here, right now, you mean what you promise.'

'But you don't believe I'll make good?'

'I…' Her hands dropped to her sides and, leaning forward, she dabbled her fingers in the soil of the forest floor, trickled it through her fingers and then sat up again. 'I don't know.'

She shrugged.

'Perhaps it's my turn to share now. I told you how my

father left when he found out my mother was pregnant. He promised her that he loved her, that they had a future.' She gestured back the way they'd come. 'Maybe he said those words at the falls. Hell, maybe they even sat here, in this very forest. But that promise meant nothing. And, you see, that wasn't the only promise he made.'

'I don't understand.'

'He came back.' Her eyes were wide now, looking back into a past that he suspected haunted her. 'When my mother found out she was terminally ill she managed to track him down. She had no one else. And he came, and he agreed to take me in. He explained that he was married, with two other daughters, but he promised—he swore that I would be welcomed, that I would have a family, that he would love and cherish me. He said that he was sorry and that he wanted to make it up to her and to me.'

The pain in her voice caused an ache that banded his chest and he reached out to cover her hand in his own, hoped that somehow it would assuage her hurt.

'So, after she died…' Her voice caught and her fingers tightened around his. 'He came to bring me to England—to my new family.'

Perhaps he should say something, Frederick thought. But he couldn't think of anything—couldn't even begin to contemplate how Sunita must have felt. The loss of her mother, the acquisition of a father she must have had mixed feelings about, the total upending of her life. All he could do was shift closer to her, *show* his comfort.

'It didn't work out. Turned out his promises didn't materialise.'

'What happened?'

'My stepmother and my sisters loathed me—I knew that from the instant I walked into the house.'

A house that must have felt so very alien to her, in a country that must have felt grey and cold and miserable.

'In a nutshell, he pitched me into a Cinderella scenario. They treated me like I was an inferior being.' She made a small exasperated noise. 'It sounds stupid, because it is so difficult to explain, but they made me feel worthless. I ate separately from them, my clothes were bought from charity shops, while my half-sisters' were new, I ended up with loads of extra chores so I could "earn my keep", and there were constant put-downs, constant reminders that I was literally worthless.' Another shrug. 'It all sounds petty, but it made me feel like nothing—worse than invisible. I was visible, but what they could see made them shudder.'

'It doesn't sound petty—it sounds intolerable.' Anger vibrated through him, along with disbelief that people could be so cruel. 'Was your father involved in this?'

'He was more of a bystander than a participant. He was away a lot on business. I did try to explain to him that I was unhappy, that I felt my stepmother didn't like me, but he simply said that I must be imagining it or, worse, he would accuse me of base ingratitude. Which made me feel guilty and even more alone.'

No wonder Sunita found it hard to take people at their word. Her own father, who had promised to care for her, had instead treated her like muck and allowed others to do the same.

'I'm sorry. I wish I could turn back time and intervene.'

'You can't change the past. And even if you could perhaps the outcome would be worse. Because in the past I got out, I escaped, and I've come to terms with what happened. I can even understand a little why my stepmother acted as she did. She was landed with a strange girl—the daughter of a woman her husband had been unfaithful with, the woman who probably was the love of his life. The gossip and speculation in the community must have been beyond humiliating for her and my half-sisters. So they turned all that anger and humiliation on to me.'

'That doesn't excuse their behaviour, or explain your father's.'

'I think my father was weak and he felt guilty. Guilty over the way he'd treated my mother…guilty that he had betrayed his wife in the first place. And that guilt translated into doing anything for a quiet life. That worked in my favour later on. I got scouted by a model agency when I was sixteen and my father agreed to let me leave home— my stepmother was happy to see me go, sure I'd join the ranks of failed wannabes, so she agreed. I never looked back and I never went back. I never saw them again. The second I could, I sent my father a cheque to cover any costs he might have incurred over the years. As far as I am concerned we are quits. I don't even know where he is.'

So much made sense to Frederick now—her lack of trust, her fears over Amil, her need to be in control. Admiration burned within him that she had achieved so much, was such an amazing parent herself.

These were all the things he wanted to say, but didn't quite know how. So instead he did what he had promised himself he wouldn't do and he kissed her—right there in the middle of the rainforest, with the smell of the monsoon in the air, and the pounding of the waterfall in the distance. He kissed her as if his life and soul depended on it.

Her resistance was brief—a nanosecond of surprise— and then, as if she too were tired of words, of this walk down a memory lane that was lined with sadness, her resistance melted away and her lips parted beneath his.

He tasted the sweet chili tang left by the sandwiches and heard her soft moan. Their surroundings receded. The call of a hornbill, the rustle of the monkeys in the trees above all melted away and left only them, encased in a net of yearning and need and desire.

He pulled her closer, oblivious of the rustle of the blanket, the unwieldiness of the branch they sat on. Nothing mattered but *this*—losing themselves in this moment of sheer bliss as he deepened the kiss, as her hands slipped under his T-shirt so her fingers covered the accelerated beat of his heart.

Who knew what would have happened if a monkey in the tree above hadn't decided to take advantage and scamper down in an audacious bid for the rucksack. It's insistent chatter and the swipe of an overhanging branch brought Frederick back to reality.

A shout from him, a darting movement from Sunita, and the monkey jumped to safety and jabbered at them in indignation.

They met each other's eyes, hers still clouded with desire, and he managed a smile. 'Well saved.'

Then there were no words. They both simply stood there, and he reached out and took her hands in his.

'What now?' he asked.

'I don't know.' She shook her head. 'Yes, I do. Let's walk. And eat and talk. But let's not talk about unhappy things.'

'That sounds good. Only happy topics—all the way back.' He held her gaze. 'And what happens then?'

She stepped forward, stood on tiptoe, and dropped the lightest of kisses on his lips. 'I don't know,' she whispered. 'I really don't.'

For a moment neither did he. Oh, he knew what he *should* do—he should lock this down now. This physical attraction was too intense, too emotional, and he didn't want intensity or emotion to enter their relationship. This marriage was an alliance and he wanted it to last. Suc-

cumbing to physical allure, allowing it too much importance, would jeopardise that.

But today he was just Frederick, not the Playboy Prince
or the ruler of a principality who had vowed to fulfil his
brother's vision. Today they were Frederick and Sunita.

And so he stepped forward and smiled—a smile that
was shamelessly predatory and full of promise. 'Then it's
lucky that I know *exactly* what to do.'

'What…?' Her voice was even softer than before, her
brown eyes wide.

'We're going to walk to the nearest station and catch a
goods train, and then take a taxi back to the villa. Then
we're going to resume where we've just left off and this
time we are not going to stop.' He paused. 'How does that
sound?'

He realised he was holding his breath as she tipped her
head to one side, and then she smiled a smile that lit her
face and ignited a warmth that spread across his chest.

'That sounds perfect. I just hope the goods train is fast.'

Frederick shook his head. 'Anticipation is half the fun.'
He held out his hand. 'Let's go.'

'Anticipation is half the fun.'

Sunita wasn't so sure of that. As they walked alongside
the train tracks anticipation streamed through her veins,
causing her tummy to cartwheel and her pulse-rate to soar.
Was *that* fun?

It was hard to tell—her whole body felt tight with need,
a yearning that it would now be impossible to quell, and
truth to tell she didn't want to. She glanced down at their
clasped hands, at the strength of his profile, the jut of his
jaw, the lithe assurance he walked with, the whole time
aware of his own scrutiny, the desire that warmed his hazel
eyes when they rested on her.

They talked—of course they did. Of films and books and politics…of cabbages and kings…but the words seemed to be filtered through a haze of awareness that glistened in the air alongside the sunlit drops of rain that sparkled from the lush leaves.

Their ascent onto a goods train seemed almost surreal as they travelled amidst the bulky cargo, and she gazed out over the variegated greens of paddy fields, the swoop of the Goan valleys, the shimmering grey of the sky, where clouds swelled and perfumed the air with the promise of rain. All the while, even as her senses stored away Nature's munificent beauty, they also revelled in Frederick's proximity, in the knowledge that soon—soon—they would be together, that for a time at least he would be hers.

Careful!

She must not let this get out of perspective, make it into any more than it was. This was a benefit of their marriage deal—a benefit that could be taken or left at will. This was physical—no more no less—and the only reason she was so on edge was because she hadn't felt like this for two years. Not since that night when all her principles had been abandoned and she'd tumbled into bed with him.

'Hey.'

She turned to see his hazel eyes rest on her face.

'You OK? We don't have to do this, you know? We have a lifetime ahead of us…'

But not like this—not as Frederick and Sunita. Today meant something different—she couldn't explain how she knew it, but she knew with soul-wrenching certainty that this was the case.

'I know, but I want this now, today…' She grinned suddenly. 'There is only so much anticipation a girl can take.'

His answering grin removed all doubts; it was a smile

she remembered from two years ago, boyish, happy, and she hadn't seen it once in the past few days.

'It'll be worth it. I promise.'

And as the train slowed to a stop she had no doubt that this was a promise she could rely on.

Twenty minutes later they arrived back at the villa and alighted from the taxi. She glanced around almost furtively, not wanting to meet Deepali or Ashok or anyone. Hand in hand, they practically tiptoed through the garden... And if Deepali did spot them she remained discreetly hidden and they reached Sunita's bedroom safely.

Once inside, she moved to the window and pulled the blackout shutters closed, then turned and moved towards Frederick with an urgency more than matched by his own as he strode forward and pulled her so she was flush against the hard promise of his body.

'The anticipation was great,' she murmured. 'But now it's got old.'

His laugh held a breathless quality. 'Tell me about it!'

And with that he tumbled her back onto the bed, and after that all coherent thought evaporated as sensation took over. The feel of his lips on hers, his taste, his touch against her sensitised skin—all caused her to moan in unabashed joy. His skin under her fingers, his shudder of pleasure, his voice whispering her name, the shucking of clothes, the urgency and the exquisite gentleness, the awe and the laughter and desire such as she had never known, all created a waving, pulsing sense that carried them higher and higher...

Hours later she opened her eyes, realising that she was being gently shaken awake, a hand on her shoulder. *His* hand. She blinked sleepily, and then sat up as the glorious dream dissipated. Frederick stood back from the bed—fully clothed, she noted with a fuzzy disappointment.

'Hey…' she said.

'Hey. Everyone's back—we need to show our faces before they wonder where we are.'

Sunita blinked, tried to compute why it mattered—they were engaged. Surely he wasn't embarrassed. Properly awake now, she propped herself up on one elbow as a sudden awkwardness descended. 'You should have woken me earlier.'

'I thought I'd let you sleep.' Now a small smile quirked into place. 'We expended a lot of energy.'

'So we did.' For a moment relief touched her—maybe she'd imagined the awkwardness.

'But now the day is over and we aren't "just" Sunita and Frederick any more. We are the Prince and his Princess-to-be and we can't repeat this.'

'This?' she echoed, as a spark of anger ignited by hurt flared. 'Define "this".'

His gaze remained steady. 'We can't sleep together again before the wedding. This engagement needs to be seen as completely different from my father's marriages—I don't want the people to believe it is based on physical attraction alone, that their ruler has been influenced by anything other than the good of Lycander.'

'Of course.'

It made perfect sense, she could see that. Of course she could. She could measure every publicity angle with unerring accuracy. This marriage would not play well with Lycander—she herself had pointed that out. So she understood that they needed to downplay their physical attraction and focus on the real reason for their marriage—Amil.

Yet his words felt like a personal rejection, as though

beneath his common-sense approach lay reserve, a withdrawal.

The knowledge…the certainty that he regretted the day and its outcome, that he regretted 'this', bolstered her pride, gave her voice a cool assurance. 'I understand.'

After all, he'd made it clear enough. Their physical attraction was a side benefit, a bonus to their marriage alliance, and she would not make the mistake of reading any more into it than that.

'I need to get dressed. Shall I meet you in the gardens?'

For a moment he hesitated, and then nodded and headed for the door. Once he was gone Sunita closed her eyes, annoyed to feel the imminent well of tears. Two years before she'd allowed physical attraction to override common sense, and now it seemed she might have done it again. But no more.

She swung herself out of bed in a brisk movement and headed across the room. Pulling open her wardrobe, she surveyed the contents and settled on a black cold-shoulder crop top over floral silk trousers. A quick shower, a bit of make-up and she was good to go.

Once in the gardens, she spotted Frederick in conversation with Eric, saw the hand-over of a package that Frederick dropped into his pocket before he saw her and walked over.

'Shall we have a quick walk before dinner?' he asked.

'Sure.'

They walked into the sylvan glade, skirting the lily pond, where two brilliant turquoise kingfishers dived, their white 'shirtfront' breasts bright in the dusk.

'I wanted to give you this,' he said, and he reached into his pocket and took out the package, undoing it with deft fingers and handing her the jeweller's box inside. 'We can't announce the engagement without a ring.'

She flipped the lid open and gazed inside. The ring had presence; it glinted up at her, a cold, hard, solid diamond. A discreetly obvious ring that knew its own worth—its multi-faceted edges placed it in the upper echelon of the diamond class. A regal ring—perhaps he hoped it would confer a royal presence on her.

Hell, it was the very Kaitlin of rings.

'Did you choose it?'

For a scant instant discomfort showed, but then it was gone. 'No. Kirsten did.'

The woman who chose his clothes. Of course—who better to choose the correct ring for Lycander's bride?

'I asked her to get it done last night. Is there a problem with it?'

'Of course not.'

In an abrupt movement she pulled the ring out and slid it over her finger, where it sat and looked up at her, each glint one of disdain. The ring wasn't fooled—it knew this was not a worthy hand to rest upon.

Sunita glared down at it as she executed an almost painful mental eye-roll. *Note to self: the ring does not possess a personality. Second note: of course I am worthy.*

She summoned a smile. 'Guess we're all set to go.' Even if she couldn't have felt less ready.

CHAPTER TWELVE

Lycander

THE CAR WOUND up the mountain road. Sunita stifled a gasp and Frederick felt a sudden surge of pride as he saw her reaction to Lycander's castle.

'Holy-moly,' she said. 'It's straight out of a fairy tale. Any minute now Snow White will wave at me from a turret or I'll see Rapunzel climb down a tower.'

Something tugged at his heart as he looked at her— something he couldn't identify and didn't particularly want to. Focus on facts…that was the way to go.

'Believe it or not, this castle has been around for centuries. It started out long ago as a wooden fortress and over the years it has been renovated, added to, and here we have it.'

'It's hard to believe I'm going to live there.'

Equally hard to ascertain her opinion on the fact, he thought.

Sunita subsided into silence as they approached the castle and parked in an impressive paved courtyard, complete with fountains, stone lions and an immense marble sundial.

'I'll give you a proper tour later. For now, if it's all right with you, I'll show you to your rooms—I've asked Giselle Diaz, the housekeeper, to get a set of apartments ready.

After the wedding we will move into the state apartments. I'll show you those later—I think you may want to redecorate them.'

Slow down. No need to turn into a tour guide. Come to that, he couldn't help but wonder at the dearth of staff there to greet them. Foreboding touched him—perhaps the no-show was connected to the emergency council meeting he was scheduled to attend right now. Convened to 'discuss'—for that read 'object to'—his marriage.

They reached the apartment suite that would be Sunita and Amil's until the wedding and he scanned it quickly. Clean and polished…welcoming flowers in place. On the surface it all looked fine, but he knew it lacked the extra touches that had abounded the one time Lady Kaitlin had stayed as a Lycander guest. Back then Giselle had been there to greet them, the flowers had been more lavish, the toiletries a tad more luxurious.

Hmm…

'I'll leave you to settle in and I'll be back as soon as I can.'

'Why don't I come with you? My guess is that your council will want to talk to you about our marriage—let's face them together.'

Frederick shook his head. 'I'd rather do it alone. I brokered this marriage—it is my responsibility to explain it to my people.'

A flash of hurt showed in her eyes and then she shrugged. 'As you wish.'

He pushed down the urge to assuage the hurt; this was *his* business and he would deal with it alone.

Fifteen minutes later he looked around the council chamber, which was informally referred to as the tapestry room, due to the needlepoint that lined nearly every centimetre of the walls. The lifework of a princess centuries before, who had toiled whilst her husband had dallied with a string of mistresses.

Each section illustrated a different theme, dominated by war and religion with plenty of fire and brimstone and gore… Presumably it was meant to be an apt backdrop for the discussion of council matters.

'Order!' called one of the council members.

Frederick looked around the table—at Marcus's assessing expression, at the rest of the council's combative stance. 'You requested we meet as soon as I arrived to discuss your concerns. Please enlighten me.'

A middle-aged man rose to his feet. 'This proposed marriage, Your Highness…we do not believe it is a good move.'

'Marcus has kept me apprised of your concerns.' He kept his voice even. 'But this marriage *is* happening.'

'But the people will not like it,' interpolated another council member.

'Sunita is an excellent publicist—I believe she will win them over.'

'How? She is a woman you barely know—a model, the mother of a baby she kept from you—but now that you are on the throne she seems happy to marry you.'

'Shades of your mother…'

'Who said that?' Frederick demanded.

'*I* said it.' The voice came from one of the elder statesmen.

'My relationship with Sunita bears no resemblance to that of my parents.'

'I beg to differ, Your Highness. I was there. Prince Alphonse fell hook, line and sinker for your mother—chased her whilst his wife, the mother of Crown Prince Axel, was dying. Their wedding was an extravaganza pushed forward because the bride was pregnant. Within months of your birth the marriage was floundering; within a few years it had ended in scandal. Your mother played him for a fool.'

White-hot anger roiled inside him. Yet the words were true—a fact he had to face.

'Are you saying that *I* am a fool? What would have happened if you had spoken to my father thus?'

Frederick made a gesture to a guard, who stepped forward without hesitation to a murmur of surprise.

'You would have been marched out and the council would have been shut down until after the wedding.'

He gestured for the guard to stop and rose to his feet.

'But I do not rule as my father did—I have listened to all your concerns and I understand them. Now I tell you this. My marriage to Sunita is to be made in good faith on both our parts. There will be no scandal. There will be no custody battle. This union will endure. This wedding is happening.'

What was he? The Delphi Oracle? But now was no time to exhibit doubt. 'I promise you all that I value your opinion. But you see, ladies and gentlemen, Amil is my son, and if I have a chance to be a father *without* taking my son from his mother then I have to take it. So the wedding will happen and I very much hope to see you all dance at it.'

Further silence, and then Marcus rose to his feet, an enigmatic look on his face. 'I suggest that is the end of this special council meeting.'

As everyone filed out Frederick ran a hand down his face and turned as his chief advisor approached. Frederick shook his head. 'Not now, Marcus. I can't take any more wedding advice.'

The dark-haired man gave a half-smile. 'I wouldn't dare.'

'Now, *that* I don't believe.'

'You should.' Marcus eyed him. 'That is the first time since your ascension to the throne that I have seen you stand up for something *you* believe in.'

'Rubbish. I have stood in this room and fought to convince councillors to support education and tax reform, to close the casinos...'

'I get that. But those were all Axel's policies. This is *your* marriage.'

'Axel would have agreed that I am doing the right thing.'

'Then maybe you and Axel had more in common than I realised.'

For a second his chief advisor's words warmed him— but only for a fleeting second. If Marcus knew the truth he'd never use such words.

Frederick rose to his feet before the urge to confess overcame common sense and tried to rid himself of the grubby feel of deceit.

'Frederick? I'll support you in this, but you will need to make this work. You need to win the public round.'

'I know.'

Luckily, he knew the perfect person to help with that.

Sunita stared down at the diamond ring that sparkled and glistened and weighted her finger. She looked around the apartment that appeared opulent yet felt oppressive, with its heavy faded gold curtains and the bowls of flowers that, though magnificent, emanated a cloying, gloom-laden scent.

These were showrooms—there should be signs and information leaflets to outline the names of the rich and famous who had stayed within these walls, to document the lives of the painters who had created the looming allegorical creations that adorned them.

The furniture was decorative—but the stripes of the

claw-footed chaise longue almost blinded her, and the idea of sitting on it was impossible. As for the bedroom—she'd need a stepladder to get up into a bed that, conversely, seemed to have been made for someone at least a foot smaller than she was.

Well, there was no way she would let Amil live in a showroom, so she needed to make it into a home.

She started to unpack—hung her clothes in the wardrobe, took comfort from the feel of the fabrics, the splash of the colours, every item imbued with memories.

She halted at a knock on the door.

Spinning round, she saw Frederick framed in the doorway, and to her annoyance her heart gave a little pit-pat, a hop, skip and a jump.

'Hi.'

'Sorry, I did knock on the main door.'

'That's fine. How did the meeting go?'

'As well as could be expected. The council understand this marriage. But we need to get the publicity right to prevent a public backlash.'

Sunita moved away from the wardrobe. 'OK. Let's brainstorm.'

Her mind whirred as they moved into the lounge and perched on two ridiculously uncomfortable upholstered chairs.

'We need to make sure the people understand why we have left Amil in India—that it is simply so we can prepare a home for him. I could talk to the local press about my plans to renovate these apartments and the state apartments. I also suggest that before Amil arrives we go on a tour of some of Lycander, so it's clear that I am interested in the country—not just the crown. I won't accept any modelling contracts straight away.'

Even though her agent's phone was already ringing off the proverbial hook.

He rose to his feet, looked down at her with a sudden smile that set her heart off again.

'Let's start now.'

'How?'

'I'll take you on a tour of an olive grove.'

'One of yours?'

For a moment he hesitated, and then he nodded. 'Yes. I'll arrange transport and press coverage.'

'I'll get changed into appropriate clothes for touring an olive grove.' In fact she knew the very dress—a long, floaty, lavender-striped sun dress.

A shot of anticipation thrilled through her.

Stop. This was a publicity stunt—not a romantic jaunt. She had to get a grip. This marriage was an alliance that Frederick had 'brokered'—a word he had used in this very room a mere hour before.

The problem was, however hard she tried—and she'd tried incredibly hard—that anticipation refused to be suppressed by logic or any other device she could come up with.

Perhaps it was simply to do with the glorious weather, the cerulean blue sky, the hazy heat of the late August sun whose rays kissed and dappled the rolling hills and plains of the Lycander countryside. She could only hope it was nothing to do with the man who sat beside her in the back of the chauffeured car.

'So, where exactly are we going?'

'The place where it all started—the first olive grove I owned. It was left to me by a great-uncle when I was twenty-one. I visited on a whim and—*kaboom!*—the whole process fascinated me. The family who lived there were thrilled as my great-uncle had had no interest in the place—they taught me all about the business and that's how Freddy Petrelli's Olive Oil came into being. I expanded, bought up some smaller businesses, consolidated, and now our oil is stocked worldwide.'

'Are you still part of the company?'

'I'm still on the board, but by necessity I have had to delegate.'

'That's pretty impressive—to take one rundown olive grove and turn it into a multi-million-dollar business in a few years.'

'You turned yourself into one of the world's most sought-after supermodels in much the same time-frame. That's pretty impressive too.'

'Thank you—but it didn't feel impressive at the time.' Back then she'd been driven. 'I *needed* to succeed—I would not let my family see me fail. I wanted them to know that they had been wrong about me. I wanted to show them I was my mother's daughter and proud of it.'

At every photo shoot, she'd imagined their faces, tinged a shade of virulent green as they opened a magazine to see Sunita's face.

'That's understandable—and kudos to you for your success. You have my full admiration and, although it may not be politically correct, I hope they choked on envy every time they saw your picture.'

She couldn't help but laugh as a sudden warmth flooded her—it had been a long time since anyone had sounded so protective of her.

Before she could respond further the car came to a halt—and right after that they were mobbed. Or that was what it felt like. Once she had alighted from the car she realised the 'mob' actually consisted of four people—a middle-aged couple, a youth and a young girl—all of whom broke into simultaneous speech.

'The crop has been excellent this year. The olives—they will be the best yet. And last year's olive oil—the gods have blessed it, Freddy!'

'It has been too long, Frederick, too long—how can you have not been here for so long? And why didn't you tell me of this visit earlier? I would have prepared your favourite dishes. Now. Bah... All we have is what I have had time to prepare.'

'Thanks so much for the links to the bikes. Oil, gears, helmets...'

'Frederick, I've missed you! Why haven't you visited?'

There was no mistaking the family's happiness at seeing him, and as Sunita watched Frederick contend with the barrage of comments his smile flashed with a youthful boyishness.

'Pepita, Juan, Max, Flo—I'd like to introduce you to Sunita...my fiancée.'

For a moment the silence felt heavy, and Sunita could feel her tummy twist, and then Pepita stepped forward.

'Welcome, Sunita. It is lovely that Frederick has brought you here. We have all been reading the papers—every article. The little *bambino* looks adorable.'

As she spoke Pepita swept them forward towards a whitewashed villa. Terracotta tiles gleamed in the sunshine and trees shaded the courtyard outside.

'Come—lunch is all ready, Alberto, sort out the drinks. Flo, set the table, Max, come and help me serve.'

'Can I help?' asked Sunita.

'No, no, no. You and Frederick go and sit.'

Within minutes, amidst much debate and chat, food appeared. A bottle of wine was opened, tantalising smells laced the air and Pepita beamed.

'Come and serve yourselves. Frederick, you have lost

weight—I want you to eat. They are not your favourite dishes, but they are still good.'

'Pepita, everything you cook is good.'

Sunita shook her head. 'Nope. Everything you cook is *amazing*.'

It truly was. The table was laden with a variety of dishes. Bite-sized skewers that held tangy mozzarella, luscious tomatoes that tasted of sunshine and basil. Deep-fried golden rounds of cheese tortellini. Freshly baked bread with a pesto and vinegar dip that made her taste-buds tingle. Baked asparagus wrapped in prosciutto. And of course bowls of olives with a real depth of zing.

But what was truly amazing was the interplay between Frederick and the family—to see him set aside his role of ruler, to see him morph back to the man he had been before tragedy had intervened and changed his life path.

There was conversation and laughter, the clatter of cutlery, the taste of light red wine, the dapple of sunshine through the leaves causing a dance of sunbeams on the wooden slats of the table.

Until finally everyone was replete and this time Sunita insisted. 'I'll help clear.'

Frederick rose as well, but Pepita waved him down. 'Stay. Drink more wine. I want to talk to your fiancée alone.'

A hint of wariness crossed his face, but clearly he didn't feel equal to the task of intervention. So, plates in hand, Sunita followed Pepita to a whitewashed kitchen, scented by the fresh herbs that grew on the windowsill. Garlic hung from the rafters, alongside copper pots and pans.

'It is good to see Frederick here,' Pepita ventured with a sideways glance. 'And now he is a father.'

'Yes.' Sunita placed the plates down and turned to face

the older woman. 'I know you must be angry at what I did, but—'

'It is not my place to be angry—this is a matter for you to sort out with Frederick…a matter between husband and wife. I want to tell you that I am worried about him. Since his brother's death we have barely seen him—all he does now is work. I know that he avoids us. There is a demon that drives him and you need to get rid of it.'

'I… Our marriage isn't going to be like that, Pepita…'

'Bah! You plan to spend your lives together, yes? Then that is your job.'

Her head spun as the enormity of Pepita's words sank in. She *was* planning to spend her life with Frederick—her *life*. She wouldn't have another one; this was it.

Closing her eyes, she forced her thoughts to centre, to concentrate on the here and now. 'I'll do what I can,' she heard herself say, wanting to soothe the other woman's worry.

Frederick looked up as Sunita emerged from the house. Her face was slightly flushed from the sun, her striped dress the perfect outfit for a sunny day. Her expression looked thoughtful, and he couldn't help but wonder what Pepita had said—though he was wise enough to have no intention of asking. He suspected he might not like the answer.

Guilt twanged at the paucity of time he had given to this family—people he felt closer to than his 'real' family.

He turned to Juan. 'Is it all right if I take Sunita on a tour?'

'Why are you asking me? It is *your* grove, Frederick— I just tend it for you. Go—show your beautiful lady the most beautiful place in the world.'

Sunita grinned up at him as they made their way towards the fields. 'They are a lovely family.'

'That they are.'

'And it's good to see your royal authority in action.'

'Sarcasm will get you nowhere—but you're right. Pepita wouldn't recognise royal authority if it rose up and bit her. To her I am still the twenty-one-year-old they taught the olive oil business. Right here.'

Sunita gave a small gasp, her face animated as she gazed ahead to where majestic lines of evergreen trees abounded. Olives clustered at the ends of branches clad with silver leaves that gleamed in the sunlight.

'The colour of those leaves—it's like they're threaded with real silver.'

'That's actually the colour of the underside of the leaf. When it's hot the leaves turn light-side up to reflect the sun. When it's cold they turn grey-green side up to absorb the sun.'

'That's pretty incredible when you think about it.'

'The whole process is incredible. The olives are growing at the moment. They won't be ready to harvest for another few months. You should be here for the harvest. It's incredible. The green table olives get picked in September, October, then the ones we use for oil from mid-November, when they are bursting with oil. It is exhausting work. You basically spread a cloth under the trees to catch the olives and then you hit the trees with sticks. The harvest then gets carted off to the mills—which is equally fascinating. But I won't bore you with it now.'

'You aren't boring me. Keep going. Truly.'

Her face registered genuine interest, and so as they walked he talked and she listened. They inhaled the tang of the olives mingled with the scent of honeysuckle carried on the gentle breeze, revelled in the warmth of the sun and the lazy drone of bees in the distance.

It was impossible not to feel at peace here. Impossible

not to note Sunita's beauty—her dark hair shining with a raven sheen in the sunlight, the classic beauty of her face enhanced by the surroundings—and it took all his will-power not to kiss her. That would be a bad move.

She looked up at him. 'I can see why you fell in love with this place—it has a timeless quality.'

'A few of these trees have been here for centuries.'

'And in that time history has played out…generations of people have walked these fields, beaten the trees with sticks, experienced joy and sadness and the full gamut of emotion in between. It gives you perspective.' She gave him a sideways glance and took a quick inhalation of breath. 'Maybe you should come here more often.'

'Because you think I need perspective?'

'Because Pepita misses you.'

'Did she say that?'

'No, but it's pretty obvious. I'd guess that you miss them too.'

'I don't have time to miss them. In the same way I don't have time to come down here—my days in the olive oil industry are over, and I've accepted that.'

'That doesn't mean you can't visit more often.' She stopped now and turned to face him, forced him to halt as well. 'No one would grudge you some down-time. And this place *means* something to you.'

That was the trouble—this place took him off his game, distracted him from his mission, reminded him of a time untainted by guilt, of the man he had once been and could never be again. When Axel had been alive.

Yet he had brought Sunita here today—*why?* The rea-son smacked into him. He'd succumbed to temptation— one more day of 'just Frederick and Sunita'. *Foolish.* 'Just Frederick and Sunita' didn't exist.

'Yes, it does. It represents the past. A part of my life that is over. For good.'

Reality was the crown of Lycander and the path he had set himself. Axel had died—had been denied the chance to rule, to live, to marry, to have children. The only thing Frederick could do now was honour his memory—ensure his vision was accomplished. Ensure the monarchy was safe and Lycander prospered.

'It's time to get back to the palace.'

CHAPTER THIRTEEN

Two weeks later

SUNITA GAZED AROUND the transformed apartments with satisfaction. It hadn't been easy, but the spindly chairs of discomfort, the antique non-toddler-friendly glass tables, the dark gloomy pictures were all gone—and she didn't care if they *were* by museum-worthy artists. Mostly it hadn't been easy because of the intense levels of disapproval exhibited by nearly every single member of staff she'd asked for help.

In truth, Sunita quite simply didn't get it—she hadn't expected instant love or loyalty, but this condescension hidden behind a thin veneer of politeness was both horrible and familiar. It made her feel worthless inside—just as she had in her stepmother's home.

Giselle Diaz, the housekeeper, looked down her aristocratic nose at her, Sven Nordstrom, chief steward, somehow managed to convey utter horror, and the more junior members of staff had taken their cue from their superiors. Whilst they listened to Sunita's instructions, they did so with a frigid politeness that made her quake.

But she'd stuck to her guns, had ransacked the palace for *real* items of furniture, and tucked away in nooks and crannies she'd discovered some true treasures.

Old overstuffed armchairs, ridiculously comfortable sofas…and now she and Amil had a home, a haven.

Sunita gazed at her son. They had brought him back from Mumbai ten days before and he had settled in with a happiness she could only envy. With a smile, he crawled across the floor and she scooped him up onto her lap.

'What do you think, sweetheart?' She showed him two different fabric swatches. 'Do you like this one or this one? For your new nursery when we move to the state apartments.'

'Dabadabad!' Amil said chattily.

'Shall we ask Daddy? That's a good idea, isn't it?'

Frederick would arrive at any moment—every day without fail he was there for Amil's breakfast and tea, and for bedtime. Otherwise he worked.

Ever since the olive grove he'd been distant, as if he'd built a wall of transparent glass that she couldn't penetrate. He was polite, kind and unfailingly courteous, and it made her want to scream. It also made her wonder what demon drove him to spend nigh on every waking hour in the council room, closeted with advisors, lawyers, education experts or engrossed in legal and constitutional tomes that dated back centuries.

Her reverie was interrupted by the familiar knock on the door.

'Come in.'

Frederick entered and, as happened each and every day, her heart fluttered and she noted the lines of tiredness around his eyes and wished she could smooth them away.

'Adadadadaa!' Amil said, and if she'd blinked she'd have missed the smile that lit Frederick's face—one of pure, unaffected joy—before his expression morphed back to neutral.

'Good evening, Amil. And what have you got for tea today?'

'He has lasagne with carrot sticks. Prepared by his very loving, very lovely potential new nanny.'

Satisfaction pumped a fist inside her as she saw his eyebrows snap together—that had at least got his attention.

'Nanny? You didn't tell me you'd chosen one from the list I gave you.'

The list that had chilled her very bone marrow—a list of extremely qualified, excessively expensive women.

'That's because she isn't on the list. But maybe we could discuss this once Amil is in bed.'

'Sure.'

'Then let's get tea underway.'

She headed to the kitchenette and soon had Amil seated in his high chair.

As she did every day, she asked, 'Would you like to feed him?'

He replied as he did every day. 'No. I'm good, thanks. It looks tricky, and I don't know how you manage to get more food into him than ends up elsewhere.'

True enough, meal times weren't the tidiest of processes—and equally true she *had* worked out a dextrous method of spooning in maximum food—but still... She wasn't sure that his reluctance stemmed from fastidiousness. As for worrying that Amil wouldn't get enough to eat, that didn't ring true either—as she had pointed out, he could always have a second helping.

Perhaps he didn't like the idea of being watched and judged.

'I can go into the lounge whilst you feed him, if you like?'

'I'd prefer it if *you* fed him, if that's OK?'

'Of course.'

Only it wasn't OK. Not really.

Just like it wasn't really OK that Frederick didn't engage in bathtime, didn't take Amil onto his lap for his bedtime story. If it were any other man she would suspect that he didn't care, that he was going through the motions. But that didn't make sense. Frederick had fought tooth and nail to be a full-time father to Amil—risked his throne, defied all advice, was willing to take a less than ideal bride.

'Say goodnight to Daddy.'

The little boy gurgled happily and she walked over so that Frederick could give him a kiss.

'See you in a minute.'

Fifteen minutes later she tiptoed from Amil's room and entered the lounge—then stopped on the threshold and cursed under her breath.

Damn. She'd left her sketchbook open on the table—worse, she'd left it open, so she could hardly blame Frederick for sitting there and studying the page.

'Did you do this?'

'Yes.'

There was little point in denial—it wasn't as if he'd believe that *Amil* had drawn a ballroom dress or an off-the-shoulder top.

'They're good.'

'Thank you—they're just sketches...doodles, really. You know how much I love clothes.'

'These look like more than doodles—you've written notes on fabric and cut. How many of these sketchbooks have you got?'

'It doesn't matter.' No way would she confess the number. 'I've always enjoyed sketching and I've always loved fashion. Ever since my mum took me on a photo shoot with her—I loved the buzz, the vibrancy, but most of all I loved the clothes. The feel, the look, the way they could totally transform a person. Sounds mad, maybe, but I think clothes have power.'

His gaze returned to the sketchbook. 'Have you ever thought about fashion design?'

'No.'

That might be a little bit of a fib, but she didn't really want to discuss it. Her sketches were private—she'd never shown them to anyone and she wasn't about to start now.

'It's just a hobby. I think my forte is wearing clothes, not designing them.'

Moving forward, she removed the sketchpad and closed it with a finality she hoped he would apply to the whole topic.

'Anyway I wanted to talk to you about my nanny idea.'

In truth, she wasn't that keen on a nanny—but she could see that if she planned to model and fulfil her commitments as a Lycander consort then it would be necessary.

'Go ahead.'

'I want to give Gloria Russo the role.'

Frederick frowned. 'I thought she worked in the palace kitchens.'

'She does. That's where I met her. I went down there to sort out how it all works—whether I am supposed to shop, or food is delivered, how and where and when I can cook Amil's food… Anyway, Gloria was really helpful.'

Which had made a novel change from every other staff member.

'She only joined the staff recently, but obviously she has been security vetted.'

'So she used to be a nanny?'

'No.'

'All the people on my list have been trained as a nanny—they have extensive qualifications and experience.'

'So does Gloria—she has four grown-up children. And, most important, Amil loves her already.'

'Amil needs a *proper* nanny.'

Frustrated anger rolled over her in a tidal wave—a culmination of being patronised all week and a need to make her own presence felt in a world she didn't fit into. *Again.*

'*Will* you get your royal head out of your royal behind? Gloria will *be* a proper nanny. She knows how to keep him safe and she knows how to provide love and security and fun. She makes him laugh, but she will also make sure he listens. At least agree to meet her and see her with Amil.'

'As long as *you* agree to meet two people from the list. Then we will make the decision.'

'Deal. You'll like Gloria—I'm sure you will. She is kind and she's down to earth and she's fun. Fun is important.' Something Frederick seemed to have forgotten. 'You must remember that—you used to be the Prince of Fun.'

'That was a long time ago.' His tone implied a lifetime rather than mere months.

'Do you miss it? That lifestyle?'

When there had been a different woman in his bed whenever he wanted, and all he'd had to worry about was where the next bottle of champagne was coming from.

'That life feels like it belonged to someone else. So, no, I don't miss it.'

'I know what you mean. My life before Amil seems surreal sometimes, but there are parts of it that I want to retain—I still love clothes, I'm still Sunita.'

Whereas the Frederick of before—apart from the occasional glimpse—seemed to have vanished completely, remorselessly filtered out by grief and the weight of a crown.

'I know that you have taken on a huge responsibility, and of course you need to take that seriously. But there are aspects of the old Frederick that you should keep. The ability to have fun, to laugh and make others laugh.'

'I've had my quota of fun.' He rose to his feet. 'I have a meeting with Marcus now, so...'

'You have to go.'

Sunita bit her lip, told herself it didn't matter. Why should it? Their marriage was an alliance made for Amil's sake—any desire for his company was both ridiculous and clearly unreciprocated.

'Don't forget about tomorrow. We have a family day out scheduled.'

'It's in the diary.' He looked down at her. 'You are sure you don't want to tell me where we're going?'

'Nope. It's a surprise.'

It was an idea she knew the press would love—the fian-cée taking her Prince to a surprise destination with their son. A way of emphasising to the people that their Prince and his Princess-to-be had changed and their party life-style was well and truly over.

She smiled at him. 'It will be fun.'

For a moment she thought he would return the smile, but instead he merely nodded. 'Goodnight, Sunita.'

'Goodnight.'

There it was again—that stupid yearning to ask him to stay.

Not happening.

The door clicked behind him as her phone buzzed. Her agent.

'Hi, Harvey.'

'Hey, sweetheart. We need to talk.'

Frederick checked the weather forecast as he approached Sunita's apartments. A sunny and cloud-free day—a typ-ical late-summer day in Lycander, perfect for a 'family day out'. The words had an alien twist to them—family days out had been few and far between in his childhood. And now both anticipation and an irrational fear tightened his gut.

Fear at the level of anticipation, and the knowledge that too much of it was tied up in Sunita, was mixed with the fear of messing it up with Amil. Somehow he had to get these fledgling emotions under control—work out which were acceptable, which he needed to nourish to be a good father and which he needed to stifle before they got out of hand.

He could *do* this—he was a past master at emotional lockdown and he would work it out. He would achieve the balanced, calm marriage alliance he wanted.

Pushing open the door, he entered. Sunita smiled at him and his breath caught. *Beautiful*—there was no other word to describe her. She was dressed in flared, delicately embroidered jeans and a simple dark blue sleeveless top, sunglasses perched atop her head and her hair tumbling loose in a riot of waves. Her vibrancy lit the room—a room that she'd made home.

Clutter without untidiness gave it a feeling of relaxed warmth, as did the overstuffed armchairs and sofas that she had commandeered from somewhere in the palace to replace the antique showcase furniture.

'You ready?' he asked.

'We're ready—aren't we, Amil? Look, it's Daddy.'

Frederick turned his head to look at Amil, who waved his favourite toy cat at him in greeting. And then he twisted, placed his hands on the sofa cushion and hauled himself up so he was standing. He turned and—almost by mistake—let go, tottered for a moment, found his balance, and then took a step…and another step…and another until he reached Frederick and clutched at his legs for balance.

He looked down at his son—his son who had just taken his first steps. Amil had a look of utter awe on his face, as the life-changing knowledge had dawned on him—he could walk! Frederick's chest contracted with pride and wonderment as Amil turned and tottered back, with each step gaining confidence, until he reached the sofa and looked to Sunita for confirmation of his cleverness.

Sunita let out a laugh of sheer delight and flew across the room, scooped Amil up and spun him round. 'What a clever boy!' she said as she smothered him in kisses, before spinning to a halt right in front of Frederick.

Something twisted in his chest as he looked at them—a strand of emotion almost painful in its intensity. Sunita's face was slightly flushed, her tawny eyes were bright with happiness and pride, and it filled him with yearning. Like a boy locked out of the sweetshop for ever—doomed always to gaze at the sweets he could never, ever taste.

He forced a smile to his lips and hoped it didn't look as corpse-like as it felt. 'He is a very, *very* clever boy.'

Amil beamed at him and that strand tightened.

Frederick cleared his throat, turned slightly away. 'So, what's the plan?' he asked.

'First up we'll do a little press conference.'

'How can I do a press conference if I don't know where I'm going?'

'You'll have to let me do the talking.' She grinned at him. 'Don't look so worried. There are a million royal duties I am *not* equipped for, but I *am* good with the press.'

The words, though casually stated, held a shade of bitterness, but before he could do more than frown she had headed for the door.

Once in the palace grounds, with a knot of reporters, Amil proudly demonstrated his new ability and she seemed totally at ease.

'Hi, all. I've decided the Prince needs a day off—because even a ruler needs some down-time. So we are off on a family day out—I promise I'll take some pics, which I'll pass on to you. As I'm sure you all appreciate we are still a new family, so we'd appreciate some privacy.'

'And what about you, Sunita? Do *you* deserve a day off? Isn't it true you're headed back to the catwalk?'

'That's the plan—but I'll let you know more about that when I know the details.'

'Don't you feel you should focus on your role as Princess, like Lady Kaitlin would have?'

Frederick felt her tense, sensed her palpable effort to relax. 'Lady Kaitlin and I are two different people, so we are bound to approach the role differently.'

He stepped forward. 'Hey, guys, any questions for me? I'm feeling left out.'

The tactic worked and fifteen minutes later he wound the meeting down. 'OK, everyone, fun though this is, we need to head off.'

Sunita delivered the parting shot. 'Amil, wave to the nice reporters. That would be that one…that one…and that one.'

Not the one who had brought up Lady Kaitlin.

Laughter greeted this, and Sunita smiled. 'Have a great day—and, as I said, the pics will be with you soon!'

Once they were alone, Sunita nodded towards one of the palace cars. 'Hop in. We're off to Xanos Island.' She paused. 'I hope that's OK? Marcus suggested it.'

That surprised him. 'I'd like to take Amil there. Eloise used to take us. Me and Stefan and Axel, and Marcus as well, because he and Axel were best friends.'

'Eloise is Stefan's mother, correct?'

'Yes. She came after my mother, and she truly tried to be a good mother to Axel and me.'

'What happened?'

'Same old story. My father decided to divorce her and it all disintegrated into an awful custody battle. It ended up that she was allowed occasional visitation with Stefan, and only if she agreed not to see Axel or me.'

'That must have been tough on you and Axel.'

'Yes.'

The comprehension that he wouldn't see Eloise again, witnessing Stefan's fury and pain—it had all hurt. The emotions had been painful, until he'd locked the futile grief down, figured out that love could never be worth this type of loss. First his mother, then Eloise—never again.

'But let's not spoil the day—I want to make this a happy memory for Amil.'

'Then let's do that.'

Her smile lit the very air and he forced himself to turn away from it before he did something stupid. Something emotional.

The car slowed down at the small Lycandrian port, and minutes later they boarded the motor boat that would ferry them across. Frederick watched Amil's curiosity and joy at this unprecedented adventure, listened to Sunita as she broke into song and encouraged the Captain to join in.

Closing his eyes, he inhaled the salty tang of the sea breeze, absorbed the sound of her song and the cry of the curlews as they soared in the turquoise blue of the unclouded sky.

Once at the island they alighted and headed over the rocks to the beach, where Sunita produced buckets and spades and a large tartan blanket that she spread out over the sun-bleached sand. Amil sat down and waved a spade with energetic abandon and Sunita grinned as she handed another one to Frederick.

'Right. I thought we'd try and do a sand replica of the

Lycander palace—but I think the hard work may be down to you and me.'

The next hours skated by, and Frederick knew he would add this to his list of happy memories. Preventing Amil from eating sand, building turrets and digging moats, the good-natured bickering over the best way to make the walls secure, Amil walking in the sand, eating the picnic prepared by Gloria—it was all picture-perfect.

'We need to consider Gloria for the role of royal picnic-maker as well as royal nanny.'

'So you really *will* consider her? Give her a fair chance?'

'Of course. But in return I'd like *you* to do something.'

Tawny eyes narrowed. 'What's that?'

'Put a portfolio together and send it to a fashion design college. Or talk directly with an actual fashion house. You said to me that Gloria doesn't need formal qualifications to do the job—maybe you don't either.'

The sketches he'd seen the previous day showed talent—he knew it.

'Those sketches had a certain something about them that I suspect is unique to you—I think you should get them checked out.'

'I'll think about it,' she said, in a voice that was clearly humouring him as she pulled the picnic basket towards her. 'Mmm…chocolate cake.'

Frederick raised his eyebrows. 'Are you trying to change the subject?'

'How did you guess?'

'I'm bright like that. Come on, Sunita, why not send them off? What have you got to lose?'

She looked away from him, out over the dark blue crested waves that sculled gently towards the shore, towards the horizon where a ferry chugged purposefully.

Turning back to him, she shrugged. 'I could lose something precious. Those sketches kept me sane—they were my own private dream growing up. They represented hope that I wasn't totally worthless, not utterly stupid. I don't want to expose them to anyone. I've never shown them to a soul.'

And he understood why—she would have been terrified of the comments from her stepmother or sisters…she would have hoarded her talent and hugged it tight.

'Then maybe now is the time. Don't let them win—all those mean-spirited people who put you down. You've already proved your success to them.'

She shook her head. 'Only through modelling—that's dumb genetic luck, plus being in the right place at the right time. Fashion design requires a whole lot more than that.'

'I understand that you're scared—and I know it won't be easy—but if fashion design is your dream then you should go for it. Don't let them hold you back from your potential. Don't let what they did affect your life.'

'Why not? *You* are.'

He hadn't seen that one coming. 'Meaning…?'

'I think you're scared too.'

'Of what?'

'Of bonding with Amil.'

The words hit him, causing his breath to catch. She moved across the rug closer to him, contrition written all over her beautiful face.

'Sorry. I didn't mean that in a tit-for-tat way, or as an accusation. It's just I see how you look at him, with such love, but then I see how you hold back from being alone with him. You won't even hold him and I don't understand why.'

There was silence, and Frederick knew he needed to tell her. He couldn't bear her to believe he didn't *want* to hold his son.

'Because of dumb genetic luck.'

'I don't get it.'

'When I was eighteen I went to see my mum. I hoped that there had been some mistake—that my father had lied to me, that she hadn't really abandoned me and that there was some reason that would explain it all away. It turned out there was—she explained that she quite simply lacked the parenting gene.'

'She *said* that?'

'Yes.'

Her hands clenched into fists and her eyes positively blazed. 'Is *that* what you're scared of? That you lack the parenting gene?'

His gaze went involuntarily to his son, who lay asleep on the blanket, his bottom in the air, his impossibly long lashes sweeping his cheeks.

He couldn't answer—didn't need to. Even he could hear the affirmation in his silence.

'You don't.' Sunita leaned across, brushing his forearm in the lightest of touches. 'I can see how much you love Amil. You are not your mother *or* your father. You are *you*, and you are a great father—please believe that. Trust yourself. I promise I trust you.' She inhaled an audible breath. 'And I'll prove it to you.'

'What do you mean?' Panic began to unfurl as she rose to her feet.

'He's all yours. I'll see you back at the palace much later. Obviously call if there is an emergency—otherwise the boat will return for you in a few hours.'

Before he could react she started walking across the sand. He looked at his sleeping son. Obviously he couldn't leave Amil in order to chase after Sunita, which meant... which meant he was stuck here.

His brain struggled to work as he watched Sunita disappear over the rocks. If he called after her he would wake

Amil, and that was a bad plan. He stilled, barely daring to breathe as he watched the rise and fall of his son's chest. Maybe Amil would sleep for the next few hours…

As if he should be so lucky.

With impeccable timing Amil rolled over and opened his eyes just as the sound of the boat chug-chug-chugging away reached his ears. He looked round for his mother, failed to see her, and sat up and gazed at his father. Panicked hazel eyes met panicked hazel eyes and Amil began to wail.

Instinct took over—his need to offer comfort prompted automatic movement and he picked Amil up. He held the warm, sleepy bundle close to his heart and felt something deep inside him start to thaw. The panic was still present, but as Amil snuggled into him, as one chubby hand grabbed a lock of his hair and as the wails started to subside, so did the panic.

To be replaced by a sensation of peace, of unconditional love and an utter determination to keep this precious human being safe from all harm—to be there for him no matter what it took.

CHAPTER FOURTEEN

SUNITA GLANCED AT her watch and then back at the sketch-books spread out on the table. Thoughts chased each other round her brain—about Frederick and Amil; she hoped with all her heart that right now father and son had started the bonding process that would last a lifetime.

Her gaze landed back on the design sketches and she wondered whether Frederick had been right—that fear of rejection and self-doubt stood in her way. Just as they did in his. Could she pursue a dream? Or was it foolish for a woman with no qualifications to put her head above the parapet and invite censure? Or, worse, ridicule.

Another glance at her watch and she closed the books, piled them up and moved them onto a shelf. Instead she pulled out a folder—design ideas for the state rooms, where they would move after the wedding.

The door opened and she looked up as Frederick came in, Amil in his arms. There was sand in their hair and identical smiles on their faces. *Keep it cool...don't overreact.* But in truth her heart swelled to see them, both looking so proud and happy and downright cute.

'Did you have fun?'

'Yes, we did.'

'Fabulous. Tea is ready.'

'I thought maybe today *I* could feed him. Do his bath. Put him to bed.'

Any second now she would weep—Frederick looked as if a burden had been lifted from his shoulders.

'Great idea. In which case, if you don't mind, I've got a couple of errands to do. I'll be back for his bedtime.'

Frederick didn't need an observer—especially when Amil lobbed spaghetti Bolognese at him, as he no doubt would. And perhaps she could do something a little courageous as well. She needed to speak with Therese, the snooty seamstress, about her wedding dress.

Lycander tradition apparently had it that the royal seamstress had total input on the design of the dress, but surely the bride had a say as well. So maybe she would show Therese one of her designs.

Grabbing the relevant sketchbook, she blew Amil a kiss and allowed a cautious optimism to emerge as she made her way through the cavernous corridors to the Royal Sewing Room.

A knock on the door resulted in the emergence of one of Therese's assistants. 'Hi, Hannah, I wonder if Therese is around to discuss my dress.'

'She's popped out, but I know where the folder is. I'm sure she wouldn't mind you having a look.' Hannah walked over to a filing cabinet. 'I'll leave you to it.'

With that she scurried to an adjoining door and disappeared.

Sunita opened the folder and stared down at the picture—it was…was… Well, on the positive side it was classic—the designer a household name. On the negative side it was dull and unflattering. There didn't seem to be anything else in the folder, which seemed odd.

She headed to the door through which Hannah had disappeared, to see if there was another file, then paused as she heard the sound of conversation. She recognised Hannah's voice, and that of another assistant—Angela—and then the mention of her own name.

Of course she should have backed off there and then, taken heed of the old adage about eavesdroppers never hearing any good of themselves. But she didn't. Instead, breath held, she tiptoed forward.

'Do you think she knows?' asked Hannah.

'Knows what?' said Angela.

'That that's the dress Therese had designed for Lady Kaitlin—she was dead sure Lady K would marry Frederick. Everyone was, and everyone is gutted she didn't. Even that engagement ring—it was the one they had in mind for Kaitlin. Lady Kaitlin would have been a *proper* princess—everyone knows that. And she would have looked amazing in that dress—because it's regal and classic and not showy. As for Sunita—Frederick is only marrying her for the boy, which is dead good of him. He's a true prince. But Sunita can't ever be a true princess—she'll never fit in.'

Sunita closed her eyes as the flow of words washed over her in an onslaught of truth. Because that was what they were—words of truth. Otherwise known as facts. Facts that she seemed to have forgotten in the past weeks, somehow. She didn't know how she'd started to look at her marriage through rose-tinted glasses. How she had started to believe the fairy tale.

Fact: the sole reason for this marriage was Amil. Fact: Frederick's ideal bride would have been Lady Kaitlin or a woman of her ilk. Fact: fairy tales did not exist.

This must be what her mother had done—convinced herself that a handsome, charming English holidaymaker was her Prince, who would take her off into the sunset and a happy-ever-after. Perhaps that was what her father had done too—convinced himself that he could right past wrongs, that his family would welcome in his bastard child and everyone would live happily ever after.

Carefully she moved away from the door, leaving the folder on the desk, then picked up her sketchbook, and made her way out of the office, back along the marble floors, past the tapestry-laden walls, the heirlooms and antiquities collected over centuries, and back to her apartments.

She took a deep breath and composed her expression—this was a special day for Frederick and Amil and she would not spoil it.

Nor would she whinge and whine—there was no blame to be cast anywhere except at herself. Somehow she'd lost sight of the facts, but she wouldn't make that mistake again.

Entering the room, she halted on the threshold. Frederick sat on an armchair, Amil on his lap, looking down at a book of farm animals with intense concentration as Frederick read the simple sentences, and made all the noises with a gusto that caused Amil to chuckle with delight.

The book finished, Amil looked up and beamed at her and her heart constricted. Amil was the most important factor.

'Hey, guys. Looks like I'm back just in time.' Hard as she tried, she got it wrong—her voice was over-bright and a touch shaky, and Frederick's hazel eyes scanned her face in question.

'You OK?'

'I'm fine.' Walking over, she picked Amil up, hid her face under the pretext of a hug. 'How did tea and bath go?'

'Well, I have spaghetti down my shirt and bubbles in my hair, but we had fun, didn't we?'

'Abaadaaaaada!' Amil smiled and then yawned.

'I'll put him to bed.' Frederick rose and took Amil into his arms. Amil grizzled, but Frederick held on. 'Daddy's putting you to bed tonight, little fella. It'll be fine.'

And it was.

Fifteen minutes later Frederick emerged from Amil's bedroom, a smile on his face, headed to the drinks cabinet and pulled out a bottle of red wine.

Once they both had a glass in hand, he raised his. 'Thank you for today. You were right—I was afraid. Afraid I couldn't be a good parent...afraid I'd hurt him the way my parents hurt me. I thought doing nothing would be better than getting it wrong. Now I really hope that I can be a better parent than mine were, and can create a real bond with my son.'

The words made her happy—truly happy—and she wanted to step forward, to get close and tell him that, show him that happiness. But she didn't. Because close was dangerous—close had landed her in this scenario where she had distorted the facts with perilous consequence.

Perhaps it had been that magical physical intimacy in Goa, or maybe it had been a mistake to confide in him, to share her background and her fears and dreams. Whatever. No point in dwelling on the mistakes. Now it was vital not to repeat them.

So instead she stepped backwards and raised her glass. 'I'll drink to that. I'm so very pleased for you and Amil.'

And she was. But to her own horror, mixed into that pleasure was a thread of misery that she recognised as selfish. Because his love for Amil had never been in doubt—it had simply needed a shift in the dynamic of their relationship. A shift that had highlighted exactly what Sunita was—a by-product, a hanger-on, exactly as she been in her father's family. There only by default, by an accident of birth.

Well, she was damned if she would sit around here for the rest of her life being a by-product.

'Earth to Sunita?'

His voice pulled her out of her thoughts and she manufactured a smile, floundered for a topic of conversation. Her gaze fell on a folder—her plans for the state apartments.

'Would you mind having a look at this? I wanted your opinion before I went ahead.'

She picked up the file, opened it and pulled out the pictures, gazed down at them and winced. Every detail that she'd pored over so carefully screamed happy families—she'd done some of the sketches in 3D and, so help her, she'd actually imagined the three of them skipping around the place in some family perfect scene.

For their bedroom she'd chosen a colour scheme that mixed aquamarine blue with splashes of red. The double bed was a luxurious invitation that might as well have *bliss* written all over it.

She had to face it—her vision had included steamy nights with Frederick and lazy Sunday mornings with a brood of kids bouncing up and down. What had happened to her? This was a room designed with *love*.

This was a disaster. *Love*. She'd fallen in love.

Idiot, idiot, idiot.

Frederick frowned. 'Are you sure you're OK?'

Reaching out, he plucked the pictures from her hand and she forced herself not to clutch onto them. *Think*. Before he looked at the pictures and figured it out. *Think*. Because even if he didn't work it out she couldn't share a room with him—that would take intimacy to insane levels, and Frederick was no fool. He'd realise that she had done the unthinkable and fallen for him.

As he scanned the pictures desperation came to her aid. 'I wondered which bedroom you wanted.'

His head snapped up and his eyebrows rose. He placed

the papers on the table. 'I assumed from these pictures that we would be sharing a room.'

Picking up her wine glass, she met his gaze. 'As I understood it, royal tradition dictates separate bedrooms and I assumed you'd prefer that.' Or at least she *should* have assumed that. 'However, obviously there will be some occasions when we *do* share—hence the design. If you want that bedroom I'll design the second one as mine. But if you don't then I'll take that one and we can discuss how you want yours to be.'

Stop, already. He'd got the gist of it and now she sounded defensive. Worse, despite herself, there was a hint of a question in the nuances of her tone, and a strand of hope twisted her heart. Hope that he'd take this opportunity to persuade her to share a room.

'What do you think?'

He sipped his wine, studied her expression, and she fought to keep her face neutral.

'I think this is some sort of trick question.'

'No trick. It's a simple need to know so I can complete the design. Also, as you know, I'll be giving an interview once the renovations are done, so it depends what you think the people of Lycander would prefer to see. We can pretend we share a room, if you think that would go down better, or…'

Shut up, Sunita.

Just because full-scale panic was escalating inside her, it didn't mean verbal overload had to implode. But she couldn't help herself.

'And then there is Amil to think about. I'm not sure that he should grow up thinking this sort of marriage is right.'

'Whoa! What is *that* supposed to mean? "This sort of marriage"? You say it like there's something wrong with it.'

'There *is* something wrong with it.'

It was almost as if her vocal cords had taken on a life of their own.

'Is this the sort of marriage you want Amil to have? An alliance? Presumably brokered by us? A suitable connection? Perhaps he will be lucky enough to get his own Lady Kaitlin. *Hell*.' She snapped her fingers. 'Perhaps we should get dibs on her first-born daughter.'

'Stop.' His frown deepened as he surveyed her expression. 'What is going on here? We agreed how our marriage would work—we agreed what we both wanted.'

'No, we didn't. I didn't want to get married at all. *You* did.'

'And you agreed.'

'Because there was no other choice.' She closed her eyes. 'There still isn't. But when Amil gets married I don't want it to be like this.'

For her son she wanted the fairy tale—she wanted Amil to love someone and be loved in return and live happily ever after. *The End*.

'There is nothing *wrong* with this.' His voice was urgent now, taut with frustration and more than a hint of anger. 'Amil will see two parents who respect each other, who are faithful to each other, who are polite to each other. There will be no uncertainty, no banged doors and no voices raised in constant anger. He'll have two parents who are there for him—I think he'll take that. God knows, *I* would have. And so would you.'

Touché. He was right. The problem was this wasn't about Amil. It was about her. *She* wanted the fairy tale. Her whole being cried out at the idea of a marriage of civility. Her very soul recoiled from the thought of spending the rest of her life tied to a man she loved who would never see her as more than the mother of his children—a woman he'd married through necessity not choice.

But she'd made a deal and she'd honour it. For Amil's sake. She wouldn't wrest Amil from his father, wouldn't take away his birthright. But neither would she stick around and moon in lovelorn stupidity. The only way forward was to kill love before it blossomed—uproot the plant now, before it sank its roots into her heart.

So she dug deep, conjured up a smile and said, 'You're right. I just had a mad moment.' She gave a glance at her watch. 'Anyway, don't you need to go? I thought you had a meeting about the çasino bill?'

He hesitated. The frown still hadn't left his face. 'We'll talk in the morning.'

'Sure.'

Pride kept her cool, enigmatic smile in place as he turned and left the room. Then, ignoring the ache that squeezed her heart in a vicelike grip, she picked up her mobile.

'Harvey. It's me. We need to talk.'

The next morning Frederick approached the door to Sunita and Amil's apartments, forcing his steps to remain measured, forcing himself not to dwell on the previous night's conversation with Sunita. But her words still pummelled his conscience.

'I didn't want to get married. You did. There was no choice. There still isn't...'

The unpleasant edge of discomfort bit into him.

Shades of his father.

He knocked on the door and entered, glanced around for Amil. Anxiety unfurled as he looked around and saw only Sunita at the table. 'Where's Amil?'

'With Gloria. I need to talk with you.'

Dressed in a simple white three-quarter-sleeved dress, belted with a striped blue and red band, she looked both elegant and remote. The only indication of nerves was the twist of her hands.

Sudden familiarity hit him—she'd had the same stance two years before, when she'd been about to leave. Panic grew inside him and he forced himself to keep still.

'Is anything wrong?'

'No. I've signed a modelling contract. Effective pretty much immediately. We need to discuss the details.'

'Immediately? But you said you wouldn't sign a contract straight away.'

'And I didn't. The first time the offer came in I refused. But now they have upped the ante and agreed to schedule the shoots around my commitments here. I'd be a fool to pass it up.'

A bleakness started to descend...a strange hollow pang of emptiness. 'What about Amil?'

'The first shoot is in India—in Mumbai. I'll take Amil with me. We can stay with Nanni. Thereafter, whenever I can take him I will, or I will leave him in Lycander with you. Gloria will be here, and I will also ask Nanni if she can come and stay.'

She handed him a piece of paper with her schedule printed out.

Frederick frowned. 'This can't possibly have been arranged since last night.'

'No. Harvey was approached a few weeks ago—right after our first press release. The brand had dropped the model they had planned to use due to her lifestyle. They thought of me. I refused—but now I've changed my mind and luckily they still want me.'

'You didn't think to discuss this with me at all?'

'No. Any more than you discuss state business with *me*. Part of our marriage agreement was that I would resume my career as long as I fitted it around Lycander's needs. I understand some people may not approve, but to be honest with you a lot of people won't approve of me no matter what I do. The people wanted Kaitlin. I can't be her, or be like her. I will not try to fit into a box I'll never tick. I spent too many years doing that.'

Frederick knew there were things he should say, things he needed to say, but the words quite simply wouldn't formulate. All he wanted to do was tug her into his arms and beg her to stay—but that was not an option.

Because Sunita didn't want this marriage—she never had. He'd forced it upon her, caught her between a rock and a hard place. Self-disgust soured his tongue, froze his limbs. He was no better than his father. He had ridden roughshod over her wish not to marry him; he'd inveigled and manoeuvred and blazed down the trail he wanted regardless of her wishes. Worse, he'd bolstered himself with pious justifications.

But it was too late to stop the wedding, to release her from their marriage agreement—it would be an impossibility, the impact on Lycander, on Amil, too harsh.

Just Lycander? Just Amil? queried a small voice.

Of course. It made no difference to him. It *couldn't* make a difference to him

Why not?

The small voice was getting on his nerves now. It couldn't because he wouldn't let it. Over the past few weeks Sunita had very nearly slipped under his skin, and that way led to disaster, to pain and loss, to messy emotions that got in the way of a calm, ordered life. That would ruin this marriage before it even got underway.

The silence had stretched so taut now he could bounce off it. One of the terms of their marriage agreement *had* included her right to a career and he would not stand in the way. So he said, 'I understand. You're right to go.'

He looked down at the schedule again, but couldn't meet her gaze, couldn't seem to quell the spread of cold emptiness through his body and soul.

'I'll talk to Marcus—if you need to miss any functions I'll let him know it's OK. I know how important this contract is for you—anything I can do to help, I will.'

'Thank you. I appreciate that.'

He nodded, and yet still that desolation pervaded him, even as that unsquashable small voice exhorted him to *do* something. *Anything.*

But he couldn't. It wasn't in him. So instead he headed for the door.

One week later—Lycander Council Room

Frederick threw the pen across his desk and watched it skitter across the polished wood. Concentration wouldn't come. The words on the document blurred and jumped and somehow unerringly formed into images of Sunita. *Ridiculous.*

Shoving the wedge of paper away, he sighed, and then looked up at the perfunctory knock on the door.

Seconds later he eyed his chief advisor in surprise. 'What's wrong?'

'Nothing. I thought you could do with a break. You've been closeted in here for hours. Days.'

'A break?' Frederick looked at Marcus blankly. 'Since when do you care about me having a rest?'

'Since you gave up on both sleep *and* food. So how about we grab a beer, shoot the breeze...?'

Frederick wondered if Marcus had perhaps already grabbed a few beers—though there was nothing in the other man's demeanour to suggest any such thing.

'Are you suggesting you and I go and have a beer?'

'Yes.'

'Why?'

Marcus shrugged. 'Why not?'

'Because I'm pretty damn sure you'd rather shoot yourself in the foot than have a beer with me.'

Dark eyebrows rose. 'Feeling tetchy?'

Damn right he was. Sunita had been gone for a week and his whole world felt…*wrong*…out of kilter. And he hated it. He loathed it that he didn't seem able to switch these emotions off. However hard he twisted the tap, they trickled on and on. Relentlessly.

'No. Just being honest. So, what gives?'

'I'm your chief advisor, right?'

'Right.'

'So here's some advice. Go after Sunita.'

'Sunita is in Mumbai on a photo shoot—why would I do that?'

'Because I think you love her.'

Frederick blinked, wondered if this conversation was a hallucination. 'Then you think wrong. You *know* all this— we're getting married because of Amil and for Lycander.'

'You can't kid a kidder. But, more importantly, why kid yourself?'

'With all due respect, has it occurred to you that this is a bit out of your remit?'

'Yes, it has.' Marcus started to pace the office, as he had so many times in the past year. 'But I'm talking to you now as Axel's best friend. I know Axel wouldn't want you to throw this away.'

Guilt and self-loathing slammed Frederick so hard he could barely stay upright. 'Hold it right there. You *don't* know what Axel would want.'

'Yes, I do. He'd want you to get on with life. *Your* life.

Right now you're getting on with Axel's life, fulfilling his vision. I think Axel would want you to fulfil your own.'

Frederick searched for words before guilt choked him. He needed Marcus to stop—he couldn't listen to this any more.

'The accident... Axel's death was my fault. *I* should have been in that car. *I* was meant to go that state dinner. I passed it off to Axel.'

'I know.' Marcus's voice was measured. 'Axel was supposed to meet up with me that night. He told me you'd asked him to go because you had a party to go to. To celebrate a buy-out that no one thought you'd pull off.'

A buy-out he now wished he'd never tried for—if he could have pulled out any domino from the cause-and-effect chain he would. Most of all, though, he wished he hadn't chosen a party over duty.

He watched as Marcus continued to stride the floor. 'So why did you take this job with me? Why didn't you tell me you knew the truth?'

'I did what I believed Axel would have wanted. Axel was my best friend—we climbed trees as boys and we double-dated as young men. A few days before the accident he was trying to get up the courage to ask my sister on a date—he'd joke that he wished he had your charm. He cared about you very much, and he wouldn't have wanted you to punish yourself for the rest of your life.'

Marcus halted in front of the desk and leant forward, his hands gripping the edge.

'You didn't know what would happen—you didn't send Axel to his death.'

'But if I had chosen not to party, not to do what I wanted to do, then Axel would be alive now.'

Marcus shrugged. 'Maybe. But it didn't pan out like that. You can't turn the clock back, but you can make the most of your time now. I think you love Sunita, and if you do then you need to go for it—before you lose her. Axel's death should show you how life can change in a heartbeat—don't waste the life you've got. Axel wouldn't want it. And, for what it's worth, neither do I.'

Frederick stared at him. Emotions tumbled around him—poignant regret that Axel had never had the chance to ask Marcus's sister on a date, grief over the loss of his brother, a loss he had never allowed himself time to mourn, and gratitude that Marcus had given him a form of redemption.

'Thank you.'

There wasn't anything else he could say right now. Later there would be time. Time to grab those beers and sit and talk about Axel, remember him and mourn him. But now…

'Can I leave you at the helm? I need to go to Mumbai.'

'Good luck.'

Frederick had the feeling he'd need it.

Mumbai

Sunita smiled at Nanni across the kitchen, listened to the comforting whirr of the overhead fan, the sizzle of *malpua* batter as it hit the heated pan. Ever since Nanni had first made these sweet dessert pancakes Sunita had loved them.

'You don't have to make me breakfast every morning, Nanni, but I do so appreciate it."

'If I didn't you would eat nothing. And you do not need to stay in with me every night. I am sure there are parties and social events.'

'I'd rather be here.'

Totally true. She didn't want to socialise; she was too tired. Sleep deprivation, combined with the effort it took to work when all she wanted was to be back in Lycander.

Irony of ironies, she wanted to be in a place that had rejected her, with a man who had rejected her. What a fool she was. But she'd be damned if anyone would know it—she'd dug deep, pulled up every professional reserve and hopefully pulled the wool over Nanni's eyes as well.

'You aren't happy.'

So much for the wool pulling endeavour.

Nanni put her plate in front of her; the scent of cardamom and pistachio drifted upward.

'Of course I am. The job is going great, I'm back in Mumbai, Amil is here and I'm with my favourite grandmother.'

'And yet you still aren't happy. You can lie to me, Suni. But don't lie to yourself.'

'Sometimes you *have* to lie to yourself—if you do it for long enough the lie will become the truth.'

Or that was her theory. And, yes, there were holes and flaws in it, but it was a work in progress.

'That still doesn't make it *actual* truth,' Nanni pointed out with irrefutable logic. 'Do you no longer wish to marry Frederick?'

'I have no choice.'

'Yes, you do. There is always a choice—however hard a one it is. If you do not love him, don't marry him.'

'I *do* love him, Nanni. But he doesn't love me.' Tears threatened and she blinked them back.

'How do you know?'

'Because he has made it pretty clear.'

'By action or word?'

'What do you mean?'

'Love is not all about declarations—it is about demonstration. I told your mother how much I loved her repeatedly, but when the time came for me to show that, to fight for her, I failed miserably.'

'But you still loved her, Nanni, and she knew that. She never blamed you—she blamed her father.'

'At least *he* had the courage of his convictions—he did what he did because he believed it to be right. I was a coward—I loved Leela, but not enough to fight for that love. It is one of the biggest regrets of my life, Suni—that I didn't fight for her, for *you*. So all I would say is think about your Frederick, and if there is a chance that he loves you then fight for that chance.'

Sunita stared down at her somehow empty plate and wondered if she were brave enough—brave enough to risk rejection and humiliation. And even if she was...

'I don't fit, Nanni. Even if he loved me I can't live up to Lady Kaitlin.'

'You don't need to live up to anyone—you just have to be yourself. Now, go,' Nanni said. 'Or you will be late for work.'

Frederick approached the site of the photo shoot, where the Gateway of India loomed in the twilight, its basalt stone lit up to create a magical backdrop, the turrets adding a fairy tale element for the photographer to take full advantage of.

The square was cordoned off for the shoot, and he joined the curious pedestrians who had stopped to watch. The people behind the cordon were packing up, so he slipped under the ropes, ignored the protest of a woman who approached

'Sir, I'm sorry, but...' There was a pause as she recognised him.

'I'm here to see Sunita.'

'Is she expecting you?'

'No. I thought I'd surprise her.'

'And you have.'

He spun round at the sound of Sunita's voice; his heart

pounded, his gut somersaulted. She wore a square-necked red dress, in some sort of stretchy material that moulded her figure and fell to her knees in a simple drop.

'Is everything all right?'

'Yes. I want to…to talk.'

She hesitated and then nodded.

'OK. I'm done here. We can go by the wall over there and look out at the sea, if you like.'

'Perfect.'

'Are you sure everything is all right?' Concern was evident in her tone now, as she looked at him.

'Yes. No. I don't know.'

And he didn't—after all, this could be the most important conversation of his life and he could totally screw it up. He could lose her.

'I need to tell you something.'

'Actually, there is something I need to tell you as well.' Her hands twisted together and she looked away from him, out at the boats that bobbed on the murky water.

'Could I go first?' *Before he bottled it.*

She nodded.

'First I need to tell you about Axel. The accident that killed him—*I* should have been in the car. He took my place because I'd decided to go a party—a celebration of a buy-out deal. He not only took my place, he totally covered for me. He told everyone that it had been his idea, that he'd wanted to attend and I'd given up my place.'

Her beautiful brown eyes widened, and then without hesitation she moved closer to him. 'I am so very sorry. I cannot imagine what you went through—what you must still be going through. But please listen to me. It was *not* your fault—you did not know what would happen.'

'I know that, but…'

'But it doesn't help. I understand. I understand how

many times you must think *if only* or *what if?* But you
mustn't. I spent years thinking what if my mother hadn't
died? What if she hadn't handed me over to my father?
What if I could somehow have won his love? My stepmother's love. My sister's love? It made me question how
I felt about my mother and it ate away at my soul—like
this is eating away at yours. You can't know what would
have happened. Axel might have died anyway. Your action
wasn't deliberate—you wished Axel no harm.'

'That's what Marcus said.'

'He's a good man.'

'Yes.'

Frederick took a deep breath, looked at her beautiful
face, her poise and grace, the compassion and gentleness
and empathy in her gorgeous eyes.

'He said something else as well…'

Suddenly words weren't enough—he couldn't encom-
pass how he felt in mere words. So instead he pushed away
from the wall, and when she turned he sank to one knee.

'Frederick…?'

He could taste the sea spray, see the expression on her
face of confusion, and hope soared in his heart as he took
her left hand in his and removed the huge, heavy diamond—a ring chosen by someone else. He delved into his
pocket and pulled out a box, purchased earlier from one
of Mumbai's many jewellers.

'Will you marry me? For real. Not for Amil, not for Lycander, but because I love you. Heart, body and soul. Because I want to spend the rest of my life with you, wake
up with you every morning. I want to live my life side by
side with you. I want us to rule together, to laugh together,
to live a life full of *all* the emotions. So, will you marry
me? For real?'

His heart pounded and his fingers shook as he opened the box and took the ring out.

Her breathless laugh was caught with joy, the smile on her face so bright and beautiful his heart flipped.

'Yes. I *will* marry you. For real. Because I love you. That's what I wanted to tell you. That I love you. I didn't think in a million years that you could possibly love me back, but I wanted to tell you anyway. Heart, body and soul—they are all yours.'

He slipped the ring onto her finger and she lifted her hand in the air, watching the red and aquamarine stones interspersed with diamonds glint in the light of the setting sun.

'It's beautiful. Perfect.'

'I'm sorry about the other ring.'

'It makes this one all the more special. Did I mention I love it? Did I mention I love *you*?'

He rose to his feet. 'You did, but you can say it as many times as you like—those words won't ever get old.'

'No. Though Nanni says we have to back the words up. That love isn't only words—it's actions.' She stepped forward and looped her arms round his waist, snuggled in close. 'You *are* sure, aren't you? Sure this is real?'

'I have never been more sure of anything. I think I loved you from the start—I just couldn't admit it. Not to you, not to myself. You see, I didn't feel I deserved this joy.'

Her arms tightened around him. 'Because of Axel?'

'Partly. But even before that. I had parents who didn't give a damn—a mother who sold me for a crock of gold and a father who saw all his children as pawns or possessions. Love wasn't in the equation. Then I saw how much pain and angst love can cause—saw how losing Stefan tore Eloise apart. It was the same with Nicky, the twins' mother. My parents, who eschewed love, were happy and everyone else who *did* love was made miserable through that love. So I never wanted love to hold me hostage. I could see that emotions led to misery—that life was easier to control without emotion.

'Even two years ago you were different. But then you left, and Axel died, and I froze every emotion in order to cope. When you came back into my life all the emotions I'd bottled up for years kept surging up and I couldn't seem to shut them down any more. I didn't know what to do. I couldn't succumb to them because that was way too scary and it felt *wrong*. Axel died because of me. He'll never have the chance to live and love, have children, so how could it be right for me?'

'I am so very sorry about Axel, but I am sure he wouldn't have wanted you to give up on happiness.'

'I think you're right. Marcus seems sure of that too. And I know that if anything happened to me I wouldn't want *you* to shut your life down. I'd want you to live it to the full.'

'Nothing will to happen to you.' Her voice was fierce. 'And if it did I would never regret loving you.'

Frederick's heart swelled with the sheer wonder that he would share his life with this wonderful woman—and share it for real. The ups and the downs…everything.

He grinned down at her. 'I am so happy it doesn't seem possible. I never believed in my wildest dreams that you would love me too. I was willing to beg, fight—do whatever it took to persuade you to give me a chance to win your love.'

'You won that long ago but, like you, it took me a long time to admit it. I think deep down I knew the day I left you on the island with Amil. I couldn't have done that if I didn't trust you completely. And trust… I always thought that was for mugs and fools. My mother trusted my father once and ended up pregnant and abandoned. She trusted him again and it didn't end well for me. Fool me once, shame on you—fool me twice, shame on me. I figured it was best never to be fooled at all. Which meant the only way forward was never to trust anyone. But I trusted *you*. Even two years ago on some level I trusted you, or I would never have slept with you. But even after the island it all seemed so hard—you were so distant. And I felt like I used to—that I didn't fit. Everywhere I went people compared me to Kaitlin and…'

'You should have told me.'

'I couldn't. After all, you said that Kaitlin was your ideal bride.'

'I'm an idiot.' He cupped her face in his hands. 'I swear to you that you are the only bride I could ever want. Not because of Amil. Not because of Lycander. But because you are you and I *love* you. You make me whole. And if anyone makes any comparisons you send them to me.'

'No need. I've worked out where I've gone wrong—in my assumption that Kaitlin is better than me. She isn't— she is just different. I need to be a princess *my* way. Need to be myself.'

'And I know that means being a model—I will support your career every way I can.'

'About that… I'd better 'fess up. I'm not enjoying it one bit. I miss you and Amil… I miss Lycander. So I will fulfil this contract, but after that I will put a fashion portfolio together and send it off. And I also want to work for Lycander. I want to make it a fashion mecca—maybe set up a fashion show. One day we could rival Paris and London… There are so many options. But, whatever I decide, as long as you are by my side I know it will be OK.'

'Ditto.'

As he pulled her into his arms he knew this was the best alliance he could have ever made—because the only thing on the table was love.

* * * * *

If you enjoyed this story, check out these other great reads from Nina Milne

CLAIMED BY THE WEALTHY MAGNATE
THE EARL'S SNOW-KISSED PROPOSAL
RAFAEL'S CONTRACT BRIDE
CHRISTMAS KISSES WITH HER BOSS

All available in ebook now!

"I know you wanted to be married, have kids the normal way. But you yourself said you weren't willing to wait to be married in order to have children. You were going to push ahead on your own. This is another option. You're my friend, and I think you're sexy as hell. Marriages have been built on less, I bet."

Her face flushed a deeper pink than her pajamas. A good sign? He found himself hoping so.

"Think about it, will you, Gem?" He raised the marshmallow he'd plucked from the jar and brought it to her open lips. "What was it Scott and Elyse said at their wedding? 'I promise not to let the sun set without telling you how lucky I feel to have you'? I can promise you that. And marshmallows. If you say yes, I promise never, ever to make you go without marshmallows."

Before she could say yea or nay, he popped the treat into her mouth, following it with a kiss he intended to be as light and sweet as the candy. And it was. Until her arms went slack, and the blanket fell, and the temptation to make the kiss something more became too much for either of them to resist.

* * *

The Men of Thunder Ridge:
Once you meet the men of this Oregon town,
you may never want to leave!

DO YOU TAKE
THIS BABY?

BY
WENDY WARREN

First Published in Great Britain 2017
By Mills & Boon, an imprint of HarperCollins*Publishers*
1 London Bridge Street, London, SE1 9GF

© 2017 Wendy Warren

ISBN: 978-0-263-92338-4

23-1017

Our policy is to use papers that are natural, renewable and recyclable products and made from wood grown in sustainable forests. The logging and manufacturing processes conform to the legal environmental regulations of the country of origin.

Printed and bound in Spain
by CPI, Barcelona

Wendy Warren loves to write about ordinary people who find extraordinary love. Laughter, family and close-knit communities figure prominently, too. Her books have won two Romance Writers of America RITA® Awards and have been nominated for numerous others. She lives in the Pacific Northwest with human and nonhuman critters who don't read nearly as much as she'd like, but they sure do make her laugh and feel loved.

Printed and bound in Spain
by CPI, Barcelona

For
Tim Blough
And
Matt Pizzuti
Husbands, fathers, true heroes.

Chapter One

One little mistake. That's what Gemma Gould had made. One little mistake…that she was going to pay for the rest of her life.

"Beer or Bellini?" she muttered, keeping her head lowered as she manned the bar set up in her parents' backyard. Today's coed bridal shower for her youngest sister, Elyse, was turning into her own worst nightmare.

"Let's go, everyone." Elyse's maid of honor stood at the Goulds' sliding glass door and clapped her hands. "Grab your burgers and your drinks and head to the family room. Elyse's episode of *That's My Gown!* is about to begin." The announcement made Gemma's blood curdle in her veins.

Perspiration trickled down her back, hot and damp and sickening. Maybe she could say they were out of peach nectar for the Bellinis and that she had to run to the market. For about three days. Or better yet, she could fake an appendicitis attack—total rupture—and disappear for a week or more.

Nine months ago, Elyse had insisted that Gemma accompany her on a trip to New York to shop for a wedding gown (the selection on the West Coast being far too limited), and they ran into one of Elyse's college friends who, as it turned out, was working as a producer on the TV show *That's My Gown!* The next thing Gemma knew, she was Elyse's "entourage," tasked with the responsibility of murmuring "ooh" and "aah" as Elyse modeled an endless parade of gorgeous wedding gowns. Simple.

Only it hadn't gone so well.

"I'll have a Bellini, please," requested the sweet, high voice belonging to one of Elyse's eleven bridesmaids, "and could you hurry, Gemma? I missed the episode when it aired on TV. I hear it's a hoot!"

Gemma smiled with her teeth gritted. *Yeah, it's a hoot, all right.* Pouring a slushy, Creamsicle-hued drink into a stemmed glass, she passed it over the portable bar. "There you go, Collette."

"Thanks," chirped the tiny brunette. "You're such a good sport to let Elyse show the episode today." She reached a toned arm across the top of the bar to grasp Gemma's shoulder meaningfully. "You know, it's very powerful the way you two have decided to embrace humiliation and turn it into something super fun. You're an inspiration."

Gemma gaped at the girl. "Thanks."

Scooping ice into the blender and pressing Crush while Collette hurried away, Gemma kept her gaze averted from the guests who were streaming toward the family room.

The fact was, until someone mentioned it ten minutes ago, she'd had no idea the episode was going to play on her parents' fifty-two-inch plasma TV during the bridal shower that *she* was cohosting.

All of her family and plenty of the other people here had already seen the episode. It had been the talk of the town when it first aired on TV. And in a town as small and, lately, as wedding-obsessed as Thunder Ridge, she and Elyse had become instant celebrities.

Morosely, she watched the blender chop the hapless ice cubes into tiny shards. *I know just how you feel.* She'd heard all the witty comments about her appearance on the show—that she, always the bridesmaid and never the bride, must have been suffering from PTBS—post-traumatic bridesmaid's syndrome. Or that, at almost thirty-four, she'd had a "senior moment" on TV. And of course there were the people who felt "just horrible for poor Elyse," whose big sister had fallen dead asleep (and actually snored) while Elyse was sashaying along the runway in her very favorite gown.

Yep, Gemma had nodded off, snored, probably even drooled a little on a national TV show. The cameraman had caught her catnap—and Elyse's outrage—on-screen. The show added thought bubbles and sound effects in post-production, making it appear as if Gemma had fallen into a stupor after a few too many strawberry margaritas at brunch and suggesting that Elyse was a bridezilla, just waiting for her sister to wake up so she could smack her unconscious again.

Good times.

After loudly sobbing out her humiliation, Elyse had decided to face the episode head-on, showing everyone she was rising to the occasion by laughing at it herself. Nonetheless, Gemma had been making amends for ruining Elyse's fifteen minutes of fame ever since.

"If you're trying to show that ice who's boss, I'd say you've succeeded."

The deep, amused voice made every muscle in Gemma's

body go rigid. *Oh, no. Noooo.* She had known, of course, that Ethan Ladd was on the guest list for this afternoon's party, but he was in town so rarely that she hadn't expected him to show up.

Go away. She turned the blender up a notch, and the noise was satisfyingly obnoxious.

"Seriously? You're going to pretend I'm not here?"

"Not at all. I'm pretending I can't *hear* you." She dropped several more ice cubes down the safety spout in the blender's lid. The crunch was deafening.

A tanned hand reached over the bar and into her space. Involuntarily, she jumped back as Ethan managed to switch off the blender.

The nerve.

He was taller than her by at least ten inches and out-weighed her by…what? Five, maybe six pounds?

Joke. She wasn't that heavy. But having been pudgy throughout her childhood and teenage years, she'd learned there were people who appreciated her "curves" and others who thought she could drop a few pounds.

Keeping her head lowered, she felt rather than saw Ethan wag his head as he stared down at her. "Genius IQ, and ignoring me is the best you can do?" He clucked his tongue.

"I don't have a genius IQ. And I'm not ignoring you," she lied, her voice as tight as her muscles. "I'm concentrating on the job at hand."

"You always were a perfectionist," he said dryly. It didn't sound like a compliment. "I think you've lost your customer base for now, though. Except for me. I'll take a soda. Please," he added after a beat.

She inclined her head to the left. "They're in the cooler. Help yourself."

"I was hoping for some ice."

"In the cooler." She still didn't look at him. Could not look at him. Because looking at Ethan Ladd had always been her downfall. Like kryptonite to Superman, an eyeful of Ethan Ladd could turn Gemma into goo, marshmallow fluff, overcooked linguine—a squishy, messy mound of something that wasn't remotely useful.

"I'll help myself," Ethan said sardonically and moved away from her line of vision.

Gemma grabbed a dish towel and mopped at the water pooling around the blender, her mind racing a mile a minute. When she'd gotten dressed for the evening, she'd felt perfectly confident about her outfit—a sweet 1950s-style red-and-white polka-dot dress with a cinched waist and full skirt. She'd paired the vintage piece with red patent-leather peep-toe pumps and wound a yellow scarf, headband-like, around her dark brown hair. Now she wondered if she should have opted for something more trendy or sedate.

Dang it. Ethan freaking Ladd—on today of all days, when she was already the underdog.

Refusing to glance in his direction, she listened to him root around in the cooler, heard the ice clatter as he withdrew his soda and the click of his no doubt expensive shoes as he walked across her daddy's stone pavers to where she stood, all her senses on red alert, at the bar.

"'Scuse me, Gem." Directly behind her, he reached around her frozen-in-place body to grab a glass, his shirt brushing the back of her shoulder. Silky shirt…bare shoulder. Her heart flopped like a defibrillated fish. Then his right arm came around, and he grasped the handle of the blender. "I like my ice crushed."

Was it her imagination or did he deliberately brush against her a second time?

"You don't mind, do you?" he asked as he shook the frosty shards into his glass, then replaced the blender.

Moving to her left, he opened the soda and poured, leaning one hip against her work space.

That's when Gemma made her fatal mistake: she looked up, and there it was—his gorgeous kisser. Whether you liked Ethan Ladd or not, it was an empirical fact that he was practically an Adonis. The last time she'd seen him had been about a year ago. She'd been standing on the corner of Southwest Broadway and Southwest Salmon in downtown Portland, waiting for the light to change, and Ethan had been on the side of a bus. Or rather, his likeness had been.

Grinning face; thick golden locks styled, no doubt, by someone who charged by the hair; shoulders that bulged with sculpted muscle; abs chiseled from granite; and his Super Bowl ring front and center as he posed with his hand resting along the waistband of what had to be the skimpiest pair of underwear in BoldFit's lineup of men's briefs.

"So, your sister seems to be enjoying herself," he observed.

Gemma's throat and mouth were so dry, she could barely speak. "Mmm-hmm."

"How about you? Are you enjoying the spotlight?" Behind the ever-present I'm-thinking-something-very-amusing-right-now smile, Ethan watched her steadily, his dark-rimmed blue eyes thoughtful.

"Not my cup of tea." She gestured toward the house. "Why don't you take your soda inside, Ethan? I'm sure Elyse wants you to see the show." That would give Gemma time to catch her breath, practice her company smile and knock back a pitcher of Bellinis.

"No thanks. I had dinner with Scott and Elyse in Seattle four months ago. Heard all about it. Naps are supposed to be very healthful."

She was a summa cum laude, had a master's degree and

taught literature at a private college, yet she rose to his bait like a trout to a lure. "I was teaching summer courses. I told Elyse I was too busy to go to New York, but she insisted, and— Why am I explaining this to you?"

"Well, I'm no psychotherapist, but I'd say you have an inflated view of your own importance."

"That was a rhetorical question! You're not supposed to answer it."

"Sorry, Professor." His grin was challenging. Maddening.

"So—" Gemma worked at affecting a disinterested tone "—should we prepare ourselves for a brief stopover, Ethan, or are you gracing the old hometown with a longer visit?" As a wide receiver for the Seattle Eagles and the proud bearer of a Super Bowl ring, Ethan was one of Thunder Ridge's favorite sons. He truly was a local celebrity, with fame lasting a lot longer than fifteen minutes. And his ads for BoldFit men's skivvies had garnered a new generation of teenage girls who were swooning over him.

"I'm Scott's best man. Have to fulfill my duties."

"Getting the keg for the bachelor party? Just FYI, Elyse will sever body parts if you hire a stripper."

He grinned hugely. "I don't know any strippers."

"Not even the ones you've dated?"

He laughed outright, not the least bit offended. "And how about you?" he asked. "You still live and work in Portland, right? Last time I was in Thunder Ridge, I stopped by to see your parents. They mentioned they don't see you as much as they'd like."

The news that he still visited her parents when he was in town did not come as a surprise. Her mother proudly mentioned it each occasion when it happened. Ethan was two years younger than Gemma and the same age as Scott Carmichael, Elyse's fiancé. He and Scott had met while playing middle school sports. Growing up with an aunt and uncle who'd rescued him from a dysfunctional situation, he'd spent lots of evenings and weekends accompanying Scott to the Gould home. Elyse and Scott were already an item in middle school, and Gemma's mom had considered Ethan a "trustworthy chaperone." Ha! She should only have known.

"My parents won't be happy until every one of us kids moves back into our old rooms—with or without our spouses and children," Gemma said, intending to dismiss her mother's complaint, but then she winced. Ethan's eyes narrowed, and she realized her parents must have told him that her engagement to William Munson, a math professor, had ended almost a year ago. "Anyway," she said with false brightness, "I come home almost every weekend."

Oh, hell's bells. Could you sound more boring?

A burst of hysterical laughter rose in the family room. Her star turn as the worst bridesmaid on the planet must be playing in surround sound.

Looking down so Ethan wouldn't see the heat that rose furiously to her face, Gemma wiped her hands on the apron she wore over her dress. "Well, I'd better go…check on the dessert." A lame excuse, for sure, but she needed to escape.

He grabbed her arm before she could leave. "Why do you let them take advantage of you?" The words were soft, but penetrating.

She blinked at his expression. Gemma had seen Ethan on TV when his team went to the Super Bowl. The whole town had watched. Ernest Dale at Ernie's Electronics had set up three TVs in the store window, all programmed for the game. Gemma couldn't have missed it if she'd tried; Thunder Ridge had turned into one giant Super Bowl party just for Ethan.

As the wide receiver, he'd caught a number of passes

and was playing well, but then three-quarters into the action, he'd missed an outside pass. He took off his helmet and threw it to the ground, the camera following him. Jaw square and tense, brow lowered, eyes penetrating, he looked very much the way he did right now—angry and disgusted.

"I don't know what you mean," she said, because she truly didn't. Her family wasn't perfect, of course not, and as the baby, Elyse could appear spoiled at times, but they loved Gemma. She was the eldest daughter, and perhaps the only one in their family tree who was logical, practical and coolheaded in a pinch. "No one is taking advantage of me. I help because I want to."

"Admirable." His eyes looked almost iridescent in the afternoon sun slanting across her parents' backyard. "But who helps *you*?"

Maybe it was his lowered voice adding intimacy to the question. Or perhaps Gemma was simply tired and vulnerable, but tears pricked her eyes. *Oh, no, no. We are not going there. Not with him.*

She had thoroughly humiliated herself twice in her life. One of those times was being replayed in the family room for everyone to see. The other incident was long past, but in many ways it had been worse, and Ethan Ladd had been responsible for it. Partly responsible. Mostly responsible.

Oh, what the hell, it had been *all* his fault. He had ruined her senior year homecoming dance. He had ruined her senior year, period. Gemma had her revenge, but she'd stayed emotionally distant and physically away from him as much as she'd been able to after that miserable night. No way was she going to give in to the weird urge to blubber into his broad chest now.

"Thank you, Ethan," she said in her best Professor Gould voice, "but I have lots of support. Right now, all I need is to make sure the cheesecake stands at room temperature for twenty minutes before we serve it, so if you'll excuse me."

"I'll come with you."

"That's not necessary."

"Yeah, it is. I brought my own veggie burger. Left it in the kitchen."

She glanced at his heavily muscled body, evident even beneath the T-shirt and jeans. "Veggie burger?" she said doubtfully, walking toward the patio door that led to her parents' ample kitchen. "Since when?" In high school, he'd once sat in their kitchen and scarfed down four hot dogs and half a large pepperoni pizza.

"I consider my body a temple." Mischief undercut his tone. He reached the door, opened it and held it open, his arm high above her head, looking down at her as she passed through. She caught his wink. "Have to make up for all those years of debauchery."

He was angling for a response. "Careful you don't change too quickly," she replied, "you wouldn't want to send yourself into shock."

Ethan's easy laughter rang through the kitchen. Her body responded to the sound, sending shivers over her skin. *Darn.*

"I was kidding about the veggie burger. I only like them if they have meat and cheese." He went straight to the refrigerator and peered in. "That's a lot of cheesecake." He began to stack the boxes in his arms.

"I'll do it," she protested.

Paying no attention, he deposited the cakes on the center island and opened the white cardboard. "Rocky road," he murmured. Knowing exactly where to look in her mother's cabinets, he retrieved a plate and fork.

"Stop!" she ordered as he began to work a knife into

the dessert. "I told you, those aren't supposed to be sliced until they've sat at room temperature for twenty minutes."

"A rule clearly intended to be broken. Like so many other rules," he purred, sliding a slice of the mile-high cheesecake onto the plate.

"I thought you were treating your body like a temple."

"I am. I'm bringing it an offering." Ethan seemed to let the bite melt in his mouth. His eyes half closed. "Mmm-mmm."

Gemma's knees went weak. How did he do that? How did he make eating look sexy? If she floated the fork through the air the way he was doing, she'd probably drop a chunk on her bosom. No wonder he'd garnered as much celebrity for his sex appeal as he had for playing football. Suddenly, Gemma felt very, very hungry, but not for cheesecake.

Fiddlesticks. Ethan Ladd short-circuited her brain and hampered her logic. It had been different when she had a fiancé. William was intelligent, educated, taught at the same college as her and was pretty much perfect for her. They'd met in the library, for crying out loud. Engaged to William Munson, Gemma had no longer thought about men who were wrong for her. She'd stopped reacting when Ethan's name came up or when she heard he was in town, working on the McMansion he'd built on four acres that backed up to Long River. She had become neutral.

She needed another fiancé, stat.

"Gemma? Hey, Gemma!"

Ethan's voice made her jump. "What?"

"I said, are you sure you won't join me?" He held his fork out to her, his eyes half closed in a way that made him look as if he'd just rolled out of bed. Or was still in it.

Oh, yes, I'll join you... "No! Absolutely not." She marched around the counter and closed the box. Reaching into the cabinet beneath the center island, she withdrew a large silver tray she had polished earlier in the week.

In a moment, today's guests would emerge from the family room, laughing and ribbing her about her appearance on TV. Elyse would be grinning on the outside, but Gemma knew her perfection-seeking sister was crying on the inside, because Gemma had marred her big moment. So she would try to make amends—again—by earning a spot in the bridesmaids hall of fame.

A few months ago, she'd ordered a book about fruit and vegetable carving online and had dedicated more hours to perfecting watermelon roses than she had spent on her master's thesis.

"I need to prepare the dessert tray," she told Ethan, waving him toward the other part of the house. "You have a legion of fans out there. Why don't you bask in the glory of being Thunder Ridge's favorite son?"

"Well, now, that's exactly why I don't want to be in the other room. All that attention tends to make my head swell, and I'm working on humility."

He gave her such a deliberately innocent expression that Gemma felt a genuine smile tickle her lips. The man was wearing a Bulgari wristwatch and designer jeans. And the home he'd built? It was so massive and completely out of proportion with any other home in the area, it shouted, *"Hey, everyone, a really, really rich dude lives here."*

Seeing her smile, Ethan leaned against the kitchen counter and tilted his head. "How about I help you with the dessert? I promise not to eat any more cheesecake. Scout's honor."

A wave of déjà vu hit her: once before, he'd offered to spend time with her, to take her to senior homecoming dance, in fact. And that had been a disaster.

Before she could courteously decline his offer, Ethan's

cell phone rang. He used Kenny Chesney's "The Boys of Fall" as his ringtone.

"Thought I silenced that." He grimaced. "'Scuse me." Into the phone, he said, "Ethan here."

While he listened to the caller, Gemma tortured herself with memories: the thrill of believing that Ethan wanted to take her to homecoming. Yes, he'd been two years younger, but there hadn't been a senior girl at Thunder Ridge High who wouldn't have jumped at the chance to date him. And Gemma, she had…well, she'd…

Oh, go on, admit it. We're all adults here.

With Ethan turned half away from her, she looked at the massive squared shoulders and sighed. Every time he'd come to her house with Scott, she'd fantasized he was there to see her. That the two of them were going to hang out, study together, talk about music and books and movies and sports teams. Not that she was into sports, but with her photographic memory it hadn't taken all that long to memorize the stats for every player in the NFL, so that if he decided he wanted to get to know her one day, she would be ready with the kind of conversation he was likely to enjoy.

"What the hell are you talking about?" Ethan's tone was sharp and concerned, jerking Gemma back to the moment at hand.

Oookay. She moved about self-consciously, withdrawing a tray of edible flowers with which to decorate the dessert while she pretended not to eavesdrop. Which, of course, she was.

"No, I was not aware. Where is she?" Ethan spoke with his jaw so tight, the words had trouble emerging. "That won't be necessary. I'll get ahold of her myself…I see. Yes, do that. I'll be available by phone."

There was silence. The heaviest silence Gemma had

ever heard. She worked at her corner of the center island, her face turned away from Ethan, wondering if she should speak. She had no idea what the phone call was about, but his distress was obvious, and she felt a strong desire to say something comforting.

When the silence had lasted long enough, Gemma finally turned to catch Ethan staring at the floor.

Suddenly he didn't look like Ethan, King of Thunder Ridge High, or Ethan the Football Star, or Ethan the Sex Symbol, or Ethan the Boy Who Made Gemma Gould Feel Like an Ugly Duckling Loser in High School. He was, perhaps for the first time in her eyes, just a regular human being. And he looked really, really alone.

"Are you all right?" she ventured. "If you need to talk—"

Her voice seemed to bust him out of his spell. "I have to go." He didn't look at her directly. "Tell Elyse and Scott I'll call them."

He seemed to hesitate a moment longer, or maybe that was her imagination, then exited through the kitchen door. And that was that.

Returning to her edible flowers, Gemma told herself not to feel compassion for the big boob. He'd just rejected her friendly—no, not friendly, simply *humane*—overture, and, let's face it, *rejection* pretty much summed up her relationship with Ethan Ladd through the years.

She shook her head hard, jiggling some sense into it. She was over thirty, had a great career, good friends. She'd had a fiancé and would surely date again. Someday. Ethan Ladd did not have the power to make her feel valuable, attractive and worthwhile or rejected and unwanted. That was so fifteen years ago.

All she had to do was get through this wedding. Then he would be gone again, her regular life would resume and her heart would stop beating like a hummingbird in flight every time she thought about weddings and true love, or about the first man who had broken her heart.

Chapter Two

Two months after Elyse's bridal shower, Gemma was in Thunder Ridge again, staying at her parents' place over the weekend, so Minna Gould, mother of the bride, would have an audience while she fretted over last-minute preparations for the wedding.

"You need to decide whether you're bringing a date," Minna insisted as they carried the dinner plates to the Goulds' cozy pale-blue-and-white kitchen. "This is the last chance to order another meal from the caterer. After this, she'll serve my head on a platter."

"I'm not bringing a date, Mom. I don't want your head on my conscience," Gemma assured her, taking the plates from her mother and plunking them in a sinkful of suds.

"Don't be silly! If you want to bring a date, then by all means—"

"Mom, I was kidding. I'm not seeing anyone."

Only twenty-four years older than her second child,

Minna Gould, née Waldeck, was still a beautiful woman. Most of the Waldeck women married young, started their families young and stayed beautiful without artificial enhancements well into their fifties.

Gemma, unfortunately, took after the Gould side of the family. The women on her father's side were outspoken with above-average intelligence, very average looks and way-above-average bustlines and butt, and they tended to marry later in life—so much later that children were often out of the question—or they never married at all. Depressing.

"I'm just saying, Gemma, that if you *do* want to bring someone so you can have more fun dancing, for example," Minna suggested, picking up a dish towel, "I'm not really afraid of the caterer. I'll dry," she said, holding out her hand for the first dish Gemma washed. Minna's hazel eyes, the only physical characteristic Gemma had inherited from her mother, sliced her daughter's way. "Maybe William would like to come with you?"

The mention of her former fiancé nearly made Gemma drop the plate. "Absolutely not."

"But you're still friends. You still work together." It was impossible to miss the hopeful note in Minna's voice.

"Mom, William and I decided our engagement was a mistake." *Lie.* William had decided they were meant to be friends only. Gemma had been perfectly (or pathetically, depending on how you looked at it) willing to accept friendship as a solid basis for marriage. "We are not getting back together." When Minna opened her mouth to interject, Gemma cut her off. "And he is not coming to the wedding."

In all fairness, Minna had no idea that a scant two weeks after he broke up with Gemma, William started dating the new, adorable French lit teacher at school, and that they were now "serious." It had seemed kind to spare her family that bit of information. They worried about her, she knew. None of her siblings, who favored Minna in looks and in character, had ever lacked a date on weekends. Only Gemma, with her Gould-given averageness and her keen interest in historical novels and theater versus, say, sports, pop culture and who won *Dancing with the Stars*, tended to struggle in the dating arena. True, she lived in a busy, exciting city, but Portland tended to skew more toward families and the twentysomething indie-music crowd. Gemma knew her options were decreasing, but she just couldn't bring herself to look online for a mate.

Okay, *lie*. She and her friend Holliday had imbibed a mimosa or two one Sunday brunch at Gemma's place, and Gemma had allowed Holly to make a dating profile for her on one of the more popular sites. In the light of stone-cold sobriety, however, Gemma had deleted it.

"Don't worry, Mom. I'll have a great time going stag to the wedding." She bumped her mother's hip. "When Dad's doing the Cupid Shuffle with Grandma, you and I can practice twerking."

"Oh, stop it, you!" Minna snapped Gemma with the dish towel. "Do you happen to know if Ethan wants to bring someone? I can't get Elyse or Scott to slow down long enough to tell me anything these days, and I can't imagine he would come alone. I saw on the cover of *In Touch* that he's been dating that redhead from the TV show about vampire cheerleaders. What's her name?"

Gemma felt a little pinch to her heart. "I have no idea."

"Well, do you know if he's bringing someone?"

"How would I know that?"

"You dated him in high school."

The pinch felt tighter. "I wouldn't call it a date," she mumbled, "exactly." Had nobody in the family ever told

Minna the truth about the single evening Gemma had spent with Ethan? Elyse knew all about the disastrous homecoming event, since she had set the "date" up to begin with. And their sister Lucy knew, because she'd seen Gemma crying, and Elyse had blabbed all about it. Even their older brother, David, knew. "Mom," Gemma said carefully, "that night with Ethan…that was more of a high school convenience thing."

"Don't be ridiculous. You primped for two hours, and he brought you a corsage."

Amazing how the memory could induce a flood of embarrassing heat all these years later. Yes, she had primped. Yes, she had been excited. No, he hadn't given her a corsage. Elyse, as it turned out, had provided the corsage for Ethan to give to Gemma. The entire evening had been Elyse's brainchild, not Ethan's.

Keeping her eyes on the sudsy dishwater, Gemma said, "Everyone primps for the homecoming dance, Mom. It didn't really mean anything."

Minna shook her head, exasperated. "Oh, for heaven's sake. Three daughters, and not one of you interested in Ethan. I don't understand it. If he'd been in town when my friends and I were in high school…"

Gemma didn't have to listen to know what came next—*we'd have been fighting over him like cats and dogs.*

Well, who said she hadn't been interested? And girls *had* fought over Ethan like cats and dogs; it was just that Gemma had never had a prayer of winning that particular battle.

"Fine." Minna shrugged. "It didn't work out, so that's that, but he always liked talking to you."

Yes, I am a sought-after conversationalist, all right. Even William still dropped in at her office for the occasional chat.

"You were the only person he spent any time with at all at the wedding shower," Minna continued. "Really, I can't imagine what would have made him run off the way he did. Are you sure he didn't give you a clue?"

It didn't feel right to repeat a conversation she probably shouldn't have overheard in the first place, so Gemma muttered, "He didn't tell me anything." That was the truth. "He said he'd talk to Elyse and Scott."

"Oh, they're both so busy, they're useless when it comes to—" Her mother cut herself off.

"Feeding you juicy gossip about Ethan?" Gemma teased.

"Oh, fine. We'll definitely see Ethan next week. I'll ask him for some gossip myself."

"Next week?" Gemma heard the panic in her own voice. She hadn't seen or heard a word about Ethan since the bridal shower, and life was much more peaceful that way.

"Gemma," her mother chided. "Please say you didn't forget the rehearsal dinner. I told you to write the date down immediately. You're not going to tell me you have one of those endless work functions or dinner with the dean."

"No, I remember the rehearsal dinner. I just forgot Ethan would be there."

"Well, of course he's going to be there. He's the best man. I'm giving you the job of calling him to confirm."

"What? Why me? Why not—" Gemma stopped herself. The more she protested, the more she would draw her mother's attention. And she couldn't claim not to have Ethan's number; it had been her job to text the wedding party to give them the time of the fittings for their gowns and tuxes. "All right."

She'd merely text him again. Wouldn't have to trade actual words until the rehearsal dinner.

* * *

Past 9:00 p.m., the General Store in Thunder Ridge was closed, so if you had a midnight hankering for a pint of mint chocolate chip or a desperate need to read the latest celebrity gossip mag, you had to drive to Hank's Thunderbird Market on Highway 12. When Gemma's sister Lucy phoned their parents' house at 11:00 p.m., asking if someone could please, please, *please* pick up ear drops for her baby, Owen, and some teething gel—"The pink gel, not the white. The pink!"—because Owen had been crying nonstop for two hours, Gemma volunteered to make the drive.

Deciding a snack would make the late-night trip more entertaining, Gemma grabbed a package of Nutter Butters, which were the best cookies on earth, then added a bag of rippled potato chips since she was going to need to crunch on something on the way home. With her basket of support foods, she headed to the pharmaceutical aisle intending to grab the teething gel quickly and go to her sister's. As she rounded the corner of the aisle, however, she nearly collided with another late-night shopper.

"Oh! My gosh. I didn't expect to see you."

"Yeah, no, me either. I'm… I had to pick up a few things." Ethan nodded to the loaded cart in front of him and then—was it possible?—he blushed. As in, a deep red infused his gorgeous face. His gorgeous, exhausted-looking face.

Why was *he* blushing? Other than seeming tired, he looked great. She, on the other hand, had been wearing a T-shirt that read Eat, Sleep, Repeat and her hot-pink emoji pajama bottoms when Lucy had called, and she hadn't seen any reason to change for the trip to the Thunderbird.

Her surprise at seeing Ethan here turned into absolute shock when she saw the contents of his shopping cart.

"Teething biscuits?" She arched a brow.

"Yeah." He glanced around, then lifted a shoulder. "I like 'em."

"Favorite locker-room snack?"

Ethan did not look happy. He looked, in fact, miserable. With one hand, he finger-combed the thick golden hair that appeared to have been mussed several times already. With the other hand, he retained a white-knuckle grip on the cart.

Gemma peered at the rest of the contents, which looked as if they'd been scooped up by a dump truck and piled in.

Coffee, milk, two four-packs of energy drinks, cotton balls, bandages, a thermometer (several, in fact, each a different brand), tissues, baby wipes—

Baby wipes? She looked closer. Yep, baby wipes. And formula! He had at least four different kinds of formula in that cart. And were those boxes of…

Oh, my goodness. Ethan was buying diapers. Disposable diapers, again in a few different brands. Plus, she spied the very item she was looking for—teething gel.

"You got the white kind," she said, pointing to the small box with the picture of a tooth. "You should get the pink. My sister says it works the best."

Frowning, Ethan followed her finger. "Really? Where is the pink one?"

Feeling as if she'd fallen asleep and was having a very weird dream, Gemma led him to the correct spot along the aisle. "This one." She picked a box from the shelf. "Worked like a charm when my nephew Owen was cutting his first tooth."

Looking as confused and frustrated as he was tired, Ethan scowled at the label, then tossed it into the cart along with everything else.

Selecting a box of the ointment for her sister, Gemma ventured, "So, Ethan, you have a toothache? And—" she nodded toward the diaper boxes peeking out at the bottom of the cart "—a problem with incontinence, perhaps?"

"Very funny." He did the finger-comb again. "Can you keep a secret?" he growled, sotto voce.

"I *can*," she replied, wondering at the strangeness of this meeting. "I'm not sure I'm going to *want* to."

When he spoke, he looked as if even he didn't believe the words he was about to say. "I have a baby."

Gemma stared at him until her vision got blurry. "A baby what?"

"You know." He made a rocking motion.

"A person? You have a baby…person?"

He nodded, and she could hardly breathe. *I'm blacking out, I'm blacking out.* Her heart flopped in her chest. "Wh-who-who is the mother?" Then she gasped. "Is it the redhead from the vampire cheerleader show?"

He looked at her oddly. "Who— You mean Celeste? No!" He swore. "Lord, no." Coming around from behind the cart, he took her upper arm, glancing up and down the aisle as if this were a dark alley. "It's not *my* baby," he whispered.

She whispered back. "You said, 'I have a baby.'"

"I do. In my house. Look," he grumbled, "I don't want to talk here. Are you done shopping?"

"I want to get ear drops for Lucy's son. He's been crying all night. She thinks he's just teething, but you never know."

Ethan's attention sharpened. "Would an earache make a baby cry? A lot?"

"Yes."

"Where are the ear drops?"

"Over here." She showed him. He handed her a box, then added one to his cart. "Let's go."

The fact that he was asking her to go to his house was

weird—and exciting—to say the least. "I can't come to your house right now. I have to take these things to Luce."

"Tonight?"

"Yes. Owen's crying."

"Where's her husband? Why are you out this late?"

"Rick is out of town. I help when I'm here."

"Aren't you already helping with the wedding? I hear you're driving up from Portland every weekend."

Was she mistaken or was there a note of censure in his tone? Instantly, Gemma felt on the defensive. "I don't mind."

Ethan shook his head. "You have three other siblings and parents who live in Thunder Ridge. Couldn't one of them have helped Lucy?"

"They all have families, so…" She shrugged.

"So you get dumped on in the middle of the night."

"It's not the middle of the night! Anyway, it's not like that. I told you, I don't mind." She sounded convincing, even to her own ears, but a cold heaviness filled her chest. *Sometimes* she minded. Sometimes she was envious of her siblings' problems and their time commitments with kids and spouses and PTA meetings. Sometimes she wished it were her living room walls that needed to be repainted *again*, because the kids woke up early one Saturday and got creative with an indelible marker. Gemma chewed the inside of her lip.

"Sorry," Ethan relented. "I shouldn't have said 'dumped.' You're good at fixing people's problems. It's natural they turn to you."

"Yes, I'm good at fixing problems," she murmured. Everyone's problems but her own.

Her thirty-fourth birthday was in September. According to her friend Constance, who taught reproductive biology to premeds, 95 percent of thirty-year-old women had only 12 percent of their original ovarian follicular cells. That was a lot of cells MIA. And everyone knew that when women reached thirty-five, fertility dropped like a rock. With no man on the horizon, Gemma could feel her ovaries shrinking to the size of raisins right here in the market.

Her gaze fastened on Ethan's face. He was even more handsome now than in high school.

Why do you have a baby? Whose is it? Clearly, the situation was a surprise. He was about to purchase half the infant-care aisle and didn't seem to know a single thing about infants.

"Who's with the baby now?"

"I hired a nanny." He frowned. "She's young."

"Oh. I'm sure she's capable." *And I am going to mind my own beeswax.* "I'd better get going," she said hastily before she could change her mind. "My nephew is really uncomfortable."

"Right. Okay." He looked at his cart and frowned. "Me, too. I'd better—" he waved a hand "—head home."

"Good luck with everything, Ethan."

"You, too."

As he picked up a box of infant cold and fever medication and stared dubiously at the label, she sped up the aisle toward the single cashier on duty. Her mother would kill her for not getting all the info on Ethan's mystery baby. Come to think of it, it was strange that he hadn't told Scott, who surely would have mentioned it to Elyse, who would have told not only their mother, but all of her former sorority sisters and everyone else who would listen. "Oh—" She turned back. "I'm supposed to ask if you'll be at the rehearsal dinner and whether you're bringing a date to the wedding."

Ethan glanced up. "Yes. And no."

"Yes to the rehearsal dinner, no to the date?"

"Right."

"Okay. Well, see you soon."

He nodded, turning back to the cold medicine, his brow furrowed in thought.

Gemma continued on her way. No date. She could thrill quite a few women with that information. And flatly refused to consider her own response.

Paying for her items and carrying the bag to her car, she tried not to think about William or about how, if he hadn't ended the engagement, they would have been married by now, attending Elyse's wedding as husband and wife and quite possibly arguing over baby names (he liked Jane for a girl; she favored Eliza). Instead, she was flying solo with shriveling ovaries, while Ethan, who apparently chose dating celebrities as his off-season sport, wasn't bringing anyone to the wedding…but did have a baby.

Forget Ethan. Forget William. And, for heaven's sake, stop thinking about your ovaries.

But she kept picturing Ethan with a baby and seeing images of him in high school, dating cheerleaders. And going out with her, Gemma. Once.

Turning the key in the ignition, she found the bag of ripple chips and tore it open. She just might require a few peanut butter cookies, too, for the lonely drive to her sister's house.

Elyse and Scott's rehearsal dinner was held at Summit Lodge, a fabulous place that could accommodate rustic or more formal affairs. Nestled into the base of Thunder Ridge, the Scottish-themed lodge allowed guests to enjoy the mountain's year-round majesty, and every December, Santa distributed presents among the boys and girls whose parents brought them to Brunch with Saint Nick. Gemma's baby sister had chosen the lodge as her wedding venue all the way back in elementary school.

Because it was Memorial Day weekend, and Oregon's weather could be unreliable, Elyse had opted to walk down a formal staircase and up the aisle between rows of guests who would be seated before one of the lodge's massive stone fireplaces. Elyse and Scott were being married by their friend Jessie, an ordained minister. The fireplace was so tall and so wide that they, their officiate and some of the wedding party could have stood inside it.

It was in this majestic, romantic environment that Gemma saw Ethan for the first time since their meeting in the market.

At their current altitude, it was a bit chilly, and in his ivory cable-knit sweater and straight-leg jeans, he fit perfectly into his surroundings. His hair glowed golden in the ambient lights, and his blue eyes held their customary laugh, but once, when he glanced Gemma's way, she thought he looked stressed.

Elyse had Gemma running around, asking so many questions and tying up so many loose ends that there was no time at all to speak to Ethan. Her sister's remaining bridesmaids, on the other hand, seemed to find plenty of time to gather around the sports star. He looked as if he were holding court, and his million-dollar smile almost made her think she'd imagined the tension. So far no one she knew had mentioned Ethan's baby news. Sometimes it seemed she'd dreamed the whole thing.

As the rehearsal finally wound up, Gemma dropped into one of the wide chairs positioned around the perimeter of the room. She still hadn't caught up on the sleep she'd missed while running to Lucy's last weekend, and at school, rapidly approaching final exams had kept her working extra hours. She was toast, and the wedding was tomorrow.

"Auntie Gem! Auntie Gem!"

Her brother David's six-year-old twins, Violet and Vivian, ran over and grabbed her hands.

"Do you wanna see the floor where we get to dance tomorrow? We know where it is! Come on, we'll show you. Come on, Auntie Gem! Come on!"

Resisting the yanking of her appendages, she instead pulled the chair with her and frowned doubtfully into freckled faces topped by curly auburn hair. "Do I know either of you? You don't look like anyone I know."

"We're your nieces!" Vivian, the bolder of the two, told her indignantly. "You knowed us since we were babies."

"You changed our diapers," Violet, the more serious of the two, pointed out.

"Really?" Bending toward each in turn, she sniffed. "No, you don't smell like those kids. They were stinky."

Both girls dissolved into giggles as Gemma cuddled them.

"We're not stinky anymore, Auntie Gem," Violet informed her. "Mommy says we have to take a bath once a year, whether we need it or not."

Gemma grinned. "Yeah, I do the same. Once a year, no excuses."

"I knew we had something in common."

The deep voice had them all raising their eyes. Ethan was looking right at her, azure gaze steady, his smile an ad company's dream.

Gemma glanced around, wondering if the groupie bridesmaids, as she was starting to think of them, were going to pop up in a second. But nope, amazingly, he was alone.

"Your fellow bridesmaids are with Elyse and Minna,"

he supplied as if reading her mind, "making sure there are enough mirrors for everyone to get ready tomorrow. First one who calls a mirror gets to use it." He arched a brow. "You want me to take you to them so you can stake your claim?"

"I'm not very competitive. I'd rather take my chances with a compact. How about you? Shouldn't you be duking it out with the groomsmen for mirror rights?"

The perfect lips unfurled into an electrifying grin. "Nah. I just roll out of bed, and I'm pretty already."

He may have been joking, but it was the gospel truth. Not that she'd seen him straight out of bed, but… Gemma sighed. It only took a glance to realize he'd been gifted. If she was plain as brown bread, he was red velvet cake.

"I think I can guess who these lovely ladies are." Ethan looked at the two girls who were staring at him, a bit intimidated. Getting down on his haunches to make his six-foot-three-inch body less imposing, he said, "Your dad is Gemma's brother. Am I right?"

Protectively, Gemma pulled her nieces closer. *That is the kind of smile for which you do not fall.*

Vivian spoke up first. "No. She's our aunt."

Ethan pursed his beautiful lips. (And, really, why were those wasted on a man? The Cupid's bow looked drawn on.) "Hmm. So that would mean your father is Gemma's… grandfather?"

"No!" The girls rocked with laughter.

"Your father is her…great-grandfather?"

"No!"

"Her son?"

"No!"

Ethan scratched his head. "I guess I'm not good at this. Never mind. What were you talking about again—

oh, yeah, bathing habits. Let's see, I try to shower when there's a full moon—"

"Okay, that's too much info," Gemma interrupted.

His devilish expression seemed to reach out and grab her. "For them or for you?"

Violet wriggled off the chair. "We want to show Auntie Gem where we're gonna dance."

Leaping to the floor after her sister, Vivian craned her neck to look up at Ethan. "You can come with us."

"Sure." He glanced at Gemma. "If we go before the return of the bridesmaid brigade, I would be eternally grateful."

"Too many adoring fans for you to juggle at once?" she asked, rising.

"Yeah, I usually have my manager do that."

Vivian grabbed her sister's hand and raced ahead with her twin. "Follow us!" she called back as they ran along the wide-planked wood floor to a carpeted hallway that led to the reception room.

Gemma walked more sedately by Ethan's side. "So, Ethan," she said, "the last time I saw you, you were taking care of a baby. Or did I dream that?"

"Do you dream about me often, Gemma?"

She looked up sharply. "Only when I have indigestion."

He grinned, but the smile faded quickly, replaced by fatigue. "I do still have the baby," he answered her.

Gemma's heart thudded strongly in her chest. Questions tumbled through her mind. She chose the most boring one. "Have you told anyone else in town?"

"No. Have *you* told anyone?"

"No, of course not. You didn't tell me I could."

He pinched the bridge of his nose. "Good. I don't think I could handle the press right now." Gazing at her speculatively, he commented, "You always did have good principles, Gemma." A hint of mischief returned to his eyes. "Except that one time."

She knew, of course, exactly what he was talking about: when she'd discovered he hadn't wanted to take her to the homecoming dance, that he'd had to be *persuaded*, she had paid him back by playing a trick on him. A rather mean—and rather effective—trick.

Preferring their current topic, she asked, "Why *are* you taking care of a baby? You said it's not yours. Whose is it, then? How long are you taking care of it?" She wrinkled her nose. "I have to stop saying 'it.' Is the baby a boy or girl?"

Ethan smiled. "Still don't want to discuss the great homecoming debacle, huh?" They walked a few more paces, following her skipping, giggling nieces. "I'm taking care of Cody—who is a boy—for someone close to me. I'd like it to keep it quiet for now. The media is a funny thing, Gemma. Journalists twist stories all the time to find a hook that will sell. I'd like to stay under the radar as long as I can."

"Staying under the radar isn't your usual MO, is it?" She winced. That sounded snarky. "I mean, the media's been good to you, haven't they?"

"I've made a good living off the media, and they've made a good living off of me. But this isn't business. It's personal."

She nodded. "Your world is different from mine. So much larger. Thunder Ridge is a fishbowl. In Portland, I work at a private college and rent a mother-in-law unit a stone's throw from campus. It can be claustrophobic at times. I thought a life like yours would be more expansive, freer. I didn't realize it could get claustrophobic, too."

Ethan stopped walking and turned toward her. "That *is*

how it feels." He nodded, almost to himself. "Sometimes when I'm in a crowd of people, there's not enough air."

"It's over here! Come here!" Vivian and Violet were waving them to the Long River Room, where Elyse and Scott's reception was being held tomorrow night.

A rare intimacy wove around Ethan and Gemma, real yet frail, like the sheerest of scarves.

"I'll respect your privacy," she said, meaning it, and wanting the delicate moment to last awhile longer.

"Thanks, Gemma."

Vivian emerged from the ballroom, fists on her little-girl hips. "Are you coming?"

"Or not?" Violet mimicked her sister's body language, though with less conviction.

Ethan relaxed enough to laugh. His eyes glinted again as he arched a brow at Gemma. "Shall we?"

"We'd better. It's not wise to cross Vivian when she's on a mission."

Side by side, they walked to the ballroom, and Gemma realized she was in no hurry to get back to the rehearsal dinner. No hurry at all.

Chapter Three

Ethan had been friends with Scott Carmichael and his bride-to-be since they were in their tweens. He thought it was great that they had stayed together and were getting married after all these years. Scott hadn't even asked him to be his best man; it was simply a foregone conclusion, and Ethan had been happy to oblige. Recent events in his life, however, were turning this wedding weekend into one giant pain in his neck.

Elyse had already hinted that she'd traded on his name to get a friend of hers from college to cover the wedding for *The Oregonian*. Ethan didn't come home to Thunder Ridge often, and when he did he valued his privacy, but he'd figured he could grin and bear Elyse's desire for a taste of celebrity. That, however, was before the Department of Human Services had called to tell him he was about to become the guardian of one very tiny baby.

"This is where we're going to dance!" Vivian pulled

her sister to the large wood-floored square in the middle of the room. The girls began to spin, watching their skirts swirl around their legs. Cute.

"Come twirl with us, Auntie Gem," Vivian invited. "It's easy-peasy-lemon-squeezy!"

"Twirl!" her sister echoed.

Ethan looked at Gemma. As long as he'd known her, she'd been serious, studious, responsible. Not exactly the twirling type. Smart in a way he could never be. He'd been at the Goulds' once, hanging out with Scott and Elyse, when Gemma and a friend of hers were studying for an English exam. He'd barely known what she was talking about, but listening to the conversation, he'd felt a pang of envy and a yearning so deep he'd made some smart-ass comment to Scott just to cover his discomfort.

Having a friend like her would have been impractical. Impossible. They'd had zero in common. And then Elyse had convinced him to ask her to the homecoming dance. He'd been a sophomore, already making a name for himself on the football team, and she'd been a senior. Elyse had insisted that Gemma needed to attend at least one high school dance before she graduated. He remembered thinking how wrong Elyse was, how bored Gemma was bound to be, especially if a bonehead like him accompanied her.

"Are you going to twirl?" he asked now, nodding to the spinning twins. Gemma might not be interested in dancing, but her skirt was made for it. Sea-foam green with alternating sections of lace from the knees down, it flirted with her legs when she walked. Her silky top was deep purple, and on her very nice feet were coral-colored shoes with just a couple of straps. All those colors might have clashed on someone else. On Gemma, the outfit looked artsy. Joyful. Suddenly it occurred to him that her clothes had always been the least serious thing about her. "I like the way you dress." He surprised them both by speaking the thought out loud.

"Thanks." She blushed, her cheeks turning a deep pink.

Inexplicably not dizzy, the girls ran over and tugged on their aunt. "Come on!"

Gemma chewed the inside of her full lower lip.

A smile tugged at Ethan's mouth. The women he knew had no problem dancing in public. They fed off the attention. Gemma, however, looked sweetly self-conscious.

Hoping to help her out, he bowed in his best impression of Prince Charming. "May I have this dance, Princess Professor?"

The girls giggled and clapped.

"I'm not a professor, yet. And there's no music," Gemma pointed out reasonably.

"You don't hear anything, Professor?" He looked at the twins. They wore huge smiles, by which he concluded that small children were a lot easier to impress than tiny babies. Or maybe it was because they were female. He didn't have a wide range of talents, but football and females? Yeah, he had that down. Tilting his head, he insisted, "I hear the castle musicians. Girls, can you hear it?"

"Yes!"

"It's *loud*!"

"Then let the dancing begin." As the twins resumed an energetic ballet, Ethan looked at Gemma. "We've danced before. I'm sure it'll come back to us."

At the reference to their single awkward dance at homecoming, Gemma narrowed her gaze. "You danced with me once. Then you spent the evening with a varsity cheerleader."

Yee-ouch. He'd forgotten that part. The cheerleader hadn't intimidated him at all. Wagging his head, he figured it was time for the apology he'd been too embarrassed or too egotistical to offer her back then. "I was a punk kid, Gemma. I didn't think much beyond the moment. Or about other people's feelings."

He'd been too busy trying to protect his own. From the moment he'd arrived at Thunder Ridge High, Ethan had struggled to appear more confident than he'd felt. Actually, it was more accurate to say he'd been struggling since elementary school. His deficiencies had simply become more noticeable in high school.

Gemma Gould, on the other hand, had been the president of the National Honor Society and captain of the debate team, had started both their school's geography bowl and Spanish club and led an after-school program called Community Kids, a group that performed socially conscious acts in their own neighborhood. Hadn't she played the flute, too?

He, on the other hand, had played football and flirted with cheerleaders. When Elyse had told him Gemma needed to go to homecoming and would write an essay for him if he took her, he'd balked at first. His fall progress report had been worse than bad, however, and to keep playing football, he'd needed to pass social studies. So he'd agreed to accompany Gemma in return for an essay guaranteed to bring his grade up. When he'd picked his "date" up that night, she'd been so nervous and he'd felt so damn awkward when she'd presented him with a boutonniere that he'd started babbling about the paper she was going to help him with, and somehow the night had turned to crap really quickly. He wasn't even sure why.

Fifteen years later, he still cringed. The more uncomfortable she had seemed, the more he'd started to act like a jerk, leaving her to find her friends while he hung out with his. And when another girl—the cheerleader with grades on par with his—had asked him to dance, he'd accepted.

Gemma had paid him back but good for his behavior that night. Even though her brand of retribution had infuriated him at the time, deep down he'd figured he deserved it.

"Auntie Gem, you're not dancing!" Vivian stomped her foot, came over and tried to mash the two of them together. "You need to start dancing."

Sliding an arm around Gemma's back, Ethan pulled her body closer to his, leaving what he deemed to be a pretty respectable space between them. Still, he could feel her go rigid.

"For their sake, hmm?" he murmured, though he realized that dancing with her was a good opportunity to get the guilt monkey off his back. "About that homecoming date," he began, surprised by the nervous adrenaline that pumped through his body. He must be overtired. "I should have danced with you more. I should have danced with you the whole night." He was merely stating the truth. He'd agreed to take her; he should have behaved like a gentleman.

"Don't be ridiculous. We shouldn't have gone to homecoming together at all."

"Maybe not," he said. "But I could have behaved better. I was young. And a jerk."

Gemma stopped moving and gently pulled her hand from his. "This—" she gestured to the dance floor "—is awkward. I mean, there's no music or anything. Maybe we should—"

"Here." He pulled his phone from his pocket, tapping it a few times, and Aerosmith's "I Don't Want to Miss a Thing" began to play. The twins were delighted. He handed the phone to Vivian—despite his better judgment—and pulled Gemma toward him again.

Her head only came up to his chin, and she kept her gaze straight ahead. Because he wasn't sure what else to say at the moment, he simply danced until she murmured something he couldn't quite make out. "What's that?"

"I'm sorry about the social studies essay."

A reluctant smile curled his lips. "Don't be. Best grade I ever got."

"You were teased for weeks. That was my fault."

"True. But I forgave you." He stared at the top of her head, wishing she'd look up. "After the initial impulse to throw you into Long River."

Ethan had felt like the world's biggest jackass when his social studies teacher, Martin Oleson, had read his paper—the one Gemma had written—out loud in class. Gemma had penned a ridiculous, but grammatically correct, essay on how participating in a sport like football increased testosterone in young men and made them want sex all the time. How could they be blamed if that's all they focused on, even when they were sitting in their social studies class? The paper had gone on to propose that school funding be put toward maintaining a library of men's magazines, which would be far more useful than textbooks to retain student attention. Ethan had been mortified. His only recourse had been to brazen the moment out, laughing along with everyone else. Humiliation had been preferable to admitting he hadn't written the paper, couldn't have penned something that articulate no matter how hard he'd tried.

Gemma lifted her face, plainly revealing the guilt she felt after all this time. "I never expected you to turn it in, you know. I thought you'd look at it first and ask for an extension so you could write it yourself."

Ethan stiffened. Look at a ten-page paper twenty minutes before he had to turn the thing in? Not damn likely. "Too lazy," he lied.

Gemma frowned. "You're not lazy. You play professional sports. You won the Super Bowl. You work during the off-season and you mowed my parents' lawn every Sunday morning for five years."

The discomfort began in his gut and spread. He pasted a glib smile on his face, as he always had in moments like this. "I'm academically lazy."

"The brain is like a muscle. It grows and becomes stronger when you use it. If you ignore academics, you may as well cut your head off."

"But my face is so pretty."

Her outraged expression both shamed and amused him. Choosing to focus on the amusement, he laughed. A big dumb-jock laugh. "Calm down, Professor. We can't all belong to Mensa. Every hive needs drones."

"Oh! That is a terrible way to look at one of the greatest gifts you'll ever have—your mind."

She had no idea how ludicrous that comment was. If his mind had come with a return policy, he'd have traded it in long ago.

"How do I make another song play?" Standing beside them, Vivian tapped on his phone.

She was right; the music had stopped. He let go of Gemma. Her creamy skin reddened as she took a step back.

"Sorry," she said. "I don't know why I went on like that." She shook her head. "Sorry."

He didn't want her to be sorry. Pretending school didn't mean anything to him had always been easier than caring. That didn't mean she should lower her standards. He'd be disappointed if she did. "You're a teacher. You're supposed to be irritated by someone like me." He smiled, but it didn't change his plummeting mood. "I'd better head home."

"Home? But they're serving dinner in—"

"I can't stay. I already told Scott." Turning from Gemma to reclaim his phone from a reluctant Vivian, he tapped the little girl's nose gently with his finger. Violet presented her nose, and he tapped it, too. "I will see you two ladies tomorrow. Save me a dance."

The girls beamed. "What about Auntie Gem?" Violet inquired thoughtfully. "She likes to dance, too."

Ethan looked at Gemma, who appeared confused. "Dancing doesn't seem to agree with us," he observed softly. "Maybe tomorrow we could try again and improve our track record?"

Her smile was uncomfortable, but she nodded. "See you at the wedding."

With a tip of his head, he strode from the ballroom, reminding himself that this part of his life—this crazy time with a baby in his house and more contact with people from his past than he usually had—would be over soon. This summer, he'd return to training camp, which was, at least, a world he understood. Being glib worked there. He'd be able to keep things light and…what had Vivian said? Easy-peasy-lemon-squeezy. Which was how he liked his life.

He would stop thinking about Gemma Gould and her intimidating brain. And her calming presence. And her beautiful awkwardness.

They were oil and water, and even he knew that combo didn't mix. Sometimes, though, when Ethan was with Gemma and there were few other people around, he had the strangest sensation that, for once, he wasn't alone.

The next evening, Gemma felt like a plump pink sausage in a bridesmaid's gown clearly meant to be worn by a woman several inches taller and at least two cup sizes smaller. Women like Elyse's other ten attendants, for example.

Seated at the long bridal table amid the rest of the exquisite wedding party, Gemma felt restless. Ethan was to her right, currently engaged in discussing football with the other groomsmen. As discreetly as she could, she reached beneath her armpits and gave the strapless bodice of her fuchsia gown a healthy tug. Oh, was she going to be glad when the final kernel of birdseed was thrown and the happy couple drove away in their glossy white limo. Despite her sister's constantly voiced worries, the ceremony had been perfect, and the reception was under way without a hitch. Still, seated at the elegantly appointed table while servers poured wine from vintage labels and placed dishes of *filet en croûte* before the laughing guests, Gemma couldn't help but feel twinges of grief.

She frowned, idly plucking chia seeds off her housemade soft breadstick. Her own wedding, had it not been called off, would have been last month. A full year and a half before the date, she'd already chosen her gown (winsome chiffon skirt, no train), her location (on the beach in Manzanita) and the food (casual-but-authentic Mexican— crab-and-tomatillo quesadillas, street tacos, carnitas… yum). She and William would have had only one attendant each, and her four-year-old nephew could have worn a pair of swim trunks and his favorite Ninja Turtle floatie instead of the toddler tux he kept trying to struggle out of tonight.

"Whoa, what did that breadstick ever do to you?"

Ethan's bemused voice jerked Gemma's attention to the crumbles of bread over the table. "Dang." She wiped bread crumbs off the white linen and into her palm, depositing the mess on her bread plate as a waiter placed her dinner in front of her. "Thank you." She smiled at the server, then looked glumly at her meal. Pastry-covered filet mignon, wild mushrooms and Yukon gold potatoes in a dill-and-Gruyère cream sauce and an individual spinach soufflé— there had to be three thousand calories on that plate.

While everyone around her tucked in, Gemma mentally calculated the odds of living long enough to hook a man and become a mother if her heart was pumping dill sauce through her veins.

"Something wrong?" Ethan spoke close to her ear.

She glanced at him. *Men*, she thought, but didn't say out loud. *Men are the problem.* In a dove-gray tuxedo that perfectly complemented his golden hair and tanned skin, Ethan had already drawn more attention than the bride. Betcha he could go home with any number of women tonight. Some of the willing ones were probably married. Love was too difficult for some and too easy for others.

"This food is a little rich," she said.

"Aw, no. Don't tell me you're one of those." He wagged his head tragically.

"One of what?"

"Bird women. The ones who barely taste their food and don't take it to go, because they don't have a dog, and there's no way they're going to eat anything more interesting than a celery stick, anyway."

Gemma gaped at him. "You're kidding, right? Do I *look* as if all I eat is celery?"

Apparently, he took her words as an invitation to let his gaze roam leisurely over the parts of her he could see while she was seated. He even leaned back a smidgen, as if he was trying to get a look at her bottom. When she glared at him, he grinned.

"You look good." He nodded to her dinner. "Eat up."

"I've seen your girlfriends," she said. "Three of them standing together wouldn't fill out a pair of size-eight jeans."

"You keep track of the women I date?"

"Of course not." She managed to sound highly offended. "My mother buys gossip magazines when you're in them."

He grinned. "I know. She has me autograph them when

I'm in town. Between you and me, I think she's selling them on eBay." He nodded, sliced off more meat, chewed, then tried the cheesy potatoes. Gemma's stomach growled. She picked up her fork and was about to give in to temptation when he observed, "So you read about me when you come home on weekends, then. I'm flattered."

Abruptly, she retracted her fork. "That is not what I mean. My mother likes to discuss topics of interest to *her*. She shows me the magazine articles. I don't seek them out." *Ooh, liar, liar, pants on fire.* Raising her chin, she amended, "I have never bought a rag mag."

That was true, actually. If she saw Ethan on the cover of a magazine, she would read it while standing in line at the market. No money ever transferred hands.

"From what I've seen," she told him, "you prefer to date women whose physical attributes directly correlate to the norm in print and other media. A norm that is dangerously out of touch with a standard attainable for the average healthy American woman."

He reached for another breadstick—his third—and lathered it with the sweet Irish butter Elyse had requested. "Could you say that again? In English this time, Professor."

"You date skeletons!" She wanted his breadstick so badly she nearly grabbed it out of his hand. For the past two months, Elyse had begged her to diet. Her best efforts had led to a loss of four measly pounds, which would be back again before breakfast tomorrow. She needed food. She wanted food.

The breadstick, gorgeously buttered, hovered between them. She pointed. "Are you going to eat that?"

Flashing his most gorgeous smile, he held it out. "I'm happy to share. And happy you're going to eat. I like you the way you are."

Unexpectedly her heart filled the hole in her stomach. He liked her. The way she was.

Don't get carried away. He offered you a breadstick, not a diamond ring. Who could blame her, though, if after a lifetime of being the "smart" sister, it felt good to have a man like Ethan pay her a compliment?

Accepting the breadstick, she took a ladylike bite. *Mmm, yummy.*

"Why didn't you get married, Gemma?"

Coughing as the breadstick paused in her windpipe, she took a slug of wine. "What do you mean?" she asked when she could talk again.

Ethan's blue eyes narrowed thoughtfully. "Elyse and Scott came to Seattle for a home game and mentioned you were engaged. Had the rock and everything."

Swell. She poked at the beef *en croûte.* "I wonder how they cook this steak without burning the pastry?" she mused aloud to change the subject.

"Too personal?" The deep dimple in his left cheek appeared. "Even for old friends like us?"

Gemma held her hands up in surrender. "Okay. Yes, I was engaged. We were supposed to have gotten married last month, but we called it off. End of story." *Sort of.*

"Your wedding was supposed to have been last month?" He whistled beneath his breath.

"It's fine. We ended it a long time ago." Shrugging blithely, she sawed at the beef.

"How long?"

"Almost a year."

He considered that. "How are you doing tonight?"

It wasn't the question that made Gemma set her knife and fork to the side of her plate, but rather his tone. How was she doing? He'd asked it so plainly, no hesitation, no lurking reluctance to hear the answer. Most of her family, except for her mother, tiptoed around the topic as if it were a land mine. "I'm all right," she answered quietly. "But sometimes I wish—"

"Ethan Ladd, you'd better save me a dance tonight." A hand glittering with rings clamped Ethan's shoulder. "I haven't seen you in so long, I almost forgot what you looked like." Throaty laughter punctuated the statement as a platinum blonde with long straight hair crouched beside them in a sequin-encrusted dress that hugged her body so tightly a bead of perspiration couldn't have fit between the material and her skin.

"You remember me, don't you? Crystal McEvoy." She batted outrageously fake lashes. "Senior year prom? Best date of your life?"

Ethan turned his head slowly to observe Crystal. "Sure, I remember you." He leaned back and draped an arm at the back of Gemma's chair. "You know Gemma Gould?"

"Hi." Predictably, Crystal glanced at Gemma only long enough to appear polite, then shifted her attention back to Ethan. "You save a dance for me." She put a hand on his thigh, obviously trying to lay claim to a lot more than a dance. "We can pick up where we left off." Crystal trailed her fingers over Ethan's chest and shoulder before she walked back to her table, swaying her hips the entire way.

"Where were we?" Behaving as if the previous moment hadn't happened, Ethan looked at her, not Crystal.

Whoa. Was he going to ignore the fact that he'd practically been groped by a woman he hadn't seen in a decade and a half? "Uhm…" She couldn't remember what they'd been discussing prior to the other woman's arrival.

"You were telling me about your engagement," he prompted.

Talk about being dumped by her fiancé after that exhibition? Not happening.

Crystal's perfume lingered in the air, but it wasn't strong enough to overpower Ethan's pheromones. Gemma had always known when Ethan was at her parents' house, even if she'd just walked in the door. Everything about the house changed. It smelled like soap and aftershave and…him. Like right now.

"You okay?" Ethan asked as the bride and groom's first dance wound down. "You look flushed."

"You're right, it's hot in here." She waved her hands at her face.

"It's probably not any cooler on the dance floor, but you want to give it a try?"

Dance? With her and not Crystal or one of the bachelorette bridesmaids? Gemma felt as if the hottest guy in school had just asked her to homecoming—genuinely this time.

"Oh, Gemma, good, you're done eating!" Her sister Lucy appeared at the banquet table, bouncing baby Owen in her arms. "Hi, Ethan," she greeted. "Gem, they're about to open the dancing, and Rick and I haven't danced without the kids practically since *our* wedding. Would you hold Owen while I get out there with my husband? Pretty please?"

Lucy was indescribably lovely, with translucent ivory skin, a dancer-like long neck and shiny dark hair she wore simply in a perfect bun. She did look tired, though.

With a rueful glance at Ethan, she replied, "Sure," even though she thought she might tear up in disappointment.

Lucy blew her an air kiss. "You're a peach." She beamed at Ethan. "She's such a peach. Okay, baby boy, over the table and into Auntie Gem's arms." An old pro at handing off kids, Lucy didn't bother to walk around the table; she merely passed Owen over the stemware. "He's fed and dry. We'll just dance to a couple of songs. Thank you, thank you," she said sincerely as she sped to her husband.

Gemma dangled the eight-month-old above her lap. The baby tried to grab her nose.

"Nasa-fa!" he said.

She turned to Ethan. "That's Owen-speak for 'nose.'"

"Quite the conversationalist." Ethan nodded, but didn't smile. And now Crystal was wriggling their way.

"Oh, Ethan," she sang.

"Come on." Abruptly taking her arm, Ethan helped her to her feet.

"Where are we going?"

"For a walk."

Guiding her past an unhappy Crystal, whom he didn't even acknowledge, Ethan led them out of the ballroom. With Lucy's baby in her arms and Ethan's hand firmly beneath her elbow, Gemma felt less like a maiden aunt and more like—just for a wee sec—a wife and mommy. Thinking about the man beside her cast in the role of loving husband and baby daddy, she realized how easily that fantasy could become a habit.

Chapter Four

As Ethan propelled Gemma away from the reception, he could practically feel the tension drain from his body. The noise, the crowd, the many pairs of eyes not-so-covertly trained on him—it made stepping through the broad double doors feel like freedom.

Up a short flight of stairs sat a private alcove and a hearth crackling with a lively fire. With a hand resting lightly at Gemma's lower back, Ethan steered her toward an overstuffed love seat.

"Here?" He made the pretense of asking, but was already loosening his tie.

"Perfect." Sinking onto the cushions, she kicked off her high heels and tucked the burbling baby into her lap. Her feet were bare, toenails some wild shade of neon orange with sparkly stars, and he couldn't help but smile as she curled them over the edge of the coffee table. Even her feet were fun.

Sitting beside her, Ethan made himself comfortable and propped an ankle on his knee. "How old is this guy?"

"Owen is eight months old today, aren't you, old man?" Gemma bounced the baby on her legs, smiling as he shrieked with joy.

"He's cute." The compliment sounded lame, but until recently his experience with babies had been limited to his teammates' kids. He'd admired them from a safe distance when they were infants, enjoyed them more once they were old enough to roughhouse or to joke around with. Now that a baby had been dropped into his own lap...hell, he was half convinced they were aliens.

"So, uh, how long before these little guys settle down?" he asked.

"Settle down?"

"Yeah, you know, when do they stop crying?"

Gemma laughed. "Gee, I don't know, maybe when they're eighteen?"

He felt like an idiot. "Okay, when do they stop crying 24/7?" For the last two months, he had witnessed misery personified as his sickly, scrawny nephew struggled to adjust to...pretty much everything.

Gemma didn't immediately answer, seeming to give his question serious thought. "What's the baby's name again?"

"Cody."

"You've taken him to the pediatrician?" she asked.

"Of course," he snapped, then ducked his head. "Sorry. I didn't mean to sound defensive, but we've been to the pediatrician four times." He was afraid he must be doing every damn thing wrong, or why wouldn't the screaming have, at the very least, lessened by now? "The last two times, I went to Portland for second and third opinions. They all say the same thing."

"And that is?" Gemma asked softly.

The very thing he didn't want broadcast all over Thunder Ridge. Ethan dragged his free hand over his mouth and considered Gemma. He didn't understand why, but somehow he knew he could trust her with the whole story. "The baby I'm taking care of is my nephew."

"Samantha had a baby?" She posed the question matter-of-factly, neither surprised nor appalled, which he appreciated.

"Yeah. I'm sure you remember from high school that Sam had a drug problem. Still does." His sister and Gemma had been in the same class, though Gemma had hung out with the brainy crowd while Sam had been part of the Goth scene. Spent most of her school lunch hours under the bleachers getting stoned.

"I'm so sorry," Gemma murmured, her hand rhythmically circling Owen's back. "Was Samantha's baby born addicted?"

Ethan could tell the compassion in her voice was the real thing, not some fabricated platitude meant to blanket her curiosity. He nodded. More and more often, he felt rage rise when he talked about it. "He's a crack baby. And he's having a pretty tough time getting through withdrawal."

"That's so hard. On both of you," she commiserated. "But there is actually some good news. I've read about this. Over the years people have found that, even though the first weeks and months can be hellish, crack babies generally thrive over time. Developmentally, they have just as much potential as anyone else. Much more than a baby whose mother drank during pregnancy."

Her confidence ignited a tiny spark of hope—the first he'd felt. The folks at DHS had said something similar, but coming from Gemma, he believed it. "How do you know about this stuff? Aren't you an English teacher?"

"Yep. And I had an exceptionally bright student who

did his master's thesis on his personal experience born as a crack baby. The paper was so good I asked him to read parts of it to the class. There wasn't a dry eye in the room when he was done."

One of the pediatricians had handed Ethan a thick photocopied study on drug-addicted infants. The papers had been less than useless to Ethan. The social worker had asked him to attend classes on babies and children whose development was interrupted, but as soon as Ethan had heard the word *class*, he'd made up an excuse to wriggle out. And so every time the baby cried, he felt the heavy weight of fear and failure. His sister had destined her son to a jagged, painful beginning, and Ethan's own short-comings made him worry that his nephew didn't stand a chance.

Gemma's story about her student gave him a glimmer of hope. He was hungry to know more.

Owen grew suddenly cranky, and she dangled him so that he was dancing on her lap.

"That student of yours," he ventured. "He's really… smart, is he?"

"Absolutely. He's one of the brightest stars in our lit program. Try not to worry too much." The smile she sent Ethan shot warmth straight to his heart. Smoothing a wild patch of hair at the back of Owen's head, she offered, "This little guy here had colic for the first two months. Lucy had to ask my mother more than once to come rescue her and Rick in the middle of the night when they were too exhausted to see straight. I helped out on weekends, too, and let me tell you, this guy could have taken down Super-nanny. Now he's the picture of health. Right, buddy boy?"

Owen blew a wet raspberry, slapping her arms with glee. When she nuzzled the baby's neck, his giggles rang out and his feet pumped like pistons.

Ethan wished he could be half as successful with Cody as she was with Owen. He'd never pictured himself with a child, not his own and certainly not anyone else's. His early years hadn't taught him about the care of kids.

"Anyway," he said now, dragging himself away from his fascination with Gemma's instinctive parenting skills, "I hope you're right. I've burned through two nannies already. The third one phoned during dinner just now, sounding miserable and wondering where to find fresh batteries for the baby swing."

"Two already quit?"

"Cody's crying can wake the dead." Even he wasn't sure he could take three more months of sleepless nights and ringing ears.

As if the word *cry* was a cue, Owen clouded up and got weepy. Gemma must have noted the dread on Ethan's face, because she explained quickly, "He's looking for his mama. I can always tell by the way he tries to cram his fist into his mouth." Rooting in the diaper bag, she came up with a bottle. "This should do the trick for a little while."

Not only did Owen stop crying, his eyelids closed. Disbelieving, Ethan blurted, "Why don't you have kids? You're great with them."

She grinned. "All I did was give him a bottle."

"No. You're a natural with babies, and your nieces are crazy about you. You're the Pied Piper. Do you want any of your own?"

The grin dropped before she forced it back. Laughing awkwardly, she asked, "Any of my own what? Rats or babies?" Her gaze flew to his, then skittered away equally quickly. "That was Pied Piper humor," she mumbled.

He saw it then—the flash of pain in her eyes, the tightening around her mouth. He'd touched on a sore spot, one that was obviously none of his business and that she'd prefer to avoid. Ordinarily, Ethan happily steered clear of personal topics. That way, he could justify keeping his own life private. Plus, he didn't like messy emotional moments. Not his thing. Even now, he could feel his cortisol spike in response to the thought of Gemma being hurt. Tallying his options, he counted two: A) rescind the question; or B) make a glib, distracting comment and pretend the moment hadn't happened.

He chose option C.

"So who called off the wedding? You or your fiancé?"

Gemma felt herself blanch. "Wait. How did we get back to that topic?"

"Before Crystal interrupted us," Ethan persisted, "you were going to tell me more about your fiancé." He gave her the look that *People* magazine, in its "100 Most Beautiful People" issue, had said "could charm a hungry boa constrictor." "Anyone you were going to marry must be a pretty interesting guy. But I'm guessing you called it off."

She wanted to lie. Oh, boy, did she ever. Swirling her fingers in the downy curls on her nephew's head, she equivocated. "What makes you think so?"

"You're picky." Eyes narrowed, he attempted to wow her with his powers of clairvoyance. "My guess? The day you went to look at wedding dresses, you had a hard time choosing something, and suddenly you realized your indecisiveness about the dress reflected how you felt about your fiancé. He was a smart guy, nice enough, but you knew you couldn't live with the way he ate corn on the cob."

At that, she actually laughed. "Corn on the cob?"

"Absolutely."

"Really. How did he eat it?"

"Like this." Ethan mimed a beaver gnawing on an ear of corn as if it were stripping a log. Gemma laughed again, harder, and he grinned back. "You knew every summer it would be the same thing—ol' Beaver Boy and his corn. You couldn't stand the thought. Not to mention how you felt about the bedtime toenail clipping."

"Eew!"

"Exactly."

His grin seemed to make her bones melt. Realizing that Owen was falling asleep, she shifted to a cradle hold while she gathered her thoughts. "The woman at the bridal salon said I chose my wedding dress faster than anyone who had ever shopped there."

"Ah. Not picky, then?"

"I wasn't picky enough, I think."

She said it so softly, she wasn't 100 percent certain he heard her until he said, "You were the one who called it off, then?" Unbuttoning the collar stud at his throat, he settled back to listen.

"No. William, my fiancé, decided he needed to make a big change in his life."

"What kind of change?"

Realizing that pride and the truth were not always compatible, she admitted, "A change of fiancées."

He swore under his breath.

"Yeah. Especially since I work with them both. William is a math professor, and Christine Marie Allard teaches French. She's the object of desire for the entire Easton College male population. Probably some of the female population, too. Lucky me, I get to see her and William eat off the same salad bar plate in the café during lunch. I snitched a bite of his vegan burrito once, and he said he thought that was 'unwise during flu season.'"

"Sounds like William needs to be slapped around."

She shrugged. "I brown-bag it now so I won't have to look at them."

"And he's engaged to Mademoiselle Allard?"

"Not yet. But he came to my office before the end of spring quarter to let me know they're headed in that direction. He didn't want me to be surprised, because that wouldn't be 'thoughtful.'"

Ethan let the silence linger a moment before venturing, "Were you in love?"

"In love enough, I thought."

"What does that mean?"

"You were right, I want children. William said he wanted at least three kids. We agreed about politics and that we wanted home with a fenced yard and a chocolate Lab named Atticus. I thought we were in sync."

Carefully, so he didn't disturb Owen's sleep, Ethan stretched his arm along the back of the sofa. "Atticus is a dweeb name for a Labrador retriever."

She jerked in surprise. "It is not."

"Is too. Labradors are a sporting breed. No self-respecting Lab wants to be named Atticus."

A smile poked at her mouth. "Mine would have."

He touched the dimple that always appeared just to the left side of her lower lip when she smiled. The contact lasted about a millisecond, but she knew she was going to feel it the rest of the night. Her bare toes curled over the side of the coffee table. *Dang.*

"He wasn't good enough for you," Ethan murmured, voice like a stroke of velvet against her cheek.

Double dang.

She adjusted Owen's tiny suit. "You think so?"

"I know so. You dodged a bullet." The air was fragrant with the subtle scents of cologne and baby and crackling wood. The buzz of Ethan's cell phone relieved Gemma of the need to figure out what to say next. Reaching into his jacket pocket, he glanced at the picture on the screen, then said, "Excuse me. I'd better take this."

She expected him to get up and walk away for privacy, but he stayed put, the phone to his ear. "Okay, take a deep breath," he said after a moment. "Have you turned on the lullaby CD?...He doesn't hate it. It—it just takes a while..." He rubbed his eyes. "I understand that he can be difficult, but you told me you have experience with—...All right, all right. I can't leave right now, but I—...Within a half hour, forty-five minutes at the max."

Gemma rubbed slow circles over Owen's back as Ethan wound up his call. She kept her gaze averted, trying to be discreet, though her curiosity ran rampant. When he got off the phone and slipped it back into his pocket, she hoped he'd tell her whether the call was from someone taking care of Cody, as she suspected, but he merely looked at her regretfully. "I may have to leave sooner than planned. I'd better get back to the reception and make my toast to the happy couple."

Disappointment thudded in her chest as their personal moment dissolved.

It wasn't all that personal, she told herself pragmatically. *He only asked you to take a break from the reception with him, not take out a thirty-year mortgage.* "I'll come with you," she said. "I have to give my speech, too."

She rose nimbly with Owen in her arms, but wriggling her feet back into her mile-high shoes proved more of a challenge. The long gown kept getting in her way.

"Here, let me help." Kneeling, he steadied her shoe with one hand, holding the back of her bare ankle with the other as he guided her into her high heel.

His intention was simply to help—she knew that—but she sensed instantly when "help" turned into *holy moly.*

Did he realize goose bumps were racing up her legs? *Oh, crumbs... I'm going to giggle.*

To save her dignity, this process had to be interrupted. "Thanks. I can get the other one mySELF!" The last syllable became a yelp as he reached for her other foot.

"Put one hand on my head to steady yourself," he told her. "Can you manage that with the baby?"

"Sure," she squeaked, transferring Owen to her hip and doing as he directed. His fingers curled around her ankle, and she gulped. His hair was as thick as her own. And it was sort of springy, with a wave. And she kind of accidentally delved into his hair a little as he slid her foot into the shoe.

Looking up, he flashed her the grin he'd perfected over the years. "Back to the ball, Cinderella?"

No, thank you. I'm perfectly fine staying here the rest of my life. But she nodded.

Careful not to walk too near him and utterly incapable of making conversation, she pretended a need to fuss with the baby, who was perfectly content to gnaw on her shoulder. The middle of Gemma's chest began to hurt. Why? Frustration? Grief, because when she went home tonight there would be no man to help her put anything on...or take anything off?

The deep ache sliced through her again. Maybe it was longing. She didn't begrudge anyone the joy of love and family, but she was getting mighty tired of waiting for her own turn. And maybe, just maybe, she thought as she held Owen closer, it was time she did something about it.

"I can't do this!" Slamming closed the heavy textbook in front of him, Ethan pounded his fist on the dining table. *"I'm stupid. I'm the dumbest kid in my class. I'm the dumbest one in the whole fifth grade. I hate school!"*

Picking up the social studies book, he threw it across the room, where it hit his mother's wooden Families Are Forever plaque, knocking it to the floor. Drawn by the commotion, Marci Ladd ran in from the kitchen, wiping her hands on a dish towel, her expression concerned but not surprised.

One look at the worry in his mom's eyes filled Ethan with crushing guilt. His uncle had told him and his sister not to give their mom any trouble right now. She'd been sick—the having-to-go-to-the-hospital kind of sick—almost all year, and she didn't need more problems. But Samantha was getting into trouble all the time, and Ethan...

"What's wrong with me?" Leaning forward over the table, he thumped his head on his folded arms and mumbled, "Sorry."

His mother's slender fingers curled around his shoulder. He could feel her trembling. She did that a lot now, as if she was no longer strong enough to control her own body. "There is nothing wrong with you. You learn differently, and the school hasn't figured out how to help you yet." She stroked his hair. "They're still learning, too. But you're fine. The coolest, funniest, kindest boy I know. And you run faster than anyone in school."

Instantly, love overwhelmed Ethan's other feelings. He dived toward his mom, wrapping his arms around her waist and hanging on like some dumb little kid while tears clogged his throat and spilled from his eyes no matter how tightly he shut them. "Don't leave, Mom."

She laughed, squeezing him in return. "Don't be silly. Where would I go without you and your sister? You and Sami are my favorite people to be with."

For a second, Ethan relaxed, but then the screaming started.

"Oh, my." His mother set him away from her, turning toward the sound with an almost robotic reaction. *"That must be your sister. Why does she do that, I wonder?"*

Ethan reached toward his mother, but when his fingers curled around her wrist, she seemed to slip from his grasp as if she were nothing more than ether. *"Don't leave,"* he pleaded again.

"Maybe she's hungry. Have either of you eaten today? I have some asparagus."

"Mom, please don't go."

His sister wailed like a banshee in the background. It actually hurt Ethan's ears. *"Shut up, Samantha,"* he shouted to her. *"Stop screaming!"*

Marci rounded on him. *"How dare you talk to your sister that way!"* Suddenly, her face wasn't sweetly concerned; it was furious and frightening. With eyes that looked dark and haunted and her lips drawn back, she snarled, *"You're ten for crying out loud. You're supposed to take care of her. Maybe if you'd fed her, this wouldn't be happening."*

The screams grew deafening. Marci disappeared from the room abruptly—there one second, gone the next. Ethan wanted to find her, but his feet wouldn't move, so he remained where he was, using all his strength to call out, *"I'll get her something to eat, Mom! Come back! I'll make her something right now—"*

As he awoke from the miserable dream, Ethan's leg jerked, making contact with Cody's crib. The already-piercing screams from Samantha's son intensified, and Ethan became aware of pain in his head as he awoke from the bad dream.

Sitting up in the chair he'd moved to what was now the nursery, Ethan felt the pain beneath his skull pound in rhythm with Cody's angry sobs.

"All right, buddy," Ethan said in the most soothing tone he could manage at two in the morning. Still groggy, he looked into the crib with a feeling he could define only as absolute fear. Cody's red face was screwed into an expression of rage. Nothing new there, but the inability to help—at all—filled him with dread.

Cody's inconsolable misery was the reason Ethan had asked each nanny he'd hired to live in, 24/7. It was also why they kept quitting.

Awkwardly, he fumbled with the baby's blankets for the umpteenth time tonight. "What happened, huh? You were asleep for a half hour. I thought we were on a roll."

He picked the baby up, knowing what was coming and trying not to wince. But, yep, the moment Ethan's large hands scooped beneath the little body, Cody went rigid, the decibel level in the room doubling.

With difficulty, Ethan exhausted the same checklist he went through every time. First, as Cody's fists and feet flailed, he checked his nephew's diaper. Then he warmed a bottle, walked the baby, jiggled the baby, turned on a CD, turned off the CD. Nothing worked. The most recent pediatrician visit had determined Cody's ears were fine, and he was nowhere near teething, so that wasn't the problem.

Finally, Ethan broke out in a sick sweat.

"Dude," he said raggedly, "I'm so, so sorry. I wish I knew what to do." With a feeling of loneliness and isolation he hadn't experienced since he was a kid, he lowered his head in exhaustion. "Dear God, what am I going to do?"

Opening his eyes at his uncle, Cody inhaled sharply, his brow furrowed, almost as if he'd heard the question and was giving it some thought. After a moment, however, his response to Ethan's plea was a shriek that threatened to shatter the windows.

With defeat threatening to engulf him, Ethan finally had an idea, and it afforded him a tiny glimmer of hope as he realized there actually was one more thing he could try.

Chapter Five

Ethan lived out of town a ways, on the other side of Ponderosa Avenue, tucked into the foothills. Gemma knew he'd built a spectacular bachelor pad that had been the talk of the town and had even been featured in *Architectural Digest*. Nothing, however, prepared her for the stunning log-and-river-rock dream that greeted her at the end of a quarter-mile, tree-lined drive.

Parking near the front of the house, she craned her neck to take in a wall of windows that rose two stories. "Wowsers."

It was barely 7:00 a.m. the morning after the wedding. At 6:00 a.m., her mother had awakened her, handing her the cordless house phone. Sleepy and confused, she'd sat up in bed, put the phone to her ear with her eyes closed and heard, "Gemma? I'm sorry I'm calling this early. Really sorry. I—I'm in trouble here. Can you come to my place?"

A baby's plaintive sobs had underscored Ethan's fatigue-roughened voice.

Deciding to act first and ask questions later, Gemma got his address, placated her rabidly curious mother with a promise to tell her *later* what was going on, then dressed quickly in pink pedal pushers and a short-sleeved blouse she knotted at her waist and headed to the local bakery, Something Sweet, where she ordered bagels, almond–poppy seed muffins and two coffees to go.

Now, as she maneuvered out of her car with breakfast and stepped onto the stone walkway leading to the house, she hoped she hadn't been dreaming and was actually about to embarrass the devil out of herself.

Ethan answered the doorbell looking as if he'd just been tackled by a weed-whacker.

"Thank God," he breathed, mopping at a blob of spit-up that adorned his T-shirt. "Come in. I just laid him down, and he's freaking."

On cue, Cody unleashed a squall that could have tossed ships at sea.

"Where's your nanny?" Gemma asked, crossing the threshold into a grand foyer.

"Number three tore out of here like a bat out of hell last night. She won't be back."

"Oh. Wow." The blue eyes and smile that had charmed a legion of women were dull and exhausted now. Gemma's attention was divided between Cody's squall, Ethan's agitation and her surroundings. Everywhere she looked, the house spoke of Ethan's success and the current chaos.

A soaring log ceiling supported enormous wrought iron chandeliers, and a double staircase curved like a parentheses toward a second-floor bridge, but on those stairs lay baby-sized blankets and towels and toys that appeared to have been dropped and left. Before them on the first floor, a beveled-glass-and-wood-trimmed hallway directed them into the great room beneath.

"He's in here," Ethan said as he led her to an immense, professionally decorated space. More toys, a box of diapers that had been ripped open and assorted laundry littered their path.

He led her straight to a crib he'd set up incongruently in the center of the large room. Appointed with an elaborate mobile and premium bedding, the crib was a luxe nest for the baby who screamed from its depths.

Over a river-rock fireplace, a flat-screen TV approximately the length of a compact car played a children's show that competed with the baby's hollering. "The baby sleeps in here?" she asked, trying not to sound disapproving.

"No. Cody has his own room. I got another crib for in here, because..." Ethan raised a hand and swirled it in the air as if he were about to say something profound, then he ended on a helpless, "I don't know. I thought he might like it better."

That was cute. "Did either of you sleep at all last night?"

"I nodded off once."

Ethan wore an expression of such utter defeat on his beautiful, drained face that she wished she could hug him without it seeming awkward. She settled for a heartfelt, "I'm so sorry," offering a sympathetic smile, then setting the coffees and treats she'd brought on a huge coffee table in front of the half U–shaped sofa. Returning to the crib, she bent to retrieve the red-faced baby from his bed. "Hey, you," she cooed, albeit loudly enough to be heard above the noise. "I bet you're a tired boy."

Cody looked at her, arched his back and howled.

Ethan plunged a hand through his hair. "Sounds like he's trying to summon a werewolf."

"Is that what you're doing, little man?" Gemma cocked her head. "I think you don't like all this light. And all this air. And all this noise." To Ethan she said, "I need a receiving blanket. And could you turn off the TV? And most of these lights." The room was awash in what appeared to be light from every source in the house.

"Sure." He picked up a remote and the TV fell silent. "I thought he might be bored, so I turned it on." An app on his phone must have been connected to the lights, because they dimmed considerably at the touch of his screen. "What's a receiving blanket?"

"Thin? Soft. Flannel?"

"Oh, yeah. I think there is a stack of those." He moved to the couch and riffled through a pile of unfolded laundry until he found what he was looking for. "This it?"

Gemma nodded. "Yup. Spread it out for me right there, will you?" She nodded to the sofa cushion.

While he did as she asked, Gemma checked the baby's diaper. Dry. That was good. And kind of impressive. Ethan must have changed him at some point. Or at several points. "Has he had any formula recently?"

"I tried fifteen minutes ago. He didn't want it."

"Okay." Pointing to a cushion next to the receiving blanket, she suggested, "Why don't you sit over there and watch."

"What am I watching?"

"A lesson in swaddling 101."

"I don't know what you just said."

She smiled. "That's okay. It'll be clear in a minute." As Ethan settled on the cushion, she laid the crying baby with his head pointed to one corner of the blanket. Fortunately, he was too wiped out from lack of sleep to protest much physically. Then she took his arms, crossed them over his chest and followed up by wrapping one side of the blanket at a time very tightly over his body, mummy-style. The last corner was at his feet. Nimbly, she twisted it several times, tucking the end in at his neck, then pressed the bundled baby to her chest and held him close with both hands. The technique had worked brilliantly with her nieces and nephews, but Cody was a baby with a different set of issues altogether. His poor little body grew rigid when he cried, and as Gemma pressed him closer and made what she hoped were soothing shushing sounds in his tiny ear, she worried that she was out of her league here and had given an exhausted Ethan false hope.

With deep inhalations and exhalations, she relaxed her own body, letting Cody feel her slow rhythmic breaths. Almost before she realized it, the cries turned to whimpers and then…

Silence.

Ethan half rose. "Is he still breathing?" Getting all the way to his feet, the big man peered down at his nephew. "Is he getting air? You've got him locked in there pretty tight."

Gemma rolled her eyes. "Shh. This is swaddling. Of course he's getting air." She kept her voice calm and even. "Aren't you, big guy? You feel mighty fine."

Cody made little snuffling sounds as his lips worked, and his eyes slid to half-mast. Gemma had to restrain herself from punching the air in victory. Very gently, she rubbed slow circles between the baby's shoulders. Lowering her voice to barely above a whisper, she explained, "The theory behind this wrapping style comes from the idea that before birth, babies are used to being held very tightly in the womb. When they're born, some babies have a problem with sensory overload. Too much light, smell or sound, or even their arms and legs being free, makes them anxious. So you bundle them up like this, turn out the lights, then sit in a rocker, like your fancy recliner over there, and hold the baby close enough to hear your heartbeat. Like this."

Gingerly, she moved to a leather recliner large enough

for two adults and lowered herself and Cody to its cushy depths, turning the baby to his side so that his ear lay over her heart. As she cupped his head in her hand and slowly rocked, she could feel the remaining tension leave his little body in several shuddering sighs.

"It's a miracle," Ethan breathed, staring in disbelief.

"Actually, it's more biology than anything." Though she believed that, she couldn't help but revel in Ethan's admiration.

"Don't move," he said, wagging his head. "Ever again."

Gemma chuckled. "Don't worry. You'll be a pro at this in no time. Just remember to hold him tight and close to your body." A thought occurred to her. "Like a football."

"Okay, I may be able to do *that*."

"Just don't spike him," she teased, gratified when Ethan cracked a smile that made him look more like himself. For the first time since she'd arrived, he seemed to be taking full breaths.

Moving to the sofa, he sat and seemed to notice for the first time the cardboard container with coffees and the snacks she'd picked up at the bakery. "Where'd this come from?"

"I brought it in with me."

"You did?" He ran a hand through his hair, and Gemma entertained herself by studying the way it curled over his ears. "I didn't even see that. I'm losing it."

"You're understandably distracted," she comforted, rocking as Cody gave the occasional small, reflexive jerk on his way to sleep. "And probably as exhausted as Cody. I brought coffee and something for breakfast, but I'm guessing you could use a hot shower and sleep more than caffeine. Why don't you get some rest? I'm free today. I can stay awhile."

Shock preceded gratitude, but he shook his head. "No, I couldn't—"

"I know, I know. You don't want to inconvenience me, blah, blah, blah." She smiled. "Listen, my day will consist either of sitting here in the Barbie Dreamhouse, rocking a baby and looking at Thunder Ridge—million-dollar view, by the way—or keeping track of how many place settings Elyse and Scott get as they open their gifts, and we eat leftover wedding cake. Guess which one I choose?"

He wagged his head, a look of wonder on his still gorgeous but infinitely tired features. "Wow. You're remarkable, you know that?"

He was leaning forward, elbows on knees, hands clasped loosely between his legs, his gaze intent and wondering. Gemma had a moment of dizzying déjà vu. As far back as high school, she'd pictured herself rocking a baby someday under the watchful eye of the man who loved them both. Now, moving slowly back and forth as Cody breathed against her, she felt for a second that all this was real. That it belonged to her.

Danger! Danger! This is not your life. You need to get your own baby...home...man. Possibly, but not necessarily, in that order.

"You should go," she told Ethan, "while he's sleeping." *And while I'm still sort of sane.* "Get some rest. Cody and I are fine."

Ethan rubbed his forehead. "I feel guilty leaving you here."

Soooo cute.

"No. Don't feel guilty. You'll be useless without rest." *Although I could think of some uses—*

Stop!

He scooted to the edge of the table, still leaning forward, his squared shoulders appearing massive, his face a study in solemnity and beauty as his gaze held hers. "As long as I've known your family, you've been a giver. I don't want to take advantage of that. But I sure can use your help right now."

She couldn't. Even. Speak. A jerky nod was the best Gemma could do. Her eyes followed him as he rose.

"I'll take a quick nap. Then I'm going to think of a way to repay you."

"'Kay."

He took a last look at his now-peaceful nephew, shook his head in wonder, gave Gemma a grateful smile and left the room.

With her hand cupped behind Cody's downy head, Gemma closed her eyes and sank into the soft cushion of the recliner. She smelled baby and expensive leather. And Ethan.

Repay me, she thought, somewhat bemused. How funny that he wanted to repay her for what was undoubtedly the most blissful moment she'd had in years.

Gemma was busy for the three hours that Ethan slept. By 11:00 a.m. she'd tidied the kitchen, changed and fed the Codester, prepared a killer three-decker turkey-avocado-and-cream-cheese sandwich, set a place at the ginormous breakfast bar and, most important, figured out how to turn a sheet into a baby wrap. Cody snoozed soundly against her while she went about her business. By the time Ethan arrived downstairs, looking semi-refreshed from his nap and newly showered (yummy soap scent + wet hair and bare feet = *Oh, mama*), she was feeling pretty much like a rock star at the whole domesticity thing.

"Wow."

Ethan stood between the family room and kitchen and

stared at all she'd done. That was the second "wow" she'd elicited from him this morning. Not bad.

"Are you hungry?" she asked. "I made lunch. Hope you don't mind that I raided your fridge."

"Are you kidding? Of course I don't mind. What is that?" He pointed not to the plastic-wrapped plate she withdrew from the refrigerator, but to the bundle wrapped securely around her body.

"That," she said, smiling, "is your nephew in a baby wrap I made from a sheet I swiped out of the laundry room. It's clean."

"He's asleep in there?"

"Yep. It's called baby wearing. I had to Google how to improvise with a sheet, but I think it's working just fine. When the twins were little, I'd wear one of them while their mother wore the other. We could get a ton of things accomplished, even give the girls a bottle, and still have happy kiddos. Being held securely against someone's body is incredibly comforting."

A slow, sexy grin crawled across his gorgeous kisser. "I bet it is."

Heat filled her, but not because she was embarrassed. "I hope you like turkey with avocado," she said to distract herself, placing his plate on the breakfast bar.

"You did not have to do this." He surveyed his lunch. "But I'm glad you did. I'm starved."

Setting a place for herself, too, she joined him. Ethan glanced at the top of his nephew's head as it peeped out between her breasts, his body securely held by the way she'd tied the linen fabric.

"Has he been sleeping since I left?"

"He woke up briefly, but I was able to soothe him pretty quickly with a snack. He fell asleep again before the bottle was empty."

"I don't believe it. She's brilliant, isn't she?" he asked the sleeping baby. Cody snuffled in his sleep. "He says, 'yes, she's wonderful,'" Ethan interpreted.

Secretly delighted, Gemma glanced down. "That looks more like, 'What-ev. 'Night, y'all.'"

"Nah. He's just super chill. He likes his pillow."

Her toes curled over the rung of the bar stool. "Any port in a storm."

"On the contrary." He looked at her, his Pacific-blue eyes exultant with gratitude and admiration. "My nephew is very discerning. And he has excellent taste in pillows."

The kindling heat burst into a full-fledged fire, undoubtedly turning her cheeks bright red at this very moment. Reminding herself that she was nearly thirty-four, not nearly fourteen, Gemma offered a philosophical shrug.

"When you grow to be a big boy, Cody," she said to the top of the baby's head, "remember that being a smooth-talking jock might be cool, but so is being a nerd."

"What?" He began to eat his sandwich. "What kind of lame advice is that?"

"It's not lame. Nerds are sexy."

"Ah." He chewed and swallowed his first big bite. "You go for the boys with a lot of book learning, do you?"

She thought about her ex-fiancé. William was a nerd—expert in his field, studious, a little awkward and quiet, with looks that had to grow on you over time. She'd felt safe with him because of that, but look at how it'd turned out. Christine Marie Allard had gone for nerds, too, and that had been that.

Gemma looked down at the little face of the baby drooling on her bosom. She swirled a finger in his fine downy blond hair. "I'm revising my wish list where men are concerned," she murmured.

"Oh, yeah?" Ethan plucked a couple of the carrot chips

she'd placed on the side of his plate. "What's topping the list these days?"

The answer came easily. "A family man."

Was she mistaken, or did he cringe a little?

"Do you want children of your own?" she asked. When his gaze cut straight to his nephew, she put a hand on the baby's back. "They don't all cry as long and hard as this guy. And he's been an angel since I put him in the wrap."

Rising, Ethan went to the refrigerator and pulled out a can of soda. "Want one?"

Gemma shook her head. Talk about changing the subject. She looked at her sandwich, a much smaller version of his, but realized she wasn't the least bit hungry—except for more information. "You said that Samantha is still addicted to drugs. Is she in a rehab facility?"

Introducing the topic of his sister clearly threw him off guard. Popping the tab off his soda, he took several long gulps, watching her warily over the rim. Lowering the can, he wiped his upper lip with the back of his hand and said, "No."

That was it? Just "no"? Rarely one to pry, Gemma figured that in this case she'd earned probing a bit. "DHS contacted you, so I'm assuming Cody's father isn't available to parent?"

Rather than returning to his lunch, Ethan leaned against the section of counter closest to the refrigerator. "We don't know who the father is."

It was clear that he loathed the admission.

Gemma felt a wave of empathy. "I'm not judging Samantha. I just wonder…if Cody's biological father isn't available, and if Samantha can't parent, will you raise Cody?"

Instantly, Ethan's scowl deepened. "Samantha *is* going to raise Cody. It's just the damn drugs—" He passed a hand over his face. "Look, we lost our mom to cancer when we were really young. And Mom was never the most…attentive parent to begin with. She had her own issues. After she died, Sam and I moved in with our uncle and aunt." He shook his head. "Aunt Claire meant well. She was responsible and decent, but she wasn't the warmest person, and Samantha had already started acting out while our mom was ill. Aunt Claire and Uncle Bob tried to help her by bringing the parental hammer down, but that pushed Sam further away. Then Bob passed away, which left Claire all alone to earn a living and take care of two kids who had plenty of baggage."

"I'm sorry. Sorry about your losing your mom. I never knew the details."

His eyes seemed bleak. "I've tried not to talk about it, because I don't want negative attention on Sam. It's easy to make a drug addict the fall guy for all the problems in a family."

"I won't share anything you don't want me to share. You're not going to be able to keep the baby secret for long, though, not in Thunder Ridge."

"I know. I need a little more time, though, before the rest of the world gets wind of this. I've got to find Sam and get her back into rehab."

"Find her?" Gemma watched Ethan closely. Guilt etched lines onto his handsome face.

"I don't know where she is." The response seemed to cause Ethan physical pain. "She left the hospital right after having Cody. I didn't even know she was pregnant."

Gemma couldn't imagine being that out of touch with one of her siblings, or having to worry about their safety with no information. "That sucks."

Ethan's head rose, and he smiled. "Thanks. It does." Pushing away from the counter, he came to stand opposite her at the breakfast bar. "Once I started making good

money, I sent her to rehab. The best places I could find."
He shrugged powerlessly. "There were a lot of celebrities.
Maybe too many distractions… I don't know. I'm going to
find someplace more basic this time."

She nodded. No one close to her had ever required
rehab, but wasn't it fairly common knowledge that the addict had to want recovery for herself in order for it to work?

"Maybe Samantha wasn't ready," she suggested gently.

"Maybe not then. She's a mother now. I know she'd be
ready if she had support, but she's running scared."

Gemma felt the baby stir against her. "How did you get
custody of Cody?"

"I don't have custody. Not exactly. DHS is Cody's legal
guardian. They consider me a 'relative foster placement.'"
Ethan turned his soda can in slow circles on the granite
countertop. "Out of the blue, I get a phone call from DHS
telling me Sam went AWOL from the maternity ward of
a hospital in Miami after the baby tested positive for co-
caine. DHS searched for over a month, and I was the only
identifiable relative they could place Cody with."

He rubbed both hands over his temples, a gesture Gemma
associated once again with guilt. "No one has heard from
Sam in over two months, which is typical when she's on a
binge. She's been known to disappear for over a year at a
time. But now, with the baby, I'm positive she's running
scared and that if I found her, I could talk some sense into
her, get her back into recovery. Some facilities let mothers
bring their children."

Another tense silence echoed in the kitchen. Gemma
thought about how this conversation had begun—with the
question of whether he would take care of his nephew if
his sister *wasn't* capable of parenting. But he didn't want
to discuss that.

A hot coil of fear threaded through the center of her

chest. She placed both hands on Cody's gently breathing body. "Well, I hope everything works out the way you want it to."

She didn't feel good about Ethan's plan, however. As the baby slept on, unaware of his tenuous future, Gemma didn't feel good about their situation at all.

Chapter Six

"Honey, you look terrible." Holliday Bailey peered at Gemma through her front-porch screen door. "Come to the kitchen and pull up a bar stool," she told her best friend. "I'm fixing us mimosas."

"Thanks."

High heels clicking, Holliday sashayed down the short hall in a leopard-print sweater set and shiny black leggings. Gemma glanced down at her own faded jeans and T-shirt and couldn't help but feel a little underdressed.

Standing in the kitchen, Gemma swallowed the nausea she'd been feeling all morning. She'd come to a decision—a *definite*, life-changing decision—today, but now she felt as if she were standing on the deck of a boat in the middle of a storm at sea. Trying to calm herself, she glanced around while Holliday rooted through her refrigerator.

Holly lived in one of the newly built condos in Thunder Ridge's growing southwest neighborhood. The decor in the unit was minimalist, cool, sparsely furnished. It perfectly suited Gemma's acerbic, smart and sassy friend and her dedicated single life.

"Your African violet is dying," Gemma noted. She reached into a cupboard for a glass to water the poor, wilted plant. "What's that?" she asked, raising her head to listen to a distinct cry.

"The cat."

Gemma blinked at her friend in shock. "You have a cat?"

"Of course not. It's a stray. It conned me into feeding it. I keep telling it to go find a motherly type, but it insists on nagging me. You want a cat? I'll throw in the violet."

Gemma watered the plant, then opened the sliding door to the patio and let the cat inside. It was small and fluffy and began purring instantly. Like a baby, but with fur. Bending down, she scooped the animal up. "It's a sweetheart. What are you calling it?"

Holliday frowned. "Cat."

Gemma shook her head at her friend. "Is it a boy or a girl?"

Holly waved an airy hand. "You choose." She handed Gemma a champagne flute and, holding hers aloft, said, "Here's to the good life." She pointed a perfectly manicured finger at the bundle twisting happily in Gemma's arms. "Which does not include pets." After clinking her glass to Gemma's, she took a long drink. "Mmm." She gestured to the modern chrome and white fabric sofa in her living area. "Have a seat. Tell Auntie Holly what's on your mind this fine Sunday afternoon. I don't suppose the dark circles under your eyes have something to do with your younger sister getting married yesterday."

Gemma thought for a moment as she sat down. "No." That really wasn't it. She was happy for Elyse and Scott and the life they were building together. The family they'd probably be having soon. "What do you think about single motherhood?"

"Oh. My. Lord. You're pregnant." Holliday's eyes were enormous. "Who? When? Why didn't you tell me you were sleeping with somebody?"

"I'm not sleeping with somebody. My gosh, slow down." Gemma took a sip of the drink Holliday had given her. "I've been thinking, that's all."

"Thinking?"

"About how I've always planned to have children someday, and I'm not getting any younger, and..." She raised her chin. "It's time to get on with it."

"This *is* about your little sister getting married. You have post-traumatic wedding disorder. Happens all the time. Single women attend weddings and wind up in the bathroom, crying because it's not them. You'll get over it." Holliday eyed her flute. "Maybe we should switch to straight champagne."

"I was at Ethan's this morning."

Holliday sat up, instantly attentive. "No way! What happened? I saw you two at the reception and thought if I didn't know better, I'd say something was brewing, but then I figured—"

At her abrupt halt, Gemma supplied, "That I'm not his type?"

"I was going to say that, yeah, but I knew it wasn't going to sound right. What I mean is you're not the *casual* type." She arched a brow. "Or was that before breakfast?"

"Don't get carried away. It's not what you're thinking. Ethan asked me to come over to help him with a..." She hesitated. "A baby."

"A baby what?"

"A baby human. His nephew. Cody." Swearing her

friend to secrecy and knowing that beneath the glib drama, Holly could be trusted with the keys to Tiffany's, Gemma filled her in on the basics of Ethan's situation, leaving out details about Samantha.

"Wow," Holliday breathed when Gemma paused, "this is better than *Access Hollywood*. So Ethan thinks you're the baby whisperer."

"When I hold Cody, I realize what I'm missing. I want to be a mother, Holly. Soon. Now."

Holliday's perfectly shaped brows drew together. "What about a husband? Haven't you always wanted one of those first?"

Gemma rubbed her chin over the cat's downy fur. "I think I'm over that. I mean, look at you. You're single. You're happy."

"You're not me. Honey, I know you love your nieces and nephews, and I'm sure holding a baby first thing in the morning is very enticing…to some people." She shuddered indelicately. "But is it possible you're confusing the baby with the uncle? Ethan Ladd is one yummy hunk of man. Even I'm not 100 percent immune, and if he called, needing your help—" She halted abruptly. "Wait, why call *you*? You don't have kids. Why did he come to you for help?" Her gaze narrowed suggestively. "You two left the reception for a while last night, didn't you? Juicy."

"It's not juicy. He's seen me with my nieces and nephews, and he wanted advice. End of story."

"They're your siblings' kids. Why didn't he ask Lucy or David? And your parents are parents. He could have gone to them."

Gemma tried to think back. Why had Ethan come to her? "We've gotten friendly lately. I think he…trusts me."

Holliday's expression changed from fascinated to concerned. "Oh, honey, be careful. I know I've been teasing you about Ethan, but I seriously doubt he's marriage material. He probably has a woman in every port, and by that, I mean airport."

Gemma felt agitation swell at the mention of Ethan's extracurricular activities. She shook her head. "You're completely jumping the gun again. I'm not interested in Ethan as marriage material. Or as anything else."

Holliday arched a brow. "No?"

Holly hadn't lived in Thunder Ridge when Gemma and Ethan were in high school, and Gemma had never told her friend about the disastrous homecoming date or its aftermath. She didn't see any point in sharing that info now, so instead she said, "You said it yourself. Probable woman in every port. Not marriage material. And not in my league."

"I never said he was out of your league. Quite the opposite, if you ask me."

"Yeah, yeah. But all I want is a baby. Maybe. Can you give me solid reasons why I should *not* under any circumstances go forward?"

"Well, there is the matter of finance. I mean you live in a studio apartment just off campus right now. You'll need a two-bedroom place—in Portland, with Portland rents. That sound you just heard was your checking account screaming. And what about your lifelong dream of going to Europe? I thought it was going to take all your extra cash and a summer job to get there."

"It was. I mean, it is. But if I don't jump into the deep end of the motherhood pool and just *do* it, I'm afraid I never will. And I don't think I can face a future where I don't get to be a mother."

Holliday pondered her words for a moment. "And you *can* face a future where you don't get to go to Europe?"

"Lots of people who have kids eventually get to Europe, too. I'll take my child with me. It'll be fun."

"Paris with a four-year-old. Yeah. You sure you don't want the cat instead?" She nodded to the fur ball that was falling asleep on Gemma's lap. "I'm told they eat less than human children, and they rarely require college tuition."

Gemma smiled. "I think you should keep the cat. I'll take the violet, though."

Holliday fell into a reflective silence. Finally, she looked hard and long at Gemma and there was none of the usual cynicism in her expression. "You should do it."

Stunned, Gemma said, "Seriously?"

"Yeah. I mean it. If this is your dream, you have to do it."

A tiny curl of excitement replaced some of the fear. "So you're willing to be an auntie? But what about all of the cons? What if we're wrong, and I can't take care of myself and a baby?"

Committed now, Holliday brushed off her worries with a wave of her hand. "You always achieve everything you set out to do. You'll be fine. More than fine. Your kid will probably be a Rhodes scholar. In fact, I see only one question mark in your immediate future."

"What's that?"

"How are you going to get the baby? I mean, there are a number of avenues for the single woman, but what appeals to you? Adoption? Artificial insemination? The old-fashioned way, with a willing partner?"

"I may need more mimosa."

Holliday nodded. "Cats are easier."

Pulling the collar of her scoop-neck T away from her body, Gemma blew cool air over her bosom. Although a pleasant breeze wafted through the open window of her upstairs apartment and propelled tiny raindrops against the screen, she was boiling hot. Anxiety did that to her. And right now, she was as anxious as she'd ever been.

"I want this. I shouldn't be anxious. I want this," she muttered like a mantra as she stared at the Portland Reproductive Options website currently displayed on her computer screen.

Women under the age of thirty-five typically have more success with alternative insemination.

If she wanted to have a baby, she couldn't mull this over too long, but the what-ifs were chasing each other through her mind like squirrels.

What if she couldn't afford to raise a child on her salary? After William broke their engagement, she'd decided to go after her PhD, and as a professor, her income would triple. But PhDs were expensive, not to mention time-consuming. What if she couldn't work, care for a baby and earn a PhD?

And the issues involved in how to become a mother in the first place—what if not knowing the identity of her child's father was too much for her to handle? What if, one day, her child had questions she couldn't answer about his or her daddy? Adoption, on the other hand, took longer, and was more expensive and more challenging for single applicants. What if she was gumming her own food by the time she became a mother? She and the baby could share strained peas.

Gemma thunked her forehead on the desk. *Help.* Why couldn't this be easier, like in the old days when you found a baby wrapped in fluffy blankets in a basket on your porch with a note that said, "Please take care of Annabelle"?

When a knock sounded on her door, she bolted up, immensely grateful for the interruption.

"Coming!" she shouted, finger-combing the hair she

hadn't yet brushed, and stopping at the round mirror above her vanity to make sure she didn't have food between her teeth. She'd been munching nonstop while she researched her options.

A glance at her watch showed her it was almost 10:00 a.m. A series of knocks sounded again. "Be there in a sec!"

Her back ached, and her neck felt stiff as she tromped to the door. Her above-the-garage apartment sat in a graceful neighborhood in Portland's southeast quadrant. She had all the privacy she wanted, but also maintained a come-over-whenever policy for her friends and coworkers.

Plastering a wide smile on her face, she opened the door. The first thing she saw was not a neighbor or a friend, but a baby.

In a car seat. Wrapped in a fluffy blanket.

Her heart began to hammer a mile a minute. *There's a baby on my doorstep, there's a baby on my doorstep! Oh, thank you, thank you, thank you—*

Hold on.

She bent down. "Cody?"

Yes, it was Cody, his sweet face scrunched into unhappy lines and crinkles. And there was no note. "Anyway, Uncle Ethan would never just leave you here."

A heavy *ka-thunk-ka-thunk-ka-thunk* on the stairs leading to her apartment made her look up.

"Hey." Ethan, as haggard as she'd ever seen him, attempted a smile that fell flat as he trudged up the steps. He lugged a diaper bag stuffed to the gills, a grocery bag and a large rolling cooler that he dragged behind him.

Quickly, Gemma scooped up the car seat and baby and carried them into her home, making space for Ethan to follow.

Setting the car seat on her coffee table, she unfastened Cody and took him into her arms. Not a moment too soon, either, as his face was screwing up into pre-squall position. In a moment, the air was going to be filled with shrieks unless she could comfort him ASAP. From the look on his blotchy little face, he'd been crying quite a lot again.

She hadn't seen the two of them in three days. After her talk with Holly, she'd known it was time to return to Portland. Satisfied—sort of—that she'd left Ethan with extensive instructions on swaddling, plus a website where he could purchase a baby carrier made especially for daddies, she'd left them with a silent prayer and hightailed it back to her own life.

Looking at man and baby now, it was clear that the concern she'd been trying to keep at bay was justified. Exhaustion had once more claimed a smidgen of Ethan's golden-boy good looks (nothing could douse them entirely), and Cody... Poor thing. He looked bereft.

While Gemma wrapped him more securely in the blanket and snuggled him, Ethan set all his baggage inside her apartment and shut the door. He glanced at his nephew with something approaching fear.

"I'm sorry," he said without preamble. "It's wrong to drop in on you. I should have called." He ran a hand over his hair. "Actually, I did call, but then I hung up. I was afraid you'd tell me not to come."

"How did you know where I live?"

"I called your mom." Before she could fully process that, he rambled, "I can't find a nanny. The agency said they don't have anyone else who's 'qualified at this time.' What does that mean—we wore them out?" He paced in front of her coffee table. "I tried the baby wrap. I just called Amazon and told them to overnight one to me. Maybe it's the wrong kind. He hates it when I wear it. I'm not kidding. If the kid could talk he'd be swearing at me." Stabbing a finger toward the small mountain of baby paraphernalia he'd brought with him, Ethan complained, "I tried a different brand of diapers, 'cause, you know, maybe he didn't like the ones he was wearing. That's a personal thing, a guy's skivvies. And I bought new formula, because maybe he's tired of the one I've been giving him and *that's* his problem—"

"Ethan, slow down," Gemma soothed, genuinely shocked to see him in his present state. "You want a glass of water? Or Alka-Seltzer? Or scotch?" She'd hoped to tease a tiny smile from him, but received only a blank, defeated stare. "Sit down." She nodded to her couch. "You look like you're going to keel over."

Nodding absently, he moved around the coffee table and stared down at the pile of travel brochures she'd left on her couch last night. She'd forgotten about the glossy pamphlets set out over the sofa cushions. For two hours, she'd studied them, wondering if the literary tour of Europe she'd planned as part of her PhD studies would be feasible if she had a baby, too. How could she ever afford both?

"Just move that stuff to the coffee table," she instructed while she went to the rolling cooler to find a bottle for the squirmy baby. When she turned back, Ethan was staring at the brochures he now held in his hands.

He riffled through them, then looked up at her with some alarm. "You planning on leaving the country?" Looking at the shiny picture on top, he frowned. "This is Scotland."

"Yeah…well… I want to do some research for my doctoral thesis, eventually. But it's spendy, and I—" It wasn't the time to mention her plan to have a child. In fact, the very thought of mentioning it to Ethan was kind of…weird.

Taking the bottle and the baby to her kitchenette, she said, "You know what they say about best-laid plans? Sometimes life comes along and interrupts."

"Yeah, I have a little experience with that." Ethan followed her into the tiny kitchen area, still holding her travel info. "But you *want* to go on this trip? Is money what's standing in your way?"

Placing Cody's bottle in the microwave, she glanced at the big football player who was currently making her apartment feel smaller than ever. For the first time since uncle and baby had arrived, Ethan looked more clearheaded, more connected. "Money. Time. I planned to make a little money by teaching summer school and tutoring over the summer, but I don't think it's going to be enough." *Not if I need to plan for a baby, too.*

The infant in her arms seemed to sense that she was preparing to feed him. He was wide-eyed now and quiet, apparently still a rare state for little Cody.

Uncle Ethan noticed. "How do you get him to do that?" He raised his hands in exasperation. "He's never like that with me, or with the nannies. Never."

"I don't know." Gemma shrugged. She looked down, sending Cody a smile as she jiggled him a bit. "Maybe he senses how much I enjoy holding him." She really did. She loved it. Her morning angst melted into the calm assurance that she was meant to be a mama, one way or another. Then she realized how her words might have come across to Ethan. "Not that you don't enjoy it. I wasn't saying that."

"You didn't offend me. I *don't* enjoy holding him. Who enjoys doing the thing they suck at?"

"You do not suck at it. You shouldn't even say that."

He set the travel brochures on the edge of her tiled counter. "Got to accept reality before you can change it."

The microwave dinged. He opened the door and withdrew the bottle before she could, checking the temperature, then handing it to her. They watched Cody eagerly get to work on his morning snack.

"Have you had breakfast?" Ethan asked, shifting his attention from his nephew to Gemma.

"Yes. Today's and tomorrow's. I eat when I'm tired. Are *you* hungry?"

"Starving. Want a cup of coffee while I grab something to eat?"

"Sure. There's a place a few blocks away that has great breakfast skillets. We can walk there. Let me get my purse."

As she went to the sole closet in her apartment, which was near the front door, Ethan said, "I like your place. It looks like you."

"Cramped and utilitarian?" she joked.

"No. Petite and unique."

Gemma laughed. "By the way, did you bring the baby wrap—" Turning as she spoke, she saw Ethan explore the wall on the other side of the kitchenette. Atop her Lucite desk, the oversize laptop screen displayed the most recent website she'd been perusing.

Yikes! Photos of babies—some with mothers, some without—dominated the screen.

"Looks like you've been doing some research," he said, and she could feel the hot flush of embarrassment. References to artificial insemination topped the screen, obviously requiring some explanation. Even a cursory scan of the page would make it clear she'd been researching sperm banks.

"Uhm, actually, I've been looking into, uh…" How the heck was she going to explain this away? Was she ready to tell him she wanted to have a baby on her own? She hadn't mentioned it to anyone in her family.

"Have you learned anything that might help Cody stop crying?"

"What?"

"Did you find some information that might help us figure out what's wrong with him?" Straightening away from the screen, he turned to her.

His question baffled her. How was she going to discover cures for crack babies on a website for artificial insemination? "Ah...not so much," she said hesitantly.

"Doesn't matter," he said, walking to the pile of baby things he'd brought and quickly locating the wrap. "He's happy when he's with you. You have the right touch. You don't need advice."

Ethan's expression, so filled with gratitude and admiration, sent shivers of lust racing up her spine. He was giving her his sexy I'm-smiling-just-for-you look.

"Is it hot in here?" she croaked. "It's been too hot in here all morning."

"Let's go, then. Looks like the rain stopped."

He handed her a baby wrap, electrifying her fingertips as they brushed his. Trying to ignore the feeling, she thanked her lucky stars that he was too distracted to realize what she'd been looking at on her computer screen. Transferring the baby and bottle to his arms so she could put on the wrap, she said, "You look like you're scared of him. Maybe he can sense that. Why don't you pretend he's a big, scary linebacker, or whoever usually tackles you. You're not scared of them, right?"

"They're not as loud as Cody."

She shook her head. "Keep the bottle in his mouth. I think he'll be reasonably happy until I can get him in the wrap."

Following her instruction, Ethan waited patiently while she arranged the material. The baby did, indeed, quietly suck on the bottle. Nonetheless, Ethan looked relieved when she took Cody from his arms and tucked him into the wrap.

Grabbing a light coat from the hall tree next to the front

door, she said, "We're ready. The restaurant isn't far, only a few blocks," she said as they exited the apartment and she locked up.

"You okay on these stairs with the baby?" Solicitously, he reached for her elbow.

I'm fine with the baby, but you're making me dizzy. Ethan looked really, really good carrying a diaper bag.

"Hunky-dory." She smiled. "Although it might help if we go down single file." *Without touching.*

"Sure. Let me go first, so I can help if you lose your footing." He slung the diaper bag over his shoulder and preceded her down the steep flight of stairs, glancing back as if she were as delicate as the wings of a butterfly.

Already she was gaining insight into how different it would be when she was doing this on her own. Struck by a pang of longing for the life she'd once planned, Gemma almost stumbled. "I'm fine!" she assured him when Ethan reached for her. She stood stock-still until he assured himself that she was okay and began to move forward again.

I am fine, she repeated to herself. *I will be fine.*

Hanging out with Cody was great experience for the day when she would hold a baby of her own against her heart. Hanging out with Cody's uncle…

That was a test of a different kind.

The streets steamed as the sun came out from behind the clouds to dry the pavement. Branches above the tree-lined sidewalks glistened, and Portlanders, undaunted by a spring shower, pushed strollers and walked their dogs. Overhead, birds chatted as Gemma and Ethan strolled through her charming vintage neighborhood. Arts and crafts–style homes from the 1930s had been repurposed into thriving cafés and boutiques and, on Thursday mornings, she bought her fresh produce at the corner farmers' market. From a block away, she could see her favorite breakfast spot, a popular bistro called Flapjacks. A line wound halfway around the block.

Gemma looked anxiously up at Ethan. "I know it's packed to the rafters, but it's worth it. Best breakfast in the southeast."

"I'm happy to wait," he said, and he did look a little more relaxed as they stepped into line behind an elderly couple who smiled at Cody.

"I bet you don't have to wait in line much," she teased, squinting up at him. "Do maître d's say 'Right this way' the second they see you?"

"No, but I almost always get a few extra fries at the drive-through."

He grinned, and she felt herself grow warm. Humble as he was, Gemma saw the people around them beginning to notice Ethan. A middle-aged man in a baseball cap nudged the woman next to him and chin-nodded toward Ethan. A teenage boy pulled out his phone and snapped a photo.

"That kid just took your picture," she whispered. "That's an invasion of privacy."

Without glancing the young man's way, Ethan said, "Nah. He was taking your picture. You want me to go break his phone for you?"

She marveled at him. "You're that used to all this attention. It doesn't faze you?"

He shrugged. "It comes with the territory, Gemma. It's not about me, it's about what I do."

"What if someone photographs you in the restaurant with egg yolk on your chin?"

A smile pushed his cheeks. He leaned forward, so close it might have appeared to onlookers that he was going to kiss her. "I trust you to wipe it off before anyone else sees it."

He is soooo gorgeous. His hair sparkled with wheat and gold threads in the sun. The highlights weren't artificial, either. She remembered the same color mesmerizing her in high school. Standing this close, she could see tiny flecks of brown in his blue eyes and the darker rims around the irises. His eyes were a little bloodshot, and it gave her a thrill to realize that only she knew the reason for it.

"I've got something to ask you," he said, his expression turning more serious.

Her heart thumped against her ribs. "Okay," she responded breathlessly. When Ethan looked at her, his attention was so focused she felt as if she were the only woman in the world. He could charm the socks off anyone, she knew that, but sometimes, lately, it seemed as if he might be feeling the attraction, too. "What is it?"

"This is going to sound like it's coming out of left field," he qualified, "and I admit it's not something I've given a lot of thought to before this morning. But I know it's right."

Oh. My. Gosh. He knows it's right? Ohmygosh, ohmygosh, ohmygosh. He *was* feeling the attraction. Maybe. Was he going to tell her he wanted to take their relationship to the next level? "Go on."

"You're Ethan Ladd, aren't you?" The older couple in line directly ahead of them turned, faces wreathed in smiles.

Gemma looked at the kindly visage of the elderly man who peered through his glasses at Ethan. Uncharacteristically, she wanted to sock him.

She felt Ethan's frustration, too, as he took a breath and nodded. "Yes."

The woman leaned forward. "Your baby is an angel. Our grandson was born a few months ago. Aren't they darling at this stage?"

Ethan glanced at Gemma, irony filling his expression as he took her hand and gave it a little squeeze. "Adorable," he agreed, and they grinned at each other. Once again, even in the middle of a crowd, she felt as if she were all alone in the world with Ethan.

The man asked him when training camp started for the Eagles, and Gemma's attention drifted to a young couple farther up in line. Like her, the woman wore a baby in a front wrap. The man stood face-to-face with her, the baby between them, and Gemma watched with a pang of longing as they kissed over the infant's pink-capped head. She glanced down at her own hand, safely enveloped in Ethan's. *This is what I want.*

As the line moved forward, the older couple turned their attention to what they wanted for breakfast, and Gemma seized the opportunity. "What were you going to ask me?"

For the first time, he seemed to realize he was still holding her hand. Giving it another squeeze, he began to speak, but was interrupted immediately by a middle-aged fan with a piece of paper, a pen and timing that made Gemma want to scream.

"Could I get your autograph for my husband and a selfie with you?" the woman asked, and Ethan, ever gracious, let go of Gemma. "Hang on for just a second," he whispered to her.

Disappointment filled her every cell as he accepted the paper and posed for a photo, the first of several as they made their way to the front of the line.

The next time they had the privacy to resume their conversation, they were seated with menus at a blissfully secluded table toward the rear of the restaurant.

Gemma's anticipation began to rise as Ethan laid his menu on the table and leaned forward to speak.

"So. This European trip. How much money will it take to get you there, you think?"

Prepared for a different conversation, Gemma groped for the thread. "My trip?"

"Yeah, those brochures you have? Trips like that are expensive, aren't they?"

She ducked her head and fussed with Cody's wrap. "When we were outside, you said you wanted to ask me something. Was that it?"

"I'm getting there."

A waiter arrived. "Hi. What can I get you to drink?"

Vodka tonic, Gemma thought, irritated. "Coffee, thanks." She smiled. Ethan asked for the same.

As soon as the waiter left, Ethan continued, "About your trip. You were telling me that you needed to get a job this summer to afford it. What are you looking at, cost-wise?"

Utterly confused, Gemma shrugged. "A lot. The trip would help me get my doctorate. The doctorate would help me afford the trip. It's a catch-22. At this point, it's probably a pipe dream."

"But you really want to go?"

I want my doctorate. I really want to have a baby. I really, really want...someone like you. It was true. Crazy, maybe ridiculous and potentially sophomoric, but sitting here imagining them as a husband, wife and baby filled her with a happiness she didn't get anyplace else. Probably her hormones acting up. "Yes," she answered carefully, "I'd like to go...sooner or later."

"So you need to make a decent wage this summer. Right?" Ethan picked up his spoon and drummed it on his palm.

"Sure. Ethan, where are you headed with this?"

As he opened his mouth to respond, the waiter arrived with two glasses of ice water.

"Ready to order?" the young man asked, his pen already poised above his pad.

"A lemon-blueberry scone, please," she said, damning her diet, but needing the carbo comfort. Ethan shifted in his chair, opened the menu, looked it over quickly and pointed randomly. "I'll have that." Snapping the menu shut, he handed it to the waiter.

"How would you like your eggs?"

"Don't care."

"Oh?"

"Surprise me."

The waiter seemed at a loss.

"Scrambled," Ethan said, tone final, trying to get back to their conversation.

"Whole grain, sourdough or rye toast, or blueberry, pumpkin or maple-bacon pancakes?"

"Really don't care."

"The maple-bacon pancakes are—"

"Fine."

He wrote on the pad. "Bacon or sausage?"

"Bacon!"

"Yes, sir. I'll be back in a second with your coffee."

As the young man finally moved off, Ethan drove his hand through his hair. Gemma reached across the table and patted his arm in an effort to soothe him. "What were you going ask—"

"I want you to move in with me!"

Slack-jawed, Gemma stared at him. Wow. *Should have ordered that vodka tonic, after all.*

Chapter Seven

That could have gone better.

Ethan hadn't planned to blurt that out, but he felt desperation crawling through his veins. "I can get another nanny," he said. "The agency said they'd find someone eventually. But…" *Just spit it out.* "Cody needs you."

The words hovered in the air between them, and he knew they weren't right. They were true enough, but they weren't the whole truth. Ethan shifted on the hard chair. He was uncomfortable in the room, uncomfortable in his skin. There was too much noise and too many people in the restaurant. He should have talked to her at her place.

"You want me to be Cody's nanny," Gemma reiterated, looking shell-shocked and…not happy.

"I know that's not what you do with your life," he responded. "I know it's not something you'd seek out. There's no reason for you to say yes. I get that. But, Gemma, DHS is breathing down my neck. The social worker doesn't think I can handle Cody, I can tell." He rolled his eyes. "Why the hell would she think I can handle him? I don't know what I'm doing, and I—" On the verge of telling her why DHS never should have placed Cody with him in the first place, he stopped. He trusted her, but he just wasn't sure he wanted her to know exactly how unqualified he was to take care of a baby. Of anyone.

"What if they take him away from me?" That fear was so strong, he couldn't contain it anymore. "They could put him with strangers. Before I can even find Samantha."

Beneath the surface of the table, he clasped his hands, cracking his knuckles to release the tension he could barely tolerate. The fact was, he shouldn't have come here. Shouldn't be laying his worries on her. She was too good, too willing to help people. Hadn't he always thought her family took advantage of her? And now here he was, doing the same. *Stand up. Take Cody. Find a new nanny agency—*

"You really believe they would take him?"

Looking up at the softly spoken question, Ethan scrutinized Gemma's face. He couldn't tell whether she was considering his request, but selfish or not, he couldn't live all alone in the anxiety anymore. "They're worried that I can't keep a nanny. And they're concerned about the future, because no one's heard from Samantha. They're talking about 'permanency planning' if they can't find her, and I haven't been able to devote enough time to looking for her. And I sure can't convince them Cody belongs with me for now when he's screaming bloody murder every time the caseworker shows up."

After that, they were silent. Cody remained asleep, and Gemma toyed with the edge of her paper napkin, seemingly deep in thought. She wore a bright red kerchief tied in a big bow around her hair. The color matched the wide belt that cinched her small waist and emphasized her hips and breasts. Nervous and exhausted as he was, he'd noticed that the moment he'd laid eyes on her today. Gemma had a twenty-four-karat-gold brain and a body that was *va-va-va-voom*, an old-fashioned term that fit her 1950s pinup figure…which had been distracting him lately. He'd dated models, long and lean, and had always figured that was his type, but now every time he was around Gemma—

Ethan gave his head a clearing shake. His fatigued brain was going to places it didn't belong. Unclasping his hands, he rubbed his eyes. "Listen, I'm sorry. I never should have—"

"Let me think about it—"

They spoke at the same time.

"You'll think about it?"

"Shouldn't have what?"

The waiter brought their coffees as he and Gemma stared at each other across the table. Guilt and jubilation fought in his mind. Any friend would tell her to run like hell, not to get mixed up in another family drama that didn't belong to her.

"Do you take milk or cream?" the waiter asked.

"Bloody Mary," Ethan answered, his eyes still on Gemma.

She nodded. "Same." Then she broke eye contact with Ethan and turned toward the bemused server. "And please hurry."

The savory aroma of onions and garlic welcomed Gemma as she let herself into her sister Lucy's kitchen. Stepping over toys belonging to both children and dogs, she found her sister in the process of getting dinner started for her family. Minna, looking as harried as Lucy, was busily cleaning out Lucy's refrigerator and freezer. Face sticky, smile wide, Owen leaned way over in his high chair, holding his arms out in greeting.

"Hi," she announced herself. "Something smells good." She'd been hoping to discuss her situation with Ethan with Lucy alone, but knew Minna would have to be told sooner or later, anyway.

"Well, it's not from this freezer," Minna announced, removing an ice-covered something or other and plunking it onto a mountain of stuff already on the counter. "What are you doing here?"

"Yeah, I thought you went back to Portland," Lucy said as she stirred what looked and smelled like her homemade Bolognese. "Can you stay for dinner?"

"Well, that's kind of why I'm here. I have news. Big fat news."

Minna set down a stack of frozen dinners and looked up excitedly. "News? Something juicy?"

"I think so." Gemma meandered toward the center island. "You know I want to go to Europe, and I need a summer job, so I was going to teach over the break, right?"

Minna looked disappointed. "Yes, dear, we know."

"Right," Lucy said as she dunked a piece of soft Italian bread in the sauce and blew on it for Owen.

Minna brandished a jar she pulled from the refrigerator. "The expiration date on this is from before you were born," she said to Lucy.

Lucy rolled her eyes. "Mom, it is not."

Nudging her glasses higher on her nose, Minna peered at the label. "Yes, it is. Moses ate this in the desert."

"Mom!"

As the two of them bickered, Gemma pulled Owen out of his high chair and into her arms. Taking the sauce-drenched bread from her sister, she said, "So as it turns out, I'm not going to work in Portland. I got a job locally."

Minna swung around. "Darling! How wonderful! We'll see you all summer, then?" She frowned at the string of freezer-burned knockwurst in her hands. "Lu? You want to keep this, honey? Just in case of famine?"

Ignoring her mother's jabs, Lucy asked, "What kind of job?"

There was an open container of frost-covered brownies on the counter. Lowering her squiggling nephew to the floor as he happily gummed his bread, Gemma picked up a brownie and examined it. "I'm going to be a nanny," she said, striving to sound offhand, "for Ethan Ladd."

Both Lucy's and Minna's heads snapped around, and they gaped at her.

"For Ethan?" Minna asked. "What are you talking about?"

"Ethan doesn't have a baby." Lucy snorted. She traded a glance with her mother, then looked back to Gemma. "Does he?"

Knocking some ice off the brownie before she took a bite, Gemma stayed on the cool, casual, low-drama track. "Mmm-hmm."

"Mmm-hmm what?" Lucy demanded. "Mmm-hmm, he has a baby?"

Slamming the freezer door, Minna scurried to the counter in intel-gathering mode. "Is it his? Is he the father? Is it out of wedlock?"

"Mom, no one says that anymore," Lucy reproved, demanding, "Who's the mother?"

Minna slapped the counter and gasped. "It's the redhead!"

Lucy's eyes got huge. "From the vampire cheerleader show?"

"No!" Trying to speak around frozen brownie, Gemma waved her hands. "No, no. It's nothing like that." She set the brownie away from her. "Please, you guys, you've got to stay calm and discreet. Ethan's in a tough spot, and he doesn't need a lot of gossip circulating around town right now. So let's stick to the facts, okay?"

Minna crossed her arms. "I don't gossip. Do I, Lucy?"

Turning from her mother to Gemma, Lucy said, "What are the facts?"

Pretending not to notice that their mother had taken offense, Gemma explained the situation as neatly as she could, telling them about Ethan getting the phone call from DHS and about being unable to keep a nanny.

"But why are *you* going to be the new nanny?" Lucy asked when Gemma was through.

"Because she's wonderful with children," Minna responded on her eldest daughter's behalf. Wearing a big smile now, she reached out to shmoosh Gemma's cheeks. "A man who's ready for a family can tell when a woman is good with children."

Lucy popped a piece of brownie into her mouth. "Like gorillas trying to mate with the best breeders?"

"No, not like gorillas," Minna snapped.

"Anyway, the male of a species typically doesn't do the choosing," Gemma pointed out. "It's the female, and even then a gorilla might—"

"Stop talking about gorillas!" Exasperated, Minna shook her head. "We are talking about Ethan now, and it's lovely that he wants to care for his family in this way. I remember his sister. She was a very good artist. Her pieces were always displayed at the school art shows."

"I remember her, too," Lucy said. "And I understand why he wants to find her and get her into rehab, but doesn't the addict have to want it, also?"

"I suppose he'll cross that bridge when he comes to it," Gemma murmured, though she'd had the same thought.

"The immediate concern is making sure DHS keeps Cody with Ethan, and for that he needs a nanny who won't quit."

"Well, you've never been a quitter," Minna said approvingly.

"What's he going to do when you go back to school?" Lucy questioned.

"Hopefully he'll be more able to take care of the baby on his own by then. And once we get Cody through the withdrawal phase, it should be easier to find a nanny who'll stay. For now, though…" She shrugged. "I seem to know how to soothe the little guy. Probably because of all the tricks I learned from you, Luce, when Owen had colic."

"It isn't just that. You're *wonderful* with children," Minna said as she tossed several mystery ziplocked bags of frozen food into the sink. "Be sure to pack your good shoes. The dainty ones with the bows on the heel."

Lucy gaped at her mother. "She needs good shoes to be a nanny?"

"To be *Ethan Ladd's* nanny." Eyes big, Minna waggled her brows.

"Hey, guys, let's not—" Gemma tried to regain control of the conversation, but Lucy persisted.

"Ma, you are not going to try to push Gemma and Ethan together. Ethan is a serial player. He is totally wrong for her. Remember the *People* magazine interview last year? Ethan said he's never going to get married or have children."

"Oh, pish tish," Minna dismissed. "He has a baby right now. He's already a family man." She pried the top off a container and gave it a tentative sniff. "Ethan will settle down once he's found the right woman. Just like George Clooney."

"Yeah, once he's found the right impossibly tall, glamorous, skinny woman with an IQ of 180." The moment the words were out, Lucy put a hand over her mouth and cast a sheepish glance at Gemma. "Sorry, hon. I didn't mean you're not—"

"Tall, glamorous and skinny?" Picking up her brownie, Gemma waved her sister's apology away. "Forget it." But even though she agreed—*really* agreed, 100 percent—with her sister's analysis of her and Ethan Ladd's couple potential, the words did sting. A thousand years ago, back in high school, she'd felt a little giddy and sort of…chosen… when she'd believed he was asking her to homecoming. When she'd discovered Elyse had bribed him to take her nerdy older sister… Well, message received.

"Anyway," she said, making a perky effort to steer the conversation back to her new employment opportunity, "for one summer, Ethan's going to pay me what I usually earn in five months. I'll be able to go to Europe and work on my PhD." And, with a PhD, she'd have enough income to raise a child on her own. She'd pondered telling them that part of her plan, too, but decided to wait. Her mother was happy, Lucy had some juicy new gossip and Gemma'd had enough stress for one day.

"Sounds good, honey," Minna said. "I know Ethan will be delighted with you."

"Yep. Well, I should probably be on my way. Just wanted to let you know I'm moving into Ethan's place before you read about it in the grocery line."

Another time, she would confess that she hoped being a nanny would be great preparation for when she had her own baby. Of course, she'd make sure there was a defibrillator nearby when she told her mother and father about her plans to adopt or to become pregnant on her own, because given her mother's penchant to see her children *married*, the mention of alternative insemination or single-parent adoption could put her on life support.

As Gemma gathered her purse and car keys, Lucy swooped Owen onto her hip and tucked her free hand into the crook of Gemma's arm. "Before you go, I have some stuff that I found really handy when Owen was Cody's age. If you're going to be a celebrity nanny, you need to be well-equipped. C'mon."

The moment Gemma stepped into the beautiful, elegant bedroom suite that Ethan had assigned her, she felt instantly at home. Though he called it the guest room, the square footage rivaled her entire apartment in Portland. The walk-in closet alone was the size of her childhood bedroom at her parents' place, and the bathroom had a glorious soaking tub and a shower that could accommodate a small army. It was heaven.

At her request, Ethan had moved Cody's crib to her room and was in the process of putting it back together so Cody could sleep in her room for the first couple of weeks.

At the moment, Cody was sleeping soundly in the middle of her bed as she bustled about, hanging her clothes in the closet and setting up the various appliances and products that Lucy claimed would make her job easier.

"Hand me that small wrench, would you?"

Ethan extended his hand without turning to look at Gemma, and she sorted through the tools on the bed before selecting a small, red-handled item. "This one?"

He took it, eyed it a second and said, "Perfect."

Perfect summed up the view on her end, too. Watching him work was, well, innervating to say the least.

His sculpted arms and shoulders were so broad Gemma felt certain that if the house caught on fire in the middle of the night, Ethan would be able to carry her, the baby and the bed they were in to safety. The sight of him was already playing havoc with her assurances to Lucy and their mother. She'd told them—never mind telling herself—that working for Ethan was strictly business. But when was the last time she'd had the urge to run her hands over her boss's back and shoulders and arms and—

Down, Gemma. His being all wrong for her—and vice versa—apparently did nothing to quash the libido.

"So, you're sure you want Cody in with you at night?" he said, frowning a bit as he tightened a bolt. "It might be better to have him in one of the other guest rooms so we can take turns. Not that I'll be much use in the middle of the night—"

Oh, I can think of a few uses...

"—since you seem to be the only one who can calm him." Giving the bolt a final twist, Ethan rose and turned toward her. "What do you say? Last chance to change your mind before I finish setting up this...what did you call it? Sidebar?"

"Side*car*," Gemma croaked, as parched as if she'd been living in the desert for a year. *Maybe I have been. A romantic desert. Maybe that's the problem. Ethan looks so good because I'm love-starved.*

She'd asked him to rebuild the crib right next to the bed, removing one side of the rails so that she could touch Cody easily in the night. She'd read all about it, and Lucy had done it with her kids. Clearing her throat, Gemma said, "It will be easier to fall asleep again if I don't have to get up and walk to another room to give Cody a bottle or change his diaper or reassure him. It should be easier for him to fall asleep again, too."

He gazed at her awhile, curiosity and admiration filling his eyes. "You know a lot about being a mother. Then again, you've always seemed to know a lot about everything." Shifting his study from her to the baby sleeping soundly in the middle of the queen bed, he shook his head in wonder. "Okay, one crib attached to the bed coming right up."

If only it were that simple, she thought, to make a request of God. *Could You please send me a man strong enough to put up a crib, gentle enough to look at a child with wonder and willing to love me for a lifetime? Thanks. Oh, and PS, the sex appeal of Adonis would not be unwelcome, though it's not a must. It's just that I'm in my thirties, I've been engaged before, but I have never felt this turned on in my life. If you don't mind my saying so.*

"Done," Ethan said as he made the final adjustments to the crib, then rose and collected the tools he'd laid out on the bed. "You're good to go."

"I certainly am."

"If you're feeling comfortable on your own, I'll leave you to unpack."

"I'm fine."

At the door, he hesitated a moment. "I'm glad you're here, Gem." His voice had lowered to a leonine purr.

Dang.

"I want you to feel at home," he continued. "Anything you need, just ask and I'll make it happen."

No doubt about it, she was going to have a hot flash right here in her thirties. "Thanks."

After Ethan left, Gemma turned to the soundly sleeping Cody. "If you don't mind, I think I'll join you," she said. "That was exhausting."

Twenty minutes later, Gemma emerged from her closet dressed in the most sedate outfit she'd put together in her entire adult life. In lieu of napping, she'd racked her brain for ways to get through the summer like the rational, professional woman she had been up to now.

Clearly her body wasn't listening to her brain where

Ethan was concerned, so she decided to send herself the message that she was here for one purpose and one purpose only—to be a nanny to Cody and to collect her paycheck—by wearing the blue suit unadorned with belts or scarves or funky seamed hosiery. Checking herself in the mirror, she gave a satisfied nod. She looked boring, but also serious and in control, like a cast member of *Nanny 911*.

In his crib now, Cody was still fast asleep. Her bedroom was unpacked and set up for business. She was dressed for success. It was time to head downstairs and set up a little space for Cody's and her meals and utensils in the pantry. Organization and professionalism would be the key to a peaceful coexistence with Ethan.

Gemma glanced at the baby monitor near the crib. On. Good. Tucking the remote parent intercom into her pocket, she stepped confidently into the hallway—and straight into her half-naked boss.

"Oops. Oh, my goodness!" she gasped. "I'm so sorry."

"About what?"

"About…uh…" Struggling to regain her professional demeanor, she tried to find something to stare at that wasn't Ethan, but it was tough. The man's spectacular damp chest was mere centimeters from her face, and he smelled fantastic, like the breezeway just outside the Bath & Body Works store at the mall.

Taking a step back, he regarded her with lightly veiled amusement. "What are you wearing?"

Tucking her chin into her collarbone, she looked down and frowned. *What am I wearing?* "I'm wearing clothes. And you're…not."

Smile lazy, Ethan glanced down at himself, then back up at her. "I'm wearing a towel. I just got out of the shower. Do you wear clothes to take a shower, Gem?"

"No." She squared her shoulders. "But I wear them when I get *out* of the shower."

His smile slid into a broad grin. "Not me. I like to get all nice and dry first."

Right. He was teasing her now for overreacting. She needed to say something professional.

"I have everything set up in my room for the baby now. The bottle warmer is plugged in next to my nightstand." Her recalcitrant gaze flashed to his six-pack and then on down to where it disappeared into the towel. "And the baby monitor is here in my pocket." His skin was smooth and perfectly tanned over muscles that rippled like rings of water on a lake.

Clearing her throat, she forced her eyes to a spot over his shoulder and feigned deep thought about the nanny gear Lucy had lent her. "I think the baby swing will come in handy. The motion will be good for...for, um—" he started to dry his hair with a second towel "—sensory issues." She had to face it: it was not humanly possible to have a normal conversation while Ethan and his abnormally perfect body were glistening right there in front of her. "Well, I'll let you get dressed."

"Actually, I'm glad I ran into you. I came out to grab fresh towels for my bathroom. Let me show you where I keep them." He pointed to a door directly behind her. "Linen closet. Right there."

Gemma glanced over her shoulder. "Ah. Very good, thank you. I will certainly need towels. Babies are messy, and...I should probably familiarize myself with the laundry room, too." She could feel him studying her.

"You going somewhere? Besides the laundry room?" he questioned.

"Me? No. Why?"

Ethan shrugged. "You seem..." Tilting his head, he assessed her. "Overdressed. Speaking of messy babies and everything."

The heat that began in her belly crawled up her neck. She tugged on her jacket, refusing to contemplate that she probably looked like a militant funeral director. "Not at all. Babies respond to physical cues. Proper professional attire sends the signal that the caretaker is calm, efficient and not prone to flights of fancy."

"Flights of fancy?" He looked as if he was going to laugh outright. "Okay. Well, you look professional, all right. I've never seen your hair in a bun before."

Gemma smoothed the sleekly drawn hair at the side of her head. The damn hairdo was so tight, she was going to need an ibuprofen. "Thank you."

He did laugh then.

Right, she realized. *It wasn't a compliment.*

"You have nice hair," he commented. "I like it down."

That was a compliment.

"See you later." Ethan turned, sauntering back down the hallway to the master bedroom.

If the front view was awesome, the view from the rear was nothing to sneeze at either. She watched until she realized she was watching, then spun on her heel, ducked back into her own bedroom and shut the door. Sagging against the wood panel, Gemma smoothed her skirt with damp hands. *Think Nanny McPhee. Channel Nanny McPhee.*

She wasn't Ethan's type of woman. And he wasn't her type of man—walking around all wet and naked and muscle-bound. Disgusting.

She wished he would come back.

Pushing herself off the door as Cody began to stir in the crib, she commanded herself to concentrate on priorities. She'd didn't need another relationship disappointment.

What she needed was to take care of this little baby and collect the money his generous uncle Ethan was paying so she could realize her dreams all by herself.

Chapter Eight

Ethan awoke early after the soundest sleep he'd had in weeks. Outside his bedroom window, several shades of green leaves and a crystal-blue sky tempted him to take a run before anyone else woke up. At least, he didn't think anyone else was up. The silence in the house was golden.

Yesterday had been weird and also kind of cool. Before falling asleep last night, he'd stared at the ceiling, trying to figure out the exact moment Gemma Gould had morphed from relaxed, capable friend and caregiver to Mary Poppins on speed. Sometime between setting up the crib and bumping into each other in the hallway, he speculated.

And about that encounter in the hallway…

Tossing back the covers and deciding to get dressed and have breakfast—he was starving—instead of a run, Ethan stretched and headed to his glass-enclosed shower, grinning like an idiot at the memory of Gemma trying not to look at his bare torso.

She had a brother, and she'd had a fiancé, so he wasn't quite sure why a man in a towel, in his own house, had thrown her off quite as much as it had. As for seeing her in that crazy getup…

He hadn't known whether to laugh out loud, hug her, loosen her hair or kiss her. The latter reaction had surprised him the most. There'd just been something so damn *cute* about her yesterday. And he hadn't had a girlfriend in a while, and he was a guy, so…

Taking a quick shower, toweling off, and throwing on a pair of jeans and a shirt, Ethan decided to get back on the old stable footing with her today. Cody's social worker was due to arrive today at noon. He and Gemma needed to present a unified front.

As he headed into the hall barefoot and walked quietly downstairs so as not to awaken her or Cody, he thought about his growing friendship with Gemma. He wouldn't have known how to get through these last couple of weeks without her and felt a tug of disappointment over the realization that once the intensity of having Cody in the house was over, he would live most of the time in Seattle again, she would return to her life in Portland and they'd probably go back to being acquaintances. The friendship they shared now would be a memory, but a damn good one. The kind of memory it was worth hanging on to.

When he hit the bottom step and turned toward the kitchen, Ethan smelled coffee. *Good man. You remembered to set the timer on the coffee maker.* He hoped Gemma liked pancakes, his specialty, because he intended to make a couple dozen. Until training camp began, he was going to do all he could to lighten her load and the mood in the house. While he couldn't prepare a gourmet feast, his uncle had taught him how to make breakfast, and he was pretty good at it, if he did say so.

Whistling, he wondered how much time he had before Gemma and his nephew rejoined the living. Maybe he'd cut up a fruit salad. Women liked fruit.

A few feet into the great room, he realized he hadn't made the coffee; Gemma had.

Dressed in another boring skirt and plain blouse, with Cody snug in the wrap he'd purchased, Gemma murmured softly to his nephew as she cracked an egg.

Entering the kitchen, he glanced at the clock on the six-burner stove that had a large iron skillet ready and waiting. It wasn't even seven o'clock, yet she gave the impression she'd been up for hours. "Morning," he greeted.

"Good morning." She looked up to give him a bright smile, but it fell quickly. As it had yesterday, her glance lowered to his chest, then skittered away.

Looking down at himself, Ethan realized he hadn't buttoned his shirt—never did in the mornings—and she was obviously uncomfortable. Again.

"I'm making blueberry pancakes," she announced without looking at him.

"That's what I was going to do." It was stupid to feel disappointed that he hadn't been able to surprise her, but he *was* disappointed. "I've got some turkey bacon to go with it."

"It's already laid out in the fry pan, if you want to turn on the flame."

His other nannies had not cooked for him. "You didn't have to do that."

"I don't mind. We both have to eat."

Ethan turned on the flame beneath the bacon, then went to fill his coffee cup. "Thanks, then." He leaned back against the counter, close to her, but not in the way. "How long have you been up?"

"Oh, a little while."

She was deliberately avoiding eye contact. When he reached over to stroke his nephew's head, Gemma jerked. It was the open shirt. Had to be. She was just as uncomfortable around him as she'd been yesterday in the hallway.

"It was so quiet down here, I thought you were both still sleeping," he commented, studying her.

"Not at all," Gemma responded briskly, beating eggs to within an inch of their lives. "Cody and I were up at six. Need to keep to a schedule. Schedules are very soothing."

"Even when they begin at the butt crack of dawn?"

A smile twitched at the corner of her mouth. Quirky, funny Gemma would laugh or make a smart remark of her own or both, but Nanny Gemma pursed her lips and concentrated on measuring oil into the pancake mix.

If she was truly so uncomfortable, the gentlemanly thing would be to button his shirt and keep a reasonable distance between them while she was here.

That's when Ethan Ladd realized he was no gentleman.

His back to the sink, he braced his hands on the edge of the countertop, forcing his shirt open a little more, and flexed his pecs. Then he pulled in his gut and grinned as color flooded her face. Did that tiny squeaky sound come from her or Cody? His money was on her.

"How did it go last night? You didn't come pounding on my door, so I assumed everything was okay."

She swallowed twice before responding. "Everything was fine. I'm keeping a log of Cody's wake and sleep times and the presumable reasons for awakening. I only had to get up once, because he was hungry. After he ate, he went back to sleep." She kept working, folding berries into the pancake batter as she talked. "You know, I think he might be getting past the worst of the withdrawal."

Ethan said nothing, waiting her out until she turned her

head to see why he was silent and thinking, *Ha, gotcha!* when she finally did.

The plain skirts and buttoned-up blouses she'd worn the last two days made her look like a cross between Betty Boop and a Franciscan nun. Gemma might be one of the most educated women he knew, but she clearly didn't understand the way a man's mind worked. The more she covered her hourglass body, the more any man was going to imagine what was going on under there.

"You gonna be dressing like that every day now?" he asked.

"Like what?"

"Like you're wearing a uniform."

"You wear a uniform when you play football," she pointed out.

"I wear it for protection." He arched a brow. "Is that why you wear yours?" Giving her the look one magazine had called his "Liam Hemsworth smolder," he added, "Because you don't want anyone to see what a babe you are?"

There was the twitchy smile again. She reached for a bottle in a warmer on the counter and plugged it into Cody's eager mouth. "Cody doesn't care what I'm wearing. Do you, Cody?"

"I don't care, either. Take it off."

"What?" Eyes wide, she stared at him.

He inched a bit closer to her while Cody made sucking sounds on his bottle. "Go slip into something more comfortable. Seriously. You're all buttoned up. Just looking at you is making me itch." Okay. So it wasn't the clothing that made him so antsy. He enjoyed women, always had. But this friendship/boss thing they had going? It was becoming hands-down the most interesting relationship he'd ever had.

"I'm trying to figure you out," he murmured.

A frown crinkled her brow. "What's to figure?"

Without consciously intending to, Ethan touched her hair. As it had been yesterday, it was slicked back so tightly, his scalp hurt just looking at it. Usually, the brown waves were loose and tousled or twisted up in some half-silly, half-sexy hairdo. Ever since high school, she'd favored giant silk flowers and polka-dot bows he wouldn't have liked on anyone else, but that somehow looked exactly right on her. This tight, scalp-punishing style was all wrong.

"Take your hair out of that ridiculous bun."

Finally, he saw the Gemma he knew, with a smile she couldn't suppress.

"I'll take down my hair," she bargained, "if you button your shirt."

Ethan's grin matched hers as he slowly—very slowly— did as she asked. "Your turn."

After a moment's hesitation, she raised one hand to the back of her head, holding Cody's bottle steady with the other. When she struggled to accomplish her task one-handed, Ethan reached around her, locating the bobby pins and removing them one by one. They stared at each other as he worked, their smiles fading and their bodies heating up. At least his was, and he was pretty damn certain that some of the heat he felt was rolling off of her.

He was a dumb jock. Dumber than anyone would probably guess. There had never been a time, would never come a time, when he'd be the right man for Gemma. But this moment felt isolated from all others, and right now he wanted to kiss her. He wanted it a helluva lot.

They were standing as closely as they ever had as her bun unraveled, releasing coils of silky hair that fell below her shoulders. Their gazes never wavered. When Ethan's landline rang, he decided to ignore it until caller ID announced in a robotic monotone, "Jeanne Randall." *Damn it.*

"That's Cody's social worker." He whispered the words.

Gemma's eyes flared briefly. "You should pick it up," she said breathlessly.

Ethan nodded. Jeanne was due at his place in a couple of hours. The phone stopped ringing, then started again. Once more caller ID announced Jeanne's name, and this time he swallowed his frustration, stepped back from Gemma and walked around his nephew and their nanny to lift the cordless phone on the counter. His heart pounded in a way that had nothing at all to do with the phone call.

"Ethan here."

While he spoke to the social worker, he watched Gemma set Cody's bottle on the counter, then use both hands to return her hair to a much looser knot at the back of her head. Frustrated that he wouldn't be able to finger-comb the long brown locks that tempted him, he saw one telltale sign that lifted his spirits: her hands were shaking almost as much as his.

An hour after Ethan had sent her blood pressure into orbit, Gemma was in the kitchen again, nervously wiping the counter as she awaited the social worker's arrival.

Ethan had seemed to come to his senses after Jeanne Randall phoned to see if they could meet earlier than planned. Hanging up with her, he'd excused himself to make a call from his office and left the kitchen without further comment, barely looking in Gemma's direction again.

Had she completely misinterpreted that whole shirt-buttoning, bobby-pin-pulling-out, bedroomy-eyes thing? That had been a sexuality-drenched moment, the kind that could steam off wallpaper. For her. But Ethan lived a very different life. Maybe he'd just been joking around. Flirting came naturally to him.

When she'd fooled herself into thinking he was attracted to her fifteen years ago, it had gotten her into a whole peck of trouble. She didn't care to go down that road again.

So she'd left a plate of pancakes and turkey bacon for him on the center island, then taken a walk around the property with Cody in the wrap. Burning off her excess energy, she'd told herself to get back to the business at hand: they had a social worker to impress.

After her walk, she fed and changed Cody, waited for him to nod off, then tucked him into his swing while she cleaned the kitchen, including the empty breakfast plate Ethan had rinsed and set in the sink. When the doorbell rang, her heart rate doubled. The baby was still sleeping soundly, and she prayed the calm would last. Rushing to the microwave, she peered at her reflection in the glass door, hopeful that she looked neat, professional and in control.

As the voices in the front hallway grew louder, Gemma turned to see a middle-aged woman with platinum blonde hair in a chin-length bob enter the kitchen on Ethan's heels.

"Gemma," he said with an expression that spoke of his nerves, "this is Jeanne Randall. Cody's social worker."

After they greeted each other, Gemma asked, "Can I get you a cup of coffee?"

"Love one." Setting a large leather satchel on the floor near the kitchen table, Jeanne smiled at the baby sleeping in the swing and settled herself into a chair. "I was just telling Ethan that the purpose of this visit is to approve your employment as Cody's nanny. After we chat, I'll leave some paperwork for you to fill out. Okay?"

"Sure." Reenacting her college waitressing days, Gemma

carried three mugs of coffee to the table. She had a feeling her smile was overly bright. Ethan's sure was.

Busily sifting through a large stack of paper, Jeanne looked up and smiled. "I can see you're both nervous. Don't be. I don't bite…too hard." With a hearty laugh, she adjusted her reading glasses to the tip of her nose and folded her hands beneath her chin, looking warm and friendly. "All righty, Ethan, why don't we begin by addressing the question I know my supervisor will be posing—'Why is this nanny going to work out when the others haven't?' This is the fourth time you're asking me to go to bat for you on the nanny vetting process. The track record is unimpressive to say the least."

Whoa. Make that: as warm and friendly as a police interrogator. Gemma watched Ethan's Adam's apple bob. The man made his living being body slammed by defensive tackles built like refrigerators, but Jeanne had just managed to make him look as if he might throw up. Gemma had the nearly overwhelming urge to reach for his hand, but she resisted.

"Cody had a rough time at the beginning," Ethan said. "It was hard to find someone with the right temperament to deal with him. The good news is I finally found the perfect fit."

Jeanne's expression didn't alter much as she tapped the pile of papers she'd put on the table and turned her attention to Gemma. "I'll need to have you fill out these forms and get them back to me as soon as possible. Let's talk about your experience a little bit. How long have you been a nanny?"

Gemma could feel the tension rolling off Ethan in waves. Praying her first interaction with Jeanne would help him relax, she took a breath and reminded herself: *be calm, be confident, be cordial.* "I haven't worked as a *professional* nanny, but I do have quite a bit of experience caring for my nieces and nephews. I used to come back to Thunder Ridge every weekend to offer respite care for my sister's son. Owen had a pretty severe case of colic as an infant. He wanted to be held practically around the clock."

Jeanne's smile was kind enough, though her tone remained firm. "Colic isn't the same as an addiction to crack, though, is it?" Removing her glasses, she chewed on the tip of the stem. "What do you do professionally?"

"I teach lit at Easton College in Portland." For the first time ever, that didn't sound very impressive.

"You have the summer off, then?"

Gemma nodded. "That's right. And, I want to say, Jeanne, that even though I haven't worked as a nanny before, the techniques I learned while dealing with Owen seem to be working very well for Cody."

"Glad to hear it," Jeanne murmured, replacing her glasses and jotting a few quick notes on her legal pad. "Okay, let's assume you have summer taken care of, Ethan. What happens when Gemma goes back to work in September? For the baby's sake, I certainly don't like the idea of having to vet another slew of nannies."

The muscles worked in Ethan's jaw. "There won't be another slew of nannies. Sam will be back by the time Gemma leaves, and we'll have her in rehab. The clinic I found supports mothers bringing children to the facility with them. They do parenting classes."

"Has there been any positive movement on your end in locating Samantha?"

If Ethan stiffened any more, they'd have to check him for rigor mortis. "I expect to hear something soon. I hired a private investigator yesterday. I was on the phone with him before you arrived."

This was news to Gemma. Jeanne's expression, however, conveyed more resignation than surprise. "Your sister hasn't responded to DHS's attempts to get in touch, either," she said, easily reading between the lines. Samantha had zero contact with her brother. "We spoke to a former roommate, who thinks Samantha left the state."

A sudden shriek from Cody had them all jumping in their chairs. The baby blinked and, realizing that he was no longer asleep on Gemma's chest, started to howl.

Gut instinct told Gemma that Ethan needed to pick up the baby, needed to prove to this woman that nanny or no nanny, he could take care of Cody until Samantha was found.

"Why don't you take Cody out of the swing while I warm a bottle?" she suggested.

Instantly, Ethan was on his feet. "I'll get the bottle."

"No, thanks. I'm trying a new supplement in his formula. Besides, I know how much the two of you enjoy your male bonding time."

When Ethan stared at his nephew, his expression as trepidatious as ever during one of Cody's crying jags, she jerked her head once at the baby and hoped her wide eyes sent the message to *pick him up!*

She hoped his reluctance was less obvious to Jeanne than it was to her as he said, "Hey, little man, Uncle Ethan to the rescue." Cody's ire increased while Ethan fumbled with the safety belt. Once the baby was in his arms, Ethan paced and cooed and jostled unsuccessfully, all the while shooting imploring looks at Gemma.

Drat. Blaming herself for encouraging the epic fail, Gemma nonetheless gave props to Ethan for his effort and hoped Jeanne did, too.

When the bottle was ready, she crossed the kitchen and took the baby. Cody only had to look at her face before he stuffed his fist into his mouth and fell silent. Kissing the top of his downy head, Gemma resettled herself in her chair with the little man snuggled against her chest. Expression owlish, Cody listened to Gemma's murmured platitudes, then accepted the bottle she offered and relaxed against her.

Unmistakably relieved, Ethan dropped back into his chair and looked at Jeanne. "See what I mean? She's like the baby whisperer."

Jeanne nodded. "I see that." Taking a long moment to study baby and nanny together, Jeanne rubbed her eyes behind her glasses, then sighed heavily. "Ethan, I know you believe your sister wants to parent her son, but that's not the impression DHS is getting." She held up a hand as Ethan prepared to interrupt. "Let me finish so you'll know exactly what you want to blast me for." Irony and understanding filled her eyes. "Conventional wisdom is that reunification between birth parent and child should be our first goal. And it is. But kids can get shuffled through the system for years waiting for parents to clean up their acts. Or maybe the parent gets clean for a while and the child is returned, only to wind up in foster care again when the pressures of life make things implode." She shook her head. "We fail kids miserably when that happens. Especially if we can prevent it."

Wariness furrowed Ethan's brow. "How do you prevent it?"

"Permanency planning," Jeanne stated. "If Samantha can't be located, or if she is contacted, but doesn't want to cooperate with DHS, we would terminate her parental rights and begin to look for the best possible placement for Cody's needs, both his present needs and the ones we can reasonably anticipate given his exposure to drugs."

The kitchen fell silent except for the soft sucking sounds of Cody working on his bottle.

Something in Jeanne's tone and physical demeanor put Gemma on edge. She looked at Ethan and saw him tensing for battle.

"I have no intention of allowing *my nephew* to be tossed around like a pigskin on a football field," he told Jeanne in no uncertain terms. "If you're going to give up on his mother, then Cody is staying with me."

"Ordinarily that's the solution we'd be hoping for," the woman agreed carefully. "In this case, though…" She shuffled through a manila folder. "You made it clear when we first contacted you that you're not a permanent resource. 'I travel a lot' and 'I'm not a daddy type' are the quotes I wrote down. And we haven't even touched on what happens when training camp and your season begin. You're struggling now."

The silence that followed rang with the echo of the damning quotes.

"We're not struggling anymore. Not with Gemma here." Adamance warred with desperation in Ethan's tone.

Jeanne didn't have to state the obvious again. Gemma wouldn't be here for the long haul.

Genuine compassion filled the social worker's brown eyes. "You want Samantha to mother her son, but historically speaking, the chances are slim. Even if she shows up eventually, her history of relapse would make the placement precarious at best, unless she's consistently and willingly in a recovery program and absolutely dedicated to being a mother. Parenting Cody may present extra challenges his whole life."

Swallowing hard, Ethan looked at Cody. His obvious struggle had the backs of Gemma's eyes suddenly burning.

With what Gemma recognized as characteristic practicality, Jeanne asked, "Have you been attending the parenting classes I told you about? And, by any chance, have you read these?" Digging in her large bag, she withdrew her copies of the *Prenatal Drug Exposure Handbook* and *Coping Skills for Parents of the Special Needs Infant*.

Ethan shifted uncomfortably. "Actually, what with losing the last nanny—" he glanced around the room, seeming to grope for excuses "—and then, you know, looking for help, I haven't really had the opportunity."

Though Jeanne's slow nod seemed sympathetic enough, Gemma could tell the woman was more than a little frustrated. "I understand the strain of single parenting—that's one of my big concerns. But, Ethan, you've had these books since we placed Cody with you. And attending classes was part of the agreement when we gave you an emergency foster certification to care for your nephew. The classes are mandatory." Resting her open palms on the stack of books, she offered, "The classes could put your mind at ease. You'll meet terrific couples—two-parent families, some of whom already have experience parenting drug- and alcohol-affected kiddos and are eager to do it again. To be frank, I'm a strong proponent of having two parents in the home when dealing with all the needs Cody could present. There's a lot of mediation for birth families, too. You could have regular contact, including visitation, with your nephew."

"I'm not going to have visitation with Cody. He's going to stay right here." Raw with emotion, Ethan's voice pierced Jeanne's practical wisdom like an arrow. Jeanne's lips thinned.

"We'll both take the classes!" Gemma blurted. "I've been thinking seriously about adopting on my own. That's one of the reasons I wanted to help out with Cody—to get 24/7 experience. I'm totally dedicated. We'll take the classes and…and catch up on all the reading. Ethan is wonderful with the baby. He really—"

Feeling her hand being squeezed as if it was in a vise, she caught Ethan's message. *Quit while you're ahead. Sort of.*

Perhaps feeling her agitation, Cody released his hold on the bottle's nipple and began to fuss.

Jeanne gathered her things. Pushing herself back from the table, she stood. "I have to say, I appreciate your attitudes. And for all involved, I hope you can do it. Without Samantha here, the department can't wait too long before preparing a permanency plan for Cody."

Chapter Nine

Though Gemma had lain awake for the past two hours, watching the numbers on her digital clock progress with agonizing lethargy toward midnight, the knock on her door was still startling. She bolted up in bed as Ethan's silhouette hovered uncertainly in the spill of hall light.

"Gemma?" he whispered. "You awake?"

Heart thundering, she gathered the covers around her and sat up. "Yes," she whispered back. "Is something wrong?"

Quietly, Ethan entered the room. The baby stirred but, thankfully, didn't rouse.

Moonlight streamed through her window to reveal the strained lines of his face.

"I can't sleep," he admitted.

"Me, either." For once, Cody was the only one who seemed peaceful.

The mattress dipped under Ethan's weight as he settled at the edge of her bed, his head lowered.

After Jeanne had left that morning, Ethan had gone for a long run, returning drenched in sweat, but no less troubled than when he'd set out. Gemma had asked if he wanted to talk, receiving a bleak, "Not right now, thanks." She'd gotten that same answer when she'd asked if he wanted lunch. He'd spent most of the day alone, sequestered in his study, making phone calls.

Twice when he'd emerged to get water and aspirin, he'd looked at Cody with such bald angst, Gemma had physically ached with the desire to help. But how? The teacher in her wanted to sit him down and insist that he read the materials Jeanne assigned. And why hadn't he attended the classes? The friend in her wanted to hug him and say everything would be okay. Realistically, however, she knew Ethan and Cody were standing on a rug that could be pulled out from beneath them, and she was scared.

After several moments of heavy silence, Ethan turned to face her. "I spent the day on the phone with the investigator I hired. No progress in finding Sam yet. I called my lawyers next, and they were able to recommend a family law group that's supposed to be tops in custody issues around adoption. I have an appointment with them in a few days, but the attorney I spoke with today said there are a few strikes against me already. First, I made a mistake telling the social workers that I only wanted to keep Cody until my sister could be found. To be honest, I didn't want to take him at all. I just wanted to talk some sense into Sam until they told me she'd disappeared."

"Those are honest reactions," she said. "But now you know Cody, and you can explain that your feelings have changed—"

"It's not that simple." He sounded as agitated as he looked. "There are things…" He stopped, seeming reluctant to continue. "It wouldn't be smart for me to try to keep Cody if the best I can give him is me and a series of nannies. No judge is going to want to picture a kid raised by nannies, anyway. Not if someone else can give him a two-parent family, like Jeanne said." His eyes were bleak as he looked at her. "The lawyer said that before I meet with him, I should think long and hard about Cody's needs and my own capabilities and commitment."

No. Gemma's heart beat too hard. *No, don't say you're going to let him go to another family.* She respected the concept of adoption—she wanted to do it herself—but losing Cody…it was wrong. It just felt wrong.

"Ethan, you only spoke with Jeanne today." She glanced at the clock and amended, "Yesterday. Isn't it too soon to make decisions? I mean, it's still possible things could work out with Samantha—"

"Things *will* work out. I believe that." As always when he spoke of his sister, his tone became adamant. "But I can't wait for her. I need to make decisions now for Cody's sake. For my own sake, too."

For perhaps the first time in her life, Gemma understood what it meant to feel as if her heart literally sank. Tears stung the back of her throat and eyes. *Silly,* she chided herself, *Cody isn't your baby. When all this is over, you'll go back to hearing about Ethan from your mother and in magazines, so get a grip.* But in her gut, she knew that little baby was exactly where he belonged.

"When I got off the phone," Ethan said slowly, staring down at his hands, "I did what the guy said—I thought about it. I prayed. Every time I asked the question, 'Am I capable of this?' the answer came back, 'Hell, no.' Cody deserves a lot more than I can give him."

Oh, Ethan.

He rubbed his hands over his face. "I guess I'm about as selfish as you can get, because I called the Eagles and made plans for early retirement. I don't have too many years left to play, anyway." He turned his head toward Gemma. "I've got to show DHS I mean business. I *do* mean business. Cody's not going to another family. He's staying with me."

He barely got the last word out before Gemma gasped in surprise and threw her arms around his neck. "I'm so glad! Oh, Ethan, you'll never be sorry. Never! I know you don't think you're a family man, or the right person for this, but you *are*. Look at how much you care about your sister, and you've always hung around my family. My mother was right—if George Clooney can change, you can, and… Oh, my gosh, I'm so relieved!"

It took a couple of moments to realize she was hugging Ethan and that he was hugging back. Sort of. His large hands were splayed across her back, holding her lightly, almost tentatively. She pulled away slowly, and they stared at each other. Unreadable blue eyes gazed into hers, and his mouth made a tiny move toward a smile.

Gemma's heart gave one extra-hard thump that served to wake her up. "So…early retirement. Is that really okay with you?"

Ethan nodded. "Yeah. I want to do it. And I appreciate your enthusiasm," he murmured, his smile appearing again briefly, "but this isn't a touchdown yet. I'm not a poster boy for the perfect guardian."

"Jeanne hasn't seen the paternal side of you yet," she pointed out. "She'll come around."

Ethan began shaking his head before she finished. His grip on her arms tightened. "Listen. You told Jeanne you were interested in adoption." Through the light and shadow, he looked at her intently. "Why did you do that? Were you trying to con her for my sake?"

"No, of course not! I wouldn't lie to a social worker,"

she insisted, then softened. "Not even for your sake." Realizing she needed to tell him about her plans, she felt the need to shift a few inches away, and he let go of her arms. Pulling the light covers up around her body again, she confessed, "I *am* thinking about adopting. Or becoming a mother some other way."

"Now?" he asked, obviously surprised, his tone somewhat less than lukewarm. "Alone?"

"Well, not *right* now. And not alone, no. I have family, I have friends. And I live in Portland. There are single-parent support groups. I'll meet a lot of great people, I'm sure."

"Single-parent support groups," he muttered. "Probably happy hour with toddlers."

"Don't knock them. You'll probably be using them yourself."

He shook his head. "Don't you remember what Jeanne said about two-parent families? She thinks they're best for kids with special needs like Cody's. She's not alone in that philosophy, either. The lawyer said I could easily come up against a judge who believes the same thing."

"Still, successful one-parent families do exist. She can't deny that."

"No. But she can make it tough on me. *I've* made it tough on me."

"Ethan." Throwing aside the covers entirely, Gemma swung her legs off the bed to sit side by side with him. Even though she wore her favorite summer pj's—shorts and a pale pink T-shirt bearing a skull and the Shakespeare quote, "To sleep, perchance to dream"—sitting beside him felt more…businesslike…than hiding under the covers. "So, listen," she said, feeling suddenly calm and practical and surprisingly alert given the hour, "you have to stop looking at the past. Forget what you've said before. Give Jeanne time to get to know the real you."

Putting both hands on his face and rubbing, Ethan made a guttural sound. "If she knew the real me, she'd take Cody in a heartbeat."

"What are you talking about?" Over the past few days, there'd been a couple of occasions on which Gemma had the strange feeling there was something not quite right with Ethan. She made a face. That didn't sound right. She didn't know what she meant exactly, only that sometimes she thought she was getting to know him well and then other times she felt she didn't know him at all. It was weird.

Suddenly it occurred to her that they were in a bedroom after midnight, involved in something hugely important together; she had every right to insist on an answer.

Turning toward him, she asked, "What do you mean Jeanne would take Cody if she knew the real you?" at the very same time he dropped his hands, looked at her and queried, "Gemma, will you marry me?"

I suck at proposals.

Mostly, that was all Ethan could think as Gemma stared at him, her eyes so huge he could see the white part even with no illumination other than Cody's night-light and the dim glow from the hall. She didn't say anything at first, but then he heard a weird choking sound.

She stood up, body ramrod straight. "Downstairs." Sounding like Minerva McGonagall scolding Harry Potter, she jabbed a finger toward the door. "We will discuss this downstairs." She took two steps, turned back, swept the blanket off the bed to wrap it around herself, then marched all the way to the kitchen, flipping on lights as she went.

Yeah, he totally sucked.

He sensed his best tactic was silence while she filled two mugs with milk, put them in the microwave, punched a button, then pulled a can of hot cocoa powder and a glass jar filled with mini marshmallows from the pantry. Unscrewing the lid on the jar, she withdrew several of the marshmallows, filling her mouth and chewing before she tilted the jar toward him. "Do you want some?"

He shook his head, which appeared to disgust her.

"Men," she scoffed. "You drop bombshells, and you don't even want to eat. William told me about Mademoiselle Allard right after we got takeout from a new Thai place. Then he left me with all the food, saying *he* felt too bad to eat anything." Shaking a handful of marshmallows at him, she said accusingly, "I ate an entire serving of *mee grob* and half a pad thai." She shoved more of the small white puffs into her mouth, making her cheeks look lumpy.

He decided to risk a beheading by easing the jar away from her, afraid she'd hate herself in the morning.

"Okay, look," he began, "I could have approached that question with more finesse—"

"Ya think?"

"—but how? It's the last thing you expected to hear. Before tonight, it was the last thing I expected to say—"

"Give me the marshmallows."

"—because marriage isn't something I ever thought I'd be any good at. Just hear me out. You want to adopt. I asked the lawyer if it would be easier for a couple to adopt Cody, and he said it's always easier for a two-parent family to adopt. Always, Gemma, even in your case."

She set her fists on her hips and challenged, "Even if they've been married for two seconds?"

"I thought about that. We've known each other since high school. Would it be so far-fetched to tell people we fell in love? And that Cody gave us the extra push we needed to make it official?"

He could see her consternation. The timer on the microwave dinged, but he doubted she noticed. Standing next to the massive island in his kitchen, wrapped in the blanket, her bare toes painted with multicolored glitter this week and her brows drawn together, she looked small and angry and adorable. And hurt. He didn't want her to be hurt.

"I can give you what you want," he said, trying to explain his reasoning. "If we get married, you'll be in a better position to adopt. I'll be in a better position to keep Cody. And I think you and I... I think we like each other pretty well."

She reached for the marshmallow jar. He held it up, compressing his lips before admitting, "I never planned to propose to anyone. I'm not good at this."

"Big. Fat. Understatement."

Strange thing about his relationship with Gemma: the more she glared at him, the more he relaxed. Feeling a smile push the corners of his mouth, he resigned himself to telling the truth, at least about her. "What I meant to say, what I *should* have said, is *I* like *you*. I feel better around you than I've felt around just about anyone. I trust you. And you look good in your pj's." His smile grew. When she'd put her fists on her hips, the blanket had slipped to reveal the front of the skimpy pink sleepwear. "Real good." Sans bra, her full breasts were impossible to miss and equally impossible not to appreciate.

Despite all the worry he'd been carrying, Ethan felt his body react. Any red-blooded male would react to the pint-size bombshell that was Gemma. Her brain added to the allure...and also made him so wrong for her, but he couldn't allow that to stop him now.

"Maybe you're not attracted to me," he suggested, voice soft, seduction mode on. "Maybe the thought of marrying me is a turnoff." He walked toward her, keeping his gaze locked with hers. He might not have confidence in his childcare skills or in the brain that too often let him down, but he was a sexy SOB, and he knew a thing or two about women—like the fact that this one was physically attracted to him and trying not to be.

Unscrewing the glass jar in his hands, he picked out a marshmallow with his thumb and forefinger. Yep, he'd caught Gemma getting hot 'n' bothered a couple of times since she'd moved in, and he'd wanted to do something about it—might have done something about it—if he didn't like her so damn much. She was the marrying kind; he wasn't. She'd been hurt already, and they were nowhere near right for each other. Plenty of reasons to keep his hands off. But he needed a wife, and she could get some mileage out of a marriage, too.

"If we go into this with our eyes wide-open, it could work," he said softly.

She seemed to have trouble swallowing. "H-how? I'm not sure what you're talking about. How long is this marriage supposed to last?"

He'd thought about that, knowing how much he needed her, which was a helluva lot more than she needed him. He would never, ever be able to raise Cody alone. It wouldn't be fair to the poor kid. It wouldn't even be safe. The real question was how long before Gemma grew tired of the game? Aloud, he answered, "I don't know. As long we both think it works for us, I suppose."

"It's crazy. What happens if Samantha comes back and takes Cody? What if one of us meets someone?"

"I won't. I've never cheated on a woman, Gemma. I sure as hell won't start with you." He set the jar of marshmallows on the granite counter. "As far as Samantha…that's a bridge we cross when we get there. She's going to need a lot of help for a long time. Cody will still need us. We may have adopted by then, too."

"We? You'd be interested in more than one child...of your own?"

"The idea is less alien than it used to be." There it was again—the urge to smile despite all the what-ifs that hung in the balance.

Gemma shook her head. "This is too much to take in. If we have children and the marriage ends..."

"We wouldn't be the first," he allowed, though he didn't want to put a child through a divorce, nor did he like the assumption that it *would* end. "I know you wanted to be married, have kids the normal way. But you yourself said you weren't willing to wait to be married in order to have children. You were going to push ahead on your own. This is another option. You're my friend, and I think you're sexy as hell. Marriages have been built on less, I bet."

Her face flushed a deeper pink than her pajamas. A good sign? He found himself hoping so.

"Think about it, will you, Gem?" He raised the marshmallow he'd plucked from the jar and brought it to her open lips. "What was it Scott and Elyse said at their wedding? 'I promise not to let the sun set without telling you how lucky I feel to have you'? I can promise you that. And marshmallows. If you say yes, I promise never, ever to make you go without marshmallows."

Before she could say yea or nay, he popped the treat in her mouth, following it with a kiss he intended to be as light and sweet as the candy. And it was. Until her arms went slack, and the blanket fell, and the temptation to make the kiss something more became too much for either of them to resist.

He started it... He was pretty certain he started it. All Ethan knew for sure was that his hands were framing cheeks as soft and smooth as the petals of a rose and that he'd wanted to taste these lips for a lot longer than he'd ever be willing to admit.

The kiss sent wave after wave of desire flooding through his body. Even though Ethan was no stranger to foreplay (although he was less prolific than the media made him out to be), he almost lost control when he felt her hands traveling up his back…then clutching his shirt.

He pulled her against him, wanting to feel the body he'd tried not even to wonder about for the past fifteen years. And it felt… *Damn.* If he moved one hand to the front of her body, he could explore her breasts; the other hand could slide to her butt and—

Whoa! She went there first, to *his* butt. The action seemed to surprise her as much as it did him. Letting go, she jumped back as if she'd suddenly awoken from a spell.

They stared at each other. Ethan realized he had one hand out, as if he wanted to pull her back, and let it fall to his side.

Her face looked…kissed. She was breathing heavily. He didn't know if she was going to kiss him again or run as fast and as far as she could.

"Gemma," he said, hoping to steady her, positive of only one thing in this moment—that he couldn't let her go. "Please. Marry me."

"I still think you need to have your head examined." Standing behind Gemma, twisting her friend's heavy locks of hair into an intricate updo, Holliday spoke her mind—for the umpteenth time since Gemma had announced she was going to marry Ethan. "Seriously. If there's a Groupon for psych evaluations, I'm buying you one."

Handing her friend a bobby pin from the small collection on the vanity she was seated in front of, Gemma smiled, the very picture, she hoped, of equanimity. "That's not a nice thing to say to someone on her wedding day," she responded without a trace of resentment.

Seventeen days ago, Ethan had proposed to her. Twice. Once before The Kiss and once after. Holliday was the first person Gemma had told, partly because she'd wanted to be completely honest with someone and partly because she'd wanted to practice saying, "Ethan and I are getting married," with a big, confident smile before she told her family.

"Ouch!" Gemma exclaimed when her friend stabbed her with a bobby pin. "If you're upset about the wedding, use words. My scalp is just an innocent bystander here."

"Sorry." Contritely, Holliday patted Gemma's head. "I'm not upset about your wedding. I'm upset about your wedding night. Explain one more time, please, why you are not consummating this marriage, which might—only *might*, mind you—make the idea of getting married for the baby's sake a bit more palatable."

"We're having a probationary period," Gemma told her friend again. "No sex for three months while we focus on Cody's needs, and I look into adoption. This way we can make decisions about all our futures without unnecessary entanglements."

"Sleeping with your husband is an unnecessary entanglement?"

"This isn't a normal marriage."

"I'll say," Holliday muttered, her expression a cross between *you need more therapy than I thought* and *whatever*.

S'okay, maybe Gemma hadn't been 100 percent honest with Holliday when she'd explained her reasons for putting restrictions on her marriage. She'd omitted her number one fear: that she was falling in love with Ethan.

She'd probably sort of almost known it already, but after that kiss—*awww, that kiss*—she'd become really concerned, and that meant she had to protect herself from heartbreak. And *that* meant no sex until she had reason to believe their relationship might actually go the distance.

"Uhm, Holl?" Gemma ventured as the redhead wound her hair still tighter around the barrel of the curling iron. "Could you relax or put down the curling iron, because I'm afraid you're going to singe me."

"Oh. Sorry." Dressed for the wedding in a vintage fifties floral cap-sleeve wiggle dress with bright red pumps and matching fire-engine lipstick, Holliday sighed loudly. "I can't believe Ethan agreed to your terms."

Well, he hadn't been wild about her terms. She'd had to make it clear—before she could change her mind and jump his bones right there in the kitchen—that there could be no kissing. *Awww, that kiss!* Under the spell of his lips moving slowly, sensuously over hers, she'd lost all sense of time and place. Never before had she been swept into such pure sensation. For several magical seconds, she'd had no idea where Ethan ended and she began. If someone had told her to describe the difference between lust and love in that moment, she wouldn't have been able to do it to save her life.

Which was why she'd slapped some rules on herself.

"This marriage has to have parameters," she told Holliday—and herself. "Guidelines."

"Yes, I'm familiar with the concept of parameters. Contrary to local rumor." The flamboyant redhead arched a perfectly shaped eyebrow. "Why ninety days? That's so looong."

Gemma chewed the inside of her lip. Why? Because if her marriage imploded over the summer—for any one of a thousand plausible reasons—then she could jump back into school to save her sanity. And because it was the first thing that came to mind when she was trying to convince

Ethan that a moratorium was not personal; it was a commonsense way to simplify a complex situation.

"Ethan understands." *Sort of.* "He agrees." *Kinda.*

Three brisk raps on the door provided an interruption, and Gemma signaled Holliday that they needed to cut this convo short. "Remember," she whispered, "my family thinks this marriage is the real deal, and that's the way it's got to stay, or I'll never hear the end of it." She and Ethan were under enough pressure.

Holliday wagged her head. "You Goulds watch too much reality TV."

The door opened. "We're here!" Minna sang. It had earlier been decided that the women would get dressed together.

Plastic garment bags rustled as Lucy followed Minna, who had entered with a snoozing Cody in her arms. Placing the baby in the middle of the queen-size bed, Minna directed Lucy to hang the garment bags over a hook on the back of the guest room door. "Where's Elyse?" her mother asked, glancing around.

"I thought she'd be with you," Gemma replied. The sudden flurry of activity was making everything seem more real, and blood roared in her ears. Only four weeks ago, she had attended her sister's wedding. Now she was having one of her own.

"You're doing a lovely job with her hair, Holliday," Minna complimented as she began to rearrange some of the strands. "Where is your dress, sweetie?"

Gemma pointed to the closet. While Minna fetched the tea-length gown, Lucy uncapped a mascara and helped herself to a section of the mirror. "I think Elyse is concerned," she ventured uneasily, keeping her eyes on her own reflection and giving the impression she was about to throw a wet blanket over the party.

"Concerned about what?" Minna asked as she removed Gemma's frothy crinoline petticoat from its hanger. "Stand up, honey," she ordered, preparing to slip the undergarment over the bride-to-be's head.

Gemma complied, lifting her arms to allow her mother to carefully ease the acreage of netting over her elaborate hairdo.

"I think," Lucy explained while coating her lashes, "Elyse may be concerned that Gemma is…settling by marrying Ethan."

Three pairs of eyes fastened on Lucy's reflection. Three voices exclaimed, "Settling?"

"'Settling' for Ethan Ladd?" Minna's expression was almost comical. "Don't talk silly. He was in *People* magazine." She shook her head. "Honestly, the ideas you girls get sometimes. My bridge club will be green when they see pictures of this house." Her voice became muffled as she encased Gemma's head and her own in a cloud of rustling fabric. "Are any celebrities coming?"

"No, Mom," Gemma mumbled. Even though she and Ethan had agreed they needed to make the wedding seem as real as they could, they'd also agreed to keep it as simple as possible. Just family and close friends.

Exasperated, Lucy jammed her mascara wand back into the tube. "Who cares if there are going to be celebrities there, Mom! Don't you think—sorry, Gemmy, nothing personal here—that this is all just a bit sudden? I mean, they went from zero to sixty in less than ten. It's unusual. That's all."

"So?" Minna, who had shown nothing but joy over the new development in her eldest daughter's life, rushed to the defense of the bride and groom. "They've known each other forever. This kind of thing happens all the time. Friendship turns to love. Look at Harry and Sally." She tugged on the petticoat. "Suck in, Gemmy, I'm going to cinch the waist on this."

"Who are Harry and Sally?" Gemma asked, wondering if she'd attended their wedding.

"She's talking about the movie with Billy Crystal and Meg Ryan," Lucy snapped. "They're actors, Mom. It's a story."

"Well, I know that." Minna put her fists on her hips. "I also know that truth is stranger than fiction." Her heels clicked on the hardwood floor as she marched across the bedroom to get Gemma's wedding dress.

"Gem," Lucy said, "Elyse and I know how badly you've always wanted a family, but couldn't you slow down a little?"

"They aren't getting married only because she wants a family," Minna argued on her way back. "Not that it isn't enough of a reason, dear," she assured the bride. "Ethan is ready to get married, and he chose a hometown girl with a good head on her shoulders and a wonderful personality. And *that's it*. Now let's all speak pleasantly."

Lucy exhaled loudly and tossed her mascara onto the vanity. Holliday reached over to squeeze Gemma's shoulder, and Gemma wondered whether the truth could be any worse than this…

"Let's get you in your dress," Minna directed, settling the fifties-inspired sweetheart bodice and red-dotted skirt into place. "Suck it in one last time while I zip you up."

Once Gemma was tightly ensconced, her mother fluffed and smoothed and tweaked, then took a step back. "You know—" Minna's smile was wobbly "—I wasn't too sure about this dress when you bought it. But, honey—" she waggled her fingers for Lucy to hand her a tissue from the dressing table "—you look absolutely beautiful. Radiant." She dabbed beneath her eyes.

Lucy moved to Holliday's side, and Gemma watched their concern transform into smiles now, too. "You really do look perfect," Lucy said as Holliday nodded in agreement, and they all snatched a tissue from the box. "I'm sorry I put a damper on things," Lucy sniffled. "If this is your happily-ever-after, I'm all for it."

"Thank you," Gemma whispered, feeling tears rise in her own eyes. She'd never imagined her "happily-ever-after" beginning as a three-month trial marriage of convenience. She hadn't imagined duping her own family. And she admitted, as the women led her to the cheval mirror standing in the corner, she was probably duping herself, too.

Because the image that stared back at her looked every inch the smitten, hopeful bride.

Chapter Ten

"Dude. Stand still."

"Right. Like *you'd* stand there and let someone effectively choke you to death." Ethan grimaced as Scott, his soon-to-be brother-in-law, helped him with his tie. They'd holed up in his bedroom for a celebratory glass of brandy and a cigar that remained unlit because Elyse had barged in and didn't like the smell.

"Yeah, well, as your best man, it's my duty to make sure your tie stays on during the ceremony. Cut me some slack. Your neck belongs in the Redwood National Park. Elyse? Give me a hand here. My fingers are too big to get this collar button closed without cutting off his air supply."

Elyse, hair in rollers and still wearing a bathrobe, slid off Ethan's bed and onto her feet. Ethan could feel the tension fairly radiating from her body as she approached.

"You all right?" he asked as she reached for his throat.

"Ethan. I realize you're my husband's best friend. And,

at the moment, you are my sister's fiancé. You also out-weigh me by more than a hundred pounds."

Ethan frowned, glancing at Scott as Elyse took the loose ends of his bow tie into her fists and tugged. Eyes wide, Scott shrugged and shook his head with a look that said, *I have no idea.*

"However," she continued, lifting herself onto the balls of her bare feet and skewering him with a menacing eye, "that will not stop me from removing your head from this beer keg you call a neck if you break my sister's heart. William put her through hell last year. He lied to her. He cheated on her. He embarrassed her in front of her friends and coworkers. And—" her lips began to tremble, her eyes filling with sudden tears "—my sister is the sweetest, most loving, amazing, fun and funny, loyal person on the face of this earth and I love her with all my heart. So if you so much as look cross-eyed at her, I swear, you will have to—" she gave a watery hiccup "—deal…with me, Ethan Ladd!"

As suddenly as she'd flared up, Elyse let go of his tie, buried her face in her hands and began to sob. Her fore-head thudded against his chest. Awkwardly, Ethan pat-ted her back and looked over her head at Scott. *What the hell?* he mouthed.

To Elyse he said, "Uh, okay. Listen. I just want you to know that I'd never, ever, intentionally hurt your sister."

Help, he whispered to Scott who stepped to his wife's side and took her into his arms.

"Hey, now, sweetheart," Scott murmured while he rocked Elyse, attempting to stroke her head over the huge, juice-can-sized rollers. "Don't you think you're being just a little bit tough on Ethan? After all, it is his wedding day."

"No, Scott!" Elyse blubbered into his shirt. "Gemma

has been hurt enough already. By me, too! I made a big deal about *That's My Gown!* and I sh-sh-shouldn't have."

"Honey, Gemma's a strong woman. She's fine. And she's happy now...so you should be happy for her. Right? C'mon, now. *Shh...shh...shh*," Scott soothed and cajoled and then looked at Ethan in apology. "Sorry about this, buddy. She's a little hormonal."

Ethan winced at the ceiling. "Too much info, man."

Scott laughed. "No, I mean...she's pregnant."

"Already?" Surprised, Ethan stared at them, instantly worried about how this would affect Gemma. First, her younger sister gets married and then, right away, she's pregnant. It would be a blow. "Does Gemma know?"

Scott shook his head. "No. We just found out this morning. We decided not to say anything until after your wedding. Didn't want to steal your thunder."

Elyse gazed up at her husband with watery eyes. "I'm always stealing people's thunder!" she cried, her head thudding on Scott's chest.

Slowly, Ethan lowered himself to the edge of his bed as it dawned on him that Elyse probably had a very good point. Gemma would be the one to bear the brunt of the hurt and humiliation if this not-quite-the-real-deal-marriage thing didn't work out. He was used to the press and accepted that they could be as brutal as a troop of Mongol warriors. His skin was thick. Plus, in situations where wealthy men and middle-class women got together, headlines tended to treat men better than women. If anyone got wind that this marriage wasn't a love affair, Gemma could be painted a gold digger.

Because Gemma was everything her sister said she was, he couldn't let her get hurt.

Sighing, he pinched the bridge of his nose between his thumb and forefinger. Since it was far too late to back out now without making everything worse—and because he had no intention of backing out, anyway—he knew he needed to drop back six and punt. As his mind rapidly scanned the possibilities, an idea came to him. A way to squelch speculation about the validity of his and Gemma's marriage. He nodded, a smile stealing slowly across his face. Yeah, a fail-safe play.

The PDA play.

Public displays of affection would not be hard to pull off today. They were logical. Necessary even. His blood began to heat at the thought. If there was one aspect of their relationship he was really becoming fond of, it was touching Gemma.

When she'd come up with her no-sex probation period, he'd wanted to shoot the idea down ASAP, but he figured that was his libido talking. Besides, she'd been adamant, and her reasons were pretty logical. Sex was a complication, she'd insisted, and their marriage was complicated enough already. With so much at stake, she wanted them to focus on the reasons for their "arrangement"—Cody's future and her potential adoption. Later, they could renegotiate.

Reminding himself she'd always been the smart one, he'd agreed. He could get sex just about anyplace, but he couldn't find another Gemma.

When it came to persuading everyone the marriage was real, however…well, she was going to have to trust the PDAs to him. That's where he had the know-how.

"Elyse," he said, after giving her a chance to blow her nose and pull herself together. "Your sister means the world to me." *True.* "The way I feel about her is… It's new to me." *Also true.* He couldn't remember another time when he'd had a great friendship with a woman. Or a time when he trusted someone so much. "I promise I will never deliberately hurt her. We know what we're doing. She's happy. I'm happy. And I want to do everything I can to make this wedding great for her. You had your day, right? Now let's give her hers." Seeing Elyse begin to well up again, he dragged a hand through his hair. "You've got to stop crying unless they're happy tears."

Elyse sniffed and nodded.

"And whatever you do, please don't tell her you're having a baby, okay? Not today. Give her some time to be the star of the show. She deserves that."

Elyse looked up at him, tremulous discovery gradually altering her features. "You really do care about Gemma." Accepting the tissue Scott passed her, Elyse blew her nose again and nodded. "I think you *are* going to take good care of her. I mean, despite all the other women you've slept with and discarded, it's different between you two, isn't it?"

"Hey, Elyse, I have not slept with and discarded—" Ethan began hotly, then saw Scott make a slashing sign across his throat: *She's happy again. Leave it alone.* Ethan nodded. Fine. "Yes, it's different," he concluded.

"Good enough," Scott said, taking his wife by the shoulders and pushing her toward the door. "I'll walk you down the hall, honey. You need to get ready, don't you?"

They began to murmur gooey endearments to each other, and Ethan made a mental note. "No baby talk" was going to be part of his pact with Gemma. And absolutely no hormones.

The wedding ceremony was slated to take place in front of the waterfall on Ethan's back lawn, for privacy's sake. Because they'd had such a brief time to plan, Gemma had stated she'd be perfectly happy with a barbecue or perhaps a potluck, keeping it as simple as possible, but Minna, of course, had been appalled. Going into overdrive, she'd called on the connections they'd only recently used for Elyse's wedding, arranging for thirty red-ribboned white chairs, a tent, tables and even a chuppah constructed of branches and woven with flowers and twinkle lights.

"Mom outdid herself," Gemma murmured as she stood

with her father before the grand glass doors leading to Ethan's backyard.

"She wants you to have the best, Gemmy girl." Hal patted the hand she'd curled around his arm. "We all do. Mother Nature is cooperating, too."

Indeed she was. The late afternoon had settled perfectly into the midseventies with a sky so celestially blue, it looked as if cherubs had painted it. The parklike lawn and abundant foliage graciously lent themselves to the creation of a fairy-tale bower for her and Ethan to be married in. It was so much more than Gemma could have ever dreamed.

From where she stood, she could see Ethan waiting for her next to Scott, and her stomach clenched with excitement as much as nerves. She didn't think her groom could see her yet, but she got a nice eyeful of him. Dark gray suit perfectly tailored to a perfect male body, his hair glittering with sunny streaks, his hands held loosely in front of him, his smile turned toward Scott as they shared a word before turning their attention to the petal-strewn white satin aisle, where Holliday began to make her inimitable way toward the chuppah as the Dream Catchers, a local group, played a sweet, stringed version of "Storybook Love."

"Mom's really happy, isn't she?" Gemma asked, catching sight of her mother beaming in the front row.

"She wants you kids to be happy." Hal patted her arm. "She thinks being married will contribute to that."

"Because she's so happy in her marriage to you." Gemma smiled up at her dad, caught by surprise when his eyes grew watery with emotion. In response, her own eyes began to fill. How many times had both her father and her mother concluded a mealtime blessing with, "And thank you especially for our family"? Minna wasn't simply excited about Gemma marrying *Ethan*; she was excited, because, as far as she knew, Gemma was about to have the very things that made Minna's life so rich.

All Gemma's siblings had found the mate who would walk with them into the legacy Hal and Minna had created— a legacy of partnership, laughter and the overwhelming, imperfect love of family. For the first time, Gemma felt that she, too, was part of continuing that legacy.

As Holliday reached the chuppah and moved into place, Gemma's heart thumped harder. It was time. The Dream Catchers began the first notes of "Wedding Song." Hal took a step forward to open the glass door, but Gemma tugged him back.

"Daddy," she whispered, "were you nervous on your wedding day?"

"I was afraid I was going to throw up my Cheerios." A poignant smile creased Hal's face. "But the minute your mother showed up, I was fine." For a moment his gaze traveled down the aisle to the man who waited for them. When he turned back to Gemma, Hal's expression was more sober. "Sweetheart, every summer when we took you kids to go diving off Stronghold Rock, your brother and sisters would jump right in, but you'd hang back, standing on that rock, shivering, looking down, waiting for the courage to jump. It was the same every summer. You'd wait and wait, and when courage didn't arrive, you'd get down from the rock and say you'd do it for sure the next summer."

Gemma frowned. She remembered that rock, remembered the heart-stopping feeling of standing with her siblings twenty feet above the best swimming hole on Long River and the yearning to go for it.

"But I did jump eventually," she defended. What was her dad getting at?

"Yes, you did," Hal allowed, his face as kind and nonjudgmental as ever. "When you were fifteen. That's a lot of summers."

Fifteen. Had she really waited that long? She'd absolutely loved it once she'd taken the plunge, but her siblings had been soaring off the rock since elementary school. She'd missed out on years of flying.

"Ethan was a good boy," her father commented, "and he's an even better man. But you don't have to go through with this if he's not the right man for you."

The desire to tell her father the whole truth hit Gemma like a sledgehammer. It would be selfish to worry Hal, though, if she planned to go through with this, anyway.

"You're telling me that if I'm going to do this, I should jump. You know me, though. I want to predict the future." She tried to sound ironic and offhand, but could feel her upper lip trembling. "I guess I've never been as brave as I wish I was."

"Ah, sweetheart." Hal touched her cheek lightly. "Courage isn't the confidence that you're going to succeed at everything. It's the faith that you'll be fine if you don't. That kind of courage is available to every one of us."

A couple of tears Gemma couldn't hold back slipped down her cheeks. Immediately Hal reached for the handkerchief he was never without. "Four women in my life means I need four handkerchiefs," he always joked. With an expertise born of experience, he dabbed the tears without disturbing her makeup.

"It's your choice, honey." He nodded toward the room's entrance and then at the glass doors leading to the garden. "Which way do you want to walk?"

Gemma took a deep breath. "Forward, Daddy. I'm going to go forward."

As soon as she stepped onto the silk runner, Gemma's eyes met Ethan's. Their gazes remained locked as he took her hand and stood with her before the officiant. Only dimly aware of the small crowd gathered on the lawn, Gemma recited the words of the wedding vow and fell under their binding spell as Ethan recited his, voice deep and certain.

Even though this wedding wasn't as real as Elyse's or Lucy's or their parents' had been, Gemma *felt* married when she heard the words, "I now pronounce you husband and wife."

To whoops and clapping, Ethan kissed the bride, dipping her back dramatically. His lips pressed deliciously to hers, stopping time and blocking out everything but the awareness that Ethan's lips were the just-right ratio of soft to firm, and that they applied the most perfect pressure, and that if this was Ethan's *fake* just-married kiss, then, yowza, would she ever love to get a taste of the real thing.

When finally he set them both upright, she was so wonderfully woozy she only vaguely heard their introduction as "Mr. and Mrs. Ladd."

They walked up the aisle arm in arm, stopping so Ethan could hug her mother and shake her father's hand. Minna had quite obviously cried throughout the short ceremony and hugged her daughter fiercely, murmuring, "You're beautiful. He's a very lucky man."

Wow. I should be a bride more often, Gemma thought. She was genuinely touched.

After the pit stop with her family, Ethan drew her over to his aunt Claire, whom she'd met for the first time a few nights ago when Claire arrived from Washington and moved into one of the guest rooms for her stay in Thunder Ridge. Claire seemed like a no-nonsense, plainspoken woman, caring but not effusive with her emotions. She'd met Cody with a stoic approval, commenting that he was a handsome baby, "like his mother." She hadn't requested to hold him and declined when Gemma had asked if she'd like to, stating baldly and without apology, "Babies make me nervous. Always have."

As Gemma leaned forward to hug the older woman now, Claire gave her a hearty thump on the back. "You're good for him," she whispered huskily in Gemma's ear, with the most feeling Gemma had yet heard from her.

A strange combination of pleasure and guilt filled her. Perhaps she needed to rethink her definition of "real." Maybe it existed on a bell curve. There were facts and there was the truth, and the truth was that in this moment she felt excited about her future, more excited than she'd been in ages.

"He's good for me, too," she whispered in return to Claire.

Escorted by the Dream Catchers' rendition of "Here Comes the Sun," Ethan, Gemma and their guests moved the party to the area covered by a sprawling white tent. In the gathering twilight, flickering candles illuminated the faces of happy family and friends as they dined on a buffet of salads, brisket, chicken in a Jack Daniel's glaze, vegan knishes and martini glasses filled with assorted pickles, all freshly made by the Pickle Jar deli's ever-growing catering division. Dessert had been ordered from the deli's own bakery, Something Sweet, and featured an elegantly lovely wedding cake with stunning sugar flowers, plus a groom's cake in the shape of a Seattle Eagles helmet.

Minna had been solely in charge of the food and the cake, and everyone was thrilled with the results. Elyse had offered to take charge of flowers and other decorations, and she, too, had done a splendid job, taking into account the dots of red in Gemma's unique gown while incorporating the vivid yellows, greens, blues and intense fuchsia pinks of an Oregon summer. It wasn't at all the wedding Gemma had planned when she'd thought she was going to marry William, but it was exactly right for her and Ethan.

Cody, dressed in his tiny two-piece "tuxedo," had cooperated beautifully by snoozing through the ceremony. He was awake for the reception, however, and Gemma insisted on taking him from her mother, missing the feel of him in her arms. Eager to be fed, Cody surprised her by calmly accepting the hubbub around him as he sucked on his bottle.

"Sit down with him, sweetheart," Ethan urged with a hand on Gemma's waist.

At the word *sweetheart*, she shot him a questioning look he either missed or ignored. He'd been using endearments liberally since their walk back up the aisle, as if the vows had included, "Do you promise to use cutesy terms of affection whenever possible?" Honestly, she hadn't thought he was the sort, but she liked it. Her fave so far was when he'd referred to her as "my pinup girl." (Sorry, Gloria Steinem.)

Leading her to their table, he pulled out her chair. "I'll get our food."

Returning with her plate first, he set a mountain of delectable treats in front of her. "I'll see if your mother can hold Cody so you can eat," he said, already looking around for Minna.

"No, don't bother." Gemma stopped him, smiling. Ethan held the baby more often now, but he still didn't feel confident holding his nephew when they were someplace where crying would be inconvenient. "Go get a plate for yourself. We're fine here."

Gemma cuddled the baby and chatted with Aunt Claire, two cousins who had driven over from Portland and the other guests at their table until Ethan arrived with another full plate of food. Instead of tucking into his own meal, however, he looked at her dish and frowned. "You haven't eaten anything."

"I'm fine."

As conversation around the table continued, with questions about football and other Seattle Eagles players tossed

Ethan's way, Gemma found herself caught entirely off guard when a forkful of brisket appeared before her lips.

"Taste this, babe." *Babe?* Ethan hovered his fork in front of her until she leaned forward a smidgen to take his offering. For the next several minutes, tempting morsels of food were airlifted her way, along with casual comments— "These potatoes are the bomb. We should try to make them at home," and "You're going to love the chicken"—as if they did this at every meal when, in fact, he'd never fed her so much as a grape before.

By the time Minna arrived of her own accord, insisting on holding the baby and showing him off to her friends, Gemma felt she'd had enough food and was ready to mingle. With her hand tucked into the crook of her new husband's arm, they made the rounds from table to table. When they'd hammered out the details of the marriage, they'd agreed to maintain the ruse that their union was a love match, but they hadn't discussed the finer points.

As they moved among their guests, Ethan kept a hand on her waist and every so often rubbed her back in languorous circles. At her aunt Edie and uncle Hugh's table, they chatted about the new composite decking Hugh installed until Ethan quite suddenly put both arms around Gemma, pulling her against him so he could bury his nose and lips in her neck.

"Ooh, you two are so adorable!" Aunt Edie trilled. "Hugh, get a picture of them."

While Uncle Hugh search his pockets for his cell phone, Gemma tried to keep her mind clear, no easy task with Ethan eliciting goose bumps on every part of her body. Once more, she wondered why, in the two weeks since his proposal, he hadn't nuzzled her neck as he was now. Nor had he pulled her close to his side and kissed her head while he was talking to other people or fed her tiny knishes from his own fingers as if he were afraid she might waste away without sustenance. It had all started after the ceremony today. Ergo, either wedding vows were an aphrodisiac for him and he was hoping to toss the ninety-day probationary period on intimacy out the window (she might be able to be persuaded), or there was something else going on. Every touch at her waist, every sexy glance in her direction, every stolen kiss made it so tempting to believe in this marriage, so easy to float through the party on a pink cloud.

When Hugh had taken his fill of photos, Ethan stepped away slightly, grinning, the glint in his eyes suggesting he'd like to rip the dotted Swiss off her body right then and there.

The prohibition on consummation…yeah, why had she insisted on that? It had something to do with keeping things uncomplicated. But at the moment, with their wedding night looming ahead like a giant neon bed, it seemed to Gemma that her no-sex-please-we're-not-really-married rule was actually making things a wee bit more complex.

Minna and Hal had gifted them with a suite at the Nines Hotel in Portland for their wedding night. They'd insisted, actually. No baby, no distractions and, according to her, no whoopee.

"May I, um, speak to you alone for a moment?" she murmured to her husband. Time to address the elephant in the room…or under the tent, as the case may be. "Excuse us," she said to Edie and Hugh, who waved them on with big grins.

Night had fallen. High overhead, stars mimicked the twinkle lights around the tent as she steered Ethan to the shadows beyond the patio area.

Facing him, she could clearly make out how gorgeous

he was in his tux, even in the night shadows. "So," she began brightly, then faltered. "So."

He leaned forward. "You look beautiful. Have I told you that?"

She laughed a little. "Yes, but thank you. Again." Nervously, Gemma fingered her skirt. "Elyse wasn't thrilled with my choice of polka dots."

"Are you kidding? There should be a law—from now on, all brides have to wear polka dots on their wedding day. You're stunning, Gemma."

Heat—*no, let's be honest here: lust*—filled her. She swallowed with difficulty. "Yeah, okay, only can you tell me what's going on here? Not that I don't like it," she hastened to add. "I like it. I like it fine. I like it…really well. It's just that…it's a bit of a surprise." He was frowning.

"What are you talking about?"

Okay, spit it out like a big girl. "What's with all the kissing and nuzzling?" she said plainly. "And the copious use of cutesy names."

"'Cutesy'?" Ethan's frown deepened. "They're not cutesy. I hate cutesy."

"Well, these have been cutesy. In a good way. I just wonder *why* you're doing it?"

The summer night seemed to hum with an energy of its own, beyond the music and laughter emanating from the tent. Ethan's gaze and his silence lingered until finally his voice emerged as velvety as the sky. "Don't you enjoy kissing and nuzzling?"

"Y-yeah."

"Me, too." She felt his fingers touch her waist again, but more lightly this time. "I like it a lot. Which is convenient since we're trying to make people believe we're average, everyday newlyweds."

"Right." A breathy laugh escaped. "I think we've certainly fooled my mom. And Aunt Edie and Uncle Hugh. You were laying it on pretty thick in there, after all." She hitched her head toward the tent. Was it as obvious to him as it was to her that she was fishing for him to say he meant every kiss and every nuzzle?

"I wasn't 'laying it on thick,'" he protested. "I was playing the part of devoted husband to your beautiful bride—" he took a step closer, looking very much as if he planned to kiss her again "—because I don't want there to be a doubt, ever, in anyone's mind that I wanted this marriage.'"

He had her at "beautiful bride." Almost.

Once Gemma's desire-addled brain processed the words *play the part of*, she realized… "You're playing the part so I won't look like I'm being jilted." *Again.* But she didn't say that. "Aren't you? If we break up, I mean, after our three-month trial period."

"Seems like the gentlemanly thing to do," he murmured, "though I wouldn't have put it quite that way." He tucked a tendril of hair behind her ear, then tilted his head. "You're upset."

"No, I'm not." *Yes, I am!*

"The point is, if things don't work out for any reason, you can blame it all on me."

"Well, then, I'm grateful. That's—" she clenched every muscle in her face, determined not to release a single one of the tears stupidly queuing up behind her eyes "—super thoughtful." He was gazing at her, concerned, and she knew she needed to lighten things up, fast. "What reason should I give for dumping your celebrated butt?"

He shook his head, but she could make out his smile. "I don't know. The sex?"

Ha! She'd bet her wedding band that no one had ever left him for that reason. "Okay, what's going to be the problem? Too much? Too little? Not of an acceptable quality?"

His smile deepened. "Yeah, forget it. You'll never leave me because of the sex."

As he continued to gaze at her, she couldn't think of a single thing to say next. Usually she enjoyed it when they teased each other. Tonight, though, she simply felt sad. "It's depressing to talk about breaking up at your wedding."

Slowly, Ethan's expression turned more serious. "Agreed. But the future is open-ended, right? We don't need to predict what's going to happen."

"Nope."

For a second it seemed he was going to touch her cheek, but the hand he'd raised lowered again without making contact.

A burst of laughter rose inside the tent when the band suggested over the microphone that the happy couple must be off somewhere "getting happier."

"Our cue to go back?" Ethan murmured.

"Must be."

Taking the arm he offered, she walked with him, side by side, to their reception.

No question about it. This was going to be the most complicated wedding night in history.

Chapter Eleven

Much to Gemma's chagrin, Minna and Hal had not only provided a suite at the beautiful Nines Hotel in downtown Portland as a surprise wedding gift, but Minna had also obviously given detailed instructions as to how the room should be decorated. The already-opulent space was filled with dozens of roses and warm ivory candles, plus a silver tray filled with chocolate-covered strawberries. An expensive bottle of champagne, wrapped in linen, sat chilling in a bucket of ice.

The sound of water streaming from the rain forest show-erhead serenaded Gemma through the closed bathroom door as Ethan bathed and she searched through her over-night case for her pajamas. After they'd returned to the reception, Ethan had appeared to be in a great mood, and she figured she'd faked "young and in love" pretty well, though she had indeed dodged a few of his more overt at-tempts to persuade their guests that he was head over heels.

"What the heck," she muttered now, tossing items from her luggage. Her pajamas were nowhere to be found, and she was sure she'd packed them last night. Instead, at the bottom of the case, she found a tiny pink bag from Victoria's Secret. *What on earth?* She frowned as she opened the attached card.

> *Gemma,*
> *You cannot wear emoji pajamas on your wedding*
> *night. You'll thank me later.*
> *Love,*
> *Elyse*

"Oh, no." Tossing the card onto the nightstand, she fumbled with the tissue inside the bag and withdrew a scrap of black lace. According to the tag, the wisp of material that looked like a child's headband was actually a "sheer lace plunge teddy." It was sheer, all right. Holding it up to the light, she could see clear through it. And plunging? Yep.

The water in the bathroom stopped, triggering a surge of panic in Gemma as she frantically tore through every pocket of her overnight case. Her sister had left her with no clothing options other than the pedal pushers she planned to wear the next day. Elyse had, however, thoughtfully provided literally dozens of condoms, which she had crammed into every pocket, nook and cranny. A cornucopia of birth control. Interesting, considering she and Ethan only had the room for the one night.

Her first task as a married woman would be to kill her baby sister.

Grimly, she stared at the wisp of lace dangling from her fingertips. No way could she wear this to bed with Ethan, not under the circumstances.

She heard the sound of toothbrushing. *Uh-oh.* She

glanced nervously around the room. Ethan would be out any minute. She couldn't wear tomorrow's pants to bed on her wedding night, and her only other choice was to climb under the covers in her wedding dress with its giant, noisy taffeta skirt and hope he didn't think she was insane.

Ohhh. It was the teddy or buff-o. "You win, you big buttinsky," she growled to her absent-but-there-in-spirit sister and wondered how to handle the actual clothing change. If she waited until it was her turn in the bathroom, she'd have to walk all the way from the door to the bed in only the teddy. With the lights on. Leaving nothing to the imagination. In front of Ethan.

Not happening. Getting to work, she wrestled her way out of the voluminous wedding dress and into Elyse's special gift. Once she had the various tiny strings and straps and lace bits where she assumed they belonged, she peeked at her reflection in the mirror.

Oh, sweet mother of everything holy. There was no lining in the bra of this thing. Nothing, not even a strategically placed seam. And she wasn't exactly built like her sister, who had spent her twenties researching "breast implants" on the internet. Darn her! Gemma wanted her cotton pj's back. She'd made such a big deal over keeping her trial marriage sex-free. What was Ethan going to think now?

After finding out his kisses and his embrace and his cutesy-patootsie names for her were nothing more than a big show—however well-intentioned—she wasn't about to risk looking like she wanted to seduce him. No, no, no. Rushing to the vanity, she found a small stack of hand towels and tried stuffing a couple into the teensy bra cups currently straining to support her. She certainly didn't need the padding, but hoped the coverage would provide some modesty. A check in the mirror told her all she needed to know: no matter how she folded or smoothed or prodded them, the towels were about as attractive as the nursing pads Lucy had worn while breastfeeding.

The sink stopped running. He'd be out any second.

Gemma was out of time. Abandoning the towels in a heap on the sink, she flew to the bed.

From the nightstand, she grabbed the stack of books and pamphlets the social worker had asked them to read and tossed everything onto the mattress, then dived beneath the covers. Hastily, she tucked the top sheet and the blanket tightly around her body and up to her neck. Her heart pounded crazily when the bathroom door opened and Ethan emerged amid a cloud of steam, wearing only pajama bottoms and looking very much like a model. Which he sometimes was.

What the devil were you thinking, marrying someone that good-looking? demanded a voice inside her head. William, at least, had looked like a normal person.

Stay cool, she chanted to herself. *Stay cool. So you checked into a romantic hotel room to sleep next to a half-naked man. It's not like it's the first time.* It was the second, actually. And William had unfortunately suffered from pigeon chest…but that was neither here nor there.

Ethan flipped off the light switch in the vanity area, leaving them in the glow that came from the bedside lamps and the various candles that burned around the room. As he came to the edge of the bed, he stared down at the materials she'd scattered over the comforter and frowned.

"What's all this?"

Gemma hoped her shrug was casual. "I thought we'd read. That's what Jeanne wants us to do, right? Study, study. So I figured we may as well get started. I'm not sleepy. Unless you are. And then I could be sleepy. Sleepy enough to… actually sleep." *Wonderful, Gemma. Outstanding display of bedtime nonchalance.*

"No, I'm not sleepy," he acknowledged, still frowning.

"Okay, then." Holding the covers to her neck with one hand, she used the other to reach for one of the books. "This looks like a good place to start. *Effects of Prenatal Drug Exposure on Child Development.*" That sounded like a libido-killer.

Ethan picked up the remote on his nightstand. "Sure. Before we knuckle down on the homework, why don't we see what's on TV?"

"Oh. Um, if you want."

He began to channel surf, asking what she'd like to watch, but Gemma didn't have much of an opinion. After settling on an action movie, Ethan got into bed and sat up against the pillows. Quickly, she scooted over, taking the covers with her, then trying to make sure he had his share while maintaining a grip, literally, on her modesty. As still as marble, she stared at the TV, seeing nothing, but noting that Ethan's head turned her way several times. He shifted a lot, too, giving the appearance he was no more interested in TV viewing than she.

Finally, during a commercial break, Gemma suggested, "Maybe we should start reading now. The day we told Jeanne we were getting married, she said we still needed to prove we're willing to do the work it will take to be awarded permanent custody of Cody. Remember?" she prodded when Ethan continued to frown at the screen. He said nothing. "We're running out of time here. Jeanne wants to see us in two weeks, and she'll be expecting—"

He clicked the TV off. "Let's not worry about studying tonight, Professor." His smile seemed half-hearted. "You hungry? We could go out."

Not talk about studying *tonight*? He never wanted to read the materials Jeanne had assigned. "Ethan," she said as he got off the bed, "we're not dressed, and getting ready would be a hassle."

"We can order room service." Picking up the menu, he gave it a glance, then tossed it onto the bed. "I bet they have a steak."

"I'm really not hungry," she said, as he picked up the phone and punched in zero. When the operator came on, he asked for room service, even though the extension was printed clearly on the phone. Probably on the menu, too. Idly, she picked it up. Yup, the number was right there at the top of the first page. A quick glance told her they weren't going to be able to order from the grill this late at night.

She stared at Ethan as he asked for a steak, was obviously given the information she'd just gleaned from the page and then had room service verbally tell him what was available. The feeling that something was wrong landed upon her as it had a couple of times before, only this time more strongly.

He set down the phone. "They said they'd be here in about forty-five minutes. If you don't want to wait, I could call them back to cancel and we could get dressed again. There are several really good restaurants close by."

She was not ready to let go of this question, niggling at her. "Do you dislike reading?" He hesitated too long. "Ethan, what's going on? We got married for Cody's sake. Shouldn't we do the work it's going to take to keep him?"

Without looking at her, he moved restlessly toward the window and stared out. "Yes. We should do the work to keep him." Ethan's voice was tight, his carved-from-granite back and shoulders rigid.

Concern, curiosity and exasperation were tossed into the pot of emotion inside her. "Ethan, talk to me. I know how much you want Cody. You've been sweating blood for him. You were willing to get married to keep him, for heaven's sake. But if you want me to help you, you can't shut me out."

His shoulders flagged and his head dropped. "I'm going to lose him."

She was genuinely stunned. "What do you mean? Why would you think—" As the possibilities filtered into her mind, adrenaline flowed through her veins. "Have you spoken to Jeanne recently? Did she say something?"

"No." He rubbed his forehead, then pushed his fingers through his hair. Slowly, he turned to face her, his next sentence emerging through a jaw so clenched, she had to strain to hear the words. "I can't read." The angst and shame in his expression was heartbreaking.

Gemma's next breath was a long, deep inhalation. She was looking at a man who had a Super Bowl ring and multimillion-dollar endorsements. He was Ethan Ladd, Thunder Ridge's favorite son.

He couldn't read.

All the things that had never made sense before began to click into the puzzle that was Ethan. A respectful, responsible teenager who blew off assignments or persuaded others to do the work for him. A man with myriad responsibilities and people who were constantly trying to contact him, but who refused to text. And who couldn't read the label on a box of baby ointment.

"The essay I wrote for you in high school. You couldn't read it. That's why you turned it in."

"Yes," he admitted tightly.

Guilt welled in her throat. He'd had no clue she'd intended it to be a joke. "But the wedding license," she recalled. "You asked me to let you fill it out for both of us."

"Because I knew I wouldn't be able to fill it out at all if I had to do it in front of you. I can read and write simple things. Unless I'm stressed, and then sometimes even simple isn't possible."

"So who filled it out?"

"Aunt Claire. She told me we could do it online, and… she helped me."

"Does she help you often?"

He nodded. "I wouldn't be where I am without her. She had no idea how bad the situation was until my senior year of high school. You can fake a lot of things, and Samantha covered for me until the drugs took over. When it came time to fake my way into a football career, though…" He shook his head. "Most players begin their careers in college. I knew I'd never survive higher education, so I figured I'd work my way up by playing semipro, but even with that I panicked and told Claire everything. Up to then, they thought I just hated school. I finally admitted I'd tried as hard as I could and still wasn't able to do what most third graders could do in their sleep." His tone grew self-derogatory. "Claire doesn't have a lot of education, but she's smart. Unlike yours truly," he snorted. "The big success story. What a freaking fake." His eyes were filled with pain. "I'm so damn sorry."

"Why are you sorry?"

"I lied to you." He looked out the window again, to the city spread out before him. "I let you marry a man who can't read a book to his nephew. Or figure out how much cold medicine to give. And you—" he glanced back at her, resigned now, but no less apologetic "—you deserve a helluva lot more. You could have married anyone."

While that wasn't remotely true, it was flattering. And yet…

I only want to be married to you.

Tonight was more surprising and confusing than she'd dreamed it would be. One thing, however, was clear: Ethan was her husband, and she found him more multilayered and fascinating in this moment than she ever had before.

"How can you say you're not smart?" she asked, genuinely amazed. "You're a businessman, you told me you helped design your house, and you strategized getting into the NFL. Then you won a Super Bowl with all that entails afterward—all the interviews and endorsement deals. I bet you've even spoken to heads of states. And nobody discovered your secret. I think you're brilliant."

He gave her a "come on" look, but she saw gratitude and a glimmer of hope in his eyes. She had some information for him, too, and was excited to tell him.

"Ethan, when I first began teaching, I had a student who sounded exactly like you. He was older than the others by several years, because it wasn't until after high school that he found out he had a learning disorder. It prevented him from learning to read the way his peers had. Once he made the discovery, he was able to acquire strategies that helped him. He went to night school, caught up and enrolled in college. Even then, we had to make accommodations to facilitate his learning. He kept growing and acquiring new reading skills. Eventually, he became a master's student."

"I saw the special ed teachers, Gemma. They tried to work with me when I was a kid, but—"

"We didn't know as much back then," she interrupted, her enthusiasm mounting. "I realize it doesn't seem that long ago, but in terms of specialized education, tremendous gains in understanding student differences are being made all the time." Bounding out of bed, she grabbed her purse, found her cell phone and got on the internet. "Wait till you see this. It's a documentary called *The Big Picture.* It's wonderful. It even helped a colleague of mine realize why she's had so much trouble reading over the years. We can watch it while we're waiting for room service." She looked up, delighted. "I know I'm talking fast. I always do that when I'm excited. What?" she asked, becoming aware he was staring at her intently. Not smiling. Not reacting to her good news. "Don't you want to watch it? It's really interesting. Richard Branson, the billionaire head of Virgin Airlines, is dyslexic, and he couldn't…he couldn't… he… Why are you staring at me like that? Why aren't you talking? Would you say something, please?"

Ethan's Adam's apple bobbed as he swallowed. "What are you wearing?"

The expression on his new bride's face would have been hilarious if Ethan had felt like laughing at that moment. Unfortunately, he'd developed a pounding headache at their wedding reception. Talking to people who had known Gemma since her childhood had finally slammed home the enormity of what he'd done: he'd married a woman who could pepper the most casual conversation with literary references. A woman so well-read, she had no trouble shifting from one conversation to the next without struggle. Unlike the man she'd married. Ethan had stood beside his wife, exhibiting his aptitude for PDAs while she discussed the latest bestseller. It had seemed most everyone wanted to discuss books with the college lit teacher. And the crazy thing? Ethan realized Gemma's mind was one of the sexiest things about her. Every touch, every kiss, had heated him up to the point of internal combustion, and when she talked books, he got so turned on, he'd almost had to excuse himself to take a cold shower in the middle of the reception.

When they'd arrived at the hotel, and he'd first taken note of the bed, he'd cursed the day he agreed to ninety sexless days of marriage. Hopping into the hotel shower, he'd kept the water as cold as possible and tried to shock the desire for her out of his system. He knew damn well, after all, that he was the wrong man for her in the long run. All through the reception, he'd begun to feel guiltier and guiltier. Living in the narrow world of Cody and his needs, where it was mostly just the three of them day in and day out, marriage had seemed possible. Advisable, even. Watching Gemma interact in the larger world, he'd known damn well that she deserved better.

When he'd emerged from the bathroom, she'd been shrouded in the sheets and blanket with only her head poking out, and he'd figured the ninety-day no-sex policy was in full effect, so whether to seduce or not seduce was a moot point. But then she'd leaped out of the bed, and his heart rate had leaped right along with her.

"You look," he said, forming words out of sawdust, "really good."

Gemma's hands flew to her breasts. She glanced down at herself and quickly repositioned the hand holding the phone at her crotch, like a cellular fig leaf.

"Elyse bought this," she hastily explained. "She took the pajamas I packed out of my suitcase, and this is all that was left. I'm going to kill her when we get back to Thunder Ridge, but I can't do anything about it now unless I sleep in my wedding dress."

So she hadn't changed her mind. Ethan turned and walked to the closet. Pulling a T-shirt from the duffel he'd deposited on the luggage stand, he tossed it to her.

Wasting no time at all, she slipped it over the brilliant garment her sister had sent along. He'd love to thank her, but lust and disappointment were going to make for a long night. His next move was either another cold shower, or... "You want to show me that video?"

His suggestion met with a relieved nod. "Yes. Yes, that'd be good." She glanced toward the bed, but they both knew watching the video in the king-size invitation to sex would be awkward, to say the least. Ethan walked to the sleek table and chairs provided for their convenience and sat down.

"Ready when you are," he said.

She joined him, notably self-conscious, but still endearingly excited as she set her phone between them and tapped Play on the video titled *The Big Picture: Rethinking Dyslexia.*

"Dyslexia?" He frowned. "Isn't that when numbers and letters are mixed up or turned around or something?"

"That's true for some people, but there are varying degrees and different forms of dyslexia. The colleague I mentioned? She has no trouble at all writing, but reading is so challenging that she was only able to get through college by taking enough notes to practically publish her own textbooks. Watch." She angled the phone toward him. "You'll see."

He did see. As the video played, Ethan became riveted by the stories of talented people at the top of challenging careers, the kind of people he'd always envied, who had been abysmal students. They had been as mystified by their difficulties as he was by his. By the time the credits rolled, he felt as if he was awakening from a bad dream.

"I can't believe it." He sounded as shocked as he felt. "Surgeons, executives…" Still somewhat disbelieving, he ran a hand over his face. "I thought I was just stupid."

Her touch on his arm felt cool and comforting. "Now you know the truth. It has nothing to do with intelligence. And it doesn't have to limit you in any way."

Ethan shook his head, but in wonder rather than negation. Feeling almost shy, he admitted, "Funny thing, I always wanted to be a high school coach once I retired from the NFL."

"You'd be an amazing coach!" Gemma sounded like she loved the idea.

His looked at her gorgeous, eager eyes. At her enthusiastic smile. "I'd never get through college."

She grabbed both his hands. "Can you see now that's not true? You *can* go back to school. You'll simply need the right kind of help. Ethan, I've known you a long time and even lived with you for a little while now. I know you're intelligent. Your expressive and receptive language skills are absolutely fine. I'm a teacher, so you can trust me on that." She gave him an adorable, impish smile.

"I wouldn't have any idea where to start." But for the very, very first time, the notion of becoming a coach…it didn't seem as crazy as it would have an hour ago.

"I know some very talented special ed folks we can talk to, and of course I'd be happy to help. I mean, after all, reading is my thing, and I'd like to work with you. I'd love it, actually."

Ethan leaned forward and kissed her hard on the mouth. Couldn't help it. He didn't want to ruin the moment or jeopardize the easy bond between them right now, but the way he felt this minute was how he'd have felt after winning the Super Bowl if he'd been married at the time. He'd have needed to kiss his wife to seal the victory.

"You really think I can be a high school coach?" he asked, ignoring her surprised expression. "Maybe I should start with something smaller, like preschool." He was fishing for another compliment, because hearing Gemma say she believed in him was as addictive as great sex.

"You'd be perfect for high school. Think of the kids you could help on and off the field."

"Kids like me," he acknowledged, the idea growing on him by the minute. His heart pumped on pure adrenaline as he realized one of the most awesome things of all. "I might be able to read to Cody."

"You *will* read to Cody."

They sat with their hands clasped on the tabletop, grinning at each other, the phone with its miraculous video lying between them. Even though he was pretty sure no normal bride and groom would choose to spend their wedding night the way they were, he felt a sense of hope and promise he'd never experienced before. Suddenly, this seemed like absolutely the sweetest way he could imagine to begin his marriage to Gemma.

Chapter Twelve

The next evening, they were home in Thunder Ridge, eating dinner together in the kitchen nook after they'd put Cody to bed. Ethan's exhilaration and their easy companionship had lasted through a half day of sightseeing in downtown Portland, but they'd both been eager to get back to the baby. With the worst withdrawal symptoms presumably behind them, Cody was the kind of delight no parent wanted to miss for long. Even though they were not parents, per se, they were certainly falling under the little man's spell.

She enjoyed studying her husband tonight, too, as he finished the meal she'd slaved over...sort of slaved over. Holliday had gifted her with a book titled *Your Dinner in Twenty Minutes or Less*, and so far it had lived up to its claim.

"Thank you," Ethan said, setting his napkin beside his plate. "That was great. For someone who says she doesn't like to cook, you've been doing an awful lot of it. Want me to take the helm tomorrow?"

"Sure." If he was cooking, she fully intended to take a front-row seat at the center island. There was a new light-heartedness that made her husband even more gorgeous. And, hello? *Husband.* Even if it wasn't "real" in the most traditional sense, dang was it fun to say! She'd already emailed several of her colleagues to share the glad tidings and so she could type *my husband.* "What have you got in mind for dinner?"

"I thought I'd treat you to a little something I tried when I did a photo shoot for boxer briefs in Costa Alegre, Mexico. It's called *salchichas y frijoles.*"

Gemma sat up straighter, grinning. "Holy ethnic cuisine, Batman. I'm impressed. What did you call it? *Sal...* what?"

"*Salchichas y frijoles,*" he repeated in a perfect accent, wagging his head. "You're such a *gringa.*" He had her practice until she could say it easily.

"So what is it?" she asked.

"Franks 'n' beans." He shrugged. "It was an all-guy shoot. And the wienies went down real easy with the local beer."

Gemma picked a cherry tomato from the relish tray she'd set out and chucked it at his head. "You realize, I hope, that *you* are now the wienie in this story."

Laughing, Ethan collected their plates and carried them to the sink. "Can I redeem myself if I tell you that our guide, who was a local, made the food and showed us how to add just the right amount of hot sauce, then smother the whole thing in crispy onions? And that it will undoubtedly be the best franks 'n' beans of your entire life?"

"We'll see." Gemma narrowed her eyes. "After that lame joke, you've got your work cut out for you." Rising, she picked up the tomato she'd thrown, then commented, "So how did you get in and out of airports and navigate foreign countries without Aunt Claire or someone else who knew your story and could help you?"

"Foreign countries are easy." He began to rinse the dishes. "No one questions a tourist's confusion. As for local travel, Claire and I practiced a lot that first year. Any uncertainty that was left, I handled with my personality." Glancing her way, he gave her a completely straight-faced appraisal. "You may have noticed I'm quite charming. Chicks dig that."

Walking around him to the refrigerator, Gemma began to dig through the veggie drawer.

"What are you doing?" he asked.

"Looking for a bigger tomato."

His laughter, rich and uninhibited, filled her with pleasure. A hug, at least, would feel so natural right now, but they'd been careful all day not to touch too much. Or *she'd* been careful, at any rate. Perhaps it had been easy for him to keep a physical distance. Gemma, however, wanted to get near him so badly, she'd have settled for moshing.

Watching Ethan commandeer the sink, she felt the wonderfully cozy sensation she'd had growing up when her father would scoot her mother out of the way after dinner and take charge of the cleanup.

"My dad used to say, 'The cook never cleans,'" she murmured.

"I remember. Hal would make us boys do the dishes, and he'd tell us good manners aren't based on gender, so if we wanted successful marriages someday we'd better be prepared to get our hands wet." He grinned at her. "Your dad's a wise man. I thought we could have the 'cook never cleans' rule in our family, too."

The room took on a hazy, not-of-this-planet feeling. The

sun was low on the horizon, streaming its waning golden light through the trees and into the windows. More than anything, though, the words *our family* wove a spell around Gemma. Mystical, intimate and exactly right.

Their motives may have been different from other couples', but saying "I do" had changed things. They talked about *their* immediate future now, *their* home. Their family.

"So when do you want to start teaching me? Want to get started tonight?"

"What?" Gemma shook her head, beginning to lose herself in the fantasy of what tonight *could* be like and requiring a few extra seconds to process his words.

"I was just wondering when we should start the dyslexia workbook we bought at Powell's today."

"Oh, right!" Making a stop at Portland's famous bookstore before heading back to Thunder Ridge, Gemma had discovered several books she could use to help Ethan while they waited to hear from the special ed teachers she'd already phoned.

"Sure," she agreed, "we can get started." On another occasion, her enthusiasm for the project would have been through the roof. Tonight, however, she wondered what normal newlyweds would be doing right now. Most likely having dessert, and she didn't mean cake and ice cream.

It wasn't natural to live in such close proximity, fully licensed to have crazy, lusty sex, but continuing to sleep in separate beds. One thing Gemma knew for sure: this was the only time she was ever going to be married to a man who had scored an eight-figure contract to model men's underwear. She could not be blamed if her mind wandered occasionally (every fifteen seconds for the past eight hours) to fantasies about what sex with Ethan would be like.

"I left the books in a bag on my bed," she told him. "Do

you mind getting them and checking on Cody? I want to get his bottle ready for tonight." *And run around the center island a few times to burn off the lust.*

"Sure. I'll finish cleaning up later." He cocked a finger at her. "Don't touch anything. Remember the rule."

For crying out loud, could he look any sexier? She swallowed with difficulty, then cocked a finger back at him. "Okeydoke."

While he was upstairs, Gemma prepared Cody's bottles, then broke her word and made quick work of the remaining mess in the kitchen. Her buzzing body demanded more to do, and she was beginning to think a jog around the island might not be a bad idea, when she glimpsed the clock and realized Ethan had been upstairs for a good twenty minutes. Maybe he was having trouble locating the books. Had she put them somewhere other than her bed? Setting off to help him look, she heard his voice as she approached her bedroom. Slowing, she peeked through the door and saw Ethan leaning over the crib, talking to the wide-awake baby, who made sweet baby chirping sounds.

"...so that's why I focused on sports instead of school. I only know a few things," Ethan told his nephew in a soft voice, "but I think they're important, so listen up. First off, you can learn a lot from football. For example, being good isn't good enough. You need heart and courage, too. And don't ever stop trying. Ever. Remember, though, that you can't win all the time. It's more important to play well with others."

Cody blew a raspberry and pumped his feet.

Ethan shook his head. "Okay, you're right. That's bull. Winning feels great. But you should also play well with others. And whatever you do, don't be just a jock all your life. Even if you're dyslexic, like me. I hear that stuff can run in families, and you might get that from me, but we'll make sure you have help. You study hard and get an education, so you'll have some options. 'Cause nothing lasts forever, you know?"

Gently, he rubbed his knuckles on Cody's tummy. "And that's it. That's what I know. Any questions?"

The baby stretched out his arms.

"You want me to pick you up? At night? That's a change. I don't know, I guess we could try. If it doesn't work, we can always go get your girl. You like her, huh? Yeah, I know, you're a ladies' man. Come by that naturally, I guess."

Riveted to the scene, Gemma watched Ethan oh-so-carefully reach into the crib. As he drew the baby to his chest in an exquisitely protective cradle hold, she felt an overwhelming sense of déjà vu. She had lived this moment a thousand times before. In all her cherished daytime dreams, in her fantasies of the perfect life, this was how it had played out—with her husband looking at a baby so lovingly, so tenderly that she felt her own love flare to life in response.

If Ethan hadn't been cooing to Cody at that moment, he might have heard her soft, quick intake of breath. Moving quickly into the hallway, Gemma leaned against the wall for support. *I love this life. I love...*

You.

It was true. Time to come to terms with the idea that she didn't simply love Ethan—good friend, caring uncle and object of her vivid fantasy life. No, she'd fallen in love with him. She was already living the life of her dreams. Or she could be if she gave herself and Ethan a chance to truly make this marriage work. In fact, this was better than anything she could have possibly imagined.

Why had she insisted on that stupid moratorium?

Damage control if this doesn't work out, remember?

Chewing her thumbnail, she thought about it for a moment, then shrugged. The "damage" was already done. Her heart was irrevocably his.

As quietly as she could, she turned toward the laundry room, where her freshly washed and dried clothes waited for her. She knew what she wanted. And it was all under this roof.

When Ethan's footsteps finally sounded in the hallway just outside the kitchen, Gemma felt her knees begin to quake. *Be brave. Nothing ventured...*

She'd put a spiral-bound notebook, a relatively simple children's story and several pencils on the kitchen table to set the stage for their...lesson. *This had better work*, she thought as she quickly donned the reading glasses she used for grading papers and positioned herself at the table. If for some reason her plan for the evening failed, she doubted she'd be able to live it down in this millennium.

As Ethan rounded the corner and swung through the kitchen door, he said, "Sorry that took so long. I had to get Cody...back...to sleep..." His voice trailed off and his movement stilled. As his brows rose, his eyes widened, then ever so slowly, the million-dollar grin unfurled.

"Hello again," she said, hoping she sounded a whole helluva lot calmer than she felt.

Ethan's gaze started at the top of her head and traveled down, making frequent leisurely stops to enjoy the scenery. And there was plenty of scenery to enjoy, as she'd donned the tiny sheer teddy from their wedding night.

As Ethan's breathing grew noticeably more shallow, Gemma thought she might forgive her sister for the pajama switch, after all. "Excited to get started on your reading lesson?" she asked.

"Ohhh, yeah." Like a lion stalking his prey, he moved

slowly across the kitchen to stand in front of her. "In fact, I think reading is going to be my favorite subject."

"That's the idea." Removing her glasses, she ran the stem along her lower lip. "I have a few learning techniques I'd like to try with you."

"Really." Reaching out, he traced the lace that ran over her collarbone and into the valley between her breasts.

She shivered, her head dropping back. "I take it you're a hands-on learner."

His palm slid over to cover her breast. "What gives you that idea?"

Gemma inhaled deeply. "Oh, just a hunch. Many dyslexic people are—" she had to swallow a moan when his free hand cupped her other breast "—quite tactile," she completed her sentence.

"Mmm." Ethan dipped his head to the side of her neck, his warm breath and the brush of his lips causing ripples of pleasure. "I had no idea there were so many advantages to this disability."

"Me, either." She allowed her head to fall back, giving him access to as much of her neck as he cared to kiss. "Might as well look on the bright side. Also, I believe strongly in the reward system. Have I mentioned that?"

"No. I bet you're a really popular teacher."

"Actually—" she gasped as he pressed his hips against hers, leaving no doubt about the effect she was having on him "—up to now, it's all been theoretical." Excitement, like soap bubbles, rose in her stomach as she felt his grin tickling her neck.

He trailed kisses along her collarbone, then touched his tongue to the hollow of her throat. She tingled everywhere. Barely able to murmur, she asked, "Did you want to start reading now?"

He growled his response. "No."

"Oh, good." Her head fell back, exposing more of her neck for him to enjoy.

Unleashed, he took her face in his hands and kissed her with a hunger that matched her own. Could it be? Was it possible he wanted this moment, this marriage, as much as she did? Hope tasted as delicious as his kiss as Gemma wound her arms around his neck. Only the hum of the refrigerator and their labored breathing broke the quiet as they made up for all the kisses they'd managed to sidestep since leaving their reception. When she was sure she was beyond the point of no return, Ethan pulled away and took a step back.

Lungs laboring, he dragged a hand through his hair. "What about the ninety-day prohibition on sex?"

She stared at him, feeling glassy-eyed, breathing just as hard as he was. "Moratorium. For educational purposes."

He reached for her again. "What about the work you set out?" He nodded to the books and papers on the table behind her.

"We'll tackle that later." In one motion, she swept everything off the table. "For now, just tackle me."

Ten days later, the afternoon sun looked like a ball of honey by the time Gemma returned home from a very special shopping excursion. She'd driven all the way to Sandy to buy the props she planned to use to set the stage for the most important night of her life. More important than her wedding. Because tonight she was going to tell the man she'd married that she loved him.

The past ten days had been better than any daydream she'd ever dared to dream.

For one thing, he'd received numerous calls about his decision to retire from the NFL and about their marriage. Though neither she nor Ethan had any idea how the information about their hasty wedding had been leaked, he seemed perfectly comfortable confirming it and adding that he was "completely happy" and "very excited about this next phase of life." It could have been a sound bite, but somehow Gemma knew it wasn't. She'd never seen him look so content.

He even enjoyed their learning sessions, which were turning out to be a revelation. Gemma would watch his broad shoulders hunch over a book, his handsome brow furrowed in concentration, and she would marvel at his humility and hunger to learn.

Then there was the sex.

Although she'd never made love without believing she was *in* love, neither had she ever experienced the passion she felt with Ethan. She'd never even come close.

Gemma was crazy in love with her husband, and he loved her, too. He must. No one could make love to her the way he did, be as attentive and caring and happy as he was right now, without loving her back.

The past couple of nights as she'd lain in his arms, warm and safe and complete, it had taken all her willpower not to blurt, *"I love you, and I love the three of us together, and this is exactly how it's meant to be forever and ever and ever, and I know you feel the same, but could you say it, please, because I'm a girl, and I reeeeeeaaaally need to hear it."*

Instead, she'd planned a night she hoped they'd both remember forever. With Cody happily bundled against her tummy and chest this afternoon, she'd shopped for groceries—including the ingredients for a chocolate body paint recipe she'd found online—and a brand-new teddy with matching bikini panties in purple lace. The skin-baring ensemble was decorated with pink silk hearts positioned in a way that made Elyse's selection look subtle by comparison. Tonight, she thought delightedly, was not going to be about subtle.

On her way back to town, she'd dropped Cody at her parents' place. They were thrilled to babysit while the newlyweds had a date night. Now Gemma buzzed with anticipation as she carried her groceries and the tissue paper–filled gift bag containing her lingerie up to the front door. Setting the groceries on the ground, she fit her key in the lock.

"Hel-looo, I'm back!" she sang, wondering whether to begin the evening with the dinner or the chocolate body paint.

"Gem?" Ethan called from the direction of his office. "I'm glad you're home. I was just about to call your cell. Stay right there."

As he rounded the corner, Gemma felt her pulse accelerate. *The chocolate body paint. Absolutely.* Her husband was…everything. Everything she wanted. *You know what? The heck with the body paint.* It would have to wait. She couldn't let another second pass without telling him all she was thinking.

"Ethan!" She ran to him before he reached the foyer. "Ethan, I have something—"

"Gemma, I've got great—" He stopped as they talked over each other.

"Oh, all right, you first," she relented with a grin, looping her arms around his waist and leaning back to look at him. "I'm going to require your full attention."

Bending down, he pressed his lips to hers in what felt like a swift, celebratory victory kiss. "Okay. About an hour ago, give or take, I got a call from Winston Rhodes, the private detective I hired to find Samantha. He tracked her down again, in Montana this time. He's actually with her right now. I spoke to her, and Gem, she's stone-cold sober. She says she's been clean since she had Cody, and she's agreed to stay put until I get there."

Slowly, Gemma's arms fell away from Ethan's waist even though her thoughts were spinning so quickly now, she felt dizzy. "Until you get there?" she asked. "You're leaving?"

"Right away." He gestured to the door, where his duffel sat, waiting.

"You're packed." Slowly, she shook her head. "You said the detective phoned an hour ago, and you're packed already...and you didn't call me?"

"I was just about to. I told you that when you walked in, remember? Gemma, I'm sorry. I had to move fast. I needed to call Claire, so she could make my plane reservations." Reaching for Gemma, he rubbed her upper arms. It was impossible to miss the excitement and urgency in his expression. "Samantha has run every other time we've gotten close. She's finally willing to talk, to see me. We can't lose this chance."

"You really believe she hasn't used drugs or alcohol since Cody was born?" Hearing the cynicism in her voice, Gemma cringed. Resentment was bubbling inside her, like poison in a witch's cauldron. But at whom was she resentful? At Ethan for not calling her immediately to tell her what was going on? Or was she resentful that Samantha was back, possibly well and ready to parent the baby that Gemma already loved?

Ethan's hands had stilled on her arms. "I do believe her. She told me she's tired of running. I think she means tired of running away from her life and responsibilities." A smile, small but heartfelt, pulled at his lips. "I think I'm finally going to be able to bring my sister home."

Smile back, her conscience told her. *Tell him how happy you are for him. For Samantha.* But "When do you leave?"

were the only words she could speak, and her lips barely moved.

"Now." He rubbed his forehead, wincing apologetically. "I've got over an hour drive to the airport."

Before her throat closed completely, Gemma asked, "Want me to take you?"

"No," Ethan responded immediately. "I'll use airport parking so the car's there when I need it. I don't have a return flight booked yet. This'll be easier all the way around." He hunched down to give her the Ethan Ladd Look, the one that implied she was the only other person on the planet in that moment. "I *will* call to keep you in the loop about everything. First priority. I promise."

She nodded, using sheer willpower to summon a wobbly smile.

"Is Cody in his car seat? I want to say goodbye and take a photo so Sam can see what he looks like. He's changed even this past week, don't you think?"

Suddenly feeling as tired as if she'd run a marathon, Gemma said, "I took Cody to my parents' house." At his quizzical look, she admitted, "I'd sort of planned a surprise date night."

Ethan squeezed his eyes shut briefly. "Aw, damn. I'm sorry."

Sensing his guilt and that he was trying to figure out amends even with everything else on his mind, Gemma told him not to worry, and she meant it. "We'll do it another time. When you get back."

Pulling her close, he kissed her again, more thoroughly this time, though Gemma's own head and heart were so full, she had a hard time responding the way she would have only a little while earlier.

When they parted, Ethan remembered. "You said you had something to tell me."

"Let's hold off. There's so much going on…"

"You sure it can wait?"

"Yep."

"All right." Getting the duffel bag, he slung it over his shoulder. "You get my full attention as soon as I'm home."

"Sounds good." His leaving, on the other hand, still sounded awful, and try as she might, Gemma could not get comfortable with this situation. Or with the feelings that dogged her as she followed him to the car to watch him drive off. Returning to the house, she felt her body begin to shake from the inside out. Lowering herself to the couch, she let the tears come.

He texted her at six that evening to tell her the plane was taking off, at nine thirty to tell her it had landed, and then phoned her at midnight. His first words were, "Did I wake you?"

"No." Gemma held the phone close to her ear. Ethan's voice was rough, deep, careworn. Instantly, she wanted to soothe him, but she'd been so nervous all night and was so tired herself that she could barely speak. Spending the evening alone at home, she'd played scenario after scenario in her mind, and in every one Samantha returned to take the baby.

Gemma had been so sure she would burst into tears in front of her parents that she'd asked them to keep the baby overnight, and of course they'd been happy to oblige. Now she clung to the phone and waited for Ethan's news.

"Where are you?" she asked.

"At a motel in Helena, Montana. I'm with Sam."

"You are? Is she living at the motel?"

"Yeah. She works as a waitress in the restaurant next door."

"I'm glad she was able to find a job." Gemma said the only thing she could think of. "So…how is she?"

"Good. Hang on a minute." His voice sounded more distant as he talked to somebody else. Samantha, presumably. "Okay, I'll see you tomorrow morning, right? Maybe I'll stop in for an early breakfast." Dimly, Gemma heard another voice respond and a door close before Ethan got back on the line. "Okay, I can talk more freely now. Sam left to get some rest before her shift tomorrow morning."

"Oh. Well, it's great that she has a job." She'd said that already, hadn't she? "Is Samantha planning to stay in Montana?"

"No!" The adamance of Ethan's response made Gemma sit up straight. "Of course not. She can't stay here by herself. She'll need support to take care of Cody. And support to stay in recovery. She's clean now, but she ought to be settled in a place where she has lots of help."

The weight of Gemma's heart seemed to drag her whole body down. There were words that needed to be spoken, facts that needed to be clarified, but her lips refused to move. Samantha was going to take care of Cody.

"Sam needs to be in a twelve-step program," Ethan continued in the face of her silence. "The counselor she had at the last place was clear that she should stay in therapy and attend as many group meetings as she can during the week. I don't think she should be working now, either. It's too much. Maybe she could take one of those parenting classes Jeanne told me about."

"That's *your* plan. Is that her plan, too?" Gemma found her voice, and clearly, Ethan was taken aback.

"She hasn't made any long-term plans, Gemma. She needs help. That's why I'm here."

"So she's coming back with you, then?"

Ethan paused. "Yes." But his tone made her wonder.

"She said that? She said she's coming back with you?"

"Gemma, Sam's been struggling to take care of herself. Staying clean, paying bills on her own. She's stressed out. She needs someone to step in and make the future less… frightening. She's too confused to make major life decisions on her own right now."

Sitting on Ethan's couch, in his living room, glancing at the ring that made her his wife, Gemma began to feel less confused. And more than a little resentful. "Ethan, does Samantha want to be a mother?"

"Gem—"

"Did *she* say she wants to come back and be Cody's mother?" Filled with an energy that needed release, she rose, pacing the dimly lit room with the phone clutched to her ear.

"She's afraid."

"Of what?"

Gemma could tell by Ethan's voice that he was pacing now, too. "I don't know. Okay? I'm not sure *exactly* what she's thinking, I just know my sister."

"Know her enough to pressure her into coming back? Because I'm wondering whether she wants what *you* want. It's obvious you'd like her to be Cody's mother. It's clear as a bell that's your agenda, but I haven't heard you say she wants it. What did she say exactly, Ethan? So far you're skirting that."

"I'm not skirting anything. She wants it! She just doesn't think she can do it. She always said she'd never abandon her kids the way our mother abandoned us. The way we grew up—" He blew out a noisy breath. "Damn it, Gemma, what's the argument here? This is why we got married, isn't it? We wanted to buy time to find Samantha and bring her back. That's what I'm doing, and now you're—"

He stopped himself from saying whatever else he'd been about to say.

Gemma closed her eyes. *I'm falling in love by myself.* That's what she was doing. Oh, Lord.

Since the wedding, she'd loved becoming Ethan's wife in body and in soul, loving him and making love. Laughing at the baby together, talking about Cody's future, what his first word would be, whether he'd prefer Disneyland or Six Flags, corn dogs (which got her vote) or pizza (Ethan's guess). It had all begun to feel so real, so meant to be.

But Ethan wasn't fighting to keep what they had. He was fighting to give it away. And he was right: they'd gotten married for precisely this purpose.

I'm the beast in this story. I want another woman's child. I want her to let me keep my family.

Her eyes were still closed and her tone was low and as neutral as she could make it when she asked, "If Samantha decides she doesn't want to live in Thunder Ridge, what then? She never liked it here, as I recall. If she decides to take the baby someplace else before you think she's ready, are you going to follow her?"

After another aching silence, Ethan concluded, "That's a long way off. We've got a lot of work to do before that would happen."

Though the call was not ended, Gemma set her phone on the sideboard that divided the living area from the kitchen. Covering her face with her hands, she blocked even the dim light from the mission lamp on the end of the long table, deriving some comfort from breathing into the darkness, as if she could hide from the world behind her own palms.

Ethan wanted a nanny. A helper. Or maybe he thought they could be a supportive aunt and uncle team, cheering Samantha on whether she wanted to be cheered on or not.

He doesn't know me. Perhaps she hadn't known herself until this moment.

Maybe she truly was selfish and horrible, but she couldn't do it.

"It's late, and it's been a long day…" Ethan's weary voice came through the phone.

Reluctantly coming up for air, Gemma dragged her hands down her face and picked up her cell.

"I should have waited until daytime to call," he said. "Let's get some sleep and talk again tomorrow."

"All right." Was he really going to be able to sleep? She wasn't counting on closing her eyes.

Neither of them said another word, and neither of them hung up. Finally, Gemma whispered, "Good night."

The cell phone began to feel as if it were burning her ear. She could hear Ethan breathing, but they were a million miles apart.

"Good night," he returned stoically, and the call ended.

As she set the phone on the sideboard again, Gemma studied her wedding band. Removing it, she held it between her thumb and forefinger. It was a beautiful circle of precious metal and diamonds, strong and supposedly everlasting. Yet all anyone had to do was hold it up to the light to see that it was empty in the middle.

Exhausted, Gemma headed upstairs to the guest room Ethan had given her when she'd first moved in. Too full of grief to put the wedding band on her finger again, she left it on the dresser and climbed into bed, the first time she'd slept there in over a week.

Dozing only briefly, she awoke exhausted shortly before dawn, woodenly washing and dressing before packing a bag for herself and one for the baby. By the time she was in her car, heading to her parents' house, she began to have a sense of unreality, as if the past ten days with Ethan had been nothing more than a very vivid dream.

Chapter Thirteen

"I told Mom not to call you," Gemma complained as Lucy sat on the bed next to her. "You should be home getting breakfast ready for your family."

"Yeah, because I won't have the opportunity to do *that* every day for the next eighteen or twenty years," Lucy cracked, handing her sister a tissue from the box their mother had set on the nightstand after ushering Lucy to Gemma's bedroom and closing the door behind. "So what happened? Mom said she and Dad were set to watch the baby while you and Ethan made out like newlyweds."

A fresh spate of the tears threatened Gemma's tenuous composure. Dabbing the tissue beneath her eyes, she countered, "Our mother did not say that."

"Maybe not those words, exactly, but it's what she meant. So what happened?"

Briefly, Gemma filled her sister in.

"He seems so excited to give Cody back to Samantha—"

Gemma tried to keep the hurt out of her voice, but was afraid that she might be failing "—even if Samantha isn't ready, and by the sound of things, I don't think she is."

Lucy rubbed Gemma's back as they sat side by side on the edge of the bed. "That sucks. I mean, not that he wants his sister to be a mother to her son, but I know you already feel like Cody's mother. It's obvious to us all."

Gemma nodded miserably. "I can't imagine giving Cody up now. And I feel so guilty! Samantha is his mother. I shouldn't want to st-st-steal her baby." More tears spurted from her eyes.

Putting both her arms around Gemma's shoulders, Lucy hugged hard. "You're not stealing him. She's his mother, but up to now you've been his parent. Of course you don't want to let go without making absolutely certain it's the right thing."

"I don't want to let go even if it is the right thing," Gemma admitted miserably.

"You will, though," Lucy pointed out gently. "I know you."

"But what then? If I believe it's the right thing, what happens after that?" She shook her head. "I won't know how to move on from that." Wiping her nose even as it kept running, she admitted to Lucy, "Cody is the reason we got married. We never said we loved each other."

Lucy obviously tried not to cringe, but failed. "How about now," she asked gently. "How do you feel now?"

"I...love him." She pressed the tissue against her nose and sobbed into it. Lucy supplied her with another wad, and when she could speak again, Gemma said, "My marriage is one-sided. Samantha could take Cody away completely one day, move out of state again, and then what do we do? What's left?"

"Oh, honey." The gentleness in Lucy's demeanor began

to evaporate. "Somehow I expected more sensitivity from Ethan. I can't believe he played the that's-why-we-got-married-in-the-first-place card." She shook her head disgustedly. "Men! Elyse never should have gotten you that teddy. Maybe if you hadn't had hot sex—"

"No." Wiping her nose, Gemma shrugged. "No, it was stupid to think I could live with him and not fall in love. I was halfway there before we said 'I do.' He just doesn't feel the same."

"Are you sure about that? Husbands can be so thick. Maybe in the excitement of finding Samantha, he wasn't thinking about—"

Gemma interrupted her sister by shaking her head emphatically. "He'd had plenty of time to think about everything when he called from Montana. I've already had a fiancé who wasn't in love with me. I'd rather not repeat the experience with my husband. Know what I mean?"

Looking almost as heartbroken as Gemma felt, Lucy nodded solemnly. "You don't have to settle for someone who's not in love with you. Ethan will never have as rich, as deep and fulfilling, a relationship with someone else as he could have with you, and if he thinks he can, then he is seriously deluding himself."

Gemma looked at her beautiful, dark-haired sister, who had met her own soul mate in her freshman year of college, and thought, *Good sister. Perfect sister for ignoring that Ethan is gorgeous and funny and rich and charming and honest enough never to have told me that he loved me in the first place.*

"If Ethan doesn't appreciate you, then he doesn't deserve your love," Lucy continued more strongly, her voice rising. "In fact, I say shame on him. He handled this all wrong. You're not his employee, for crying out loud, you're his wife. Really, he's not nearly good enough for you, Gem. In fact, you are worth a hundred Ethan Ladds!"

"Knock, knock," Minna trilled as she opened Gemma's bedroom door. Balancing a small tray with a plate of scones and small pot of her homemade lemon curd, Minna smiled sweetly as she set the tray on Gemma's old desk and handed out paper napkins. "This is just like the old days, when you girls would cuddle up in here and talk about boys, and I'd bring you a snack."

Lucy traded a look with Gemma. *Yeah, just like that.* Both women jumped when their mother ordered, "All right, go home, Lucy. You're not helping here."

"What?" Confused, Lucy protested, "What do you mean I'm not helping? Mom, were you eavesdropping outside the door?"

"Please," Minna huffed, affronted. "With your megaphone voice, I've never had to stoop to eavesdropping. Now run along, sweetie. I want to talk to Gemma alone."

Gemma gave Lucy a microscopic shake of her head. *Do not leave me alone with Mom.* The only info she'd given her mother was that she and Ethan had a disagreement about something, and she hoped she and Cody could stay in her old room for a few days. She didn't want to have a more extensive conversation than that with Minna, who still thought Ethan was God's gift to her eldest daughter.

"You told me to come over," Lucy pointed out. "Besides, I want a scone."

Minna's perfectly drawn brows drew together in an ominous portent. "I didn't want to have to point this out in so many words, but it's time you children realized that Daddy and I know a *lot* more about what is going on in your lives than you think we know. So shoo, Lucy, and I mean it." She passed the plate she'd brought with her. "Take a scone with you."

Shrugging apologetically at Gemma, Lucy obeyed their mother. Wrapping her scone in the paper napkin Minna handed her, she said, "I'll call you, Gem. Maybe we can go for a walk later."

"Okay."

And then Gemma was alone with her mom, who seated herself in the desk chair and studied her daughter frankly.

"I fibbed a little to your sister," Minna admitted. "The truth is I *don't* understand everything between you and Ethan. I'm not sure what you're arguing about right now, but that isn't the point, anyway." Taking a scone, she halved it with a butter knife, then spread lemon curd on top. "The point is you got married, and that's serious business. Don't believe it when people say you can move on if you're bored or you grow apart." She waved the knife. "What kind of nonsense is that? The reason you get married in the first place is so you can stay with someone long enough to be sick of the sight of him."

"Mom!" Gemma sputtered in protest. "Does Daddy know you feel this way?"

"Of course. He agrees with me. Besides, I'm not saying we feel that way now. I'm saying we *have felt* it. Everyone has. You have to remember that marriage isn't only a relationship between two people. It's a relationship between the couple and the marriage itself. You're looking at me like I'm crazy." Shrugging, Minna handed the scone to Gemma. "Eat," she commanded, licking her thumb. "I'll try to explain."

A faraway look entered her eyes. "Most of us, when we're first married, want to believe we're in such a great love affair that divorce is unthinkable. But that's phooey. Love plays hide-and-seek. Sometimes it hides for a very long time, believe you me. So you have to decide to love your marriage as much as you love the other person, to take care of it as if it were your child. You promise to be there for it even when it's making you crazy, and it promises to grow and mature and someday make you very proud. And it will. Marriages get stronger and more beautiful with trouble and time. Just when you think it's too difficult, that you're all done with him, he'll get that little wrinkle between his eyebrows while he's trying to fix the toaster and in an instant you realize you're still in love." Minna gave a shivery wriggle. "And that's delightful. In fact a couple of weeks ago, I was looking at your father as he was getting out of the shower. He had tiny droplets of water all over his skin, and I—"

"Oh, no! No, no." Gemma covered her ears. "I don't need to hear any more. I get it."

She gazed at her mother, her rag-mag loving, gossip-sharing mother, and thought, *Wow. Just when you think you know someone.* "What you said is really beautiful, Mom," she complimented, meaning it. She was even envious, wondering if she'd ever know that kind of relationship. "But I'm not sure it applies in this case. I mean, it's not like I've fallen out of love with someone." Her nose began to feel twitchy again, and her eyes stung. "I haven't. I've…I've…I've…only just realized I'm in it."

Once more, tears began to flow down Gemma's cheeks. She lowered the scone, then lowered her head, surrendering to the sobs she couldn't control. Minna muttered, "Oh, dear. Oh, dear," as she rocked her daughter gently. "I suppose I know even less about your marriage than I thought I did," she said when the worst of the storm had passed. "But I know you. I think you want this marriage, this family, very much. Do you know that of all my kids, you've always been the most giving? The one who let others decide what movie to watch or what flavor ice cream we should have. I always loved that about you."

"You did?"

Minna stroked her daughter's hair. "Yes. Now I'm telling you to quit it. This is the time to have what *you* want, Gemmy. Ask yourself what that is, and then fight for it."

Gemma pulled back to look at her mom. "What if that means not winding up with Ethan?"

She could see her mother struggle with that question, but in the end Minna said staunchly, "So be it. I love you."

"I love you, too," Gemma returned. "When did you get so smart, Mom?"

"Right about the time you started feeling dumb." Giving her daughter's arm a squeeze, Minna rose to collect the goodies she'd brought upstairs. "Sooner or later love makes us all feel like ninnies." Her smile was tolerant. "Are you staying here tonight or going home, sweetheart?"

Since Ethan's house did not feel like "home" to Gemma at the moment, she answered, "Staying."

Disappointment flashed briefly across her mother's expression, but she nodded. "All right, then. Your father and I will take care of the baby. You take the day to yourself."

Gemma decided not to argue. It wouldn't help anyone if she cried every time she held Cody. She needed to process the facts and how she felt about them. She needed to consider what came next.

Her mother thought she didn't ask for what she wanted in life. Was that true? And if she did ask for what she wanted in a marriage, would Ethan be able to give it to her?

He hadn't asked her opinion about the situation with Cody before he'd sped off, nor had he asked when they spoke at midnight. He hadn't considered her concerns or hopes at all. Instead, he'd reminded her that theirs was a marriage of convenience.

A surge of self-disgust filled Gemma's stomach. She'd agreed to marry Ethan Ladd so she could have a taste of the life she dreamed about. A small, tantalizing taste. While other people sat down to feasts, she settled for crumbs.

It wasn't enough, not by a long shot. Not anymore.

So what was she going to do about it?

Hands balled into fists, Ethan stood in the bedroom Gemma had shared with Cody until she'd moved into his master suite. He hadn't spoken to her since midnight yesterday. Phoning this afternoon to tell her he was catching a flight home had elicited no response at all, and then he'd walked into an empty house, where he showered, unpacked, antsy with fatigue and uncertainty, then he'd waited downstairs for his wife and Cody to show up.

The dinner hour had come and gone with no sign of them and no word, even though he'd left another message, asking when she'd be home. By nine, still with no response, he'd started to get worried, so he'd phoned her parents' house and spoken with Hal, asking her father if he knew where Gemma was.

"I think she was planning to stay here tonight, son. She's out with Lucy right now. Why don't you try her cell?"

Ethan wasn't certain what had prompted him to fly up the stairs to the guest room at that point, but he had, and that's when he'd found Gemma's wedding ring sitting loudly on the dresser.

"What the hell?" he said now, unclenching his fists to snatch the ring up and look at it disbelievingly. She took off her wedding ring, then went to stay at her parents' place? With Cody? Why?

She'd been upset with him he last time they'd spoken, yes, and maybe he should have stayed on the phone with her, but the pressure he'd been under had felt nearly unbearable. And by the next morning, his sister's fury had made Gemma's resentment seem like a hug by comparison.

Shaking his head, Ethan walked heavily to the bed, lowering himself to the edge of the mattress. He'd maneuvered around two-hundred-and-fifty-pound linebackers, but navigating relationships with women...*forgettaboutit.*

Couldn't keep a nanny. Couldn't help his sister. Couldn't hold on to his wife.

Without warning, angry words from the past two days lodged in Ethan's brain. *You want life to look the way you think it should, and when it doesn't you refuse to accept it!* Fed up with his trying to persuade her to return to Oregon, Samantha had blown up this morning when he'd shown up for breakfast toward the end of her shift.

I'm trying to keep you from making the biggest mistake of your life, he'd argued.

No, Sam had shot back without missing a beat, *you're trying to re-create the past, not fix the present. The present is fine. Cody is fine. You said so yourself.*

Ethan's knuckles cracked as he pressed one fist into the palm of the other, hard. It was true that the present had been good, better than good, until a couple of days ago. Cody had improved so much in the past week or two that he now behaved, according to Gemma, like most other babies. Ethan enjoyed hanging with the little dude and even felt disappointed at times that he was sleeping so much.

What a change. And all the credit went to Gemma.

Inside his closed fist, Gemma's wedding ring dug into his palm. Jumping from the bed as if it were aflame, Ethan set the diamond band on the dresser and stalked from the guest room to the master suite. No other woman had ever been in this bedroom. Somehow he'd known instinctively that his home in Thunder Ridge wasn't meant for casual encounters, yet he hadn't intended to marry, either. Shame over being unable to read had persuaded him not to let anyone get too close. As for kids... Once he'd imagined his own children's humiliation when they realized their father was functionally illiterate, he'd known a family of his own was not in the cards.

Now Ethan looked at the dresser and mirror combination that had been chosen by his decorator. There was nothing personal on it. Not a photo stuck into the frame of the mirror. Not a card or memento on top. Nothing to show someone loved him, or that there was somebody here he loved.

He stood for a long time until a key in the front door lock shook him from his inertia.

Moving without thinking, he sprinted out of the room and down the stairs as if he'd realized the game-winning ball was in his hands. The second he saw Gemma standing in the foyer, wearing her bright yellow sundress and the flip-flops that had glassy red ladybugs—ladybugs, for crying out loud—glued along the straps, his confusion cleared. The pieces of his life fell into place as if he'd turned just the right section of a Rubik's Cube, and suddenly everything made sense.

"Before you say anything," he pleaded when Gemma looked up and saw him, "hear me out." Without waiting for her assent, he sped on, talking as he closed the distance between them. "I get it now. I do. I should have talked to you about Sam. I didn't want to, because I knew you'd tell me the truth. And I was afraid to hear it."

The tiny furrow between Gemma's brows gave her the appearance of someone either confused or fed up. He prayed it wasn't the latter as his urgency grew. "I tried to convince Sam to come home," he admitted. "When she refused, I kept pushing. She said I was trying to rewrite history by controlling the future." He shook his head. "I refused to listen. Then I saw your wedding ring…and I knew."

"My ring?" Gemma glanced at her left hand. "Where—Oh, yeah."

"Sam's right. I *was* trying to fix the past. From everything I told her, she knew Cody already has the kind of family she and I missed out on as kids. She says that's what she wants for him, and why fix what isn't broken anymore?" Ethan took a very deep breath. "She saw more clearly than I did that having a family to come home to every day, one that fills you with pride—that's my dream now. Not hers. The thing is, I never thought I could have it, Gemma, not with my background or with my—" he raised a fist to his head "—screwed-up brain."

"Your brain is *fine*," she defended hotly.

Ethan smiled. "That's my girl—champion of the underdog."

Her tiny smile gave him a bit more hope. "I don't think I would ever refer to you as an underdog."

"I am, though. When it comes to relationships, I'm way behind. I need some tutoring."

He tried to gauge her reaction, but for the first time in his memory Gemma's expression was shuttered and inaccessible. She wasn't going to make this easy on him. All he could do was take a leap of faith.

"I don't want to lose you. I don't want to—I *can't* lose what we have." Voice rough with emotion, he pressed on, figuring he had nothing to lose by laying it all on the line. "You, me and Cody…it's who I am now. Who I want to be. Gem, without you, Cody and I are just two lost dudes looking for a light to drive home by. You're it. You're our North Star. We need you." He waited for her to process his words. Some kind of reaction built behind her eyes, but she stayed silent. *Tell her the truth*, an inner voice urged. "*I* need you."

Ethan felt as if his intestines were being tied into square

knots as he waited for a response. When none came, he knew he'd blown it. He hadn't understood what was right in front of him, hadn't treated it as something better than anything that had come before or might possibly come after. And now the only woman he'd ever fallen in love with was looking at him like—

His heart seemed to struggle to beat.

Gemma was looking at him like maybe it truly was over.

He still hasn't said, "I love you."

Not anticipating the scene she'd just walked into, Gemma had listened carefully to everything Ethan had to say. She'd watched him carefully, too. The muscular Adonis who made love the way he played football—with great technique and exquisite passion—had yielded to a man who seemed uncertain and even a little desperate.

He needed her, and she didn't doubt his sincerity for a second. The problem was, needing her wasn't enough.

"My mom told me I've always settled for less than I truly wanted," she said after a long pause. "I've thought a lot about that, and she's right. I'm not willing to settle anymore."

When Ethan's brows dipped so low that he appeared to be in danger of obscuring his vision, Gemma had to steel herself against a powerful tug of compassion, and while compassion was fine, it was not a solid foundation for marriage, at least not the kind of marriage she knew she wanted.

"Our marriage began as an experiment," she said, not unkindly. "We accepted that the future was a big question mark. And then there was the whole ninety-day trial thing."

"We can go back to that," he interjected, "if that's what

you want. For now." He was so adorably desperate, she almost relented right then and there.

"No, I don't want that." She shook her head. "I made a decision about us before I came back here today. And you may as well know that my mind is made up."

"Gem—" he tried to intervene, but she stayed the course.

"Wanting to be married is an important ingredient in a long marriage, but it's not enough. I wanted to be married to William, after all, didn't I? But it was pretty easy for him to leave, and my heart didn't break when he did." There was a powerful yearning inside her, and she allowed it to infuse her voice. "I want to know my heart can break. Maybe that sounds ridiculous, but I've played it safe too long. From now on, I want to love so much that I scare myself. I want to know I can break someone else's heart, too. I want to be crazy in love right from the get-go."

Adopting the sternest expression she could, Gemma took two steps forward. "And that is why I am not going to settle for you saying—" she made air quotes "—you 'need' me. Need, shmeed." She jabbed a finger at his ridiculously broad chest. "I want to hear, 'I love you, Gemma. I don't want to live without you.' Because that's how I feel about you, you big lug. I have everything I've ever wanted right here, right now, and if I have anything to say about it, you and I are going to be together until we're sick of the sight of each other. You got that? Because—"

She had no chance to finish the sentence.

Pulling her against him, Ethan kissed her in a way that made rivers of heat course through her veins.

"I love you, Gemma," he murmured against her lips. "I don't want to live without you. So don't make me." He rained kisses over her face. "I can't believe I didn't say it already. I'm an idiot. I love you."

"I know you do," Gemma whispered, weak in the knees.

Reaching up, she put her palms on his cheeks. "Once I calmed down and thought it over, I knew you loved me even if you didn't realize it yet."

"I realize it." Lowering his head, Ethan began to plant kisses along the side of her neck. "Oh, boy, do I realize it."

Gemma reflexively hunched a shoulder against the delicious shivers that raced across her skin. "Maybe you should stop doing that for a sec?" she said as she felt herself falling into a sensual haze.

"Why?"

"So we can finish talking."

"Bad plan," he growled, pulling away to look into her eyes. "Gemma, I love you. You love me. We're married for better or worse. Forever. Right?"

Thirty-two trillion cells in her body jumped for joy. "Right."

The confirmation made his eyes smolder, and he held her tighter. "Then the rest is just details. We've got a lifetime to work those out."

"Wow." She nodded. "You make really good sense."

"Yeah." His head lowered toward hers again. "My wife says I'm a pretty smart dude."

Smart enough, as it turned out, to lift her into his arms and carry her upstairs. Depositing her in the master bedroom, he retrieved her wedding band and sank to one knee before her.

Joyful tears pricked Gemma's eyes. *I might have to get used to tears of joy for a while*, she thought as the reality hit her: she was living her wildest dream.

"Gemma Rose Gould Ladd," Ethan said in the gorgeous, deep voice that would someday read to their children, "there's a lot I don't know. But I'm sure of this—marrying you was the best move I ever made. I promise to appreciate every bumbling step in our journey together. And if I forget, I promise to let you remind me. Most of all, I promise never to forget how damn lucky I am to have fallen in love with you in the first place." He hovered the ring at the end of her finger and asked, "Will you stay married to me?"

She nodded so hard to that she almost made herself dizzy. "Yes! And I promise to remember how lucky I am to love you so much that I don't ever want to say goodbye. I will stay married to you, Ethan Jonathon Ladd, until we're sick of the sight of each other. And way beyond that."

He rose. "Hey, that's the second time you said that. We are never going to be sick of the sight of each other."

Smiles filled Gemma's heart as she recalled her mother's wisdom. "Yeah, we will be." Looping her arms around her husband's neck, she promised, "But then one day I'll watch you get out of the shower, and it'll all be fine again."

Ethan shook his head, baffled. "What?"

"I'll explain later. We have to pick Cody up at my parents' place in a few hours, so we'd better get started."

He cocked a brow. "Started on what?"

"Working on a sibling for him."

A slow smile crawled across Ethan's face. "So soon?"

"Well, we may need to practice awhile before we get it right. Besides, I'm thinking we should build our own football franchise."

Laughing, Ethan picked her up again, and they landed on the bed together. "I like the way you think, Mrs. Ladd. Have I ever told you that your brain is one of the sexiest things about you?" He began to unbutton her dress.

She looked down, where his fingers brushed against her breasts. "That's not where my brain is."

"I said *one* of the sexiest things. And now—" the small yellow buttons gave way beneath his fingers "—we're going to explore the other things." Ethan's head dipped to her chest. "All of them. Giving a great deal of attention—" he followed the opening of each button by tasting her skin "—to each."

"Oh, this is a fine plan." Gemma's fingers threaded through her husband's hair as she cradled the back of his head. Releasing a blissful sigh, she commended, "A very, very fine plan."

Epilogue

Three years later

"Read *Seymour the Serious Dragon*!" Bouncing in one-hundred-and-eighty degree arcs worthy of an emerging gymnast, Cody Ladd treated his new big-boy race-car bed more like a trampoline than a place to lay his blond head at night.

"How about a different story?" Ethan suggested, approaching his son's book collection.

"No! Seymour! Seymour! Seymour!"

"Enough jumping. Put your bottom on the bed." Ethan pointed to the mattress. When Cody complied, he scanned the shelves for the requested picture book.

Ethan had developed a serious case of flop sweat the day Gemma had suggested the floor-to-ceiling shelving and began stocking it with enough juvenile literature to start their own library. Unable to read the majority of the books his wife had chosen, he'd felt the crushing sense of inadequacy that had dogged him most of his life. But Gemma, with her characteristic optimism and unwavering faith in education, had promised everything would be fine.

"Is Mommy coming?" Cody asked.

"She already kissed you good-night, sport, remember?" Returning with the book, Ethan tucked his son under the car-covered sheets and red blanket, then sat on the edge of the bed. "Mommy's studying really hard tonight."

During the school year they lived in Portland, where Gemma continued to teach, but they spent summers right here in Thunder Ridge so Cody could connect with family while his mother worked on her PhD. Almost three years after their hasty wedding, Ethan still figured Gemma was worth twenty of him. She rarely missed Cody's bedtime routine, but tonight she'd asked for a little time to herself, and he was glad to oblige.

Opening the book on his lap, he held it up. Cody loved the illustrations of Seymour, the dour-looking dragon who learns he has it in him to choose happiness. "'Seymour was a serious dragon,'" Ethan began, reading off the page even though he practically knew the story by heart. "'He smiled once a year, and that was only because his mother made him…'"

With Gemma's unwavering support, he had turned the hurdle of dyslexia into a stepping stone. His reading skills had improved to the point that he'd registered for next fall's semester of community college, something that would have been unthinkable before Gemma had set him straight on viewing his limitations as growth opportunities. Two years of community college would bring him closer to his dream of earning a BA and a teaching credential, which he hoped someday to turn into a career as a high school football coach. Pretty high flyin' for a dumb jock who couldn't read *Green Eggs and Ham* a few short years ago.

By the end of the story, Cody had turned onto his side and closed his eyes, lips puffing softly as he settled into sleep. Closing the book and kissing his son, Ethan left on the night-light and decided to head downstairs to Gemma's office to see if she needed anything—a shoulder rub, perhaps, which might turn into some neck nibbling and possibly upper-body privileges—before he left her to her work.

Walking down the broad upper-floor hallway, he smiled at the thought of a little hanky-panky before he hit the books himself and almost, almost missed the sight in the doorway to the master bedroom.

One hand on the wrought iron stair rail, Ethan halted when he noticed Gemma leaning against the doorjamb. "Hey," he said, "I didn't know you were up here. I thought you were down…stairs. Holy moly." For a few seconds no sound emerged from his open mouth as he pointed at what Gemma was wearing. Finally he rasped, "Is that what I think it is?"

She smiled. "Mmm-hmm. Does it bring back memories?" Her voice was deliberately sultry.

Ethan swallowed. She-yeah, it did. Leaving the top of the stairs, he moved toward the master bedroom. "What I remember," he said, referring to the barely there negligee she'd worn on their wedding night and again the first time they'd made love, "is that I didn't get the chance to take that off you."

Before he'd even stopped moving, he reached for her, and Gemma slid into his arms. He wasted no time beginning to explore the lush body beneath the transparent material.

"Did I ever thank your sister for giving you this?" he muttered as his lips found the most sensitive part of her neck, the spot that always made her hunch her shoulders against the goose bumps that raced across her skin.

"I think we still owe them a thank-you note."

Ethan smiled against her neck. "I'll get right on it."

Gemma clutched his shoulders as he kissed his way toward her breasts. "Did Cody go to sleep easily?" she asked, her voice breathy.

"Mmm."

"Did he want to hear *Seymour the Serious Dragon* or *Danny Gets a Dog*?"

"Seymour." Ethan blazed a trail of kisses from the top of one beautiful breast to the other. Gemma tilted her head back, and he moved lower...

"I like the name Danny—oh, my!" She gasped as he tasted her nipple through the sheer material. "So, uh, do you like the name Danny?"

Ethan lifted his head. "You really want to talk about this? Now?"

"Kind of." Gemma's doe-brown eyes sparkled. "Unless you have something better in mind."

"Much," he growled. In one swift move, Ethan picked her up and carried her to the bed. "Do you still have to work?" He prayed she'd say no, because he had revised his plans for the evening, and they would last most of the night.

"I'm not working tonight."

Depositing her on the mattress and following her down, he slowly traced a design from the top of her stomach past her belly button. "I thought you said you had things to do."

"I did them already. I also like the name Eden for a girl. Sounds like Ethan."

Bracing himself on his hands, he hovered over her. "All right, what's going on?"

Gemma slipped her hand under his pillow, withdrawing a box tied with shiny silver ribbon.

Ethan bolted up. "It's our anniversary! Aw, damn it, I'm sorry."

"It's not our anniversary." She bopped him on the shoulder. "You boob. That's almost a month away."

"That's what I thought. So what is this?" He took the slender box she pushed at him.

"Open it."

Sliding off the ribbon, he lifted the lid and—

"No. Really?" She nodded. "Really?" he asked again, because it was completely unexpected. For three years they'd been trying, unsuccessfully, to get pregnant. Life with Gemma and their son was so rich, so full of possibilities, that his heart had broken more for her than for himself. But now—

"What do you think?" She bit her full lower lip, brow beginning to furrow adorably with concern. "I know we're super busy, and you need to focus on college in the fall and Cody starts preschool. And of course I'm working on this PhD, which I don't mind postponing, but it might be wiser to simply…mmm hmm hmm mmm…" Words lost amidst his kiss, Gemma's entire body melted when he tossed the positive pregnancy test to the side and showed his wife exactly how he felt about becoming a parent with her. Again.

Her arms curled around his neck, and her body slid lower on the bed. "I guess you're okay with it, then," she murmured when he pulled back to stare at her smooth belly.

"Our baby's in there," he said in wonder, loving the thought.

She nodded. "For the next seven months." She twirled a finger in his hair. "Have I told you lately that I'm crazy in love with you, Ethan Ladd?"

It was the damndest thing—he began to grin at the exact moment he felt the back of his eyes start to sting.

Gemma was carrying part of him and part of her beneath her heart. And Ethan figured he was the luckiest guy on earth, because he was going to carry their family inside his heart for the rest of his life.

* * * * *

Don't miss the previous books in
Wendy Warren's
THE MEN OF THUNDER RIDGE *series*
for Mills & Boon Edition!

HIS SURPRISE SON and KISS ME, SHERIFF!

Available now wherever Mills & Boon books
and ebooks are sold.

MILLS & BOON®

Cherish™

EXPERIENCE THE ULTIMATE RUSH OF FALLING IN LOVE

A sneak peek at next month's titles...

In stores from 19th October 2017:

- **Newborn Under the Christmas Tree** – Sophie Pembroke *and* **The Rancher's Christmas Song** – RaeAnne Thayne
- **Snowbound with an Heiress** – Jennifer Faye *and* **The Maverick's Snowbound Christmas** – Karen Rose Smith

In stores from 2nd November 2017:

- **Christmas with Her Millionaire Boss** – Barbara Wallace *and* **A Cowboy Family Christmas** – Judy Duarte
- **His Mistletoe Proposal** – Christy McKellen *and* **His by Christmas** – Teresa Southwick

---

Just can't wait?
Buy our books online before they hit the shops!
www.millsandboon.co.uk

Also available as eBooks.

MILLS & BOON®

EXCLUSIVE EXTRACT

Beautiful, young widow Noelle Fryberg is determined to show her Christmas-hating boss, millionaire James Hammond, just how magical Christmas can be…Could she be the one to melt his heart?

Read on for a sneak preview of
CHRISTMAS WITH HER MILLIONAIRE BOSS
the first book in the magical **THE MEN WHO MAKE CHRISTMAS** *duet*

He'd lost his train of thought when she looked up at him, distracted by the sheen left by the snow on her dampened skin. Satiny smooth, it put tempting ideas in his head.

Like kissing her.

"Don't be silly," she replied. For a second, James thought she'd read his mind and meant the kiss, especially after she pulled her arm free from his. "It's a few inches of snow, not the frozen tundra. I think I can handle walking, crowd or no crowd. Now, I don't know about you, but I want my hot cocoa."

She marched toward the end of the aisle, the pom-pom on her hat bobbing in time with her steps. James stood and watched until the crowd threatened to swallow her up before following.

What the hell was wrong with him? Since when did he think about kissing the people he did business with? Worse, Noelle was an employee. Granted, a very attractive, enticing one, but there were a lot of beautiful women working in the Boston office and never once had he contemplated pulling one of them against him and kissing her senseless.

Then again, none of them ever challenged him either. Nor did they walk like the majorette in a fairy band.

It had to be the drone. He'd read that concussions could cause personality changes. Lord knows, he'd been acting out of character for days now starting with agreeing to stay for Thanksgiving.

It certainly explained why he was standing in the middle of this oversized flea market when he could—should—be working. Honestly, did the people in this town ever do anything at a normal scale? Everywhere he looked, someone was pushing Christmas. Holiday sweaters. Gingerbread cookies. One vendor was literally making hand-blown Christmas ornaments on the spot. Further proof he wasn't himself, James almost paused because there was one particularly incandescent blue ornament that was a similar shade to Noelle's eyes.

The lady herself had stopped. At a booth selling scented lotions and soaps wrapped in green and gold cellophane. "Smell this," she said, when he caught up with her. She held an open bottle of skin cream under his nose, and he caught the sweet smell of vanilla. "It's supposed to smell like a Christmas cookie," she said. "What do you think?"

"I like the way your skin smells better."

Don't miss
THE MEN WHO MAKE CHRISTMAS:

CHRISTMAS WITH HER MILLIONAIRE BOSS
by Barbara Wallace
Available November 2017

SNOWED IN WITH THE RELUCTANT TYCOON
by Nina Singh
Available December 2017

www.millsandboon.co.uk